FADE TO CLEAR

FADE TO CLEAR

LEONARD CHANG

THOMAS DUNNE BOOKS / ST. MARTIN'S MINOTAUR ♒ NEW YORK

THOMAS DUNNE BOOKS.
An imprint of St. Martin's Press.

www.stmartins.com

Excerpts from Kierkegaard's texts taken from:
Either/Or: A Fragment of Life, vol II, translated by Walter Lowrie. Princeton University Press, 1944.
Fear and Trembling, translated by Walter Lowrie. Princeton University Press, 1941.
The Journals of Søren Kierkegaard, ed. and trans. by Alexander Dru. Oxford University Press, 1938.

Library of Congress Cataloging-in-Publication Data

Chang, Leonard.
    Fade to clear : an Allen Choice novel / by Leonard Chang.— 1st ed.
       p. cm.
    ISBN 0-312-30845-0
    EAN 978-0312-30845-2
    1. Private investigators—California—San Francisco—Fiction. 2. San Francisco (Calif.)—Fiction. 3. Kidnapping, Parental—Fiction. 4. Custody of children—Fiction. 5. Drug traffic—Fiction. I. Title.

PS3553.H27244F34 2004
813'.54—dc22

2003069678

First Edition: May 2004

10 9 8 7 6 5 4 3 2 1

FOR MIRA AND ED

PART I

EITHER/OR

One

Allen Choice, a.k.a. "the Block," is getting tired of guns. He listens to his partner, Larry, fast-talk a Jamaican gangster, a sparkling bald black man with a gold earring and a nine-millimeter aimed at Larry's temple, a gangster who has caught Larry and the Block in this Oakland warehouse filled with stolen computers and peripherals. Larry is saying in a tight voice, "I'm telling you we ain't cops. We're just PI's. Check the ID in my pocket. We're working for Supremica and were just looking for their stuff. That's all." Larry's large, protruding forehead glistens under the bright security light. The Jamaican wears a tailored blue suit with a white shirt and blue tie; he's crisp and clean and alarmingly calm. A silver bracelet slides down the back of his hand as he lowers the gun toward Larry's groin. Larry suddenly talks faster, telling the Jamaican, "We didn't know what was in here. We can leave and pretend we saw nothing."

"But you did see everything," the Jamaican says in a deep, pleasant voice.

The Block sighs.

The Jamaican turns to him and asks, "What's your problem, Chin?"

The Block says, "Why do you keep calling me 'Chin'?"

"Chin. Chinese. Chinaman."

"I'm not Chinese. I'm actually Korean."

"Man, shut the fuck up," the Jamaican says. "Get on your knees like your friend. Move slowly, or your big-faced friend here might get hurt."

"I have the Supremica contract in the car. It's proof we're working for them."

"The only proof, Chin, is your brains on the floor."

The Block doesn't quite know what this means, but follows the Jamaican's instructions, kneeling, his hands clasped behind his head. The Jamaican has already taken their weapons, the Block's SIG and Larry's Smith & Wesson. The Block says, "The last thing we want is cops. We broke in here illegally. We could lose our licenses."

"You sure did fucking break in here, Chin," the Jamaican replies, pulling twine from a small crate and throwing it toward them. "And now you're gonna tie up Big Face nice and tight. His hands behind his back."

The Block does this, and meets Larry's eyes. The Block has a hidden gun—a small Raven P-25 in his ankle holster—and waits for some kind of cue from Larry. Larry shakes his head a fraction of an inch and then turns to the Jamaican, who flips open a cell phone. Larry says, "Shit, who're you calling?"

"Shut the fuck up, Big Face." The Jamaican dials a number. Larry's gun, a nickel-plated .44 Magnum S&W 629, sits on a crate next to the Block's SIG. The Block calculates his odds—the Jamaican has three guns, the Block has one small pocket automatic—and decides to wait this out. He sees Larry also searching for angles, checking the distance between them, the Jamaican, and the exits. The glaring security spotlight makes it difficult to see beyond the fringes, where gray shadows blanket stacks of crates. The musty smell of sawdust makes the Block's nose itch. As he ties up Larry's wrists, the Block uses an easy slipknot and puts in Larry's palm the end of the twine, which should free him if pulled hard enough. Larry nods, but continues staring at the Jamaican.

This is the third time the Block has had a gun aimed at him since partnering up with Larry. He used to be a bodyguard for ProServ, protecting Silicon Valley executives, and considered that job dangerous, yet this seems equally hazardous. He says to Larry, "I'm getting tired of guns."

"You and me both," Larry replies.

The Jamaican aims his gun at them and tells them to shut up. Then he says into the phone, "It's me. We got a problem."

Allen thought he would have a quiet night. Picture him just a few hours ago in a café in north Berkeley, listening to the buzz of conversations around him. He holds his mug in both hands, leaning forward, his hair damp from a quick shower and tickling his neck, his navy blue button-down shirt dotted with water. The soft background jazz music is punctuated by the snap of newspapers, clinking mugs, and latté orders yelled across the front counter. Picture him sipping his coffee and staring out the window onto Solano Avenue, watching pedestrians along the sidewalks. The acrid smell of burnt coffee beans is oddly refreshing. He is beginning to relax after a tiring day interviewing employees at Supremica, and looks forward to seeing Serena. He thinks, Now I can rest.

His name is Allen, but his old high school nickname, "the Block," seems to follow him wherever he goes. He no longer looks like a wooden block with squared shoulders and a thick midsection, blocking all incoming forwards as an aggressive fullback on the soccer team, yet the name has stuck. He believes most people find the name Allen boring, and accepts his nickname with some resignation. He is called the Block and all its variations—Blocky, Blockman, and Larry occasionally calls him Blockmeister or simply "B."

He has been working the inside end of the Supremica case, and interviewed almost three dozen people today. His head aches. Larry is grunting the opposite end, checking out the black market for stolen computer equipment, but neither of them has made much progress after a week of digging. Allen believes they'll find something soon; Larry does not. Larry, in fact, seems depressed these days, and Allen suspects it's linked to Larry's recent fortieth birthday, which Larry insisted they not celebrate or even acknowledge.

Allen is a private investigator, licensed by the Department of Consumer Affairs' Bureau of Security and Investigative Services. He is also a licensed Private Patrol Operator and Security Guard, and has a Firearms and Concealed Weapons Permit. He's a member of the Private Investigator's Guild, the Executive Protection Society, the Black Book Society, and the Center for Corporate Espionage. He has so many licenses, permits, and memberships that he needs a list to keep track of renewals. His life has been validated and certified; he exists as a stamp of approval for a yearly membership fee. Sometimes he wonders what he was before all these licenses. What was he before all these official papers filled his drawers? Before the state of California, the San Francisco Police, the Department of Justice, and the FBI downloaded his vitals and his fingerprints (the FBI had asked for all known aliases, so of course he had typed in his nickname; now even the U.S. government knows him as the Block), his photo scanned and transmitted—what was he before all this documentation?

He was, well, a kind of block: inert, immobile. Or perhaps the metaphor is more dynamic: he was a block floating on a river. He was drifting, swept slowly by the currents. He watched activity on the banks, but was himself unconnected; he had no paddle, no oars.

But all this is changing. He is getting serious with his girlfriend, Serena, who is supposed to meet him tonight at the café. Allen, more than any other time in his life, is suddenly alert and aware and affected by his surroundings, by the people around him; he is very conscious of how he feels and who he is becoming. Last week she mentioned in a very casual way the difficulties of sleeping over at each other's apartments—Allen lives in the city, in the Richmond district; Serena lives in Berkeley—and how maybe sharing an apartment might be more convenient and cost-effective. Allen is acutely aware of feeling uncertain, tentative, perhaps a little fearful. He wonders about the approaching river, if he is now heading toward a pivotal fork.

Allen is thirty-three years old and has been dating Serena for almost a year and a half. He doesn't think he's afraid of commitment. He hopes he's not held hostage to any of those clichés of bachelorhood, of panicky responses to monogamy. He in fact yearns for stability. His last relationship broke up because he had been thinking too long term, whereas his ex, Linda, had wanted more freedom. He is, however, amazed by how quickly he and Serena have progressed, and worries about possible incompatibilities. He thinks, Is this what it's all about? He projects his relationship years ahead and anticipates problems; minor differences between them balloon over time. They love each other, and he believes this to be true, but sometimes he can't help wondering why he's not more, well, giddy. Perhaps he's getting older, more mature. Perhaps he's being careful; he doesn't want to get slammed again. Perhaps he's not really in love, but afraid of loss and loneliness.

The smell of burnt coffee beans is not the smell of trouble, yet when Serena is over thirty minutes late, Allen senses something is wrong. Sometimes he searches for larger meanings in small moments and makes connections between disparate occurrences; thus, Serena's being late means that something in the chain of events leading up to her arrival has been disrupted, and this will in turn domino into other difficulties. Everything is always connected. This he learned the hard way, when he, prior to his becoming a PI, investigated the death of his own father and an accident involving his ex-girlfriend's brother. He no longer believes in the randomness of incidences, or isolated accidents. Everything has a purpose. Everything is webbed, with small vibrations on one strand echoing onto others.

When Serena walks briskly into the café, forty-five minutes late,

Allen watches her, but also watches everyone else watching her. She is quite watchable. Men stop talking. Women give her a quick eye-flick up and down, taking in her clothes, her stride. Serena has a confident, bold walk, and prefers short skirts; this evening she wears a black short skirt with a red sweater; she stomps toward him in knee-length black boots with thick heels. The energy of the café suddenly shifts in her direction as she moves noisily across the floor. Allen smiles, his mood lighter, that small rush of affection energizing him. Serena, oblivious to the subtle looks toward her, meets his eyes and smiles back. She does a quick hop for her final step, and grabs his arm as he stands to meet her. They hug and kiss, and she pulls up a chair next to his, leaving her hand on his neck. "Sorry I'm late," she says.

"You were worth the wait," he says, liking the warmth of her hand. They sit down, legs touching, and he notices a wisp of her hair falling toward her eye. He leans forward and brushes it aside. "You look gorgeous."

She rolls her eyes, but smiles. "You better be careful, or you might actually score tonight."

Allen laughs and squeezes her knee. A couple at the next table glances over at them, and Allen wonders if he is shallow to think that being with an attractive woman makes him look better. He notices that Serena has gelled back her short, black hair, which accentuates her high cheekbones, and as she sips his coffee, she peers at him over the mug. Her eyes have a playful look. She says, "I got an e-mail from my mother."

Allen has never met her parents, but likes how close Serena seems to be with them. "How are they?"

"They're coming out here next week. A short visit."

His heart gives off one loud thump, then resumes its normal beat. He says, "Why?"

"They say it's a vacation, but I guess they want to see me."

"And me too, I guess," he says.

"You sound thrilled."

He shrugs, and wonders if this is the trouble he has been sensing tonight. Maybe Serena was late because she had responded to the e-mail, which in turn got her caught in rush-hour traffic. Everything is connected. He begins to link her parents' visit to her comments last week about real estate and the rental market, how now is the perfect time to find a place together. Invisible threads hang all around them. He waves his hand around his head, trying to clear them.

"What was that?" Serena asks.

"A bug," he says.

"You don't want to see my parents?"

"Of course I do."

"It's just strange that we've been going out for almost two years, and they haven't met you."

"New York is far."

"They offered to fly us out last Christmas."

"My job . . ." he trails off.

"Oh, come on," she says. "You could've taken a few days off."

He looks out the window. He sees a man singing to himself as he passes by.

"Hey," she says, poking his ribs. "What's up?"

He asks, "Are they expecting me to speak Korean or something?"

"No. I've prepared them."

"They're not going to scold me for not being more Korean?"

"They probably will."

"Great," Allen says.

"Don't worry. You'll like them. They'll love you."

Serena's job as a computer programmer at Angest Software requires her to connect her company's programs to the Web, and she is always worried about "scalability," or the ease with which her code can be amplified on larger and more complex systems. The thought of moving in together forces Allen to consider the scalability of their relationship.

Can this work long term? Can they eventually marry? Why isn't this a certainty in his mind? He says, "How long will they be here?"

"They're talking about a week, maybe more."

"More?"

Serena frowns and waggles a finger at him. She turns her head so she can stare at him from the corner of her eyes. Allen thinks of this as her "laser look," which she gives him whenever she disapproves of him. He preempts this by saying quickly, "I guess it's time. I'm just a little nervous. That's all."

She faces him squarely, and says, "Let me tell you they're delirious I'm dating a Korean guy. Okay? They're into the ethnic ties, and they're biased to like you."

Biased? He prefers no bias, positive or negative, since he believes in a meritocracy, of earning your goodwill or ill will based on your present actions. The fact that Serena's parents want to like him puts more pressure on him. What if he disappoints them? He changes the subject and asks what she wants to do tonight.

"I really want to work out," she says.

He smiles. "Good. Me too." Allen is about to suggest a quick, light dinner, when his cell phone vibrates. The only person who calls him is Larry, so he answers it while Serena finishes his coffee. When he asks what's up, Larry says, "Yo, B. Found something. I'm in Jack London at this warehouse, and I think a bunch of Supremica's stuff might be in here. I need your help."

Allen thinks, Ah, the real trouble

Serena sighs when he tells her he has to drive into Oakland, but he promises to meet her at her apartment in a couple of hours. They make plans for an easy three-mile run tonight, and he leaves the café. Allen, since dating her, is in the best shape of his life. They have an alternating running and working-out schedule, with one night overlapping, and if this seems annoyingly healthy, it is. Allen and Serena might not have that much in common, but when it comes to exercise, they are closely in sync. A few months ago Allen walked out of the shower and Serena told him he was getting ridges on his abdomen. He looked down in surprise. He went to the mirror and was startled by what he saw. When had this happened? There were benefits to dating a fitness freak.

One problem as Allen sees it, and he thinks about this as he drives down Martin Luther King Boulevard to avoid the freeways, heading to Jack London Square to meet Larry—one problem that might blossom between them over time is that outside of exercising they have few inter-sections of interests. When he first met her Serena claimed she wanted a quieter, more stable life; Allen no longer thinks this is true. She used to be a frequent raver, and still likes going out to clubs, barhopping with the new circle of friends she quickly established once moving up here from LA. They are all in their late twenties, single, attractive, and monied. They drive Jettas, BMWs, and Audi convertibles. If the car you drive is a reflection of yourself, then what does it mean for Allen to drive a secondhand Volvo station wagon with its wheel wells rusting?

He has no idea how to talk to Serena's glittering friends. One of them frequently hires Baxter & Choice for boyfriend background checks, so Allen is usually safe talking about work and tips on checking out potential mates. They listen to music he has never heard of. They know the best wine bars in the city. A wine bar, Allen has learned recently, is a bar that serves just select vintage wines by the glass.

Nevertheless, Serena's friends are funny, entertaining, warm. They tell great stories. They complain about work in a way that is always amusing. They talk about their boyfriends and horrible dates with Allen sitting right there, giving him some insight into his own relationship. Sometimes another boyfriend is there, though usually there isn't, since Serena seems to be the only one with any kind of serious boyfriend. Serious. Yes, they are serious.

But there is something fundamentally missing in his interactions with Serena's friends. Other than having almost nothing in common, they seem puzzled by him. For some reason Allen's comments are conversation stoppers. He isn't sure why this happens, but he will often feel the pressure to contribute to the dialogue, so he will say something, and everyone will hesitate. They will look at him, nod and then there will be an awkward silence that Serena will quickly fill.

The last time this happened they were talking about philosophy. Allen is excited by this topic, since he has been reading more philosophy ever since abandoning his own carefully constructed but ultimately ineffectual framework he called *removement,* which tried to explain his sense of strangeness with everyone and everything around him. Since then Serena, who took philosophy courses in college, directed him to a few primers on philosophy, and he picked this up as a hobby. He never finished college, had never taken a humanities course, so he finds this fascinating.

Serena's friend Margie was talking about her new outlook, her new philosophy, and Allen perked up. She said, "I've decided not to worry about the future anymore. I'm going to enjoy myself here and now and live for the moment."

Allen remembered his readings, and said, "That's interesting."

Everyone turned to him. He hadn't said much all evening.

"I'm reading Kierkegaard, and he talks about life in that style. He calls it the aesthetic realm. He believes you're never in control of your own self when you're living like that because you're guided just by pleasure and avoiding pain."

Margie blinked.

Serena grinned at Allen while shaking her head.

Margie said, "That's nice."

Well, there is something to be said about the pursuit of pleasure and the avoidance of pain. The Block has had dozens of deep-tissue bruises from his work, the kind of bruises that shine in multishades, ranging in the spectrum from pale red to deep black. He has had broken ribs, fractured tibias, sprained joints, and perilous concussions. In a couple of cases he has been hit so hard that he blacked out before he could truly feel the depth of pain of such a blow. So when he and Larry are caught at the warehouse, the Block thinks only of escape.

All this begins, however, with Larry's phone call. When Allen meets him outside this warehouse, Larry tells him about a black market contact who noticed a recent wave of computers and peripherals being fenced out of this warehouse off Jefferson. After over a decade of PI work in the Bay Area, Larry has amassed a small network of fences, grifters, and small-time thieves who are often willing to help out for a gratuity.

Allen studies the warehouse. The windows are translucent, but the faint, lonely glow of a pale security light inside hints at emptiness, vacancy. Larry gives Allen a rundown of the security system—low-tech contact breakers on the windows, and basic mercury switch motion detectors on the doors and garage.

"Wait. You want to break in?" Allen asks.

"We should check inside. My guy said they were moving stuff out fast." Larry ties his long salt-and-pepper hair into a ponytail. He says, "We don't touch nothing. We just go in, see if Supremica's stuff is there, then call the cops."

"Just to confirm?"

"Yeah. Can you disarm the alarms?"

"Probably the contact breakers on a window, but is there a skylight? Are the upper windows alarmed? It might be easier. We also need to see if there are any motion detectors inside."

"Yeah, forgot about that."

"Hold on," Allen says. "You sure about this? We can wait and watch and see what goes on here."

Larry sighs. "I'm tired, man. I don't want to sit here all night. I just want to get this fucker done with and close the case."

"But the billable hours are nice."

"Yeah, I guess," he says. "Can we just check the roof? Come on, B., just check."

As they circle the warehouse, Allen worries about his partner. Within the past two years since they officially partnered up, they have been shot at twice, and Larry has been beaten up by a pair of angry bikers. It seems that the intensity of their troubled clients has grown exponentially; no longer attracting divorce cases or simple tail jobs, they are now getting blackmail victims, protection rackets, and even—as in the case with the bikers—a drug-related job where Allen and Larry were supposed to find out why a marijuana dealer's shipment kept getting stolen. No, it wasn't legal, and it was the only time B&C took an unofficial case like that, paid in cash, off the books. After the beating Larry swore off doing favors for friends of friends. They keep trying to gravitate toward worker's comp cases, witness interviewing, and the occasional corporate job like the Supremica one, which will pay their overhead for the next three months.

Two years of this is wearing them down. More so with Larry—who has been in the business for almost thirteen years now—than Allen, who feels like he is still learning how to be a private investigator. But even Allen is alarmed by the dangers of their profession. He wants to do safe background checks. He wants to do missing persons.

True, he worked in executive protection for a few years, and that was undoubtedly dangerous, but it involved a different kind of risk. Once he finished his threat assessment, and began protecting a client, he had prepared for almost every contingency; his role was clearly defensive, not too unlike his soccer days. Whereas with Larry they are barely able to write up a threat assessment because everything they do is offensive, searching forward, encountering the unpredictable and unexpected. In essence, they *want* the unexpected, a break in the case, a new witness, a new clue, and that propels them even further into unknown territory. This shift in perspective is something Allen hasn't quite gotten used to.

So Allen is unprepared for this. When they scale the back wall using the iron security grilling over an office window, and find a skylight on the roof, Larry begins prying open the metal frame. Allen says, "Whoa, whoa. I thought we're just going to check."

"Don't see any alarms connected to this. Do you?"

"No."

"We'll look down from up here," Larry says, using his thick fingers to bend back a corroded metal bar at the base of the skylight.

"Jeez. Doesn't that hurt?" Allen asks.

"Yeah, it does, actually." But Larry keeps pulling on the bar, slowly exposing a seam where the window frame meets the black tar roof. He crouches low, his huge torso and thick arms bulging against his tight button-up shirt. Larry, at six-foot-two and 250 pounds, has the bulk and strength of a pro wrestler, and with his long hair, thick eyebrows, and large nose, he sometimes reminds Allen of a classic Neanderthal man. Larry is occasionally blustery and overbearing, but Allen likes him because he is always direct and earnest. Larry doesn't seem to have the patience or capacity for subterfuge.

Larry looks up, the moonlight shadowing his face. He says, "Hey, you wanna help me or what?"

Allen nods and grabs the bar with Larry. They pull it off, then manage to slide a large windowpane from the skylight, but the scraping noise worries Allen. He says, "If they have sound detectors, we're screwed."

"It's just a shitty warehouse. You saw the basic crap down below." He peers down through the open skylight for a moment, then pulls his head out, and says, "Way high up. And pretty dark. I got rope in the truck. Can you fit through this?"

"Are you kidding?"

Larry stands up and sighs. "B., I'm sorry I had to call you away from your woman. But the sooner we check this out, the sooner we can go home. I'm fucking bushed."

Allen looks at the narrow opening, thinking, My woman? He says, "I can fit. You have a flashlight?"

"Yeah. Just go down, look at what's there, and I pull you back up. In and out."

"Let me check the alarms inside first."

Larry nods, and walks toward the edge of the roof. "Be right back."

The Block, while waiting for Larry to return with rope and a flashlight to participate in an illegal act that could jeopardize their careers, looks out over toward Jack London Square, the marina lit up and the adjacent stores bright and active. He sees from his vantage point pedestrians moving across the piers. The weather this summer is warmer than usual, but he feels a pleasant cool breeze. He wishes he were working out with Serena, but then remembers the news of her parents visiting. The Block doesn't work well under pressure, and can already imagine himself screwing up. He will say the wrong thing or underwhelm them in some way. And he will be overtly self-conscious of his lack of ethnic ties. He can't speak Korean, and knows very little about Korean culture; Serena says he is a *gyupo,* an Americanized Korean. Serena, however, speaks the language and actually studied in Seoul for two summers, and this mere fact puts Allen at a disadvantage with her parents. He is starting in negative territory. He is an ethnic dunce.

Shaking this off, and peering into the open skylight, he thinks he hears a thumping sound down below. He waits, listens, but it's quiet. He squints into the fuzzy darkness, the security lights near the front barely illuminating beyond a small circle of an office. This is stupid. They should wait until morning and just watch the place; they will know soon enough whether or not it is a fencing operation.

Larry returns with a coil of nylon rope and a thin halogen flashlight. Allen says, "I thought I heard something down there."

"That was me. I double-checked if the doors were locked." He throws the rope down and aims the flashlight into the warehouse. "You know alarms better. Do you see anything?"

Allen peers in next to Larry, taking the flashlight and searching along the entrances for a control panel. There, next to the front door. He sees the blinking red light even from this distance, and searches the corners and along the walls for infrared motion detectors. He also looks for the small indentations on the walls for the newer microphone-alarms that feed live audio to an alarm-monitoring station. Other triggers: laser breakers, vibration monitors, and, of course, video cameras. But there is nothing.

"Looks pretty clean to me," Allen says, peering down at the crates and stacks of cardboard boxes. "Just the doors and windows are rigged. There's a lot of stuff down there. Pretty weak alarms for all this stuff."

"Not if it's hot," Larry says.

"Good point."

"Want to go for a look, B.?"

"Not really."

"Blockmeister, it's cake. You'll spiderman down there and see if there are any of Supremica's computers and shit. It'll take two seconds."

"You think the Supremica IDs are still on stolen equipment?"

"Don't forget the high-end stuff have the production stamp near the serials."

Allen picks up the coil of rope and runs it to the edge of the roof, tying one end to a section of pipe that's adjacent to the low surrounding wall. Larry throws the other end of the rope down through the skylight and tests Allen's knot, pulling and yanking. Larry nods.

Allen shoves the flashlight into his pants and lowers himself feetfirst through the narrow window opening. He tears the sleeve of his shirt on a piece of metal framing. He sighs. It's a new shirt. Wrapping his legs around the rope he goes down hand over hand, feeling his pants ride up into his crotch. Halfway down he begins swaying too much and stops, pulling out the flashlight and peering at the floor. About twenty more feet to go. He looks up. Larry is watching. Allen continues sliding down with one hand.

When he reaches the ground he stops and listens. Quiet. He searches the walls for motion detectors, any kind of extra alarms. He looks along the floor for pressure-sensitive mats or trip wires. Again, nothing. Odd. Unusually lax. Allen surveys the layout: on the far side are high stacks of crates lined up in rows; on this side, near the garage doors and main entrance, is a makeshift office with two desks and file cabinets. Next to the makeshift office, long metal shelving stacked high with cardboard boxes, computers, and electronic equipment run in narrow parallel rows. Allen hurries to the shelving to check the computers.

Supremica is an EMS, an electronic manufacturing service: they build computers and equipment, assembly-line style, to the computer company's specifications, then the computer company slaps its logo on the handiwork. Because of high turnover and a wide variety of customers, Supremica didn't notice large numbers of finished and unfinished computers and components disappearing from the quality-control checking stations. With the potential for bad publicity and their clients jumping to more secure competitors, they hired B&C Investigations to look into the matter carefully and quietly.

Allen moves along the shelving and checks the computers—laptops and CPUs—but doesn't find any of Supremica's labels, nor is there the "S" in the production numbers adjacent to the serial number plates and stickers. He looks at the routers, another product Supremica sources, and picks up one the size and shape of a large book, checking the back. He finds the "S" and examines the other routers. All Supremica.

He turns and is about to call up to Larry when he hears a voice say softly, "Don't fucking move, Chin. I've got a gun at your head. Hands up high. Slowly."

Allen then realizes why there isn't much electronic security. The warehouse has the oldest kind of security around: a guard. This guy must have heard them on the roof and hid, waiting to see what Allen and Larry did.

"Come on, Chin. Don't fuck with me."

Allen nods and slowly raises his hands.

Two

Running with Serena gives Allen an inexplicable pleasure, because it combines two aspects of his life that he enjoys the most: exercise and the intimacy of a woman. The first time he saw Serena, almost two years ago, was when she had returned from a long, sweaty run, and he still feels that thump of desire when he sees her like that now, a sheen over her muscled arms and legs. And when they run together, they talk quietly, in between breaths, usually staring forward, allowing for unguarded musings; they are less self-conscious of the other person's reaction to whatever they are saying. They are just talking into the forward air. Occasionally one of them might say something that is startlingly honest and requires a glance, a quick check of reactions, and then a continuation of the thought. Serena once told him she is turned on when she goes through car washes, and wants to try a quickie in one. Allen admitted that his irrational fear of dogs sometimes even includes Serena's placid German shepherd, who occasionally gives Allen suspicious looks.

They don't always converse, but both of them seem to save a lot of their discussion for the runs, which just recently occurred to Allen as a form of therapy. They haven't yet argued on a run, though that might be simply because an argument requires the summoning of energy that is better saved for the three to five miles. So they talk, they listen. Allen isn't sure how this started, or why both of them feel freer with their words during this time, but he now needs these evening runs with her.

In fact, as Allen now kneels on the floor, his hands clasped behind his head, the Jamaican gangster on his cell phone talking to his boss, Larry beside him, Allen is already thinking of how he will tell Serena about this on their run tonight. His knees are hurting from the concrete floor, and he hopes this doesn't mess up his pace. It isn't until he turns to Larry and sees the trickle of sweat running down Larry's temple that Allen snaps back to the situation.

He realizes that he could've avoided all this by taking down the Jamaican immediately, but Allen was so surprised by the well-dressed guard that he complied. He put his hands up, and with the nine-millimeter aimed at his mouth, let the Jamaican take his SIG from his belt holster. Then the Jamaican ordered Allen to call Larry down from the skylight. It turned out that Larry, after some grumbling, *did* fit through that small opening, and Allen now wonders if Larry sent him down here first on purpose. Larry's tolerance for risk seems to be deteriorating.

Allen's knees are aching badly, and he tries shifting from side to side, giving each knee a few seconds of rest. He knows that he and Larry will be in worse shape if the Jamaican's friends arrive. He meets Larry's eyes, then stares at their guns on the crate. His best chance is for the Jamaican to put his gun down when he ties Allen's wrists; Larry can then undo his knot and go for a gun, and Allen can pull out his Raven. It has to be timed perfectly, or else the Jamaican might grab his automatic and start shooting.

Allen's palms sweat, his adrenaline pumping through him. As soon as the Jamaican gets off the phone, he'll probably tie Allen up. Allen glances again at Larry, hoping he'll know what to do. Larry shakes his head, and whispers, "I don't know about you, but I'm getting really sick of this kind of shit." The Jamaican notices this quiet interaction, so he walks swiftly over to them and kicks Larry in the midsection and tells him to shut up. Larry doubles over, though Allen suspects Larry is exaggerating because not only is Larry's midsection strong, but he seems to have anticipated the hit and fallen back prior to the actual blow. Larry then turns to Allen and gives him such a tired, resigned look that Allen is shocked. Larry looks old. His eyes are exhausted.

"No more talking to Chin," the Jamaican says.

Allen stops rocking on his knees, staring at Larry.

"Keep your hands up, Chin."

"Stop calling me Chin, for chrissakes," Allen says.

The Jamaican stares. "What the hell you say?"

Allen says, "Stop calling me Chin. I'm not Chinese."

Larry turns toward Allen. The Jamaican says, "Chin, I call you whatever the fuck I want to call you."

"Oh, tough guy with a gun," Allen says.

The Jamaican's face hardens, and he says into the phone, "Just get the fuck over here and bring Marlon. I don't know what to do with them." He flips his phone closed and turns to Allen. "You want a little trouble there, Chin?"

Allen hopes Larry is ready to free his knots. Allen's ankle holster has a strap buttoned over the grip, so his movements need to include pulling off the strap, then grabbing the gun, and he has to do this without anything catching or snagging. Allen says to the Jamaican, "What are you going to do, tie me up and kick me, too?"

Anger flashes in the Jamaican's eyes, but then quickly disappears. He studies Allen for a second, then laughs a deep, booming laugh, his gold earring blinking in the security light. He says, "Now you're trying to be the tough guy, Chin?" He motions to Allen with his gun. "Get on your stomach, your hands behind your back, legs spread."

Allen turns to Larry, who meets his gaze with a level stare. *Okay.*

The Jamaican says, "Don't be checking with Big Face. Just get on the fucking floor." He stops, looking back and forth between them, then says to Larry, "Hold on. Move away from Chin. And you also get on the floor, on your stomach. I got to check your hands."

Damn. Allen tries to think of an alternative plan, but doesn't have enough time. The Jamaican is already moving toward Larry, about to find the loose knot.

Allen rolls onto his side, curls up to reach his ankle holster, and quickly unlatches the strap. He pulls out his Raven as the Jamaican turns to him, startled by the movement, and Larry then yanks free his hands and leaps up. The Jamaican swivels toward Larry, and Allen flicks off the safety, aims the Raven at the Jamaican, but Larry tackles him, and they both go down. Larry struggles for the gun, and Allen rushes toward them, trying to avoid the line of fire, and yells, "Don't move!" He aims the gun at the Jamaican's head.

They both stop fighting. The Jamaican says, "Motherfucker," but lets go of his automatic, and Larry yanks it free. Larry stands up, kicks the Jamaican in the stomach, and says, "Your turn to roll over, asshole."

"You guys don't know what you're getting into, man."

Larry pulls out the Jamaican's wallet and checks the driver's license. To Allen he says, "Harry Dubois."

"We should get the hell out of here before his friends show up," Allen says.

"Yeah, let's tie up this guy—" Larry stops and turns toward the front entrance. He holds up his hand. A scraping sound. Movement. The iron front door squeaking. Allen hurries to the crate, grabs his SIG, and holsters his Raven on his ankle. When he passes Larry's revolver to him, the Jamaican—Harry—suddenly sprints up, and races away, yelling, "They got guns, Marlon! They're armed!" He disappears into the shadows, darting around crates.

Larry says, "Let's go."

Allen hears the iron front door slamming shut, urgent voices bouncing through the warehouse. Larry has a gun in each hand, cowboy style, though they are mismatched—shining nickel next to a blunt black. They run toward the rear, and Allen scoops up the flashlight from the floor. He shines it ahead of them, and clicks it off when they see the Exit sign over the double doors. Larry backs into the wall, peering into the darkness, and Allen pushes the door but finds it locked. He checks the latches above and below, and sees a large bolt connecting into the floor. He pulls the bolt out and opens the door, which trips the alarm, a siren screeching. More security lights blink on around them.

Allen looks out onto an empty parking lot, and Larry yells, "Go! They're coming in the front!"

Allen jumps out and sees a man in a suit rounding the corner of the warehouse. The man stops and raises his gun, and Allen quickly lets off two shots, which go wide and hit the wall, but that's enough to send the man back. Larry runs with Allen, and they head for a darkened corner of the lot, where the fence meets another property. The alarm dies out. Voices emerge from the warehouse, and Allen sees three men running toward them. He quickly begins scaling the fence.

Larry says again, "I'm so sick of this shit."

Allen looks back at him, then jumps over the fence. Larry follows. The men yell at them to stop. Larry jumps down and follows Allen across the loading area of another warehouse, which leads onto a street. They hear the men also climbing the fence. Larry wheezes as he jogs behind Allen, who asks if he has his cell phone on him.

"In the car," Larry says in between gasps. "Yours?"

"Also in the car," Allen says. "Let's go toward the square. More people there." He looks back into the darkness but can't see the men who are after them. Allen holsters his SIG and tells Larry to do the same. They hurry along the sidewalk, more traffic moving along the streets the closer they get to the marina. Larry says, "Sorry, man. This is my fault."

"Let's just get some help."

"I gotta say, B. I'm thinking of getting out of the biz."

Allen glances at him in surprise. "What?"

Larry sighs. "Getting sick of this."

But then an Oakland police car cruises in their direction, and Allen hurries out into the street, flagging it down.

The police car pulls up beside him. "Something wrong?" the officer asks.

Allen says, "Yes, sir. Something's very wrong."

By the time the Oakland Police converge on the warehouse, the Jamaican gangster and his friends have long disappeared, but all the equipment is still there, and B&C Investigations is credited for breaking this large-scale fencing operation. When the local news station vans appear on the scene, Allen lets Larry do all the talking and tells the lead investigator, Lieutenant Rollins of the Criminal Investigations Division, that he'll finish his statement at the main Oakland Police Department. Allen doesn't want publicity. He had way too much of it three and a half years ago when, during his stint in executive security, he stumbled into an illegal importing scheme that ended up involving his family, even his dead father in a tangential way. Allen prefers invisibility. Larry can talk up their firm. Allen is sure that Larry will also creatively justify their illegal breaking and entering.

He leaves the crime scene and drives over to Serena's apartment in Berkeley. She isn't home, so he lets himself in with his key and changes into running gear. Serena's dog, Gracie, follows him around the living room, clicking on the hardwood floors. Allen has a shelf in her closet, and always has extra workout clothes here. Stretching out in front of the TV, the ten o'clock news coming up, he discovers his body still shaking from the excitement, the residual adrenaline slowly working out of his system. He walks around her apartment, African masks hanging on the walls, mahogany and cherrywood furniture darkening the track lighting. Her living room window overlooks Martin Luther King Boulevard; Allen stares down at the cars speeding in the narrow two lanes, commuters rushing home late.

A teaser on the TV says, "A multimillion-dollar high-tech fencing operation in Oakland is discovered. More on the ten o'clock news, coming up next." Allen continues stretching on the floor. He wonders if Larry is serious about quitting. They have barely begun the partnership, and Larry has even mentioned trying to restart the executive protection end, something they abandoned a year ago because the Silicon Valley economy crashed. Allen isn't sure if they are ready for that, but with business picking up, it can still be an option.

Allen suddenly realizes that Larry, after turning forty, is losing his edge. Allen saw this at ProServ, seasoned bodyguards taking easier assignments, worrying about their health benefits, and letting the young Turks move up quickly. The problem here: Allen isn't a young Turk, and without Larry's backup, this job would get even more dangerous. Tomorrow he'll sit Larry down and figure this out.

He hears the key in the door, and Serena walks in. She smiles when she sees him sprawled out on the floor. Gracie pads over to her, and Serena crouches down to scratch her neck. Serena, in black Lycra tights and fluorescent orange wrist and ankle bands, her running outfit, tilts her head at Allen. "Hey, you're here."

Allen notices the sweat on her face and hair, her movements slow and stiff, and he says "You went running."

"Oh, no! Were you waiting for me?" she asks. She sits down next to him to stretch her legs, and Gracie nestles by Allen's side. He leans over to Serena and kisses her sweaty neck; he then blows lightly to cool her.

He says, "I told you I'd be back in time to run with you."

"I called your cell, but you didn't pick up." She leans forward and her joints crack. "Tia rang me and she wants to hang out tonight, so I had to run earlier."

"Larry and I had a little trouble."

"What kind?"

"No big deal. But I was kind of looking forward to our run."

"Sorry. Want to come out with us? Janine will be there, too."

Allen considers this, trying not to appear disappointed. Nothing seems to be going right this evening. Why is everything off? Having a gun aimed at his face might account for that. He stands up. "I guess I'll head home and run there."

The TV plays a commercial. Serena stands up as well. "You don't want to stay the night?"

"You'll be out."

"I'll cancel. Or you can come with." She glides over to him and touches his arm. "Hey, what's wrong? You okay?"

"I'm feeling out of whack. I need to run. I think I'll just head back into the city—"

"You know what? I can do another run." She tugs on his shirt toward the door. "Come on. Let's work that wackiness off."

Allen smiles. This is why he likes her so much. He says, "You're great. But no, you go on. We'll hook up tomorrow night for a workout at the gym, okay?"

"Deal."

Allen gathers his clothes, and says, "You can be really nice, you know that? I love you."

Her eyes brighten. "I love you, too."

It's the postexcitement funk. He has felt it many times before. Adrenaline crashing, senses dulling, he feels the funk descending after a stressful job. When he worked at ProServ and came off his shift from a tense guarding job, he'd get this. Everything seems gauzy, fuzzy. There's a film of wispy white and grey coating the city as he drives across the crowded Bay Bridge and inches his way to the Richmond district. Taillights, streetlamps, and blinking store signs leave trails across his vision. The heaviness in his chest is the aftermath of the warehouse action, he knows, though he can't help connecting it to Serena as well. He worries about their future. He worries about meeting her parents.

Allen lives off Clement Street, around the corner from the New May Wah Supermarket and near Green Apple Books, where he has been buying used, well-worn, and student-highlighted copies of Kierkegaard and introduction to philosophy texts. He finds that reading them, as difficult as they are, distracts and challenges him, not too unlike his long runs, and sometimes he'll look up from a book, and realize that a couple hours have passed effortlessly. He wants answers. He wants perspective.

Allen looks forward to a quiet evening, relieved for not accepting Serena's invitation to join her and her friends. His studio apartment, part of a six-unit building on Sixth and staggeringly overpriced at $1200 a month, is cold and dark. It's next door to a general store that sells everything from discounted cigarettes to carpets, and every night he hears the owner chatting in Chinese with customers on the steps outside, their voices rising to his window.

He dumps his bags onto the floor and begins stretching out in the dark, ignoring the blinking red light on his answering machine. He is not home. He is not here. He is out running in the night. He is free from the daily bothers of work and life. He is flying. He intends to run to Golden Gate Park—one of the reasons why he chose to live in this neighborhood—and wraps a fluorescent orange strap around his chest for cars to see him. He has almost been hit a few times.

Then, the run: leaping down the steps and onto the pavement, the cool city air, a light fog descending. Down Sixth, past Geary. A few more blocks, and he meets Fulton, but instead of going into the park, he finds that tonight he likes the movement of cars along the street so continues on Fulton toward Ocean Beach. It occurs to him that he and Larry could've been killed tonight, and this delayed response, the sweat breaking out on his back and neck, the sudden flushed and throbbing sensation in his head, isn't just from the run. He is familiar with this feeling as well, since it usually accompanies the postadrenaline crash.

Run faster. Run harder. He tries to laugh off the events, and says "Chin" aloud. Where did that come from? Maybe it's a Jamaican thing. Maybe it's supposed to be an insult, like "chink." Chin. Chink. Why did Larry mention leaving the business? Does he really want to quit? Allen doesn't know if he can handle the jobs by himself, which means looking for a new firm. He can't stomach a job search, not now. Oh, and Serena's parents are coming. They'll love it if he is unemployed. They'll want to know if Serena is marrying him. They'll want to know how serious this is. She'll then want to know as well. And Allen will need to know. Yet he doesn't know. He knows he loves her, but nothing else is certain. They haven't talked about marriage or even about moving in together, though they've both come close. They've substituted it for innocuous euphemisms. They are really "committed" to one another. Is that weak? Is that spineless? He wants to be with her. And it's true that he and Serena would cut their costs by moving in together. But this thought scares him. He has never lived with anyone, and wonders if it's as simple as signing a lease and moving his belongings. But it's a path toward a goal. He needs to be sure about the goal. Doesn't he?

Allen debates this as he nears the beach. Thoughts swirl. The sweat on his face chills him. He has a craving for sweet rice cakes, stocked at a number of the Asian bakeries on Clement, another reason why he wanted to live in this neighborhood. He anticipates this simple pleasure, and forgets about everything except the feeling of his legs straining, his breath steady, his heart thumping in rhythm with his steps. He crosses the highway and runs along the gritty sidewalk, the sound of the crashing waves rolling over him. He speeds up. He lifts off. He soars.

"Why didn't you tell me what happened?" Serena asks, calling Allen just after his run. "I saw the news report and couldn't believe it. Larry was on TV? What was this about some fencing warehouse? You two found it?"

"Yeah," Allen says, stretching his legs. Sweat drips down his face.

"You should've said something. I wouldn't have left you. Are you okay?"

"I'm fine."

"Allen, why didn't you say something? Was I supposed to read your mind?"

"No. I just . . . I just wanted to go running."

"But—" Serena sighs. "I don't like it when you get like this."

"Like what?"

"All internal. All solitary."

Allen realizes that only two hours ago he had a loaded gun pointed in his face. He says, "You're right. Are you at home?"

"I'm at the Mallard in Albany. With Janine and Tia. You want to come back over here?"

"No, thanks. I'm tired. I want to shower, get some rest."

"We need to talk, Allen," Serena says.

A talk. He suddenly feels like going running again. He says, "Okay. Tomorrow night. When we work out. Okay?"

"Okay."

They hang up. He plays the messages on his machine and hears Serena asking him to call her back. A newspaper reporter requests an interview with him. And then Larry comes on, and says, "Yo, B. Where are you? Just heard our voice mail at the office. Be there tomorrow at ten. You got an appointment with your ex, Linda. I think she wants to hire us. Okay?"

Allen replays the message. Then he calls Larry's cell, but no one answers. He checks the voice mail at the office; Larry has already erased all the messages. His ex? Linda? Allen thought she was in LA. Linda. He can't wrap his thoughts around this. Why would she want to hire him?

He walks into this bathroom and runs the shower. He barely feels the scorching hot jets on his sore back.

The last time he saw Linda, she was wearing a baseball cap to cover her shaved head—she was recovering from a head injury that had required surgery—and sat him down and told him she was staying in LA, without him. They were breaking up. This was not unexpected at all. Their relationship had been faltering long before that moment. But it was difficult hearing it finalized like that.

Linda Maldonado was a journalist with the *San Jose Sentinel* when Allen first met her four years ago. She helped him look into the details of his partner's death, and they ended up dating for almost two years. They broke up while he was helping her and her family in Los Angeles, and he hadn't heard from her since then. He never fully understood why they split up, though he knew her previous marriage had soured her on long-term relationships in general, and at the time she had recently turned thirty, suddenly realizing that she wasn't happy where she was. She quit her job and planned to stay down there after inheriting some money from her late father.

Yes, Allen still thinks about her often, and has resisted sending her an e-mail or calling her parents' condo to find out how she is. He once entered her name in the online databases B&C subscribes to, searching for any news articles by her, but nothing recent came up. Her old *Sentinel* articles were available online, and he glanced at the headlines with an odd nostalgia, since he had read most of her stories when they had first been published.

As he prepares for bed, Allen again considers the connections of seemingly random coincidences. That Linda called today couldn't have been an accident. Today is the day that Serena's parents told her they would be visiting. Today is the day Allen and Larry had a breakthrough with the Supremica case.

Allen pulls out Kierkegaard's *Either/Or* from his stack of philosophy books on his night table. He flips the pages to see where his fingers lead him, and he come across a passage, the word "marriage" stopping him: "However many painful confusions life may still have in store, I fight for two things: for the prodigious task of showing that marriage is the transfiguration of first love, that it is its friend, not its enemy; and for the task (which to others is very trivial but to me is all the more important) of showing that my humble marriage has had such a meaning for me, so that from it I derive strength and courage to fulfill constantly this task."

Allen checks the cover. He rereads the passage, then closes the book. He thinks for a moment about the prospect of marriage with Serena. Why does that scare him so much? It's not staying with one person that alarms him—no, it's staying with one person who might leave him later.

It's staying with the wrong person. Allen reopens the book and tries to read another passage, but can't focus. He replaces the book on his night table. If he were a superstitious person he might be spooked by that passage, but he isn't. This just confirms his theory of the purposefulness of events. Everything means something, though he knows not what. He turns off his light and sinks into his pillow. He feels a small flutter of nerves at the thought of tomorrow's meeting. He falls asleep and dreams of being chased by rabid pit bulls.

Three

When Allen was nine years old he made collect calls to strangers. He would dial through the operator and wonder if the person answering the other end would accept the charges. This was before the automated recordings, before the myriad of options available now; this was when he had to reach up to dial the random numbers, and the operators, upon hearing his voice, softened theirs and addressed him as "son" or "dear."

"I'd like to make a collect call," he told the operator.

"Your name?"

"Allen."

"Just a moment, dear," the operator said, and he heard the ringing.

"Hello?" a voice would answer.

"I have a collect call from Allen," the operator said. "Do you accept the charges?"

"Who?" the voice answered.

"Allen," the operator repeated. "A collect call from Allen."

"I'm afraid I don't know an Allen. Allen who?"

"What's your last name, dear?" the operator asked Allen.

"Allen Choice. It's me, Allen Choice."

"Sorry," the voice on the other line said. "I don't know an Allen Choice."

"Are you sure you have the right number, Allen?" the operator asked.

He liked the operator saying his name. He answered, "I think so."

"Sorry, dear."

He heard the other end hanging up, then the operator disconnected him.

He wasn't sure how this had started; perhaps it was when his aunt had made a collect call to his father, and he learned the protocol. There was something liberating about making calls without money. He liked hearing the other end respond.

Allen was being shuttled to and from his aunt's and his father's places. His mother had died when he was born, and Allen's father—a driver at a shipping company, often on the road for two or three days at a time—worried about his being alone for too long. His aunt Insook had regular hours as a bookkeeper, so Allen usually stayed with his aunt during his father's trips. He would eventually move in with his aunt when his father died the next year.

Allen never called from his own phone, but from pay phones around the neighborhood. He liked phones away from noisy traffic, but near other people. Malls were good. So were parks and playgrounds. Sometimes he used his real name, sometimes not. He usually dialed random local numbers. He hoped to reach a young woman, because the only time someone had ever accepted the charges was a young woman who had said, "You know, the telephone isn't a toy."

He was stunned that the person had taken the call.

The woman said again, "It's not a toy."

He said, "I know."

"Does your mother know you're doing this?"

"No," he answered.

"You sound really young. How old are you?"

"I'm not that young."

"Okay, Allen," she said. "Don't do this again, okay? It wastes money."

"Okay," he lied.

Sometimes he tried to convince the person answering the phone to accept the charges. If a woman's voice came on and said she didn't know Allen, he would say, "It's me, Allen. Don't you remember me?"

"Son," the operator would say, "you can't speak right now. Please wait."

"I'm sorry, I don't know an Allen," the woman would answer.

"You do. It's me. Remember me?"

"Son," the operator would say again. "Stop talking."

"No, I'm sorry, Allen. I don't know you."

"But it's me, Allen—"

And usually the operator would cut them off.

Some weekends he'd be stuck at his aunt's, but she'd be either at church or with her friends, and he'd wander around Lake Merritt, watching the families picnic on the grass. He'd find the phones near Lakeside Park and watch other kids playing Frisbee or flying kites. He'd listen to them yell and laugh and chase each other. He'd walk to the nearest phone, lift up the handset, and dial "0" and a random phone number. He'd say to the operator, "A collect call from Allen." And he'd hear the distant ringing. He'd wonder if this would be a good one, if this would be a taker. He'd wonder if maybe this person would not only accept the call but talk to him. He and the operator would listen to the ringing once, twice, thrice, and when someone picked up, he'd think, Maybe this is the one.

As Allen drives to work he wonders why he has been getting more nostalgic lately. It isn't as if he's longing for a simpler time, since he knows that it was probably more difficult back then, with the turmoil of loss surrounding him. Perhaps the issues confronting him were more elemental—traumatic, yes, but dealt with in straightforward ways. Loss, absence, and loneliness seemed now, from an adult perspective, focused problems. They were challenged with his individual and direct childhood responses. Lonely? Make collect calls. The problems now, like meeting an ex-girlfriend who dumped him quite painfully, seem messier, more complicated. Knowledge of history and circumstance, the complexities of memory and interrelated emotions—these add extra burdens.

B&C Investigations sits in an alley a few blocks south of Market Street in a small converted warehouse between Eighth and Ninth. Larry found the space at a discount in the wake of the dot.com collapse, and convinced the landlord to build a conference room and private cubicles. For just the two of them, the space is actually too large, but Larry wanted room for expansion. He had visions of a large PI and security firm, with him and Allen as copresidents, though Allen isn't sure if this is still true.

Allen arrives early, and suddenly views everything through Linda's eyes, or at least a stranger's eyes who'll judge the firm by the environs, and he realizes how dirty the alley is, garbage in the gutters, the sidewalks stained. He smells urine. A junkie in a mud-splattered winter parka shuffles across the street, the same man who occasionally sleeps in their doorway. The facade of B&C has swatches of painted-over graffiti, white zigzags over gang tags. Mashed and gnarled cigarette butts lie in a heap by the steps, reminding him of dead insects.

Allen enters the cold office and immediately checks the voice mail. There are a few more inquiries, potential clients who saw Larry on TV, but nothing from Linda. He sorts through the past week's mail addressed to him, mostly junk and PI-related solicitations, then begins writing up the Supremica status report. He eyes the clock. He has an hour before Linda arrives. He looks down at his clothes—dress pants and a button-down Oxford—and wonders if he should've worn a suit.

He is about to check his hair, but stops himself. What are you doing? he asks himself. She is a potential client. That's all.

Shaking this off and focusing on his report, Allen hears Larry coming in, and calling out, "Yo, Blockman, you here yet?"

Allen stands and looks over the cubicle divider. Larry ambles in, taking off his sport coat and throwing it onto the waiting area sofa. He says to Allen, "What're you working on?"

"Supremica update."

"Chuck it. We got fired."

"What?"

"They didn't like the publicity we caused."

"But we found their stuff!"

"Yeah, but companies might be suing them now. Our contact, Hilles, was pissed as hell." Larry shrugs, then laughs. "Who cares? We probably got enough new clients for the rest of the year."

"You were on all the news stations?"

"No. Just Channel 2, 4, and 20. But that was plenty."

"So what was that stuff last night about quitting?" Allen asks.

Larry's smile disappears, and he says, "Oh, sorry about that. I was feeling pretty shitty."

"So you're thinking about it, though?"

Larry nods slowly.

"Why?"

"Just getting tired of all this, B. I'm freaking forty years old and have been doing this same shit for too long."

Allen understands this, and nods. He says, "All right, but what else would you do? And what about me and the business?"

"Hell, the business is easy. There's a guy for the books, a guy for the taxes, a guy for the benefits. You know, you met them. They do most of the business stuff. For us it's just getting the clients and doing the grunt work."

The grip of responsibility tightens around Allen's throat. He says, "I don't know."

"And it's not definite. Alls I'm saying is that I'm thinking about it."

"I thought we were going to be partners, expand, all that."

"If I did step back, I'd still help out. I'd never just walk off."

"And what else would you do?"

Larry looks down at his shoes for a moment, then says, "Not sure."

Allen leans forward, hearing something more in his voice. Allen has been getting better at teasing out the nuances in Larry's tough-guy speech, and says, "You have an idea, though. What, apply for the FBI or something?"

"No. Nothing like that."

"Not security?"

"Nothing near it."

Allen waits, then says, "Well?"

"You know what I've always wanted to do?"

Allen shakes his head.

Larry shrugs his large shoulders. "I've always wanted to be a chef."

Allen blinks. "What?"

"A chef, like Jacques Pepin on TV? You know? Making all those cool dishes."

Allen tries to picture Larry, an oversized pro-wrestler type, trying to dice onions with his thick hands and wearing a chef's hat over his long hair. Larry's forearms are so large that people at his gym call him "Popeye," and Allen imagines this huge, muscular man talking to a TV camera about preparing a soufflé. He starts to laugh, but stops as soon as he sees Larry's hurt expression. "Sorry," Allen says quickly. "I just never imagined . . . I never thought of that. I've never known you to cook."

"Dude, I cook. I just don't tell anyone about it."

Allen studies him, and finally says, "That's great, Larry. But you're going to leave me to drown."

"No. I'm just thinking about it. That's all."

Then the front door opens, and Linda walks in.

Linda Maldonado used to have long, black curly hair that fell to her shoulders, the tight curls filtering the light behind her, and that's how Allen always pictures her, so he's momentarily disoriented to see her with short hair, the curls close against her scalp; she's also wearing a long, sheer, gauzy skirt. She used to hate skirts. Allen stares at the brown-and-black fabric clinging and stretching around her legs as she walks across the office. Her matching short-sleeve blouse is snug against her body. When she sees Allen leaning against the cubicle divider, she stops. She smiles, her dark red lipstick contrasting with her white teeth. "Allen?"

"Hi, Linda."

"You've lost weight," she says.

"You've kept your hair short," he says, noticing that her face seems tan.

After a pause, Allen moves across the floor and they hug awkwardly, quickly. Linda turns to Larry and says, "Nice to see you again."

"Likewise," Larry replies.

"I saw you on TV last night. Very commanding."

Larry grins. "Thanks."

She says to Allen, "But you weren't on?"

"He took off," Larry says. "He don't like the publicity."

"I guess that's true," she replies. "You look good, Allen."

Allen feels shy. He has trouble meeting her eyes, and says, "Come, let's talk in my office."

"How've you been?" she asks as she follows him into his cubicle. "It's been a while."

"I'm fine. I didn't know you were back up here. You left LA?"

"A few months ago."

Allen points to a chair next to his desk. She sits down and crosses her legs. Allen decides not to go behind his desk, and takes a chair diagonal to her. He says, "You look great." He notices that she's wearing lipstick.

"So do you," she says. "You've slimmed down."

"Running."

She nods. "Still going on those night runs?"

"Yes," he says, thinking of Serena. "So, what're you doing up here? Are you back for good?"

She stares across his desk, her eyes losing some focus. "A bunch of reasons. The most important is why I'm here to see you. It's for Julie. She needs some help."

Allen notices the deflection of the question, the "bunch of reasons" veiling something, but he thinks about Julie, Linda's stepsister, and says, "Why isn't she here with you?"

"We're interviewing different PIs."

"Ah," Allen says. "Competition."

"We have a lawyer guiding us on this."

"On what?"

"Remember Nora, Julie's daughter?"

"Sure."

"Her father abducted her."

Allen sits up. "Kidnapped?"

"Abducted. Parental abduction. Custody problems from the divorce."

"Is she in any danger?"

"No. I don't think so. We just don't know."

Allen glances at Linda's left hand and is startled to see a diamond ring. He asks, "Is that an engagement ring?"

Linda looks down for a long moment. She then answers, "Yes, it is."

He tries to find the right question to ask, but his mind blanks. He clears his throat, then says as professionally as he can, "So tell me what you'd want B&C to do."

Linda's stepsister Julie had divorced her husband Frank last year, and though the divorce seemed to be amicable, their joint custody of nine-year-old Nora began running into problems when Julie wanted to leave the Bay Area. There were also money issues, centering around Frank's stock options not being fully revealed in the divorce asset disclosure papers, and Julie now suing for a larger share and complete access. Linda explains to Allen, "It was getting ugly. They were both using custody of Nora as a bargaining chip."

"So Frank took her?" he asks, still trying to focus. Engaged? Linda?

"He has joint custody, and one weekend just disappeared with her."

"And the police?"

"We went by the book. There are actually a number of procedures to follow with the police and the FBI. Nora's entered into the NCIC—"

"Their missing person file?"

"That's right. The National Crime Information Computer. A judge issued a contempt order for Interference with Custody, so there's a felony warrant out for him, and the FBI just issued a UFAP, Unlawful Flight to Avoid Prosecution. Frank is toast if we ever find him."

"Did he change identities?"

"He had to. He left no trace. He cashed out all his savings and brokerage accounts. We're working with the lawyer and the DA to track down possible offshore accounts, but it's really difficult."

"And you need a PI to do more legwork."

"Not just legwork. There are some things we just don't have legal access to."

Allen pauses. "Legal access?"

"We're restricted in some areas, especially with Frank's family members. Accounts, vitals, DMV, things like that."

"Restricted because it's illegal," Allen says.

"Yes," Linda replies.

"And you want B&C to break the law?"

"Absolutely not," Linda says. "But I know you guys get creative."

"Where'd you hear that?"

"From other PIs. I also checked up on you two. You guys work a lot with Gold, Yamashita, the law firm."

Allen says, "We do a lot of their interviewing and case prep work."

"Yamashita's brother is a friend of a friend. He told Julie and me about you two bending the rules a bit."

He shakes his head, and says, "That's not a good reputation to have, actually. Maybe I should talk to Kenji."

"You're missing the point," she says. "Frank's broken dozens of laws, and yet we're hampered by those laws. We have to go by the book. You don't."

"We're expensive," Allen says.

She replies, "Money's not a problem."

"It must be nice to be able to say that."

She looks at him squarely. "It is."

Allen glances at her ring, then says, "So this interview is to check whether or not we'd go along with it?"

"Yes. With the help of the DA we can look into Frank's records, but we can't do anything about his friends or family, and we know they might know something."

"Did he leave the country?"

"Possibly, but we alerted the Department of State and the passport office, making sure Nora can't leave the country. But we just don't know."

"How long has he had her?"

"Four weeks."

"Trail's getting cold. The police—"

"Have plenty of other things to worry about. Frank and Nora are in their computers, so if he's ever matched, they'll stop him, but they and the FBI aren't actively looking."

"So it's up to you," Allen says.

"It's up to me."

"Why would he do this? As a fugitive he'll have to run forever."

"Not necessarily. He was smart. He must have made up a new identity. We think he's been planning this for a while. All his accounts are empty, and he left no trace. But I don't think he fled the country. I think he has a new life somewhere in the States."

"How is Nora going to handle this? Would she go along with it?"

"Nora adores her father."

"Oh."

"But she also loves her mother. It's just that Frank could make it into a game. Julie thinks Nora would play along. Or worse, he could lie to Nora, tell her Julie died or abandoned her. *That* thought drives Julie crazy. What do you think? Can you do it?"

"I'll have to talk to Larry. Who else are you considering?"

"A couple other PI agencies, one that specializes in skip tracing."

"Sunset PI?"

"That's the one."

"They're good."

Linda says, "When Julie and I saw Larry on TV last night we knew we had to contact you guys."

"Yeah. We had a little excitement. I guess you can call it another 'creative' case we had."

Linda asks, "So, how've you been?"

Allen shrugs. "Fine. How's Julie holding up?"

Linda lets out a slow sigh. "Not so good."

"Where are you staying?"

"Right now at a hotel in Union Square. Actually really close by." She hands Allen a slip of paper with phone numbers listed. "My cell is on that, too. Let me know if you're interested. We can talk more later. I should get going."

They stand. Allen says, "So who's your fiancé?" He points to her hand.

"You don't know him. I met him in LA, but he also works up here. His name's Gabriel." She uses the Spanish pronunciation.

"An angel."

"Of sorts. Investment banker."

Allen smiles. "How is an investment banker like an angel?"

"He brings lots of money to people."

"Ah."

"He's also *my* angel."

This startles Allen, who even after plenty of time and distance away from her is bewildered by any endearments aimed at someone else. He looks away. "That's great," he says quietly. "I'm happy for you."

Linda studies him, then leans forward and kisses his cheek. She squeezes his shoulder and walks out of the cubicle. She waves to Larry, who is reading the morning paper, and she heads toward the exit. Allen watches the fabric of her skirt stretch and relax with each step. For some reason he remembers the time when she had thrown out her back and they needed to sleep on the floor, using blankets as a makeshift mattress. She lay down with three pillows under her knees, and could barely turn her head to the side. He stroked her hair and they joked about quitting their jobs and living cheaply in Mexico. They talked about living on the beach and Allen learning Spanish. They talked about sunbathing nude and eating fresh fish and vegetables all day.

As Linda walks out of the office, the door closing slowly in her wake, Allen quickly suppresses a glimmer of fear that his life hasn't started yet.

Larry doesn't like the idea of taking on a job in which the client expects illegal methods, though Allen reminds him about the marijuana case and the angry bikers. Larry winces, and says, "Yeah, exactly. I vowed no more of that crap."

Allen considers this. Can he actually turn Linda down? She helped him when he needed it, and this case is serious. Whatever ambivalence he might feel toward her, this is about a kidnapped young girl. He says, "It's her niece. I know Nora. She's a good kid, and I have to help."

"I know, but you got to be careful."

"I will be."

"You should up our rates."

"Maybe," he replies, knowing that he should probably bring in more money.

"You're taking on more risk."

Allen sighs. "I know."

"It's your license at risk."

"*My* license," Allen says. "Not ours?"

"This is your deal, B."

"You're not helping out?"

"If you need backup, I'll be there, but this sounds like a lot of grunt work, data searches and stuff. I'm going to be following up on the new clients we got. I might need your help on those."

"You serious about leaving the biz?" Allen asks. He needs reassurance. The thought of Larry leaving him alone with this company is too much for Allen at the moment. "Tell me what you're thinking."

Larry nods. "Eventually I'll go, yeah. Not for a while. There's the money situation I got to think about."

"Give me a time frame."

"A year maybe?"

Allen says, "All right. You better start teaching me the ins and outs."

"Blockman, you'll know so much about the goddamn business that you'll be sick of it."

"I don't know. It seems like we're doing a good service. How can you get sick of it?"

Larry rubs his stomach, and says, "Just wait."

Okay. So Linda is engaged. Allen tries not to feel stunned by this news, which contradicts everything Linda told him in the past, that she didn't want to marry or settle down, that families and stability were something she had tried and repudiated. You would think that after almost two years Allen would've achieved enough objectivity to view Linda and their former relationship dispassionately, yet this news stings. He takes it as a personal affront: she did not want to settle down with him. She did not want *him*. Okay.

Allen calls Linda's cell and tells her he'll take the case, but they have to work out a contract. Linda asks him to meet her and Julie at their hotel later that afternoon, so for the rest of the day Allen helps Larry cull through potential clients, then begins his research on parental abductions.

The numbers surprise him. The last time the Justice Department studied parental abductions over a decade ago, they found that more than 350,000 cases occurred in a year, and with divorce rates rising among two-income households, and custody battles becoming more complicated, the figures are now definitely much higher.

As Allen studies the profiles of abductors, he figures he'll handle this as a difficult skip trace, i.e., tracking down someone who owes money. Unlike an adoption search, of which Larry and Allen have done a handful, the subject here is actively covering his trail. Larry used to do more skip traces when he was starting out, but moved into the higher-paying corporate side within the last few years.

Allen tries to gauge the difficulty of this case. He met Frank a few times with Linda—they went over to Frank and Julie's house in Walnut Creek for dinners—but Allen never had more than a few superficial conversations with him. During one of their dinners Frank explained his job as an executive at a credit card company, and revealed to Allen, who at the time was just beginning to work as a PI, the many flaws the current credit card fraud detection system had.

"We eat a lot of losses," Frank said while holding up his fork. "A smart thief could probably live his whole life moving from one stolen card to the next without getting caught."

So, Frank has money and planned this for a while. He knows the financial trails and is motivated to disappear completely. Now a fugitive, he has too much at stake to be caught. He has eluded Linda, a former investigative reporter, for four weeks, and she's resorting to PIs, whom Allen knows she dislikes. She had made that clear when they were dating, disapproving of "garbage-hunting" PIs like Larry.

Allen begins to make checklists. Linda told him she had already used the police and FBI for the legal route, and she had checked the main information sources for Frank, the vital records, the DMV, and bank records. Because Frank is a fugitive, the DA can subpoena almost every private record of Frank's. Allen draws a chart with three levels of going underground: first, with the same name and social security number, but simply moving around before anyone catches up; second, with a new name and new social security number, establishing a new identity and new life; and third, with no name and no social security number, dealing only in cash and leaving no trails of any kind. If Frank went to the third tier, moving anonymously, not contacting any relatives or friends, and paying only cash, he'll be impossible to find. Going internationally would constitute a third-tier disappearance. Allen will have to prepare Julie for that possibility, even though Linda discounted it.

He lists a number of questions to ask Linda and Julie, then prepares a tentative contract, raising the daily rate and the retainer. By the time Allen finishes his prep work it's midafternoon, and he packs up to meet with his new clients. Putting on one of the ties he stores in his desk, he checks himself in the bathroom mirror and fixes his messy hair. He wishes he had brought his sport coat. With his dark slacks and white shirt he looks like a waiter.

His mind is filled with information about parental abductions, so when he leaves the office and immediately sees a woman crossing the street toward B&C he doesn't fully register her until she waves. He stops, staring at her blue skirt and blazer that seem incongruous with the dirty alley. Serena. He waves back and thinks quickly, unsure of what she'll think of his new client.

"Hi," she says, approaching. "I was just coming to see you." She pokes his arm and smiles. "I had a meeting in the financial district. Why are you wearing a tie?"

"I'm about to see a new client," he says. "Sorry, but I've got to run."

"I wanted to apologize for last night. I should've waited for you."

Allen says, "It's fine. I was the one who changed our plans at the last minute." He hesitates. "The new client is someone you know."

"Who?"

"Linda."

Serena says, "Linda? Linda who?" But then the name shifts something in her eyes, and she straightens up. "Linda, your ex-girlfriend Linda?"

He nods. "Her niece—technically her stepniece—was abducted by Frank, Julie's ex. It's a divorce custody thing."

"I thought she stayed down in Marina Alta."

"Her stepsister lives up here." Allen gives Serena a quick summary, and says, "I'm meeting with them now to work out a contract."

"Why your firm? Especially with your history? Isn't there a conflict?"

Allen shakes his head. "It should be fine." He glances at his watch. "But I should get going. We can talk about it tonight."

She leans forward and kisses him, then draws back. "Chanel."

"What?"

"She wears Chanel No. 5."

"Linda?"

"I smell it."

Allen's neck warms up. "Uh, well, we hugged. That's probably why."

"Mmm," she says. "We should definitely talk tonight."

He tries to read her expression. She has a half smile, an amused expression, but her eyes are probing. He mumbles an apology for having to leave and touches her arm. She tells him to go, not to be late, and he scurries off.

The address Linda gave him is a small bed-and-breakfast off Stockton, in a tiny cul-de-sac next to an upscale women's clothing store and an Italian deli. The narrow three-story building, a converted gray Victorian with blue window trim and shutters, seems squeezed on both sides, and falls under the shadows of the taller office buildings and stores across the street. Allen enters the main lobby. A young woman at the front desk smiles at him. He tells her he has an appointment with Linda Maldonado in 2C, and she picks up the phone. "You can wait in the adjacent lobby," she says, pointing through a doorway.

Allen sits down on an overstuffed sofa. Running into Serena rattled him, and he didn't expect to feel so guilty, even though he hasn't done anything. The fact that Linda is engaged rattled him; Larry's wanting to leave the business rattled him. He is getting thoroughly rattled. He needs time and space to think.

Linda enters the lobby wearing a light brown blazer with the same skirt as earlier, and calls him over. She says, "We're in a small conference room upstairs." They ride a tiny elevator to the third floor, and walk single file down the hallway. Linda says over her shoulder, "Our attorney will want to ask you some questions first."

"Sure," Allen replies, staring at her short hair.

She turns around, and Allen looks away. She says, "Be prepared for Julie."

"What do you mean?"

"She doesn't look so good."

As they enter the small conference room, Julie and another woman stand up. Allen is shocked by Julie's appearance. He tries not to reveal any expression when he says hello, but Julie, once slightly chubby in a healthy, pinkish way, must have lost thirty pounds, and has a gaunt, skeletal look that frightens Allen. Her once full and curly blond hair has become stringy and wispy. Allen smiles and shakes her hand, which feels like a piece of tissue paper. The attorney, Charlene Bickford, has hard eyes that appraise Allen for a moment before shaking his hand. She is in her fifties, with short graying hair, and her face has an athletic leanness that Allen sees at the gym all the time. Her firm handshake confirms this for him, and she says without any preamble, "Can you give me your DCA license number so I can check your PI status, Mr. Choice?"

Allen asks that she call him by his first name and hands her his business card, which has the relevant information. She glances down at it and nods curtly.

Julie says, "We can't afford to make any mistakes."

"How are you?" he asks.

"I've been better."

"What'd you think of Sunset?"

"Assholes," Julie says. "They treated me like I was some idiot housewife."

Allen notices the stacks of documents on the conference table. Charlene says, "Some of those are for you if we decide to work together."

"Let's talk business, then," Allen says.

They all sit down, and Charlene tells Allen that she specializes in family law and custody disputes, and that they've exhausted all the legal means for finding Frank and Nora. Allen consults his notes, and says, "Linda mentioned you got Nora into the NCIC, and you've put a UFAP on Frank, but what about the Federal and State Parent Locator Service?"

Charlene gives Julie an approving nod. Linda says, "Yes, we're going to, but that info is updated once a year, so it'll kick in after six months, and only if Frank gets any kind of state or federal aid."

"Which is unlikely," Julie says.

"All right, why don't you tell me what else you've done, and I can tell you what I can do."

"Maybe we should talk about rates and the contract first," Charlene says.

Allen pulls out the template with his proposed rates and slides it to her. She reads it with Julie. Julie says, "Whoa. You're expensive."

Linda leans over to them, and says, "This is a lot more than you used to charge."

"It's more than normal, given the risks that I'm anticipating. Linda filled me in on what you expect."

Charlene says quickly, "I don't know what Linda said, but let me make this clear: You are not to do anything illegal or anything that will jeopardize our case against Frank. Even if you should locate Nora, you're not to do anything except contact us immediately, and we'll contact the local authorities. Is that clear?"

Allen checks with Linda, who nods slowly at him, and he understands that this is a necessary disclaimer. He says, "It's clear, but I'll still be taking risks."

Julie says, "Three hundred a day plus expenses will add up."

"A ten grand retainer, Allen?" Linda says. "Are you joking?"

"Actually, it's a better deal than you think. We usually charge anywhere from $75 to $100 an hour, but I'm thinking a daily rate because of the legwork and possible travel involved."

"No sliding scale? No guarantees?" Charlene asks.

"We can renegotiate after the retainer is gone, depending on how difficult the case is turning out. It might be tougher than I'm expecting."

"You mean *raise* the rates?" Linda asks, and laughs. "Jeez, Allen. When did you become so mercenary?"

Allen sighs, feeling a twinge of guilt, and explains, "Last night I had a nine millimeter aimed at my face. I've decided to start asking for what I deserve."

"But this won't be like that. It's a complicated skip trace. No guns," Charlene says.

"I'm going to be talking to relatives, friends, people wanting to hide him. I wouldn't rule out physical danger."

"Okay," Julie says. "I'll pay it."

"Wait," Linda cuts in. "I'm sure we can negotiate—"

"Listen to me," Julie says. "Every goddamn day we don't find her, it's another day he brainwashes her. Do you understand? He could be telling her I'm dead or didn't want her or even worse! I'm not going to quibble over a few bucks." To Allen she says, "You find them, and you find them fast. I'll pay anything."

Linda and Charlene glance at each other. Linda nods. Charlene sighs, and says, "All right, Mr. Choice—"

"Please call me 'Allen.'"

"All right, Allen," Charlene says. "You're hired."

Four

After briefing Allen for almost an hour, during which Linda, Julie, and Charlene fill him in on the time line and their actions up to this point, they hand him a thick stack of documents to review. Linda accompanies Allen downstairs as he carries the sheaf of printouts and photocopies, the records of every legal and investigatory move they have made thus far, even listing insignificant and unproductive phone queries. Allen now has a full evening of reading and planning, and considers canceling his workout with Serena. But it's one of the few things he looks forward to. He turns his attention to Linda, who is telling him about how the police and FBI receive so many of these parental abduction cases that there is nothing they can do except wait for Frank to make a mistake. "If he's ever pulled over for a parking ticket or something like that, he's nailed."

"If he's using his own name."

"I know. That's the tricky part. You're going to have to think like a fugitive."

"I didn't want to say anything to Julie, but if you've done all the first-level searches and haven't come up with anything, then you're right: he must have changed identities," Allen says. "This looks like paper tripping to me."

"I know," Linda replies. "That's why we hired you."

"But I shouldn't tell you guys everything. Charlene made that clear."

"Right. Anything illegal could hurt us. But—and this is off the record—you do what you have to. I don't think Julie can take much more of this." She stops at the doorway, and says, "Thanks for this."

"I'm getting paid well," he says, still not used to her short hair. But he does like how her slim neck is exposed, revealing a dark necklace with a pendant.

Linda says, "I know this might seem kind of . . . awkward." She motions her hand between them.

"Why?"

She smiles. "Gee, why do you think?"

"So am I ever going to meet this Michael?"

"Gabriel," she says. "Eventually. What about you? Are you seeing anyone?"

He pauses, then says, "Serena."

Her head jerks up. "The woman from Santa Ana? The party girl?"

Allen laughs. "Yeah. She moved up here for a job."

Linda raises her eyebrow and folds her arms. "Well, well, that's a surprise."

"Is it?"

She grins. "Maybe not. She was totally after you that time."

Allen had flown down to LA with Linda to help look into her brother's death, and Serena had been their first lead. As his and Linda's relationship deteriorated, he became closer to Serena. He says, "You weren't too happy about my spending time with her."

"I wasn't." Linda shrugs. "Is it serious?"

"It could be. I'm not sure."

"That's nice, Allen," she says. "I'm glad to hear it."

"Maybe we can all have dinner together," he says, half-kidding. When he sees Linda's uneasy expression, he adds, "Or not."

"Will you give us daily reports?" she asks.

He notices her shift away from the subject. "If you want. I tend to do weeklies, but I can e-mail you dailies if you'd like."

"I'd like."

"Can I ask you a question, a personal one?"

She studies him, and says slowly, "Uh-oh."

"I was just wondering: you once told me you didn't want to get married, settle down, anything like that. Remember?"

"I remember." Her expression softens, and she lets out a small sigh.

"What changed?"

She walks with him out onto the street, and glances up at the darkening sky. The slight chill in the air makes her hug herself. She says, "People change, Allen. I spent almost a year thinking about things, doing a little traveling, and then met Gabriel. I changed. Haven't you?"

Allen says yes, but isn't quite sure about this. Has he? He glances at the cars driving by. How is he supposed to gauge change? He is probably calmer, more focused. He doesn't let career and personal problems bother him as much, and yet he feels essentially the same. He has no sense of major movements or shifts in perspective or outlook. This worries him. Should he have changed more? It seems that Linda always forces him to think about himself. He says, "It's good to see you again."

"Oh, you'll be seeing more of me. You haven't gotten rid of me yet."

"What do you mean?"

"You think I'm not going to follow this case closely for Julie?"

"Follow it? You mean my reports?"

"I mean that and more, maybe even helping you."

He and Larry have strict rules about letting clients get too involved. He says, "I already have a partner."

"Forgive me if I say that Larry doesn't instill a whole lot of confidence."

Allen realizes after a second that she's serious, and he says, "Hey, he's really good at his job."

"I'm sure he's great when he has to push around a witness," she replies. "But he's not the most subtle thinker."

Allen frowns. "You've never liked him, and that's not fair."

She gives him a half shrug.

He says, "I can't do this if you're hovering all the time. I have to do this on my own."

"Not hovering. In the wings, waiting, if you do need help. Don't forget that I know a lot about digging for information about people—"

"That's not why you're hiring me."

She says, "I know, but you can see we're getting desperate. It's Julie."

"She looks really bad." He nods.

"You've heard of Parental Alienation Syndrome?"

Allen just read about that in the background material. He says, "When the abducting parent bad-mouths the other parent to the kid, and messes the kid up."

"Exactly. Julie is losing it. Four weeks have gone by. Do you understand why this is so urgent?"

Allen says he understands.

"Did you know that the more time goes by, the better the chance for the *kidnapping* parent to get custody?"

"Why?"

"Because it's too disruptive to the child. The kidnapping parent can actually argue that. Julie can't see this, but I can. We can't let this go on any longer."

"I'll go through all this material tonight and get started first thing in the morning. I'll find them. Don't worry."

Linda touches his arm. "Thank you, Allen. Hey, I knew I could count on you."

Allen immediately thinks of Serena and how he is going to explain all this. He gives Linda a quick smile and hurries back to his office.

Has he changed? He wishes he could see himself more objectively. Perhaps if he had mental snapshots of himself over the past two, four, even ten years, then he'd have a better measure of change. He knows this: when he first met Linda he was much less sure of himself, of his job, of everything really, and when they broke up two years later, he found himself becoming more focused. He shook himself out of his initial depression and, with the help of Serena, began feeling more certain of everything around him. He settled into his new job with Larry, and he found that he liked the methodical and quiet tasks that comprise the majority of a PI's work. He likes spending time with Serena. When they aren't working out or with her friends, they go to bargain matinees or read in coffee shops, Allen pushing through his philosophy texts or work-related material, and Serena reading novels or Hollywood gossip magazines, her admitted vice.

Once, just a few weeks ago, after an extended workout, they went to the café on Solano and sat by the window, the dark street creating a faint mirror, and Allen looked up from Kierkegaard's *Sickness Unto Death*. He stared at Serena, who was wearing a purple sweater and a matching purple barrette in her hair. He caught her grinning to herself as she flipped the pages of her novel. She looked up and met his eyes. She said, "Jane Austen's a hoot."

And Allen thought, This is so nice.

Before Allen has a chance to think about this or about Linda and the new case, Larry sits him down as soon as he walks into the office and tells him that the Oakland Police called with more information about Dubois, the Jamaican who caught them at the warehouse. "He's wanted for two murders," Larry says. "We might've gotten ourselves mixed up in some bad shit."

"Are you sure it's the same guy?"

"They faxed over a mug shot. It's the same guy."

"What does this mean?"

"They told us to be careful. They're worried about retaliation."

"Man, Larry, I don't have time for this."

"This guy is some kind of low-level grunt for this loosely organized gang. They're based in LA, deal mostly in drugs, but have been branching out."

"Jamaican?"

"Mix. West Indian. Anyway, the Oakland PD just wanted to let us know. They're getting some good PR mileage from the warehouse bust, so we're not in trouble for breaking in."

"Good," Allen says, and tells Larry about Julie's case. When Allen reveals the daily rate and retainer, Larry's eyes widen.

"Not bad, Block-o. Keep that up and we'll be rolling in it."

For the rest of the afternoon, Allen wades through Julie's notes. She even logged their expenses on a spreadsheet and printed that out as well. Charlene's legal fees alone have cost Julie over fifteen grand thus far, and Allen feels a tinge of guilt for charging her so much. This prompts him to work harder, and he separates the notes that deal with Frank's friends, relatives, and work contacts. Linda has already run all kinds of header searches—going through the various credit and vital record bureaus—to get all of Frank's information, previous addresses, debts, credit cards, birth and marriage records. Through the DA they also subpoenaed all of Frank's bank and brokerage records, insurance policies, health insurance records, medical and dental files, DMV and IRS records, and pretty much anything and everything that Frank dealt with over his lifetime.

Frank is rich. Before he emptied his accounts he had almost one million in stocks, bonds, and mutual funds, and his retirement accounts had about half a million, and that was after the divorce settlement in which Julie received almost $800,000 in cash. Frank's money trail begins with the checks written out to him after liquidating his accounts and then depositing them into a Guatemala bank, but that's where the trail ends. Julie's notes reveal her problems trying to access any information in Guatemala, the financial secrecy laws forbidding all access. Allen needs to read up on money laundering to understand what Frank could've done with the cash.

The best shot, and Linda knows this as well, is for Allen to dig into Frank's family's and friends' records, looking for money transfers. Also, if Allen can get access to their telephone records, maybe even e-mails, he'll be certain to find some kind of contact with Frank. He checks the addresses of Frank's brother and sister, both in the Bay Area, and Frank's parents, in Seattle. Frank also has an old college friend in New York, and coworkers in the city. Linda didn't conduct much research on these people, and Allen intends to start with them in the morning.

He realizes with a jolt that it's past six, and that he has to hurry back to his apartment, grab his gear, and head to Berkeley, no doubt fighting rush-hour traffic. Larry is still in his office, and Allen asks him how the client meetings went.

"I'm thinking about taking on a corporate espionage case. I'll let you know what I decide."

"I might not have time to help out because of Linda's sister."

"You taking off?"

"Plans with Serena," he says, putting on his coat.

"Must be nice."

"What?"

"Hanging out with her."

It startles Allen to realize that Larry is lonely. He says, "Maybe this weekend you can join us. I'm sure she's got stuff going on with her friends."

"Thanks, Block. We'll see. I might be signing up for night and weekend classes."

"Night classes?" Allen says. "Cooking?"

Larry says, "Yeah. I might start off with pastries." He grins. "So what's it like working for Linda now?"

"A little strange."

"She's still got something for you, B. I saw it."

Allen checks if Larry is kidding, but he isn't. Allen says, "No. She's engaged."

"Big deal. She can still be attracted to you, can't she?"

Allen waves this off. "I'm happy with Serena."

Larry folds his large arms and leans back in his chair, which groans under his weight. He says, "You're still a young guy, B. When you hit *my* age you start thinking of settling down. At your age you have some fun."

Sighing, he tells Larry he'll see him tomorrow and packs up his papers; he'll continue this later tonight before he goes to bed. He feels a strong desire to be with Serena.

When Allen was thirteen, three years after his father died, and Allen was living with his aunt, he began to ride the BART trains into the city without telling her. He'd get on at the Lake Merritt station and transfer at Twelfth Street. Sometimes he'd get off at the West Oakland stop because he liked how high the concrete platform was, the view of industrial Oakland fascinating. He could stare at the cranes in the distance for hours. During the weekday the platform was often empty, and he'd jump down onto the tracks and lay pennies on the rails. After the next train passed through, he'd retrieve the flattened and warped coins, bright and sparkling with the edges broadened and elongated, reminding him of shiny copper moths.

But it was San Francisco that intrigued him. He usually went to the Powell Street station and wandered around Union Square, or got off at the Civic Center to visit the library. His aunt never knew about these trips. No one did, until tonight, when he tells Serena about it while working out.

Serena's gym is a Nautilus on San Pablo, usually crowded in the evenings with professional bodybuilders and weight lifters gathering around the free-weight areas, huge men and a few women with hundreds of pounds on their shoulders as they do squats, their massive legs quivering. The iron bar actually bends down on both sides from the weights. Veins bulge from their necks as they shake and sputter to lift the last rep.

Allen and Serena begin their routine on the machines, occasionally saying hello to other regulars they've come to know. When they plan a long run after the workout, they focus on their upper bodies, and to-night they do their usual arms and back sequence. After he tells her about the BART rides, she asks, "Wasn't that dangerous?"

"I was a teen. I was also getting bigger, so I probably looked older."

"That makes me a little sad," she says. "I wish I'd known you back then."

Allen glances at her, but doesn't reply. Serena hasn't mentioned Linda yet, though Allen is waiting for the conversation to begin. During the lat pull-downs she tells him about a new project she's working on with programmers from another company on a joint project, which was why she had the meeting in the city. Allen hears the segue before it arrives, and she says, "So how did your meeting go?"

A small part of Allen wants to tease her, to be intentionally vague and elliptical, but he sees her expression in the mirror—her eyes scruti-nizing him for any suspicious signs—and he knows that he'd better resolve this quickly. She's in the middle of her second set, her grip tight. He spots her, and says, "Tiring. It's going to be a complicated case. But it's all business. You have nothing to worry about."

"Why would I worry?" she asks. One of the weight lifters groans loudly, his voice carrying across the gym. The sounds of slamming iron plates mingle with the whirring of the treadmills on the second-floor balcony.

"Because she's my ex-girlfriend," he says.

"What was it like seeing her again?"

"Strange. She kept her hair short. She's engaged."

Serena finishes her set and climbs off the seat. "Really? To whom?"

"Some investment banker."

"Interesting," she says, eyeing him. "Didn't you say she didn't want to marry or anything like that?"

Allen nods. "That's what I thought. I guess I was wrong."

"How do you feel about it?"

He lets his voice become casual. "People change," he says, but then realizes he is echoing Linda and adds, "That was a year and a half ago. It feels like a different life. I'm completely over her."

Serena looks down at her hands, checking her callouses, and says, "You're sure about that?"

"I'm sure." He reaches over and touches her cheek. "You're very cute when you're jealous."

She studies him. "It's just that I know she had some kind of hold over you."

"Like a hypnotist or something?" He laughs.

"Actually, I was thinking more like a witch." She then punches him lightly in the arm.

Allen begins his set of pull-downs, and Serena spots him from behind. His back is sore from climbing in the warehouse last night, and he's secretly glad that they were fired from that case. Although Larry prefers corporate clients, Allen—having done nothing but corporate jobs as a bodyguard—sees more meaning in personal cases, like Julie's. Here he can actually do something good for Nora, for Julie, for Linda as well. He resolves to work extra hard on this case. Looking at Serena in the mirror, Allen suddenly isn't sure if she thinks Linda is returning to Los Angeles, that this meeting wasn't a singular occurrence. Did he mention to her that Linda would be monitoring the case with Julie?

Allen tries not to worry about this. The case is important. Nora's well-being is important. He remembers Nora as a sweet kid who liked to read a lot. The last time he saw her was down in Marina Alta, at her grandparents' condo, suffering from her parents' separation. Frail and thin, with severe blond bangs, Nora always had a book in her hand, and the few conversations they'd had were about her books. Allen stops his workout, and says, "Nora must be having a bad time, being on the run with her father."

"That's horrible. Why would he do that? What kind of man is he?"

Allen says, "Never got to know him well. He always seemed wrapped up in his work." He tells Serena about the time he was at Julie and Frank's house, before the divorce, when he and Linda went there for Julie's birthday party. Allen met their friends, older couples with children and mortgages and 401(k) plans, their conversations about the stock market, insurance policies, and private schools. Despite being the same age as Julie, Allen felt young and stalled. He didn't have a retirement account and had no idea what a Roth IRA was. The couples looked at him with some uneasiness. When they explained it to him, he still didn't quite understand. He was too free, unattached, unburdened. Even Linda had a retirement account.

"But you have one now, don't you?" Serena asks. They move on to shoulder presses and the lateral fly machine. "Didn't Larry do that for you two?"

"Not yet," Allen says, and decides not to mention Larry's possible departure. "We're supposed to do one by the end of this year."

"Was Nora at the party?"

"Yes. She was about five, and really shy. She hid in the hallway whenever her parents tried to introduce her," he says. "But when no one was paying attention she'd sit at the top of the stairs and watch everyone, taking in all the adults."

Allen stops his set, struck by this image. Nora sat with her elbows on her knees, her chin resting on her laced fingers.

"What's wrong?" Serena asks.

"I hope she's okay," he says. "She's a good kid."

Their run begins at Serena's building on Martin Luther King, and they head north onto Alameda and up into Kensington, a small town adjacent to Berkeley. Moving along a mix of main and side roads to avoid traffic, Serena has on her fluorescent wrist and ankle bands that bounce and swing, seemingly bodiless, in the darkness, and Allen wears criss-crossing reflective straps on his back, a big "X" marking the spot to drivers. The terrain is a long, low-sloping hill that peaks at Colusa Circle, then descends until they hit their goal and turn back. The residential neighborhoods are filled with large single-family houses with tiny strips of yard and crooked, warped sidewalks. A cool, foggy breeze chills them until they find their pace, and Allen waits for that moment when his heart speeds up to the right rhythm, his leg muscles loosening.

It's better with a partner. They move in sync, limbs loose and their pace perfect at a nine-minute mile. Serena speaks only after she, too, finds her rhythm, and their breathing evens out. She says, "I talked to my mom today."

Allen doesn't reply. Unless she turns to him with a question, he doesn't have to. This odd protocol developed on its own somehow. And they speak in quieter, breathier voices, in part because of the running but also because of the stillness around them. It's almost ten o'clock, and on a weeknight it's never very active up here. Everyone seems ensconced in their homes, the glow of soft, curtained lights spilling onto the sidewalks.

Serena says, "She and my dad will be staying in a motel on University. They're talking about a few dinners with us, maybe a museum or sightseeing day or two."

Allen lets out an involuntary sigh, which causes her to glance at him. He says, "Sorry."

"I'm a little nervous about the whole thing, to tell you the truth," she says. "They've never met anyone I've gone out with before, except once in high school, but that was nothing. I'm not sure what to expect."

Allen imagines squabbles, small sleights, a confrontation. He tries not to sigh again.

"I just wanted to warn you," she continues. "My mom can be very nosy. She's not good with boundaries."

He waits for her to elaborate, but when she doesn't he asks, "How so?" They run through Colusa Circle, a mini circular intersection with a few restaurants and shops lining the perimeter, and a stronger wind from the Bay kicks up and slows them down. The sweat on his face cools him.

"She's probably going to ask you about us."

Like a chess player Allen anticipates the conversation three, four, even five moves ahead. The strategy is to use Serena's mother as a way to broach this topic, and Allen knows his next question is supposed to pinpoint what her mother will ask, and the answer will be something about their future, and he will be required to answer this on some level for Serena. He smiles to himself. He knows her well enough to anticipate her train of thought. He says, "Listen, I *have* been thinking about us, but I haven't come to any conclusions yet."

Serena's pace breaks for a moment, then she moves back into their rhythm. She stays quiet for a full minute, then laughs gleefully. She says, "Jeez, am I that obvious? Am I that transparent?"

"I just know you well," he says. "And honestly, I'm thinking about it."

"I know you are. I know you well, too."

"Oh? What am I thinking?"

Serena says, "I probably shouldn't say."

This worries him. "Why not?"

"Because you'll deny it."

"Not if it's true."

They run downhill now, their pace quickening, and Allen's curiosity is stronger than his fear of what she might reveal. "Tell me."

Serena says, "Linda's engagement shocked you, and you can't stop thinking about why that guy and not you."

Allen's cheeks flush, and his immediate impulse is to deny, deny, deny. Yet if he's truthful with himself he has to admit she's right. He says, "It's not that I still have feelings for her . . ."

"Maybe not deep feelings, but you still have a little something for her."

Allen squeezes his eyes shut for a second, running blind, then opens them. He jumps a curb. He ignores her last comment, and says. "Maybe I was a little surprised by her news, yes."

"How long is she in town for?"

Ah. He replies, "I'm not sure, but she might be sticking around for the case."

"Wait. Couldn't that be a while?"

"It could."

"Where is she staying?"

"A bed-and-breakfast near Union Square."

"And where's her fiancé?"

"Around. He apparently works up here as well as in LA. I actually suggested we all have dinner some time, but I don't think she liked the idea."

Serena says, "And Julie, the sister? She lives up here, right?"

"Walnut Creek. She's selling the house, or trying to. She's at the hotel with Linda."

"And you don't know how long the case will take?"

"Not yet. I'll have a better idea in a few days."

They both fall quiet as they near the turnaround point if they want to do three miles. Neither of them slow down, and they run past the high school football field, which means that the next point will be the five-mile loop. Allen wasn't prepared for five miles, but doesn't say anything. They usually push for five miles once a week, but never on the same day they work out at the gym. His back and shoulders are sore from lifting, and he tries to keep his arms loose as he conserves his energy. He relaxes his form.

Early on in their dating Serena once mentioned her concern that she was a rebound woman, that they had begun seeing each other immediately after his breakup, that there might have even been an overlap, though the specifics were murky, even for Allen. He quickly reassured her that his and Linda's relationship had been deteriorating long before

Allen met Serena, and "rebound" implied something temporary or precarious, and he didn't feel that way about them.

Now, as they run in the late-evening quiet, the streets empty as everyone in the brightly lit homes prepare for bed, Allen remembers Larry's comment about his being with Serena. He turns to her; she glistens when they approach the streetlamps, her reflecting ankle and wrist bands dancing back and forth. He thinks, It *is* nice.

Allen says quietly into the wind, "One of the best parts of this, besides that weird endorphine high I get once we turn around and have to go up the hill, is when we get back to your place and stretch out." His legs hurt now, but he doesn't slow down. He says, "When we stretch out together, and I massage your hamstrings and calves, then I lie on the ground and you step on my hams, digging your heels in, putting all your weight on me." Allen's legs tighten up quickly, and he finds that having Serena step on his legs while he lies on his stomach loosens up his muscles, and they are less sore the next day. He says, "Yeah, that's my favorite part."

He then glances at Serena, who stares ahead and smiles.

That smile, a secret pleased smile that Allen sees in her quieter moments, is revealing because he's privy to it only when they're intimate. A small, thin-lipped distant smile that Allen isn't sure she's even aware of, it offers a brief window into her thoughts that appears and disappears quickly. The first time he saw it was shortly after they began dating here, after she had moved to Berkeley, and they had gone to a club in the city. Serena had heard about this small bar with a dance floor from a coworker, and that night a blues band played loud rockabilly that rang in Allen's ears hours after they left. While dancing he thought of the few times Serena had taken him to raves down in LA—he had been helping Linda search for information about her brother, which was how he had met Serena—and he realized that with Serena he had always had *fun*.

This was something he knew he needed more of, since he never seemed to be able to relax and simply play. Serena helped him do that.

During a break they waited on line for the bathroom, the din of deafened people yelling their conversations surrounding them, and Allen didn't even try to talk. He met Serena's eyes, and winked. He moved closer to her and wiped some of the sweat off her brow. This gesture surprised her, and she looked down shyly, and smiled. He remembered the smile for its swiftness, because it flashed away as she mouthed the words "come here," and she pulled him closer, and they kissed.

Now, when they return from their run, sweating, out of breath, their limbs humming from both the earlier workout and now the five miles, Allen immediately begins stretching on her floor, her dog Gracie resting her head on her paws and watching them. Serena says, "Time for your favorite part?"

"I can do you first."

"No, I wouldn't want to make you wait for your favorite part," she says, grinning.

He turns over and she slips off her running shoes. Slowly she lowers her heel into his hamstrings and digs in. Allen sighs with pleasure, which makes Serena laugh. He feels the heat from her foot.

The cell phone on top of his duffel bag vibrates, the small red light on the side blinking. Allen stares at it, his legs tensing, and Serena says, "Now, what?"

"It must be Larry."

"Again? Is he going to bug you every night?"

"I should check," he says.

"Hey, I wanted to hang out tonight."

"We will," he says, sitting up. "Let me just check." He crawls to his bag and answers the phone. "Larry?" he says.

"Hey, B. You gotta come down here, to the office," Larry says, his voice shaking.

"What? What's wrong?"

"Someone torched the office."

"What?"

Larry curses and says, "Burned the place up, man. I just got here. It could've been an accident, but I'm guessing it was that Dubois guy. Goddammit, everything's burnt or soaked. The firemen put it out, but there's not much left. We're kind of fucked."

Allen lies back on the floor and closes his eyes.

PART II

PROTECTIVE THEORY

Five

Perhaps in the future the Block will point to this particular moment in time as the Recognition. He knows the ephemeral nature of relationships, the quickness with which lovers can split up; he knows the bonds of family are illusory, that just because you are related to someone doesn't mean you are really *connected*. He knows to be wary of the romance of attachments to people or places or even to pets, since he has never experienced longevity with any of these. And yet in hard, tangible property, in papers and files and books, in letters and notes, in proprietary *things* that can be locked away and time-capsuled, he thought there was at least some degree of permanence.

And yet there is almost nothing left in the burnt-out office.

The Block has never lost anything in a fire, has never even experienced a fire larger than one in a fireplace, so he isn't remotely prepared for the destruction. He once saw the aftermath of a large fire—a particularly strong memory is of visiting the remnants of a Korean restaurant for which his aunt Insook had been an accountant, and seeing only parts of the blackened frame of the building, and the kitchen equipment still standing amidst ashes—but he has never had a personal connection to a fire loss until now.

He drives back over the Bay Bridge and to the office, his legs aching whenever he uses the clutch to shift gears. The traffic is backed up, and while he stares out over the string of taillights blinking red he tries not to take inventory of everything in the office. Larry's unsteady, tired voice reverberates in his head, and Allen knows the fire is bad because Larry, although prone to exaggeration, wouldn't overstate the damage. Not their office, their livelihood.

The only case file that Allen needs at the moment is Julie and Linda's, and he took that home with him. All the other cases are closed. But then there's his research from past cases, his books, his extra clothes, and all the office equipment: three computers, a fax machine, phones, printers, a copier, and the mini stereo system. Are they insured for this? Allen isn't certain. He usually leaves those details to Larry.

His professional contacts are stored in his computer database. But there is even more: he left all his bodyguarding textbooks and reference guides in the office, most of them from when he first started in the business, almost six years ago. These books are out-of-print or limited editions published privately for training purposes by the executive protection firms themselves. There is no way to replace those. More: he remembers that all his licensing paperwork sits in the office files. He wanted to keep his professional life all in one place, and it made sense to keep everything in the office. More: he saved personal e-mails from Serena on his computer. There is that long and funny e-mail describing a college reunion she attended, and it makes him smile now to remember her descriptions of her former classmates. He suddenly feels the loss.

When Allen arrives at the alley, his thoughts colliding anxiously, he finds his usual entrance blocked off by fire engines and police cars. He parks illegally across the street. Small crowds cluster on the sidewalks, and the smell—the smell is something that surprises him. A mix of burnt tar and wood, an acrid odor that makes his eyes water. Allen rushes past a policeman who grabs his arm and says, "Whoa, whoa, where are you going?"

"This is my place. I have to talk to the firemen."

The officer lets Allen go, and he runs around the fire trucks, their idling engines rumbling. The wet streets glisten. He stops. The front facade of the building is blackened, and the edges of the roof are charred through, jagged beams exposed. Thin trails of smoke drift upward. The adjacent buildings are streaked with sooty water, but nothing seems burnt. Firemen in their ashy coats and helmets walk out of the open front door, dragging hoses. Allen looks wildly around for someone in charge. A fireman with a cleaner helmet and no coat stands beside a smaller truck, talking on a two-way radio. Allen hurries over and says, "This is my office. Is my partner here?" He reads the "SFFD" on the man's helmet.

"He's with the arson investigator inside." As he says this Allen notices Larry emerge from the doorway wearing one of the firemen's helmets. Behind him another man in jeans and a nylon jacket, also with a helmet, walks out with a video camera and clipboard.

Larry meets Allen's eyes and shakes his head. He speaks briefly with the investigator, then walks to Allen, saying, "Totally arson. Freaking gasoline cans still there. Not too tough to figure out."

"How they'd get in?"

"Broke through the back window, torched everything. The fire guys put it all out before it spread to the other buildings, but everything inside is gone." Larry takes off the helmet and rubs his forehead.

"We have insurance for this, right?"

"Yeah, but they're going to send over their own investigator, to make sure we didn't do this."

"We?"

"Yeah. If there's any doubt, we're screwed."

"But the Oakland Police warned us about Dubois."

"Yeah. That's going to be important, but no way they're going to cut us a check until everything's sorted out. It might be a while."

"How bad is it?"

"Take a look. Everything's gone," Larry says, motioning Allen to follow. They move to the doorway, and Allen looks in. He needs a few seconds for everything to register because he doesn't recognize anything. There are no visual clues, no familiar signs. He feels the residual heat rolling out in uneven waves. Then, slowly, as his spatial memory anchors onto the layout of the large room, the charred cubicle walls serving as the points of reference, he sees his burnt desk and melted computer. Water drips from the ceiling where a large portion has been burned out, a jagged hole opening to the sky. White smoke circles up from heaps of blackened ashes where the bookshelves used to be. Heat and a damp smokiness drift toward him. He thinks, All my books. "The files?" he asks, his stomach tightening.

"When it cools off we'll check, but most of them are probably burnt or soaked."

"What . . . how . . . ?"

"Alls I know is I got a call from the alarm company at home. They said the fire alarm was going off and they called the fire department. By the time I got here, it was totally in flames, but they managed to get it under control and keep it from spreading." He points to the back. "There are two five-gallon cans of gas back there. The arson guy is calling this a crime scene."

"You told him about Dubois?"

"Yeah. He's talking to the Oakland PD right now."

"How did Dubois know who we were?"

Larry winces. "Probably saw me on TV."

"Fucking great," Allen says. "Perfect."

"If I knew he was going to do this, I wouldn't have—"

"Yes, you would've. You love being on TV." He points to the street. "There are more TV vans coming right now. You're going to go on again? You're going to invite more shitheads to come after us?"

Larry steps back and holds up his hands. "Hey, easy. This ain't my fault."

"All my contacts, all my files. Even my files from ProServ, which I stored here in ease we moved into executive protection. Everything."

"I lost my stuff, too, Allen."

"But you're already checking out. You want to be a goddamn cook. I'm just getting started—"Allen turns around and punches the air, walking away before he says something he regrets. He hears Larry call out, "Yo, come on, B," but Allen ignores him and breathes deeply, calming himself. The bitter air hurts his throat. Surprised by his own anger, he just finds all this so wasteful. If it was an accident, bad wiring, a random spark, he might not even feel as lousy, but someone did this intentionally and for a stupid, vindictive reason. This didn't have to happen.

He walks down the alley and turns the corner, the streets quieter here. He sees three men sitting in a doorway and passing a bottle wrapped in a paper bag. He asks them if they saw anyone in the back of the building before the fire began.

The three of them look at each other, then shake their heads. One of them with a Giants windbreaker drinks from the bag, then holds it up to Allen. "You look like you need a sip."

Allen waves it off. "Thanks, but no. You guys didn't see anyone?"

"Just the firemen and cops," the third one says.

Allen thanks them and circles the block, returning to the alley, cooling off. The two large fire trucks have left, but a police car and a San Francisco Fire Department car remain. Larry is talking to the police officer. TV news cameras set up across the street, the spotlights shining on correspondents with microphones, doing their feeds for the late editions. The top of the vans have satellite dishes on telescoping poles. Larry approaches Allen, and says, "The evidence team is on their way. Don't worry. We'll figure this out."

"Sorry. I didn't mean to blame you."

"The only open case is Linda's?" he asks.

"Yes, but I took the files home with me."

"You did?" Larry says, surprised. "Good thinking. I had a few new files started that got burnt, but nothing that can't be redone. It's just all the records that's a pain. I'll take care of all this—the insurance, the landlord, all of it. Okay? You just work on Linda's case."

"What about Dubois?"

Larry sighs. "Yeah, that might be a problem. I'll talk with Oakland PD, but maybe this was payback, and that's all we'll hear from him."

"Maybe not."

"Let me worry about that. You can still access all our databases online. You got a computer, right?"

Allen says, "Serena gave me an old one, but I don't have Internet access."

"No?"

"I did everything here," he says. "E-mail, searches, everything." Allen remembers the dozens of Linda's old *Sentinel* articles he downloaded a while ago. Why did he do that, and why did he mourn the loss of them?

"Can Serena help set you up?" Larry asks. "I'll e-mail her all the password and access info."

Allen nods, exhausted.

Larry gives him a gentle push. "Go home, Allen. I'll take care of this. You rest up for tomorrow. We both got a lot of work to do."

Allen stares at the news vans across the street. He feels oddly distanced from everything. The long research day, the workout, the run—all these are hitting him now. He sees a news reporter with a cameraman behind her, heading in his direction. He turns and flees out of the alley and to his car.

And then, as he drives back to Serena's, an odd sensation overcomes him. He feels his body lighten, his head floating. He thinks of all the things in the office that are now ashes or pieces of melted plastic and metal. He gives up hope of recovering any of those important books or e-mails or files. Everything is gone. Why should he be upset at these losses? They are just things—books, pieces of paper. The bodyguarding texts don't need to be replaced, since he knows most of the information in them anyway. It's just a sentimental attachment to his career progress. He remembers a chapter entitled "Protective Theory" that lays out the theoretical framework for preemptive security, how the entire mind-set of bodyguards is anticipatory, and Allen wonders why his own life doesn't have that sense of preparation, why he doesn't foresee these kinds of hazards.

Here is a hazard: you can lose everything in a blink. Any attachment you thought was enduring is, in fact, fragile. Nothing lasts. And with this understanding Allen realizes he needs to anticipate the future loss by reveling in the present. Isn't that the only way to prepare for the inevitable?

He notices that the traffic on the Bay Bridge has thinned, and suddenly wonders why he is driving back into Berkeley when he lives only fifteen minutes away from the office. He chose to drive all the way back to Serena's. He didn't even think about it. But of course it makes sense—he wants to share this with her. He wants to tell her what happened, and he wants her comforting response.

As he drives into the East Bay and toward Berkeley, he thinks again of his aunt and that Korean restaurant. The memory, now overlaid and strengthened by the image of his charred office, gnaws at him. At the time, only eleven or twelve years old—shortly after his father had died and his aunt had reluctantly taken him in—Allen was chafing at his aunt's authority, and didn't understand the purpose of that visit. The novelty of seeing a burnt building wore off after a few minutes. But now he wonders if his aunt was trying to teach him something. Didn't she remark on the suddenness of tragedy, especially after his father had died so recently?

He can't remember. And this is tainted by the knowledge of his aunt's complicity in his father's death that he learned of only years later. Maybe she was feeling guilty and tried to justify her role by pointing to the unpredictability of such events. Maybe she actually didn't say much but simply took him there and stared out over the ruins. Maybe she just said, "Look."

Why is it that whenever he thought of his aunt a veil descended, shrouding details? Images of his father crystallized, and yet everything about his aunt was colored by his confusing mix of resentment and sorrow. He hasn't heard from her since she left the country, possibly to Korea, four years ago, and the fact that she's probably his only living relative somehow makes her disappearance more acute. He isn't even sure if she's still alive.

How appropriate that he thinks of her in a time like this. She represents the instability of everything. She is Yang. But who is Yin?

Allen parks his car and hurries up to Serena's apartment. He lets himself in and hears the stereo playing blues. Gracie sits up when she sees him, and he walks into the warm, brightly lit living room, the African masks smiling at him. Gracie trots over to him and he scratches her head and kisses her neck. Gracie nuzzles him. He whispers, "Where's your mama? Where's your pretty mama?" He listens. He looks. *This* is home, isn't it, he thinks. This is why he drove here. He hears rustling in the bedroom and hurries down the hall. Serena is sitting on the bed, a magazine in her hand. She stands up and asks him what happened. The cuffs of her pajama legs are rolled up, exposing her bare pale feet. Her toenails are red. He stares at them, and finds them lovely. She says, "Are you okay?"

Serena is his Yin. She curls her toes. He looks up and sees her anxious eyes, her need to share in whatever he is experiencing as she searches his face for clues. He blurts out, "I think it's time we move in together."

Her body immediately goes into a defensive crouch as she looks at him with shock. She says, "What?"

He repeats himself.

Her eyes, surprise drifting to pleasure, lock on to him, and she straightens up. She rests her hands on her hips, and begins to nod. "Oh, really?"

"Really." He glances down at her feet, and smiles. He looks up, and says, "I mean it."

She smiles. "Well, well."

Six

To run, to fly. Even in his dreams, Allen runs. He finds himself running downhill faster and faster until his legs blur and his body lifts off. He loses control and begins spinning. He wakes up with the sheets tucked neatly around him, Serena's side empty, the apartment quiet and still. The peace of the early morning soothes him. He hears Gracie clicking across the floor, then she rests her head on the foot of the bed, watching Allen. "Where's your mama?" Allen asks. He pats the bed next to him but Gracie doesn't jump up. She only seems to do that when Serena is around.

Allen rolls over to the night table and sees Serena's note: "Set up the computer per Larry's specs. It's asleep. Just press a key. DSL always on. See you tonight! Love, S." She underlined "Love." He smiles. He walks over to the desk and wakes up the computer, and recognizes the familiar interface he used at the office. Last night he briefly described to her their on-line sources, and after checking Larry's e-mail she said, "Looks like an intranet. How does he know about this?"

Allen shrugged, and asked her to explain it to him.

"It's a peer-to-peer intranet, a 'sub' Internet that goes to people's own computers, making miniservers."

Allen said, "He once told me it was like a sewer tunnel system of the Internet."

"Not quite, but close. It's more like private roads and homes. Anyone can download this peer-to-peer program, but he gave you all the specific IP addresses, logins, and passwords to access certain servers. What's on them?"

"Information brokers."

"Illegal information?"

"Sometimes, yes."

Serena nodded. "Cool."

Today is a research day, and after making himself a pot of coffee Allen sits down with Julie and Linda's notes, and begins drawing up "to do" lists and a rough flowchart of his alternative searches if he starts hitting dead ends, something he fully expects. Although he doesn't want to duplicate Linda's work, he feels he has to review every step she made to double-check and catch anything she might have missed. She did the standard identifier searches, locking on to Frank's name, social security number, and address as the foundation for the financial and credit searches, then expanding that with the help of the District Attorney to getting Frank's bank and brokerage accounts. One thing that Linda didn't look into was searching for Nora's name in new schools, and checking with her old school to see if her files had been transferred anywhere. He makes a note of this.

Every few minutes he thinks of a reference book he needs to consult but then realizes it was probably burnt. This disconcerts him for a second or two, and he tries to get back to work.

Gracie lies at his feet, looking up whenever Allen sighs and leans back in the swivel chair. Allen can't stop thinking about last night's discussion. He occasionally stares out of Serena's window and winces at the memory of it. He doesn't regret what he said, but he regrets how he said it. How wild-eyed he must have looked!

After he blurted out that he wanted to move in with her, and she studied him for a moment, still smiling, she then seemed to realize with a jolt that he was upset. She said, "The fire. What happened? Are you okay?"

He told her most of the office was gone, and said, "I'm . . . I'm a little rattled."

She pulled him toward the bathroom, and said, "You look dazed." She turned on the shower and began undressing him. He kept babbling how he suddenly realized what was important to him, that *she* was important to him, and that he could see this now. No, he had always known she was important to him, but he had figured out his feelings. He wanted only to be with her.

When she shed her pajamas, he stopped. "What are you doing?"

"To get the smoke out," she said, pulling him into the shower with her, and he felt the shock of the warm water. They faced each other, water dripping down their faces, and he stared at her breasts. He reached out to touch her. She gently took his hand, and said, "Relax, just relax."

He relaxed. She turned up the hot water, and the jets thrummed the back of his head. He saw Serena through blurry streams. The heat permeated his neck, spreading through his body and loosening his muscles. His words bubbled out as he said, "I'm talking crazy, aren't I?"

"First tell me about the office," she said.

With his eyes closed and Serena's fingers shampooing his hair, he told her what had happened, what was burnt. He told her about losing his temper with Larry, though Larry had kept calm, and how suddenly the impermanence of everything had hit him. Serena soaped his body, and Allen said, "Hey, you don't have to do this."

"I want to," she said. "Go on."

"Why are you being so nice to me?"

She laughed. "Because you're obviously in shock."

"So you think I don't mean it?"

She pressed up against him, and said, "You mean it. So do I. I'd love to live with you."

Allen blinked out the water and kissed her. He said, "I hope it leads to something more."

She gave him an incredulous look and shushed him. She continued soaping his chest and arms. As she moved farther down he began getting an erection, and she laughed. "At least not all of you is in shock."

He told her that he knew what she was thinking, that he was being impulsive and would regret this later. He told her his life was filled with decisions like this, something that he pondered for months, then with some kind of triggering moment that pushed him in the direction he had been intending all along. He reminded her of his dropping out of college, how he had been premed at his aunt's insistence—a condition of her paying for his tuition—and he hated it for two years until he was sitting in an organic chemistry class, and suddenly stood up and walked out. And that was the end of college for him.

Serena said quietly, "Yes, but a lot of your decisions are prompted by negatives. You left college because you hated it. You became a bodyguard because you didn't like regular security. You worked with Larry because you didn't want to be with ProServ or Black Diamond or whatever those companies were. And you want to move in with me because the alternatives are scary. I don't want this to be an escape from something. I love you, and I'm touched by this, but I want you to want it for positive reasons."

Allen thought, Hm, could this be true?

So all morning while he reviews Linda and Julie's notes, going over their searches and looking for any holes, he can't stop reviewing his own actions and looking for holes in his decisions. If it's possible to separate decisions with positive and negative motives, and negative motives are somehow the lesser of the two, then Allen's track record isn't very good. He thinks about rats in a maze and the difference between a food incentive and an electric shock penalty. Has his life been the avoidance of electric shocks?

No. He knows of one decision that's positive. He was in a state of mild contentment, not fleeing from anything, when he started dating Linda. They spent weeks together, searching for information about his father's death twenty years earlier, and during that time they grew closer. There were no electric shocks propelling him toward her.

Is this true of Serena?

Allen shakes this off and focuses on his work. He finishes reviewing the notes, and except for the school oversight, he doesn't find any new avenues. He then begins compiling lists of Frank's friends and family, and conducts slow, methodical background searches on all of them, beginning with immediate family members. By the time he finishes with Frank's family—Diedre, an older sister in San Rafael; Richard, a younger brother in the city, and Frank's parents, Marilyn and Doug, in Seattle—it's late in the afternoon and Allen has been working nonstop for eight hours.

The only references that Julie and Linda gave him are the names and addresses of the family members, but with those "indentifiers" he logs on to the various on-line database and search companies B&C subscribes to and finds their social security numbers. Not unlike a car dealer checking the credit of a potential customer, Allen then downloads their credit reports, and systematically checks the state and federal criminal records, real estate and property records, liens and civil judgments, driving and vehicle records, and even marriage records. The depth of access depends on the state in which most of the records are kept—California has tougher restrictions for DMV and Vital Records, for example—but Larry has, after a dozen years in the business, alternative methods.

Using the information brokers via the intranet, Allen sends in requests for more background, the easiest being Frank's parents in Seattle, where the Washington privacy laws are less stringent. Some of the requests, paid for by B&C's credit card, won't be fulfilled for twenty-four to forty-eight hours, but some information is e-mailed to Allen almost immediately.

He needs more time to organize and study the data coming in, but the most interesting tidbit is Frank's brother Richard, who lives in the Cow Hollow neighborhood in the city; he was in prison for four years on charges of selling drugs to minors, firearms possession, and the use of a gang in a criminal conspiracy. Allen will ask Julie more about him.

He looks up at the clock, startled to realize that he missed lunch. He stands up and sees Gracie sleeping on the rug. He swoons, dizzy from all the computer work, and sits on Serena's bed. Larry hasn't called yet, and he worries that this can only mean that most of the things in the office are unsalvageable. Gracie opens her eyes and stares at him. He says, "Positive, negative decisions. What does it matter? All that matters is whether I'm happy. Right?"

His cell phone vibrates on the table, and he grabs it, expecting Larry with an update, but instead he hears Linda say, "Where are you? Your office phone just keeps ringing."

He hesitates, not sure if the fire will somehow make the firm look bad. Then he tells her about the arson, and that he's working from Serena's apartment.

"Was it Frank? Could he have done this?" she asks.

Allen, surprised, says, "Frank? How would he even know about us?"

"I don't know. Sometimes I got the feeling that he was monitoring us."

"How?"

"Not sure. Just a feeling."

"Is he capable of something like this?"

"I don't know. I didn't think he was capable of kidnapping."

"Larry and I have a pretty good idea who it was," he says, telling her briefly about Dubois. He then asks her about Nora's school records.

"We thought of that, but we couldn't ask every school in the country. And I'm guessing Frank might have changed her name, too."

Allen says, "Maybe, but any new school she goes to will ask for transfer records. I was thinking about asking Nora's old school to see if they had requests for a record transfer."

Linda is quiet. Then she says, "Damn, I totally forgot about that."

"I was just reading this Family Educational Rights and Privacy Act, where the school—"

"Has to tell the parent if the records were sent off. We knew about that, but we were so wrapped up in finding Frank that we let that slip. I have to go."

"Wait. Why'd you call?"

"We have your retainer check. Can we meet tonight? You can update us in person."

"I might have to take care of things with the fire."

"Just for a few minutes. We can buy you a quick dinner. Come by around six."

Allen, knowing Larry will want that retainer as soon as possible, agrees.

Linda says, "I should go. I want to follow up this school thing right now."

"Wait. Isn't that my job?" Allen asks.

Linda pauses. "You're right, but let me do this. We're going crazy over here."

This might happen more often, and Allen says, "We should talk tonight to clarify my duties. I think we need to draw some lines. Okay?"

"Sure. Of course. I got to go now." She hangs up.

Allen feels uneasy with the messiness of this case, and also realizes that as an ex-girlfriend Linda has more latitude as a client than he might normally allow. He or Larry would never let a client take on any of the research, yet Allen has just done that.

He sits on the floor and scratches Gracie's ears. He says, "I hope this isn't a mistake."

Last night, after Serena had shampooed his hair and soaped his smoke-smelling body, she dried him off and led him to bed, the air tingling his skin, the sheets crisp and cool. They curled up naked, shivering. Allen hugged her, feeling her smooth skin glide electrically over his. He moved on top of her, nestling in between her legs, and kissed her lightly on her nose. "Warming up?" he asked.

"Heating up," she said, and ran her finger lightly down his back.

"So you're saying I should reconsider moving in?"

"You should think about it. I want us to, but not like this."

"Like what?"

"You freaking out about loss."

Allen laughed. "Okay."

"Also, I want you to wait until you've met my parents. You might not be so willing to live with me after that."

He thought about it, then said, "No. It doesn't matter. They're just parents." He realized that on some level she was nervous about this meeting, and he found it endearing. "Too bad I don't have anyone to introduce you to."

"Did Linda ever meet your aunt?"

Allen told her that Linda had met his aunt in a professional capacity as a reporter while she was working on the story of his father's death. The tangled investigation of the twenty-year-old accident and his aunt's involvement had brought them together. He added, "Linda interviewed her a couple times."

"You know I'm a little uncomfortable with her around."

"I know," he said, pulling the covers over their heads.

"I just want you to know that."

"I do." Allen squared his face over hers and tried to discern her expression in the dark. All he saw were fuzzy shapes, the curve of her nose, the outline of her ears. His eyes slowly adjusted, and he thought he noticed a glint in her eyes as she stared up at him. He kissed her on the lips. Cocooned in the sheets, their bodies slowly warming, he nuzzled her neck, and whispered into her ear, "No, *this* is my favorite part."

She wrapped her arms around his back and pulled him closer. Allen used to worry he was crushing her, but she wanted him on her. She had once said, "I like it. You're not as heavy as you think." So now he lowered his chest against hers, and she let out a small sigh and raised her hips a fraction of an inch, her hands pulling him tighter. They sank into the mattress. The sheets seemed to inhale and exhale with them, and they kissed again slowly. His legs were tired from the earlier run, and as he began rubbing against her, the faint pains in his thighs familiar and oddly comforting, he was, despite the fire and the events tonight, inexplicably content. He kissed her neck, her breasts, and she ran her fingers through his damp hair, and when they made love, he almost laughed aloud, a deep sense of elation washing through him.

Seven

As he drives into the city to meet Linda and Julie he finds himself missing Serena. She seems to intuit what he needs, and last night, were it not for the fire, would've been a perfect evening: to run, to shower, all with Serena. He called her before leaving the apartment, telling her that he had to pick up the retainer check and also visit the B&C office, where Larry is still cleaning up. He isn't sure how long he'll be, but he promises to meet up for a run around eight o'clock.

Even the sight of the burnt-out office can't bring Allen down. He drives into the alley and parks at B&C, the yellow crime scene tape still crisscrossing the blackened front entrance. He hears Larry talking to himself inside. Knocking on the doorframe and ducking under the tape, Allen sees Larry crouched on the ground with stacks of burnt files. Allen asks how it's going. The scarred and scorched walls are brighter in the daylight; strips of melted paint hang down jaggedly. The water and soot have mixed and dried into veinlike tributaries, branching down in gray-and-black crusts over the crumbling Sheetrock. He inhales the ashy smell.

Larry wears a baseball cap, his hair tied and threaded through the back. His face is streaked with dirt and sweat, and he grimaces at the mess at his feet. He rubs his eyes and squints.

Allen accidentally steps on a charred piece of wood. He asks, "You've been at this all day?"

"No. I got started late because the arson guys didn't want me touching anything until they were done."

"Did they find anything?"

"Partial prints on the back window, but the fire and water damage pretty much ruined everything."

"And Dubois?"

"Yeah. Everyone's looking for him." Larry stands up slowly, his knees cracking. "Not much left, Block-o."

"Those files? From the cabinet?"

"Scorched and soaked. Some of the ones deep in the middle are okay, but most of them are burnt. Sorry."

"And the equipment?"

"Oh, forget about it. Hunks of junk."

Allen sighs.

Larry says, "Talked to the insurance people. They're being careful, what with Dubois as the suspect. But it's not like we were insured to the hilt. We had basic business and office insurance."

"But will it cover everything?"

"Hope so. I'm dealing with paperwork."

"Thanks for doing it," he says. He notices Larry's subdued expression, and asks, "Are you all right?"

Larry shrugs. "Whatever. But anyway, how's it going with Linda's case?"

"Slow. Still backgrounding."

"E-mail me a copy of the status reports, okay? And let me know if you need help. I won't be taking on any new clients until this insurance crap is sorted out."

Allen worries about money. "We have enough for the business?"

"Clients?"

"Funds."

"Yeah. We're skating on Supremica's fee. We'll be fine."

He tells Larry he has to go now to pick up the retainer check.

Larry gives him the thumbs-up sign and squats back down, sorting through wet pieces of burnt paper. He hunches over. Allen watches him from the doorway; Larry reminds him of an overgrown kid absorbed with his marbles on the sidewalk, but he moves slowly, painfully. Allen is surprised to realize that even within the past four years, he has noticed that Larry is getting a little older, losing some of his eager energy. They first met in Monte Vista, when Allen was working a ProServ babysitting job for an executive, and Larry was bodyguarding another executive at the lunch meeting. Allen didn't like Larry then, his blustery unprofessional attitude annoying everyone, but now Allen knows it's a defense, a way for him to push through uncertain and intimidating situations. But back then he was definitely more alert, quicker, and more engaged with the work. Perhaps it's just the string of bad clients, and now this fire. Allen calls out, "Hey."

Larry looks up.

"It'll be fine. All this—it'll be okay."

Larry nods, and says, "I know, Blockman. Thanks."

The check that Linda hands over to him while they are at dinner is for double the original ten-thousand-dollar retainer. Allen gawks at figure, and says, "Twenty? This is a mistake."

"No. Julie and I talked it over. We wanted to make sure money wasn't an issue. We liked how you caught the school record flagging, which we just did with Nora's old school. If her records are requested by anyone, we'll know. I can't believe we let that go by, and we like how thorough you're being."

He has never held a twenty-thousand-dollar check before. He says, "I might not even need all this. You sure you don't want to go in smaller increments?"

"We're sure." Linda glances at her sister, who nods. Julie says, "We knew about FERPA, but just assumed that Frank wouldn't contact Nora's school. It was a careless assumption."

"He probably won't," Allen says, surprised that Julie seems paler. Her cheeks have sunk in even more. He adds, "If he really started paper tripping, he won't leave that kind of trail."

"But you never know," Linda says. "It's these kinds of amateur mistakes that I want to avoid. So we definitely want you on board, and we don't want money to be an issue."

He holds up the check. "It's not."

They are at a small Italian restaurant off Market, only a dozen tables crowded in a dark candlelit room with purple tablecloths and napkins and highly polished silverware. Julie and Linda have been here a few times before and know their waiter, Raymond, by name; they order their "regular" pasta salads, while Allen, starving, fills up on breadsticks and devours a veal parmesan. He feels the weight of the check in his breast pocket, and surreptitiously pats it to make sure it's still there. Italian opera filters down from the ceiling speakers.

Julie says, "So we flagged Nora's records. Anything else we missed?"

"Not that I can see. You guys were pretty comprehensive with Frank. But I have questions about Frank's family."

"Let me guess: Rick," Julie says. She finishes her glass of wine and motions to a waitress for a refill.

Allen says, "Is that his nickname? Does he go by that?"

"Yes. Rick is the black sheep—well, *was* the black sheep until Frank became a fugitive," Linda says. "We don't know a whole lot about him yet, but of course Julie has heard the stories about him from Frank."

"His criminal record," Allen says.

Julie nods. "Drug dealing. We both tried talking to him, but he's not saying a word."

"Tell me what you know."

Julie describes her preliminary talks with Frank's family, and the only one who was remotely friendly to her was Diedre, Frank's sister. Diedre, with two young children of her own, couldn't help but be a little sympathetic, though she refused to reveal even if she had spoken to Frank recently. She had just said, "I don't want to get involved in this. I'm sorry."

"Rick was the worst," Julie says. "He told us to fuck off. The parents were just scared. I know they know something. They all do."

"Tell me about their relationship. Who would Frank turn to?"

"Oh, Rick definitely," Julie says. "Rick owes him." She goes on to describe how even though Frank is the middle of the three siblings, he was the most responsible and ambitious. Rick turned to Frank on many occasions for money or advice or even a place to stay, and it came down to this: Rick would do almost anything for Frank. Julie says, "I told the police and the DA about Rick, and I know they tried to question him, but no dice."

"What does he do right now for a living?" Allen asks.

"No one knows," Julie says.

"Yes, we do," Linda replies. "He owns that diner."

"A tiny one," Julie says. "He lives in an expensive part of the city, drives an expensive car, and runs a small diner. Tell me what's wrong with that picture."

"So I should definitely dig a little with him," Allen says.

Julie suddenly looks exhausted, her body sinking back into the chair. Everyone becomes quiet. The background opera music grows louder above them.

"You know what?" Linda says, glancing at her sister. "Let's finish up here, walk you back to the hotel, and I'll take Allen out for a drink and fill him in more. You've had a long day."

"I should be here there, too," Julie says.

"No, I can handle this. I'll tell you everything when I get in, but you need to rest."

Julie nods, staring at her plate of tortellini, which she hasn't touched.

After they drop Julie off and find a bar farther up on Grant, Linda tells Allen, "She's getting worse. She's barely eating or sleeping. I can't imagine what she's going through." Linda orders a glass of Merlot, and finishes half of it while Allen is still waiting for his beer.

"She's lost a ton of weight since I last saw her," Allen says. They are sitting close to each other and he notices a few small wrinkles at the corner of her eyes; it startles him. She's only thirty-one. It has been a year and a half since he has seen her, and he wonders what his own signs of aging are. A few gray hairs, perhaps. Small wrinkles of his own. He should thank Serena for keeping him fit. He says, "The first time I met her she was actually plump."

"The first time? Oh, right. In Mill Valley, when she gave you a ride. You didn't make a good impression with her."

"I was a mess," he says, remembering that he had been beaten up while investigating his father's death; he had needed a ride to his aunt's house while avoiding the police. Julie couldn't conceal her disgust with him.

"Man," Linda says. "That was, what, four years ago? I can't believe how much we've changed."

Allen nods. "It's true."

"You seem happier," she says to him. "I mean, compared to then."

"I am."

"Good. I'm glad."

"And you?"

She says, "I'm better than I was when we broke up. That was a bad time for me."

Allen wants to tell her that he can't blame her. Her brother had died, and everything around her was tainted by that. But rather than bringing all that up, he says, "I remember when I first met you. Remember? You were interviewing me about the Florentino shooting. You were so young."

She smiles. "I was. Man, I was green. I also thought I knew everything back then."

The waitress arrives with Allen's beer, and he takes a slow sip while trying to figure out what she means by that. She knows less now? He isn't sure if he can ask. He recalls her being aggressive and eager, her job more important than almost anything else. But once her career stalled, she seemed to lose her urgency. Now that she doesn't seem to be working, he's not sure how she has retooled her life. He says, "Well, I've noticed you wear skirts now."

She looks down and laughs. "It's true. I've learned to like them."

He stares at her relaxed expression. She seems more at ease without her sister, and Allen realizes how difficult all this is for them. "How's your mother, especially after Hector and all that?"

"She coped. She's very strong. But this kidnapping has galvanized them. You should see the condo. It's command central. Both my parents are retired, so they're following all this closely. In fact, Julie's probably talking to them right now."

Allen says, "Tell me more about Julie's divorce and how it came to this."

Linda orders a second glass of wine and settles into the chair. "Of course," she says, and summarizes some of what Allen knows, that Frank and Julie separated and reconciled before this, but then their fighting turned bitter, usually revolving around money. "And it was money that was the final issue in the divorce. It seems like a petty point now, given what's happened, but it was all about valuing and reporting Frank's stock options, and full disclosure."

"Were they always fighting?"

"No," Linda says. "Before Nora they were great. Having the baby put a strain for a while, then it seemed to quiet down. But when she started school they began fighting, and it just got worse and worse. They both had affairs—"

"Julie did?"

Linda wrinkles her nose and nods. "She'd kill me if she knew I was telling you this. But yes, with some musician in Oakland."

"Did Nora know?"

"Nora knows a lot, though she'll pretend she doesn't."

"Is that a 'yes'?"

Linda sighs. "Yes. I'm sure she knew a little."

"Tell me more about Rick."

"A loser. A sniveling bottom-feeder who leeched off his brother. Julie hated him, and he hated Julie."

"But he would help Frank in any way he could."

"Definitely."

"I should start with him."

"I figured."

"Is he dangerous?"

Linda looks up at Allen, then nods slowly. "Yes."

They continue talking about Frank's family, Allen slowly getting more details, like Frank's mother having a nervous breakdown and being hospitalized when he was younger. The three kids were left to take care of themselves while the father struggled with a dead-end managerial job. Frank, despite being the middle child, took control, whereas Rick became a juvenile delinquent. He began selling dope when he was fifteen, dropped out of high school after his first big deal, and moved to California by age eighteen. Frank stayed at home, went to college, then graduate school, and married Julie shortly thereafter. Diedre married and settled in the Bay Area after her brothers made it clear they weren't returning to Seattle. Linda said, "Frank and Rick were always close.

Rick rarely listened to their father. Diedre was often the peacemaker. And that's pretty much how it stayed even as adults."

Allen keeps glancing at Linda's engagement ring, and thinks about his and Serena's relationship. He's not sure if he's moving in with her; her reaction was unexpected. He pictured her leaping into his arms, and instead she was stepping back warily. Is this a negative decision? He says to Linda, "Are you going to tell me about your fiancé?"

Linda straightens up in the booth and blinks. Her expression seems to shift as she breaks eye contact and runs her finger over the rim of her wineglass. Are these kinds of questions inappropriate? But they dated for two years, and surely this gives him some license? When the silence lasts a bit too long, Allen says, "Sorry. I was just looking at your rock."

"My rock?" She touches her hand. "I see. Well, you haven't told me much about Serena."

"You know her."

"Not really. I met her once, remember. You did all that rave stuff without me." She gives him a small smile, and says, "Sorry I was so difficult back then."

"There was a lot going on."

"I've thought about calling you a few times."

He tilts his head. "Why didn't you?"

"Guilt. I thought you were angry with me."

He doesn't want to admit that she's right. He nursed a small, bitter wound for a few months before finally letting her go. He escaped into his new job position with Larry and began dating Serena. Much of that time is foggy in his memory; he seems to recall going to the gym often with Serena. He looks across the room and notices a row of customers sitting at the bar, a few of them swiveling on the stools as they talk to each other or check everyone out. Allen realizes that this is a pickup place, with most of the men and women coming here after work. He says, "So you don't want to tell me about Michael?"

"Gabriel," Linda says with a half shrug. "Not much to tell."

Allen can't understand this reluctance. "Well, Serena and I might be moving in together."

"Really? Wow. That's huge," she says.

This stops Allen. Is it huge? He stifles a flicker of nervousness.

"Congratulations," Linda says. "That's a step before marriage."

He nods. "Maybe."

"You deserve to be happy," Linda says. "You always wanted that, didn't you? Family and the whole deal."

"And you?"

"I've been thinking about it. I'm getting older, after all."

He says, "I want to ask something about the case. When I told you about the fire, you first thought of Frank. You mentioned a feeling of him monitoring you. Tell me why."

She hesitates, adjusting to this change in subject, then nods. "Two things that happened earlier. One, a few weeks ago we noticed some files were missing from the Walnut Creek house, some of Frank's personal letters and things like that. They were there before, but then were gone."

"Someone went in?"

"Someone who knew where to look. Yes. It's possible we misplaced it because Julie is moving everything out of the house, getting ready to sell it, but we still can't find those letters."

"And the second thing?"

"Someone was calling Julie's voice messages and retrieving them. She knew that because the messages were no longer new, but saved, and she hadn't listened or saved them herself. She quickly changed the key code, but someone was trying to monitor her messages."

"When was this?"

"About a week after the kidnapping."

"How much information did Frank get?"

"You think it was Frank?" she asks.

Allen says, "Of course it was."

"The letters might have had some information about his going away, but we're not sure. And the messages were from Charlene, who was beginning to coordinate the legal actions."

"If that ever happens again," he says. "If you suspect he might be calling in from somewhere, trying to get your messages, then get the phone company to put a trap on the line."

"A trap?"

"A trace. They'll log all incoming calls."

"You mean if Julie hadn't changed the key code and we had a trap on the line—"

"You might have been able to trace where the call came from, if it was Frank. Though I suspect he's not dumb enough to call from his exact location."

"Still," Linda says, "we should've tried that."

"If it was early on, he's probably moved."

Linda pulls out a pad and pen, jotting this down.

"One more thing," Allen says. "In your notes I didn't see any reference to traveler's checks."

"What?"

"It's a long shot, but you might want to check American Express and the main banks Frank used, and find out if he bought traveler's checks. If he did, they can tell you when and where the checks were cashed, giving you at the very least his general location or movements."

"Damn," she says. "I didn't think about that."

"It's a small thing I learned on another skip trace. But I thought you said Charlene specialized in this."

"The legal part, not the investigation part."

Allen checks his watch, and says, "I've got to go now. I'm meeting Serena."

"Wait. What about your status report, and what you're going to do tomorrow?"

"Today I just went over your work and began looking into Frank's family. Tomorrow I'm going to focus on Rick, maybe even visit him."

"What time? I'd like to go."

This startles him. "No. Definitely not."

"Uh, Allen. You still have that check for twenty grand? I think I'm going with you."

He pulls out the check and places it in front of her. "First of all, there was nothing in the contract Julie signed about her or you accompanying me. Second, your presence will shut Rick up and even make him hostile if I do see him. He knows you. He doesn't know me. Third, you hired me to do a job. I can't do my job with you watching every move I make. You can do the smaller things like looking into American Express, but everything else I do alone. Or take back this retainer and tear up the contract. We don't have to do this."

Linda's expression hardens as she stares down at the folded check. She then looks up at him; he remains calm. He knows she won't tear up the check. But he also knows she won't back down.

She says, "How about I stay away if you do talk to him, but I just drive? I can be the driver."

"You'll be more useful taking care of other things, like the traveler's checks."

"Julie will do that."

"I don't want you second-guessing me—"

"Please, Allen. I need to be doing something. I need to be *working*. I promise I won't second-guess you. I just want to feel like I'm helping move this forward."

Allen considers this. He does hate driving in the city, and parking is always difficult.

Linda quickly adds, "I won't be seen. I'll drop you off wherever, and you just call me on my cell to tell me where to go. I just want to be useful."

"One condition," Allen says.

"Anything."

"If I feel you're interfering with the investigation, I tell you to leave, and you leave immediately, no questions asked."

"Of course."

"No." He leans forward. "Look at me."

She does. She grins, which makes Allen even more serious.

"I know you," he says. "I mean this. If I say 'Go,' you go without saying one word. You just go. This is very important."

She holds up her hand in a mock oath. "I understand. I promise. You say go, and I go." She then offers her hand to him. "Deal?"

They shake, and he says, "Deal." He wonders how he is going to tell Serena that his ex-girlfriend will be participating in this investigation.

Eight

The logistics of commitment often confuse the Block. Is it a truth universally acknowledged that a couple in love never have thoughts about another? Does love obviate other friends, other people? Since he has never been in love before—he might have been close to it with Linda, though he's no longer sure—and this terrain with Serena is unexplored and vaguely frightening, he gropes forward slowly, hands waving in front of him, toes inching along the ground.

He considers this when he pisses off Serena.

Allen arrives at Serena's apartment late for their run, and when he explains why, that he was with Linda, Serena looks at him without much of an expression, and says, "Don't worry about it." He suits up, and they run up toward Tilden Park. Once they hit the steep slope on Marin Avenue—the street and sidewalk angled at almost forty-five degrees—they struggle uphill, and she asks how the case is progressing. Allen tells her what he has been doing and planning, and when she asks if Linda will be accompanying him, he says, "Probably."

"Probably?"

"Yes," he says. "Though I'll be limiting her role."

"I see."

He glances at her, but in the darkness he can't tell how she's reacting. His thighs are burning, and he has trouble catching his breath. "Tomorrow she's going with me when I check out Frank's brother."

"Do you know what you're doing?" she asks quietly.

He isn't sure he hears her correctly, and says, "What?"

She repeats herself.

"I don't know what you mean."

And then she doesn't speak for a few blocks. Allen stares forward, the urge to confess welling up inside him, and he begins talking into the wind. He says, "I know how it looks. My ex-girlfriend. And I know that when you consider that I just asked us to live together, it seems strange. You might even connect my asking us to live together as guilt or something."

He feels her glance at him, then look ahead. They are now moving in rhythm, slowing as the incline levels off for a few blocks. He coughs and tries to shake off the pain spreading to his calves. He says, "But she just isn't a factor in any of my decisions. And I actually didn't want her tagging along, but they just wrote B&C a twenty-thousand-dollar check, and as long as she follows some ground rules, I can't really say no. I mean, it's her niece, Julie's daughter. I can't blame them for wanting to be active. But for me it's work. Nothing personal. It's just work."

"Was it work with me?" Serena asks.

Allen doesn't reply; he has lost his train of thought. Cars whine in low gear as they climb past them.

Serena says, "Have you forgotten how we met? How you were down in Los Angeles looking into Hector's death? And you needed my help? That was work."

"That was different."

She sighs and shakes her head. She then laughs to herself. "Oh, Allen."

"What?"

She stops running. Allen stumbles forward then backs up. "What's the matter?" he asks.

Her face, shining with sweat, breaks into an indulgent grin. "Allen, do you like playing with fire?" Headlights shine across her forehead, and her eyes glisten.

"No."

"Don't you think I'd feel a little threatened by this?"

"By Linda? But there's nothing going on."

She scratches her head, staring at him incredulously. She says, "Wow."

"What?"

"I don't know whether to be mad at you or to laugh at you."

"Look, nothing's going to happen."

She steps toward him and reaches out with her hand, touching his cheek lightly. Her fingers are cool against his sweaty skin. "I'm going to turn back now and shower and read. I want you to stay at your apartment tonight. Okay, honey?"

"What?" Now he's completely confused. "Are you mad at me?"

"I want you to think about this. Think about it this weekend. Don't forget my parents are coming next week." She blows him a kiss and begins running down the hill.

He says, "Wait. Are we fighting?" But she disappears around a corner.

The next morning Allen can't shake the disturbing memory of upsetting Serena, but she isn't taking his calls, and when he meets Larry to give him the retainer check, Larry notices something is wrong. First he eyeballs the figure, then says, "You okay, B.? You'd think a humongo check like this would make you happy."

"I'm fine," Allen replies, looking around the office. "Any progress?"

"Some. Don't worry about it. You look tired."

"Didn't sleep well."

"Worried about the case?" Larry asks.

"No, not really. Worried about . . . life."

Larry glances at him, then laughs. He says, "Yeah, that'll do it," and punches Allen in the arm. He tells him he's going to deposit the check, then finish salvaging what he can from the office. Allen is supposed to meet Linda here and waits outside. His legs ache because he finished the run by himself last night, pushing himself. He just rarely sees Serena upset, and so it's even more alarming to him to witness her cool and calm annoyance with him. She usually seems to let nuisances glide off her. Sometimes he wishes she would raise her voice and maybe curse more, because he'd be certain of how she feels; now he's bewildered. Last night after he returned to his own apartment, he paced back and forth, going over his words and trying to pinpoint his transgression. He doesn't feel as if he has alternatives; Linda is his client, and she and Julie are paying a lot of money.

His tiny apartment seemed smaller and darker. He decided to sleep on his sofa, his feet hanging off the edge. He thought it might be nice to have a dog like Gracie around. He listened to the lonely street noises on Clement until they died down after midnight.

Linda drives up to the building in her rental Toyota and looks at the crime scene tape. She's wearing tiny oval sunglasses and flicks them up to the top of her head and smiles brightly. She leans out of her window, and says, "New decoration?"

Allen has forgotten about her sense of humor. He frowns. "Very funny. Yes, we decorated with gasoline and a match."

"You'll have to change the name to reflect this new look."

Allen tries to think of something witty, but nothing comes to him.

Linda says, "B&C is now called Burnt & Charred Investigations."

He sighs and climbs in. "Cow Hollow, please."

"Yes, sir."

Rick Staunton lives in the upper half of a Victorian on Filbert, one block north of the strip of high-end boutique stores along Union, the

Cow Hollow area. Allen tells Linda to drive around the block and pass the house a few times so he can get a sense of the layout. He doesn't tell her that he's also looking for the garbage bins, which are in a narrow alley in between two houses. This is part of the PI job he knows Linda dislikes. He's also checking the accessibility of the yard or the windows, the distances and views from the street.

After getting a sense of the apartment layout and what Rick can see from his windows, Allen asks Linda to drive them to the diner on Laguna. He called the diner this morning and found out that Rick would be there right now. Linda parks down the street where they have a line of sight with the front entrance. The Pacific Diner has large front windows with booths inside and a counter curving along the back. Allen sees that most of the booths are filled, and there are waitresses in brown uniforms walking quickly with trays.

"What are you going to do?" Linda asks.

"Not sure yet."

She sits back and waits. She says, "Are you okay?"

"What? Why?"

"You look a little out of it."

He doesn't answer her, and turns back toward the diner. Yes, he is a little out of it. A small part of him wants to tell her what's happening, but that makes him feel disloyal.

He notices that the diner is getting more crowded. This might be a good time to check it out. He climbs out of the car and tells Linda to wait for him. Surveying the street and seeing a few pedestrians turning the corner near a bank, Allen tries to blend in with the other passersby and pauses in front of the diner windows. It's a brunch crowd, with breakfast platters filling the tabletops. A family with three kids sits by the first window, and Allen watches a young boy eat his bacon with his fingers. The boy smears a greasy finger along the window. The boy's mother yanks his hand back.

Allen looks over his shoulder and sees Linda in the car. He walks to the front entrance, pauses, then opens the door and is hit by the rich smell of sausages. Silverware clinks, the kitchen sizzles, pots and pans clatter. The buzz of voices. Allen moves through the diner and sits at the counter on an uneven square stool. A woman in a ketchup-stained apron nods to him from the other end, pouring coffee for another customer, and says she'll be with him in a minute, to which Allen smiles.

A waiter tends to a table in the corner, but he's a younger man, early twenties, and Rick is in his late thirties. Allen spots another man in a tie at the cash register station ringing up a customer. The man, lean and wiry with a goatee and mustache, speaks to the customer and runs a credit card through a machine. Julie doesn't have any photos of Rick, but described his height and build and said he usually keeps his curly brown hair cut very short.

The waitress behind the counter asks what he wants, and Allen orders a breakfast special with coffee, then says, "Is that Rick, the owner?" He points.

"Yeah, you know him?"

Allen nods. "Used to. He works the register?"

"Sometimes," the waitress replies, and hurries off with his order. Allen leans against the counter and watches Frank's brother. Allen isn't sure what he's going to do, but wants to see Rick in person before deciding. He knows he'll have to do some Dumpster diving tonight, and isn't looking forward to it. He also knows that he might have to try some illegal methods to get more information, and this knowledge depresses him. Why can't his job be more like Serena's, where she shows up at the office, writes software code, then goes home and forgets about it?

He tried calling her a few times this morning, though she didn't pick up. They usually spend their Saturday mornings in bed, sleeping in, then reading the advance edition of the Sunday *Chronicle,* which Serena picks up at the deli down the street. Fresh coffee, bagels, and a week's worth of interesting junk mail also add to their morning. Serena plays her favorite CDs on her bedroom stereo while Gracie waits patiently for her morning walk. For Sundays, they are too restless to stay in bed again and end up heading to Marin for a hike or reading at the beach.

This morning he felt the absence, the incompleteness of his routines as he ate a bowl of cereal and planned the day's work. He wanted to apologize for last night. He knew what he had done wrong; he knew he should've been more sensitive to her reactions. He just didn't know what to do next. He'll call her tonight, and they'll talk.

Allen stares at his plate of scrambled eggs, sausage, toast, and hash browns, and after a contemplative moment when he considers how bad this meal is for his body, he devours it. The eggs are watery, the sausages too salty, the toast cold and hard, and the hash browns greasy, but he hasn't eaten something this delicious in a while. He wants another helping, but stops himself. Instead, he orders a bagel with cream cheese for Linda, leaves a tip at the counter, then walks to the register with his check. Rick is still there.

"Was everything okay?" Rick asks him.

Allen says it was fine. He studies Rick, who has a hard jaw and taut skin over his cheekbones. His white shirt has small faint grease spots near the pocket. Rick has faded tattoos on his forearms, his sleeves rolled unevenly to his elbows. Allen says, "I've seen you somewhere before, haven't I?"

Rick glances up. "Maybe."

"Aren't you Diedre's brother?"

Rick stops counting out Allen's change. He says, "You know Diedre?"

"I taught high school for a while. I knew her from there."

Rick smiles. "Yeah, Dee's a teacher. Maybe we did meet some time. You in Marin?"

"Not now. I used to be. I thought you were some kind of banker or something?"

He shakes his head. "No, that's the other one. I own this place. What's your name?"

"Allen," he says, holding out his hand to shake. "You are . . . ?"

"Rick." They shake hands. Rick grips him tightly, trying to crush his knuckles.

"How is Diedre?" Allen asks, not flinching. "I haven't seen her in a year or so. Still teaching I guess."

"Yeah. I saw her last weekend."

"Her kids doing okay?"

"Yeah. Little brats, but okay. Where'd we meet?"

Allen pauses. "Someone's birthday party, maybe?"

Rick nods, appraising Allen. He counts the change again and hands it to him. He says, "I've never been to any of Dee's parties."

"Oh. Maybe it was something else."

Rick gives Allen a nasty smile, then says, "Who the fuck you kidding? What are you, a cop? Did that bitch Julie send you here?"

Allen almost laughs. "What are you talking about?"

"You don't think I'd remember some Jap friend of Diedre's? You think I'm stupid?"

Allen looks at him calmly, then shakes his head, "Hey, I just thought you looked familiar—"

"Yeah, yeah. Tell it to that dyke lawyer. Let me guess. You're some burnt-out cop doing a favor for Julie. Give me fucking break. So you found me at my diner. Big fucking deal." His gaze focuses behind Allen, and in the mirror Allen sees more customers approaching. Rick lowers his voice and says, "Get the fuck out of here. If there weren't people around I'd kick your fucking teeth out."

Allen has an odd, pleasant feeling about this, a reaction that cancels out Rick's hostility; the anger is a sign that Allen needs. Rick likely keeps in contact with his brother. This is the right track. This is progress. Allen says, "It was very nice meeting you."

Rick shakes his head, staring at him. "Fucking bitch Julie. I ought to shut her up. Her sister, too."

"But you know where Frank and Nora are, don't you?"

His eyes meet Allen's. There's a deadness in his gaze. "Go to fucking hell."

Linda thanks him for the bagel and waits for him to tell her what happened, but Allen just says, "Drive back to his place. Park down the street. I want to go on foot."

She pulls out of the parking space and drives back up past Union and onto Filbert. Allen had let the "Jap" remark slide, but now it's bothering him. There's always something like that hovering near him, some remark or look or feeling. Sometimes he'll actually forget about his race for a day or two until something like that reminds him—a well-meaning clerk asking where he's "from," a double take when he's in Marin or even farther north and the only Asian around. It's good living in the Richmond district, though, since there are enough Asians that no one really notices him. And in Berkeley, near the university, there are so many Asians walking around sometimes even he's a little surprised. But now he remembers the arrival of Serena's parents, who seem to think he's not Asian enough. Not Korean enough. All the mental confusion exhausts him.

Linda can't find a parking space near Rick's apartment, so he tells her to drive around and meet him back at this corner in thirty minutes. He can see her wanting to ask what he's going to do, what happened at the diner, her posture leaning forward and hesitating, words beginning to form but then halting. He says, "Please let me do my job. I'll fill you in later."

She nods and drives off.

The brown-and-yellow Victorian, in between another similar gray one and a more modern brick two-story, has telephone and electrical wires running to it from the utility pole—different from the shops on Union with their lines piped underground—and Allen follows the telephone line to the main circuit box on the side of the building, next to the alley with the plastic garbage bins. He walks casually down the driveway and opens the top flap of the garbage bin. Half-full with plastic garbage bags. The smell of something rotting blows around him and he closes the lid quickly. He opens the recycling bin. Newspapers. He needs to check the garbage pickup days. He inspects the telephone interface, which runs three separate lines into the house. Then he leaves, not wanting to be seen lingering here.

Walking around the block, Allen looks for alternative access to the backyard. The houses and small apartment buildings have been built almost touching one another, though every few houses there are narrow alleys or gaps. He can probably find his way to Rick's house from the other side. He plans the surveillance: external phone tap; maybe even an internal long-range wireless mike, but that will mean getting inside; an Infinity bug would be perfect, but he has to research the latest versions. He'll need untraceable equipment, which will be expensive, and he'll have to dig up B&C's burglar tools. He needs to take another closer look at the house in the evening, tracking not only Rick's movements but those of the downstairs neighbor and the nearby houses. He has to consider all angles of access.

He walks slowly back to the corner, and thinks, So now it begins.

Nine

arry left a note for Allen at B&C that all the salvageable files are now at Larry's loft in the Mission, so after picking up his car and agreeing to talk to Linda later, Allen heads to the loft. Larry purchased the apartment in the early nineties before the loft craze took off and while real estate prices were depressed. The value of this small high-ceilinged one-bedroom unit, one of four in a converted warehouse, has tripled over the past decade, and when Larry sells it, he can use the proceeds to pay cash for a house almost anywhere in the Bay Area. But he isn't selling. He likes the grit of his neighborhood, the cheap restaurants, and being within walking distance from BART. He has furnished the loft with black metal chairs and tables, and has a huge entertainment system with a flat-screen TV.

Even though Allen has been there a few times before, he notices now the well-stocked kitchen with the large center island, shiny steel and copper pots hanging above. He has never really thought about the cookware, and just assumed they were for show. He sees two wooden knife blocks side by side next to the large sink.

"You use all those pots and pans?" he asks.

Larry grunts from the corner of the living room, where he is sorting files and setting up a temporary office in the corner. "The copper only for special dishes. They radiate heat more evenly than stainless steel, but they're freaking expensive."

"You *are* serious about cooking."

Larry looks up. "Dude, I told you that."

"I know. It's just . . ." Allen shrugs.

"Yeah, whatever," Larry says. "Look here. This pile is your stuff. Not much left, though." He points to a wet stack of burnt papers and manila folders.

As Allen searches through them, finding that these are all old case files he shoved to the back of the filing cabinet, he says, "I'm thinking of bugging Frank's brother, the ex-con."

Larry smiles. "Yeah? What kind?"

"Not sure. Maybe the Infinity?"

He says, "Going all out. It's expensive."

"Deep pockets."

"You'll have to get inside."

"I know."

"If you get caught . . ."

Allen nods. "The network interface is on the side, no lock, so I can put a tap there, but I want to hear more."

"You know there's a new Infinity out, no first ring."

"So no hang up? I was worried about that."

"Yup. And it's small, man. Duplex plug that you can hide at the wall."

"Where do I get it?"

"Use the intranet and go to the Professional Outlet in my bookmark. You can order on my computer."

The Infinity transmitter, sometimes known as the "third wire" or "Harmonica bug," is an ingenious device that connects to a telephone and turns the telephone itself into a bug. What's particularly useful is the phone can remain on the hook to bug the room, and, more importantly, you can call in from any phone to activate and listen to the device. Earlier versions required the caller to dial the number, then either input a code, which was risky, since the person on the other end could simply pick up, and the caller would have to pretend to be a wrong number. Allen says, "It's strange to be working this end. I'm so used to *counter*surveillance."

Larry replies, "That's the thing about this job. You got to be flexible." He turns toward him. "Just don't get caught."

Allen sighs. "I know. Are all the tools still in storage?"

Larry grunts yes, then kicks aside the stack of files, which fall over in one wet clump. He says, "All no good. And we got to make a decision about the office. I talked to the landlord. He'll need a few weeks to fix up the place. We don't got to pay rent, but we got to tell him if we still want it."

"We have a choice?"

"Yeah. It's up to you."

"To me? Why?"

"He'll want a new one-year lease."

Allen waits for more, but when Larry remains quiet, he realizes the implication: a one-year lease and Larry is scaling back. It's Allen's decision because Allen will be running the firm next year. The weight of responsibility settles down heavily on him, and he says, "Will he raise the rent?"

"Probably a little, but not much. The commercial rental market is in the dumps."

"Why don't you negotiate a good lease. Factor in us putting in all new security and stuff like that. Then let me know."

Larry salutes. "Sounds good, boss. See? It's easy."

"And the insurance?"

Larry says, "It's going to take a while. Believe it or not, they're suspicious that we paid our premiums early."

"What?"

"The past few payments we were a little late. This time we were early, and then the cause, Dubois, was really convenient. It's almost as if they want to wait until Dubois is caught and confesses."

"We lost a lot of equipment."

"Don't worry. We'll sue if we have to, but I don't think it'll come to that. I'll take care of it."

"I'm still not sure about your leaving the business."

"Hey, Block-o, I'm not leaving. Just toning down. Just easing back. That's all."

Allen's not sure he believes this, but goes to make some calls, preparing for tonight.

Allen drives across the Golden Gate Bridge, heading up to San Rafael. After ordering the Infinity, special rush delivery to B&C's private mailbox, he called the city and learned that the garbage pickup in Rick's neighborhood is on Monday mornings. He also retrieved the tools from the storage closet and tried getting Rick's schedule from the diner. But the woman on the other end told him that she couldn't give that information out. Rick is being more careful now.

He calls Serena's cell phone again, but she doesn't answer. The voice mail message comes on. She has caller ID and he suspects that she sees his cell number and is letting it ring. He then calls Linda and tells her he needs someone to follow Rick around and log his movement today. "Wait," she says. "Where are you?"

"Just crossed the Golden Gate. I'm heading to Diedre's place."

"Why didn't you wait for me?"

"It's more productive to split some of the tasks. I noticed there wasn't that much about Julie's neighbors in Walnut Creek. You guys spoke with them, right?"

"Yeah. The police did, too. They didn't know much."

"All the neighbors?"

"Yes. The entire street."

"They didn't know Julie and Frank well?"

"Do you know your neighbors well?"

"Good point. And the neighbors at Frank's place? That was also in Walnut Creek?"

"An apartment, and yes, we talked to the people there. But Frank hadn't been there long, and never talked to them."

"Okay. Rick should still be at the diner. Just don't be marked."

"Is this busywork?"

"A little. I'd do it myself, but I want to talk to Diedre."

"Why can't Larry do this?"

"Because he's dealing with the fire."

"We're paying for this."

"You're paying for me, and I can tail Rick myself, but I thought you said time and speed are important."

"Aren't we paying for Larry?"

"No. It's in the contract. You're hiring me, and I'm under the B&C umbrella, but if you wanted both of us, that'd up the daily rate, and that'd eat away at the retainer quickly. All I need is a log of where Rick goes and what he does. Can you do that?"

"Why?"

"I'm going to have to break into his place, and I need a sense of his routines."

"You're going to what?"

Allen hesitates. "Actually, never mind. You can't know what I'm doing. You told me that."

She's quiet for a moment. "Okay. I'll help. Oh, and Frank did buy traveler's checks, but he hasn't used any."

"And you told the bank to call you as soon as he does—"

"Of course, but it might just be emergency travel money. We'll see. It was a good tip, though."

"You're going to get your money's worth."

"It sounds like it."

He hangs up and hears some tools sliding in the trunk. He emptied the Mission Bay storage closet and is nervous about carrying all the burglar tools, which, if he is pulled over by the police, is suspicious enough for Allen to be taken in for questioning. And if there were any burglaries in the vicinity, he could become a prime suspect. He took a quick inventory before loading up: glass cutters, wire cutters, splices, pick guns, picks, jimmies, nylon rope, twine, climbing harnesses, slings, belays, carabiners, wire gates, gloves, mini drills, electric screwdrivers, slim-jims, guitar string, an ohmmeter, a voltmeter, an infrared detector, electrician's tape, duct tape, masking tape, Scotch tape, a mini telescope, mini binoculars, mini night-vision goggles, and a mini 35-mm camera.

He drives carefully, thinking, What cop would pull over a Volvo station wagon?

Diedre Gordon lives in the Terra Linda section of San Rafael, a suburban community with low, slanted-roof homes strategically built so no house would face directly across the street from another. Allen leaves the 101 and winds around curved blocks and quiet, smooth side streets, searching for Diedre's address. He's surprised by how still it seems there, the yards empty, and almost no pedestrians on the sidewalks. It's a little eerie, actually, after coming from the noise and activity of the city. Allen has never lived in a quiet suburb, and isn't certain he can stand the silence. He needs signs of life outside his apartment. Finally, he sees a man walking a dog. Allen pulls over, and asks where Willowwood Drive is.

The man points ahead and gives Allen complicated directions involving three turns. Allen promptly gets lost again, and continues driving for fifteen minutes before hitting Willowwood by accident. He pulls up to Diedre's address, a yellow-and-brown ranch-style house, and stares at a metal gate—the front entrance—leading into what seems to be a small courtyard.

He looks around at the neighbors' quiet houses and approaches the gate. He rings the doorbell, and hears the voices of two young girls clamoring inside. They burst out of the front door and stop on the walkway when they see Allen through the metal grilling.

"Hey," he says. "Can you get your mother?"

They blink and stare, then simultaneously turn and run back in, yelling, "Mom!"

A tall, frizzy-haired woman with a pleasant and curious smile walks out. She says, "Good morning."

"Hello. Are you Diedre Gordon?"

She nods. "Yes. Do I know you?" She's wearing jeans and a gray University of Washington sweatshirt.

"No. My name is Allen Choice, and I'm a private investigator."

Her face tightens, and she steps back a few feet from the gate.

Allen says quickly, "I know, I know. I'm really sorry to bother you at home. I promise this won't take—"

"You're working for Julie Staunton?"

"Yes. I know you've spoken with her, and she said you were so helpful—"

"I can't talk to you. I just can't. I'm sorry."

"Mrs. Gordon, I understand what a difficult situation you're in. It's just that Julie is getting desperate. Surely you can see how something like this would upset—"

"Please," she says urgently. "Please don't."

Allen pulls out his business card. "How about you don't answer anything you don't want to? This is just background information for me. That's all. We can talk right here. Or anywhere. Just for a few minutes. I drove up here from the city."

"You shouldn't have."

Allen sees her wavering, and says, "You will not be jeopardizing your brother. Just background. You know, stupid things like how close a family you were and whether or not you think Nora will be okay—"

"Of course she'll be okay! Frank loves her tremendously!"

"See? Things like that. The view I have is Julie's, and I know it must be a little skewed. I need the whole picture. Give me Frank's side. I haven't heard Frank's side."

She considers this. Then she says, "Not here. I'm meeting a friend for coffee downtown on Fourth Street. Afterward I'll talk to you, but only for a few minutes."

"Time and place."

She checks her watch. "Three-thirty. Meet me on Fourth and A Street. I can't talk long."

"Thank you."

"Don't thank me yet." She turns and walks back into her house.

Diedre is late. Allen sits on the edge of a concrete planter in front of a café, watching the traffic drive by and occasionally jotting notes to himself. He wants to determine how close Frank is with his parents, and Allen needs a stronger sense of personality—whether or not Frank is methodical and patient enough to live anonymously for an extended amount of time. Allen writes in his notebook, "Routines like gyms or favorite kinds of restaurants? Favorite places traveled to in the past? Ask Julie. Ever talked about wanting to live in X?"

Few people can be so ascetic that they'd give up everything they liked in the past. If Allen changed his identity, he wouldn't give up working out or running; he couldn't live in a shack in an isolated rural town; he'd have to live in or near a city. It's these kinds of inclinations that Allen has to discover about Frank. Allen sees himself as a kind of radar, slowly homing in on Frank, but right now the signal is too weak for any real triangulation.

He pulls out his cell and tries to call Serena again for the third time. He leaves a voice message, asking her if she's still mad at him and if they could please talk. He hangs up. They've had small arguments before, but neither of them has ever been angry to the point of yelling. There is something unusually civil about their disagreements. With Linda, she might raise her voice, point at him, and tell him what she was angry about, and although he didn't like it, although he wanted to flee, at least he knew where he stood. With Serena, she'd look at him slyly, and say, "Are you sure you mean that?" Allen would be more confused than ever.

He can't even remember the last fight they had. They recently disagreed about where to spend a weekend away—Allen wanted to stay near the Bay Area and Serena wanted to drive down to Joshua Tree—but they compromised by camping in Tahoe National Park.

A sedan with tinted windows pulls up to the curb ahead and idles. Allen sits up. The rear door opens, and Rick steps out. Allen jumps to his feet, tensing, and looks around. Rick holds his hands up, and says, "Take it easy. We need to talk."

"Diedre told you?"

"Called me as soon as you left her house. We can talk in here," he says, pointing to his car, "or in there." He nods to the café.

Allen walks to the café entrance and waits by the door. Rick shrugs and says something to the driver. He follows Allen in and to a small round table by the front window. They sit down, and Rick clears his throat, sitting back and relaxing. He says, "My sister is too nice. She can't say no."

"I just wanted to talk to her."

"Yeah, I know. By the way, I shook the tail you put on me." He grins, his lips chapped.

"Did Diedre tell you what I wanted to talk to her about?"

"Yeah, some bullshit about wanting Frank's side. Give me a fucking break. I know how you private detectives work. I mean shit, you're just a half a step above the cons."

Allen thinks about his plan to bug Rick's apartment and has to smile. Rick says, "See, you know it, too."

"What did you want to talk about?"

"I'm supposed to look out for Diedre, and in a way, for Frank. I want you to stop."

"I can't."

"Sure you can."

"I'm just doing my job."

Rick shakes his head. "Get a different one. Get a real one."

"Like selling drugs to kids?"

Rick's face becomes blank, then he says, "Well, well. So you've been doing your homework. Those *kids* would've slit their mothers' throats for a fix. But that don't matter. You can still do your job, but not so good."

Allen realizes that Rick doesn't know about the past relationship with Linda. Rick views Allen as just some PI hired off the street. Allen says, "They're paying me a lot."

"I'm sure they are, with Frank's fucking money."

"Julie's money."

"So it's about money?"

Allen says, "He kidnapped Nora. He stole her from Julie. It's not about money."

"Do-gooder? No, that ain't you. Tell you what. Just think about it. Come up with a figure." Rick stands up slowly, and fixes his leather jacket.

"A figure? To back off?"

"A big figure to stay on and do a bad job."

"Help an asshole like you? Are you kidding?"

He looks down at Allen and smiles. "You know you're not the first PI on this case, right?"

Allen tries not to look surprised, but isn't successful.

Rick says, "You didn't know that? I guess that makes sense. Second string is never a good feeling. You should find out what happened to the first one." He stares hard at Allen, and adds, "You've been warned."

Allen calls an emergency meeting and drives back into the city, heading for Julie and Linda's bed-and-breakfast. The exorbitant retainer now makes more sense. It isn't generosity; it's insurance. It's fear. It also means that Julie's notes have been edited for Allen. The previous PI was deleted, and possibly his or her work attributed to Linda or Julie. Allen keeps his anger in check as he fights the traffic on Van Ness. He'll wait until he hears their story before reacting. Rick could've been lying or testing Allen. There could've been another PI who simply quit after dealing with them; Allen can imagine something like that happening.

He forgot about Linda's craftiness. She was a good reporter because she knew how to lie smoothly, how to give the subject what he wanted, and relax him, soften him. Allen had seen her at work many times, and he should've realized that with such an important case she would handle Allen carefully, and that would include omitting disquieting details like a previous PI.

He can't blame her. He might have done the same thing, given the stakes. But why him? There are so many PIs in the area. Probably because she can participate in the investigation with him, but not with anyone else. She can control him.

Allen lets out a tired sigh and feels the conflict of wanting to quit this case but knowing the importance of it. He likes Nora. He can picture her bewildered by all this. Allen remembers vividly his own childhood around that age. His father had died in an accident at work, and the unreality of loss permeated his life. Allen could not seem to get any kind of grip on the world, and turned inward. He lived with his aunt Insook, who would be a disinterested guardian until Allen hit high school, then their relationship worsened. It would take decades before Allen understood why she took him in but resented him. But at that age Allen was just beginning to understand the reverberations of death.

He feels now the urge to be with Serena. Then he remembers what she said about negative motivations, and he realizes she was wrong. He isn't lurching in her direction in an attempt to avoid something else; if he were avoiding something, his instinct would be to withdraw, to hide out. In fact, that used to be his first reaction to everything, but he's growing. He's maturing. He's jumping in Serena's direction because of her. He wants to be with her. He thinks of it as part of the protective theory principle. He's not *re*acting. He's *pre*acting. He loves her.

With this knowledge Allen feels better. He doesn't allow Julie and Linda's subterfuge to bother him. This is a job, and he can't let his personal connections hinder him. He knows what he has to do. He knows how to take control of this situation. He has to be willing to walk away, no matter what his feelings for Nora or Linda may be.

Ten

Allen senses the tension in the conference room immediately, Linda and Julie standing up upon his entrance, both asking what is happening, why he needs to see them like this. He studies their expressions, trying to determine the extent of their lying to him, and hardens himself. Their eyes are confused. They glance at each other, then wait for his answer. He weakens for a moment when he sees Julie's sallow cheeks. But he can't let this go. He can't work like this. He tries not to worry about Nora. He says, "I'll deduct the charges to date and return the balance of the retainer to you by tomorrow. It'll be on a B&C check."

Linda turns to Julie, then says to him, "What? What're you talking about?"

"I'm quitting the case," he says.

"No!" Julie says. "What's the matter? What happened?"

"As much as I like Nora and want to help, you two haven't been honest with me, and I cannot work for clients who lie to me. It jeopardizes me, and can jeopardize Nora. I'll fax over a formal letter of resignation; it's in the cancellation clause in the contract."

"Wait a minute, wait a minute! What's going on?" Julie asks. She says to her sister, "What did you do?"

"Me?" Linda says.

Allen says, "You didn't disclose to me that I'm not the first PI on the case. You doctored your notes. You lied to me."

They freeze. Julie snaps her head toward Linda, whose gaze remains fixed on Allen. He sees a red flush fill Julie's pale cheeks. Linda says, "Okay. Just hold on. Before you do anything rash—"

"I talked to Rick."

This stops them.

"You what?" Julie finally says.

Allen replies, "I was supposed to talk to Diedre, but Rick showed up."

"What did he say?"

"I'm no longer on this case—"

"All right," Julie says. "We didn't say anything about that. I'm sorry. It's just—"

"You didn't *say* anything? You edited your notes to me. You didn't give me any of this other PI's reports. Something's going on here, and I don't like it."

Julie says to Linda, "I told you this would happen. I *told* you."

Allen moves toward the door. "Sorry, but I'll be going. I'll messenger over the check tomorrow."

"Wait, please." Julie lunges across the table. "Just hear us out."

"It's my fault," Linda says quietly. "Julie didn't want to do it."

"Do what?" Allen says.

"Lie to you. But I know you. If you knew what happened, you would've focused on that first, and we're running out of time. We have to find Nora."

"What do you mean 'what happened'?"

Julie says, "Will you sit? Will you hear us out?"

Allen hesitates, then sits.

Julie says, "We hired a large detective agency out of Los Angeles. They have branches all over the country. We thought that would help."

"Which one?"

"Tyler Brennan and Associates."

"They don't have an office in San Francisco," Allen says, though he knows they use two local agencies as affiliates.

Linda says, "They still have connections here, and we didn't think Frank would stay in the area anyway."

"What happened?"

"The lead investigator, our contact, resigned. He then OD'd," Julie says.

Linda looks down.

Allen lets this settle for a moment, not having expected this, then says, "What?"

Julie says, "He overdosed on heroin."

Allen sighs. "You better start from the beginning. And you better tell me the truth."

With the help of their lawyer, Julie and Linda moved quickly as soon as Nora was abducted; they immediately hired Brennan and Associates to coordinate the investigation, and their PI contact, Earl Bascome, was the one who showed Linda and Julie the numerous procedures they needed to follow in conjunction with their lawyer and the District Attorney. And it was Bascome, not Linda, who conducted most of the background searches on Frank.

"Why couldn't you?" Allen asks Linda.

"I no longer have access to a lot of databases. You forget that I haven't been with a newspaper in almost two years."

Allen nods. "Do you have Bascome's reports?"

"He only filed twice. He was on the case for a week and a half," Linda says. "Then I took over until we came up here."

"What happened?"

Linda turns to Julie, who tells Allen that ten days into the case, as Bascome began doing precisely what Allen has just started, focusing on the family, Bascome handed in a resignation letter to Brennan and Associates, packed his things, and moved to New York.

"Just like that? What was his reason?"

"He said he was retiring," Julie answered. "He was only forty-five, though."

"Then what?"

"Then," Linda says, "he was found in a hotel room dead. He OD'd on heroin. The police ruled it accidental."

"I can't believe this," Allen says. "You don't think Rick was involved? A former drug dealer?"

"It was in New York, and the police said Bascome had a history of drug use," Linda says. "We thought it was just a bad coincidence."

"So why didn't you tell me?"

Julie clears her throat, and says, "It didn't directly involve you."

"It's my fault," Linda says. "I knew you'd be distracted by it."

"Well, yeah," Allen says. "Of course. Why did he resign? Did Frank or Rick get to him? Was it really an accidental overdose? Can you account for Rick during that time? How deeply did the police look into it?"

Linda gives her sister a look that says, *See what I mean?*

"Jesus," Allen says, raising his voice. "It's called being *thorough*. He could've been bribed or threatened to resign, then killed. Don't you understand that you put my life in danger by not telling me? That I'm not adequately prepared? It was *foolish* and *stupid* and *amateurish*." The words make them flinch.

His neck is heating up, his head pounding, and he realizes that Rick had the advantage over him at every encounter. Everyone seems to know more than Allen, who says, "What else haven't you told me?"

They hesitate.

As soon as he senses them holding back, he stands up and walks to the door. He says, "That's it. I'm off the case. You find another sucker." He leaves the conference room and trots down the hallway, hearing

Julie call his name. He ignores her. He feels relieved. No illegal break-ins. No ex-cons to call him "Jap." He can spend more time with Serena, meet her parents, and maybe pick up a few of those easy corporate jobs Larry said were coming in. His life will be simpler, and he feels his steps quicken toward the elevator.

When did Linda get so underhanded? It was undoubtedly in part because of the stakes, of Nora's safety, but Allen is disturbed that she'd lie so baldly to him, that she'd endanger him like this. Didn't she care about him at all? Obviously not.

Julie runs out into the hallway after him, but he doesn't slow down. She calls out, "Allen! Wait! Please!"

He reaches the elevator and presses the button. She runs up to him and grabs his arm. He turns to her, and she grips tighter, her bony fingers clawing into his biceps. "I'm sorry," she says. "I don't know what I'm doing. We thought it would be easier to let you think you were the first. Please don't go. Please."

"I can't do this. It's already complicated enough with Linda and my history—"

"Please, Allen," she says in a low voice. Then she lets go of his arm and begins to cry, covering her eyes with her forearm. "Shit," she says, controlling her voice. "I don't know what to do, Allen. I'm losing my mind. I'm really losing my mind. I'll double your fee. I'll pay anything. Just don't go."

Linda appears in the doorway and watches them. He meet her eyes. She mouths the words, "I'm sorry."

He frowns and shakes his head at her.

Julie notices this and grabs his arm again. She whispers, "I won't let her do that again. I promise. Just talk with us. Please, Allen. It's my daughter. It's my only daughter. You know her. You've met her. She needs your help."

Allen studies her, then says quietly, "All right. I'll talk."

She nods quickly and wipes her eyes. "Of course. Come back. We'll talk."

———————

Allen has trouble concealing the animosity he feels right now, and tries to relax himself by leaning back in his chair and staring up at the acoustic-tiled ceiling. He reminds himself that this is about Nora, not about his ego. He directs his questions to Julie, and says, "Tell me exactly what you know about Bascome."

She tells him that he was in his middle forties, divorced, and did have a history of drug abuse, though the police investigating the death learned from his former coworkers that he had supposedly been clean for years. "He was unhappy at the agency, so his resigning wasn't a surprise. No one knew why he moved to New York, except that he was born and raised on the East Coast. The police considered this a case of relapse and shooting up too much heroin. His body couldn't take it."

"No sign of force or a fight," Linda says. "Open-and-shut case."

"Then why keep it from me?"

Julie answers, "We didn't want to distract you."

"You thought I wouldn't take the case if I knew?"

"No," Linda says. "Just that you'd want to focus on Bascome first, and we don't have time."

"Were there any other PIs you worked with?"

Julie says, "We tried working with Bascome's replacement at Brennan, but found that we needed someone from the Bay Area."

Allen thinks, I was third choice. He says, "Is there anything else you lied to me about? Concealed or withheld?"

Julie turns slowly to Linda, and says, "Tell him."

"It's not relevant."

Allen says, "What the hell? I don't need this shit." He stands up.

Julie says quickly, "Linda's not engaged. She lied to you because she was worried about your former relationship. She wanted you to think she was engaged so there would be no messiness."

Allen is momentarily confused. He turns to Linda, who is staring down at her pad and pen. He says to her, "Wait. You're not engaged?"

Julie replies for her sister. "No, she's not."

He says to Linda, "You didn't think I was over you or something?"

Linda looks up. "I don't know. I thought it would keep everything professional."

"So there is no Michael?"

"Gabriel. No. He doesn't exist. I made him up."

"Made him up?" Allen repeats, bewildered. Made up an imaginary fiancé? He recalls her reluctance to talk about him. He also thinks of Serena's uneasiness, and he wonders if everyone believes that he still has feelings for his ex. He can't believe Linda would go to such lengths to shield herself. His chest tightens with hostility. He says curtly to her, "I want you to continue monitoring Rick. Just log his movements. Stay well out of sight."

"What are you going to do?" she asks.

He turns to Julie. "No more daily reports. Weekly is standard. I work alone. If you two want to help, I'll tell you what to do, but that's all you do. I'm going to call a New York PI we sometimes subcontract work to. He'll check out Bascome's death. That's coming out of the retainer. From now on I run this case without any interference or second-guessing. I also want all your notes. *All* of them. And the minute I feel like I'm losing control, I'm out. Is that clear?"

Linda sits up, and says, "Now wait a minute—"

"It's clear," Julie says, shooting her sister a sharp look. "It's very clear."

Allen turns to Linda, and says, "Is that clear?"

Linda folds her arms, but nods.

He stands up and checks his watch. "That's it for today. Linda, see if you can find out Rick's work schedule somehow."

"Wait," Julie says. "So you're still on the case?"

He moves toward the doorway, and says, "Yes. For Nora's sake, I'm still on the case."

It's humiliating to think Linda had to make up a fiancé for his benefit, that on some level she thought Allen wouldn't be able to work with her without this protection. Did she think he wouldn't be able to control himself? That her presence would overwhelm him? If the idea weren't so pathetic, he'd almost laugh. Instead he drives to Serena's in a grim and sober mood, muttering to himself.

He says aloud, "You don't think I'm over you? Well, I'm certainly over you now."

Then he realizes he's talking to himself and turns on the radio. He listens to the news for a few minutes and switches to a classical music station. He thinks about how careful Serena was after she had moved up here, when he had finished his case down in LA, and they started seeing each other. He didn't want to talk about Linda, and yet she seemed to be the undercurrent of many of Serena's questions, no doubt Serena's way of gauging his residual feelings for his ex.

Serena actually left him alone for a few weeks, since he had to prepare for a PI exam, then figure out his new role as Larry's partner. She seemed to settle and thrive in her new job immediately, finding a circle of friends and even (Allen learned later) dating a few men from her office. Yet she waited for Allen, and he would never quite understand why, though he was definitely grateful.

He remembers how nervous he was when he called her after his exam. He felt as if he were asking her out for the first time, since they never quite had a normal dating period. They had stumbled into a relationship while she had helped him down in LA. So when they went on what felt like a first date to Tilden Park, an afternoon picnic that Allen had concocted after overhearing someone at the gym mention a similar outing, Allen found himself feeling shy and uncertain. He stumbled over his words. He tried to find the right mix of friendliness and intimacy, and ended up sounding stilted. Serena stared at him curiously, and at one point asked, "What's wrong with you?"

He told her he was nervous.

"What for?"

He explained how this felt like a first date, and he wasn't sure how to act.

She stared at him for a full minute, then began laughing. She reached out and touched his neck, then kissed him. She told him to relax. She said, "That's wonderful, but I'm afraid you've already seen me naked, so this can't be a first date." They kissed again.

It's this complete ease with him and others, an inherent, instinctual ability to socialize and soften, to put Allen at ease, that he loves about her. He needs to spend time with her. He needs her. He finds parking off Martin Luther King behind her building and climbs out of his car. Linda and Julie fade from his mind. He's getting better at compartmentalizing work. He's anxious to tell Serena the new situation with Linda, how they will not be working together, and he wants to reassure Serena that he understands why she was annoyed.

He cuts through her parking lot to enter her building from the back. He notices that her Volkswagen Beetle isn't in her parking space and is disappointed. He'll still wait for her, though. He hasn't seen her since last night, and misses her.

He pauses. He misses her after one day?

Skipping up the stairs two steps at a time, he makes a mental note to bring Larry up to date. Larry knows the New York PI better than Allen does, and can handle contracting out the Bascome inquiry. Linda was right that he'd want to check this out first, but she didn't realize he could handle more than one investigation at a time.

The thought again of her subterfuge grates on him. He tries to sort out his levels of annoyance, and being lied to is only part of it; he has seen Linda lie, especially when she used to be a reporter and was lulling an interviewee into revealing more. She has even lied to him before in subtle ways, withholding certain truths for convenience. No, what bothers him is that she gave him no credit, no benefit of the doubt that he would know how to handle the Bascome case and that he would be able to *resist* her.

He walks down the hallway to Serena's, laughing to himself. What a high opinion of herself. Poor Allen wouldn't be able to contain himself around her, so she had to pretend she was engaged. She had to wear a big fat diamond ring.

Allen stops. Serena's door is ajar. She never leaves her door open because Gracie would get out, and he has goaded her into the habit of locking doors and windows, one of his pet peeves, given his line of work. The wood around the doorknob and jamb is splintered. Now he isn't sure if he saw Serena's car in her parking spot. He doesn't have his SIG with him, but he reaches down to his ankle holster and pulls out his Raven.

Moving to the opening he listens for anything inside, but hears nothing. Anxious at the thought of Serena in any kind of trouble, he pushes the door in, his mouth dry. He lets out a slow breath, calming himself, and slowly peers into the apartment. At the sight of books and furniture sprawled across the floor, he calls out Serena' s name, and steps in. He repeats her name more urgently, and runs into the bedroom, which is also in shambles, but what draws his attention is the spray-painted side wall with "warned you asshole" still dripping black from the bottom of the letters. He looks wildly around and notices the blood trails on the floor, drag marks leading to the bathroom. He yells her name and runs to the door, yanking on the handle, but it's locked. He bangs his fist on it and yells Serena's name again, telling her it's Allen, open up. He shoves his gun into his belt and rears back, raising his leg and trying a quick front heel kick to the door, which shakes the wall. Why the hell is it locked? He kicks it again. He hears some wood cracking. He backs up and runs into the door with his shoulder, feeling the doorjamb give an inch with a splintering shudder. An image of Serena lying on the tiles inside flashes in his mind, and he curses and runs back farther for a long head start and charges into the door, and slams so hard into it that he splits it into two, the jagged wood scraping his back and arms as he falls through the broken door and stumbles across the tiles and into the sink. He sees Gracie on the floor, next to the bathtub, but he doesn't see Serena. Then he realizes that Gracie is absolutely still and hasn't reacted to his violent entrance, and he leaps down to her, puddles of drying blood around her. He says, "Oh, shit," and tries to move Gracie, but she's heavy and her eyes are open. He searches for the wound, finding her neck matted with dried blood. A cut throat. She probably waited for a pat on the head, maybe even looked up eagerly when the person pulled out a knife and scratched her ears. He's not sure why they dragged her into the bathroom and locked the door, unless it was to make Allen think it was Serena. Allen leans down and tries to close Gracie's eyelids but they remain open. He still worries about Serena and pulls out his phone, speed dialing her cell. She answers on the second ring, and he asks her if she's all right. She says, "Yes. Why?" He sighs with relief. Then suddenly he's unsure how he's going to tell her about this and how this is his fault and he curses quietly and rests his hand on Gracie's cold forehead, telling Serena he's got bad news.

PART III

FEAR AND TREMBLING

Eleven

After getting Allen's message about the break-in, Serena returns to her apartment and immediately arrives to a crime scene investigation. The Berkeley PD's Robbery Detail have taken over, and are dusting for prints and canvassing for witnesses, and Lt. Georgia Marius is taking Allen's statement. Allen sees Serena run into her living room, looking around, and he says to her, "I'm so sorry about this—"

"Gracie? Where's Gracie?"

Allen already told her on the phone that Gracie had been killed, not wanting to spring it on her, and he points to the bathroom. He begins to apologize again, but she runs past him. He excuses himself from the lieutenant and follows Serena, who dodges a technician photographing the graffiti.

Allen hears her cry out, and when he hurries into the bathroom, Serena is crouched down and holding Gracie's head in her arms. She says quietly, "Why would they do this? She wouldn't hurt anyone."

"They were warning me."

"With a dog? With an old, friendly dog?"

Allen says quietly, "They locked this door, and I thought it might have been you inside."

She looks up, startled. "Oh."

"They took your computer."

She lowers Gracie's head and closes her eyes. "This has to do with your work, with the case you're on?"

Allen says yes.

She looks up at him and says, "But why would they hurt her? She's an old dog. . . ."

Allen kneels down next to her, holding her arm, and feels a growing anger toward Rick. Allen knows he has to end this as soon as possible.

The lieutenant finishes taking Allen's statement, and the crime scene technicians gather the evidence—though Allen knows Rick would've been careful not to be linked to this—but Allen soon discovers that his own apartment has been broken into, revealing a coordinated plan to steal his and Serena's computers. The case notes that Linda and Julie gave him, including his progress reports, are gone. Rick knew not only where Allen and Serena live, but when they were out, and now Rick has a record of everything that Julie and Linda have accomplished thus far. For the next few days, it seems like everyone is trying not to be mad at Allen. Julie and Linda are appalled that Rick now has all their notes, but they haven't blamed Allen—at least not in his presence—for his lack of security precautions. Serena is still shocked by Gracie's death, and only once mentions the fact that all this has happened because of Allen.

Allen and Serena slowly clean both of their apartments. He installs at Serena's a multicontact breaker alarm system protecting the door and windows. To resist tampering, Allen hides the control panel in the closet, and buries the lead wires behind the wood molding along her walls. She will have thirty seconds upon entering her place to disarm the system. Serena seems reassured by this, but still prefers to stay with

Allen at his apartment, which had a low-level door alarm that had inexplicably malfunctioned. Allen was hardly at his apartment, and had probably let the alarm's independent battery backup falter. Allen now upgrades everything.

He worries about Serena. Her mood darkens once she returns to her routines and finds Gracie noticeably absent. Allen meets her after work, and he keeps calling her from his cell phone, checking on her. She sounds listless. She doesn't feel like running. He's glad her parents will be visiting.

Serena has Gracie's body picked up by a mortuary in Orinda that also cremates pets, and a day later she retrieves the remains in a small urn and returns to Allen's apartment for a quiet dinner. She tells him she knows she has been overcharged for the cremation and urn, but she needs some kind of ceremonial ending. Gracie's death feels unresolved. "You know I had her since she was a puppy," she tells him.

Allen says he knows that. He wants to apologize again, but she seems to be getting annoyed whenever he brings up his job. He says, "A friend who was moving gave her to you?"

"That's right. Flora. She moved to Toronto. I've lost touch with her, though."

Allen says, "I wanted to talk to you about your parents coming."

"Yes. I hope you have more free time."

"Things are dangerous now," he says, thinking about that moment when he wasn't sure if it was she in the bathroom. "I'm trying to finish this up as soon as possible, but just in case, why don't you guys go to Napa or Sonoma?"

"You mean leave town?"

"For a few days."

She gives him her laser look. "And I take it you won't go with us?"

"I'm about to begin a deep surveillance—"

"We have to talk about this job of yours."

Allen nods. "It's not usually this bad. You know that."

"I remember in LA you were almost killed in the Santa Monica

Mountains. You and Larry have drug dealers as clients. It's getting worse."

"Larry is scaling back. When I take over, it's going to be completely different. Boring and steady. That's how I like it."

She doesn't look convinced, and frowns.

"I'm going to be much more careful," he says. "I'm so sorry about Gracie. Once this is over I'm not taking anything else potentially dangerous."

"Isn't there always some danger in what you do? Why not something else?"

Allen sighs. "I've always done this. Security, executive protection, that kind of thing."

"I know, but that doesn't mean you have to do this forever."

"True," Allen says. "But this PI stuff is something I like. I'm helping people. I'm doing something good for people."

"There are lots of ways to help people."

He thinks about why he can't let this job go. He says, "I told you about my father wanting to be a doctor. He wanted to help people."

She nods. "He studied medical textbooks on his own."

"Instead of being a doctor he delivered imported T-shirts. That's not going to happen to me. I'll never be a doctor, but I can help people like Julie. I can help her by finding Nora."

Serena seems tired. She is about to reply, stops, then says, "We don't have to deal with this now. But I can't get my parents to Napa before they look around here."

"Linda used to make fun of PIs," Allen says. "But she didn't understand. Yeah, it's seedy. Yeah, it's sometimes dirty. But we do something for people who turn to us. They come to us when no one else can help them. What's wrong with that?"

"All right," she says. "Don't get upset. I just worry about you."

Allen becomes quiet. He *is* getting upset. Why doesn't anyone like his profession? Why does he always have to defend it?

"I'm going to miss her," Serena says, her voice unsteady. He feels another spasm of growing hatred toward Rick, and he also finds himself resenting Linda. She pulled him into this, lied to him, manipulated him. He hasn't told Serena about Linda's deceptions, hasn't mentioned Bascome's death, but he was concerned enough to get Larry to look into it. Larry has New York PI contacts and can find out pretty quickly what happened. Until he knows for sure, he isn't going to conclude anything. But how could Linda have withheld this? He finds that all these thoughts keep swirling around him. He thinks about Rick.

While he safeguards Serena and her apartment, he simultaneously plans on hitting Rick. A Dumpster dive reveals nothing. He empties Rick's garbage into two large bags a few hours before the early morning pickup, drives to the B&C alley, and spreads out a week's worth of discarded food, cans, bottles, wrappers, coffee grounds, and shredded paper. Rick shreds *all* the paper, even the junk mail.

He then asks Linda and Julie to continue detailing Rick's current movements, which they do, and Linda even boldly walks into the back office of the diner when Rick isn't there, copying his work schedule from a bulletin board. His hours are generally in the afternoons, though twice a week he supervises the evenings, and one night he closes at 2:00 A.M. When Linda reports this to Allen, he prepares for a break-in. He wants to finish this case immediately, and can no longer endanger Serena. His guilt over Gracie and his fear for Serena's safety prompt him to consider quitting this job, but he decides that one good piece of information can end the case. All he needs is Frank's location.

Allen conducts another more detailed security analysis of Rick's Victorian, noting that there are no alarm systems that he can see, no window sensors or tape, no control panels or security lighting, and no stickers or signs. Rick has a side entrance leading up to the second floor, and the windows on the second floor are the least secure but most inaccessible.

The downstairs neighbors are a young professional couple, and Linda logs their activities over the weekend as well, though Allen isn't too worried about them.

Allen is ready.

Serena falls asleep early the night Allen plans to break into Rick's apartment. She kisses him good night and sinks into her pillow. She still prefers to stay over his apartment. Her breathing steadies, deepens. He slowly lifts his arm off her, and she rolls over, curling up. He lies there for a while, his mind buzzing, and finally crawls off the futon and wanders around his apartment. All the books are shelved haphazardly, since he cleaned everything quickly. He doesn't really care about the loss of his computer, which he hardly used. In fact, the whole apartment feels superfluous. He realizes that Serena's place is more home than here.

He sees his stack of philosophy books staggered on a lower shelf. He aims the desk lamp toward his side, and turns it on. He chooses one of the Kierkegaard texts he has been avoiding, *Fear and Trembling,* because of its religious undertones. As soon as he read the references to a Bible story, Allen put it aside. But now, as he tries to calm himself before tonight's activity, he grabs the book, sits up on his pillow, and reads.

Twelve

The night of the break-in is unseasonably cold, arctic air sucked into a
low front and blowing through northern California. Allen worries
about rain, but the cold is probably more distracting, with his fingers stiffening and his face dry and numb.

Allen can't directly involve Linda or Julie in anything illegal, so he
asks Larry to be backup while Allen infiltrates the apartment and plants
the bugs. The first one, an Infinity transmitter, is the size of a matchbox
with a male and female duplex plug, allowing Allen to slip the device at
any plug juncture in Rick's telephone line. He can even attach it outside
at the interface box, but that would weaken and degrade the signal from
the phone. So Allen has to get inside. As a precaution he also plans to
install a second bug, a standard mini–FM transmitter in the phone; this
will pick up room conversations and, Allen hopes, both sides of a phone
conversation. The problem with the FM transmitter is the power supply. Either he has to use a small battery with the danger of its running
low after twenty-four-hour continuous transmissions, or he has to siphon

Rick's electricity. The problem? House current creates a hum that interferes with the bug, so Allen also needs an AC filter in addition to the mini–AC/DC converter. If Rick has a small phone, all this won't fit, and Allen will have to install the device elsewhere; he'll lose the incoming phone conversations. In that case he might also try to install a tap in the telephone interface box outside.

Allen realizes how complex surveillance is compared to his former job. As a security consultant all he needed were the RF bug detectors, the wiretap and teletap detectors, the various pulse sensors to identify transmissions, and he simply had to conduct a few sweeps through a room to accomplish the job. Sure, he had to read up on the latest advances and buy the newest sensors, but working defense was much easier than offensive.

"You're definitely Spider-Man from now on," Larry tells him as Allen pulls on gloves and a ski cap. He tightens his climbing shoes, checking the sticky rubber soles, and rubs down his stretch sweat suit to make sure it won't snag on anything.

Allen puts in his earplug and turns on the two-way radio, adjusting the volume. He motions to Larry's handheld unit, and Larry tests it: "One, two, three. You read, Spidey?"

Allen speaks into his wrist, "Okay. Don't fall asleep now."

Larry smiles and starts the car.

As Larry approaches the dropoff—three houses down from Rick's, where Allen can slip through unnoticed and enter Rick's backyard—Allen feels the adrenaline juicing him. In the past he and Larry have broken into a few different offices, not including the Oakland warehouse, for corporate espionage cases, and though this is a fact rarely acknowledged by PI agencies, these kinds of break-ins occur on a regular basis. During the dot.com mania when Larry had his own firm, he did a number of solo break-ins, working for competitors wanting a look at a start-up's hard drive and files. The start-up companies rarely had anything but minimal security—they often didn't even have furniture.

But there is more at stake here. That Rick knows something about his brother and Nora's location is almost a certainty, and now it's a matter of unearthing this information. With it, he can finish the case and stop taking on these kinds of dangers.

Allen tries to calm himself by thinking about something else. The Bible story Kierkegaard analyzed was the one about Abraham and Isaac. Abraham, to show his faith to God, was planning to sacrifice his only and beloved son Isaac. Kierkegaard believed that the key to understanding this story would help him understand the religious sphere. Allen thinks Abraham was probably just deluded.

Larry says, "I'll have the scanner set to the SFPD, but I won't contact you unless there's clear danger."

Allen nods. "You'll have trouble finding parking in front of the house, so you'll have to figure that out."

"No problem. Don't worry about me. You sure you don't want to do more prep?"

"No time."

"Okay, B. Just play it safe."

Allen glances at him, surprised. "You worried?"

"Nah," Larry says, though not very convincingly. "You sure Linda's watching him now?"

"Yes. Check your cell again. In fact, plug it in and recharge it just in case. She'll call if Rick leaves the diner for any reason, even for a smoke."

"I know, but will she flake?"

"No."

"You sure?"

"Yes. She'll do it right." Allen briefly wonders if Julie is going to get anything more from Rick's sister. It seems to Allen that Diedre wanted to talk to him on some level, so he told Julie to try again, alone. She had previously gone with Linda, and Allen told Julie to make another personal appeal for help, mother to mother. They are all doing their jobs, and now it's up to Allen to move the case forward.

Larry pulls over. He plugs the cell phone into the cigarette lighter outlet, and the green light blinks on. "It's already all charged." He glances at his rearview mirror. "You ready?"

Allen says, "I'm ready."

Larry turns on his police scanner, and a dispatcher's voice immediately comes on. He lowers the volume. Allen says, "It'll be cake. I'll be in and out."

Larry says, "All right. Radio silence unless there's trouble."

Allen climbs out of the car and hurries into the side yard of the neighbor's house, his tight climbing shoes making him feel light-footed. He hears Larry driving off. He stops at the end of the yard, where a high wooden fence separates this property from Rick's. He looks around and listens for activity in the surrounding houses. He thinks he hears soft jazz, a woman singing, and recognizes it. Serena's Saturday morning music consists of jazz and blues singers, and although he doesn't know their names, he knows their voices. There is one woman with a tired and worn voice, whose singing seems painful to her. Serena likes her for that reason, and Allen now hears that voice coming from one of the neighbor's windows as he climbs over the wooden fence, glides across the narrow lawn, and pauses at the side of Rick's house.

He heads to his entry point: a high corner window. The only problem is that this window faces an adjacent three-story apartment building. A few apartments look out at Rick's, and Allen has to be careful, since anyone can peer out and see him. All the windows are dark right now, though, and he guesses that after midnight on a weekday most of the residents are asleep. The tricky part is getting up to Rick's second-floor window, roughly thirty feet off the ground.

He hurries to the other end of the Victorian, where an electrical utility pipe runs down the side. The pipe is bolted against the wall with "U" rings and seemed secure during last night's scouting. He looks around—part of this area is visible from the street—and begins scaling the wall, making sure the coil of rope attached to his belt doesn't snag. He tries not to pull the pipe outwards, but instead concentrates on pulling down where the strength of the bolts should hold. Slowly, he scales the side of the house, digging his rock-climbing shoes into the crevices of the wooden siding, surprised that he can pull himself up so easily. He is definitely stronger from working out with Serena.

The pipe creaks. He stops and hangs still. One of the tools in his knapsack digs into the small of his back. His forearms ache, sweat trickles down his temples, but by resting his foot on one of the "U" rings, he eases the strain on his hands. He tries to become a fixture of the house and stops breathing for a minute. All quiet.

He continues up, and has to stop every few feet when the pipe moves a fraction of an inch in its rings, creaking against the side of the wall. It isn't loud, but he knows the downstairs couple are home, probably asleep. He isn't sure where their bedroom is. He pulls himself up a foot at a time. When he reaches the roof he climbs carefully over the flimsy gutter and crawls along the rough and gritty shingles, keeping his profile low. He sees his breath in the cold air. The sweat on his face feels icy. He is thankful it hasn't rained.

He pulls out the climbing harness, nylon straps that fit around his thighs and waist, steps into it, and double loops the buckle. He attaches the carabiner, a thick oval ring, and the rappel device, a small metal housing for controlling the rope tension, then uncoils and hangs the rope around the chimney, grabbing both ends so he can pull the rope down from below. He threads the carabiner and belay for an easy rappel. Moving to the area of the roof directly over the entry window, he looks at the opposite building and the roofs around him. Everything is quiet. He presses in his earpiece, making sure it won't slip out, then crawls to the edge of the roof, checking the metal gutter where his rope will make contact. No rough or sharp edges. He tugs on it and it holds tight, but he'll have to ease his weight over the thin aluminum. The wrong angle might pull the gutter off.

As he goes slowly over the edge, holding the rope taut and trying not to jar the gutter, his arms and back straining, he thinks he hears voices carrying from one of the yards below. He freezes. Larry hasn't radioed him, so it can't be Rick. Allen tries to pinpoint the direction of the voices, and estimates it to be two houses over, and it's a woman's voice yelling, and a man's voice answering. An argument. Second floor. No direct line of sight, but the voices bounce in between two houses and off the apartment building. Allen checks his watch. Fifty minutes. Plenty of time.

He begins rappelling down to the window, this familiar sensation of descent troubling him. The last time he went down a rope was at the Oakland warehouse, and he had a gun shoved in his face when he landed. He stops at the window, using his feet to brace himself. He turns and checks the apartment building for activity. He looks down and around the adjoining houses. Then he grabs the window ledge and pulls himself close to the glass. It's a simple double-hung with a latch lock in the middle rails. He peers along the edges, searching for signs of contact alarms or motion and sound detectors. Most alarm systems don't secure second-floor windows simply because it adds to the installation expense, and the second floor is considered inaccessible.

The side pocket of his backpack has a modified slim-jim just for this kind of lock. Even a thin butter knife would work here. Larry had cut the slim-jim from an aluminum shop ruler, so it's thin and strong, and can slip in between the meeting rails to jimmy the latch open. Allen does this now, though the seal is tight and he worries about paint damage. He finally shoves the slim-jim through the crack and saws the latch open. The drawback is that he can't relock the window from the outside, and Rick, if he's observant, might notice the unlatched window and suspect something.

Allen checks for alarms again. This time he risks using a penlight to peer along the sash. No, he can't see any contact breakers. Just in case he pulls down the top half, since most alarms are triggered by the bottom, and quickly runs his fingers along the surrounding interior jambs, searching for a breaker or switch. Clean. He wipes the soles of his climbing shoes and steps over the lowered window.

Thirteen

Allen enters Rick's apartment, climbing into what seems to be a breakfast nook. He thinks of Serena sleeping in his apartment, his Kierkegaard book lying next to her. He feels a moment of dislocation, an image of Serena in her tank top curled up on his pillow, her mouth slightly open and the small knot of muscle on her shoulder flexing. She usually sleeps on her side, her hands clasped under her cheek. He knows that her reservations about his job are a product of her concern for him, that it's not like Linda's distaste for the profession.

Allen steps lightly into Rick's kitchen. His fingertips tingle, and he thinks, But I like what I do. Allen shines his penlight and checks the windows and walls, searching for any kind of sensor, but there's nothing except old sailboat prints and water stains on the ceiling. Linda didn't notice any dogs during her stakeout, but Allen remains still and listens. After a minute he moves through the rooms slowly, still checking for alarms, wired mats, motion and infrared detectors. As he suspected, it's

just a low-tech house. He makes a quick mental map of the layout, ori-
enting himself to the front. There's a living room facing the street, two
bedrooms, a kitchen, and a bathroom. He can't find the phone.

Then he sees the base of a cordless phone set in the living room and
curses. The Infinity won't work with a cordless; this kind of phone acti-
vates only when someone turns the handset on. He worried about this
when he received the Infinity schematics. He sighs. He can only bug the
room with the regular FM transmitter.

He searches for a good location for the transmitter. He notices a
small telephone stand in the adjacent hallway with an answering
machine. Perfect. He checks the power supply of the answering
machine, and examines the step-down A/C adapter outputted three
volts at three hundred milliamps. The FM transmitter will run on this
easily, but he has to split the current, so he pulls out the variable split
transformer that would enable him to connect both the answering
machine and the bug. Using his mini screwdriver to reset the voltage on
the variable, he then cuts the answering machine cord and attaches the
leads to the new transformer, shoving the old one into his bag. Then he
attaches the transmitter leads to the second set of mini screws. Now
both the answering machine and the bug share this one new power supply. He plugs it in. The answering machine beeps and clicks back on.
Allen buries the bug wire amidst the other cords, and uses the strong
double-sided tape to attach the bug underneath the table. The only
thing different now is this new transformer in the wall socket: it's larger
than the old one, but he doubts Rick will notice.

His earpiece hisses static, and Larry says, "Downstairs neighbor just
came out."

Allen stops. He presses the TALK button on his wrist, and says,
"Copy."

After a moment, Larry radios, "He's looking up at the apartment.
You might be making noise."

"Copy," he says. The hallway has wooden floors. Perhaps he's creaking too much. He remembers that he left the rope strung through the window. He walks quietly back to the kitchen. He says into the mike, "Is he checking around the house?"

"Not yet."

Allen pulls on one end of the rope, which he looped around the chimney, and coils it around his arm as he brings all of it in. This precludes this exit. He closes the window, relocking it. His slim-jim has scratched up the latch, but it's minor.

Larry says, "He went back in. Keep it quiet."

"Copy."

He attaches the coil of rope to his backpack and moves through the apartment, hoping for another phone, but there isn't any. Rick just uses the cordless, so the Infinity is useless here.

He checks his watch. Twelve-forty. He's taking too long. Twenty minutes left. Even less if Rick leaves work early. Allen still wants to do a quick search for any links to Frank's location, so he hurries to the bedroom and sees a desk. He takes a mental snapshot of the books and paperwork lying on top, making sure he won't leave anything out of place, then begins looking through the drawers. Restaurant business. Bills. Old newspaper clippings about Rick being arrested for dealing drugs. Pornographic magazines. Allen's latex gloves slip on some of the manila folders—he can't thumb through the paperwork very fast—but realizes these are old items. He closes the cabinets and repositions some of the papers.

On top of a bureau is an old spiral notebook, thinned from pages having been torn out. He picks it up and leafs through it, the spiral wire warped and tarnished. The remaining pages have scribbled notes, columns of dates and numbers in the five- and six-digit range. At the bottom of one page is: A name: "Rafe Luong: 01-01-674-444-1119." Farther below are two words: "New contact."

Allen copies this on a scrap piece of paper and shoves it into his pocket. He suddenly remembers the answering machine and wants to check it for messages. He returns to the hallway and presses PLAY, but the mechanical voice says, "No messages." He has another idea, and checks the cordless phone base, pressing the PAGE button and hearing the faint ring coming from the bedroom.

His earpiece crackles, and Larry says, "Time to wrap it up. Linda called. He's leaving the diner and is now walking home."

Allen presses his wrist, and says, "Copy." He hurries to the bedroom and finds the phone on a chair. He presses REDIAL and listens. The phone on the other end rings twice, and a tired, gnarled voice answers, "What?"

Allen hangs up. He radios Larry, "Is the tape recorder handy?"

"Are you moving? Come on."

"Hook up the tape recorder from the FM receiver to your earpiece. I'm going to send a touch-tone number that I want you to record."

"What? You gotta get out of there now."

"Just do it. Plug your earpiece into the recorder mike. Record for ten seconds."

"Jesus. Hang on." After a moment, Larry says, "Ready?"

"Record for ten seconds, then come back on."

"Count to five and begin."

Allen hears the disconnection, and counts to five, pushing the cordless handset's earpiece into his wrist mike and turning up the volume. Then he presses REDIAL again, and the seven-digit number sounds off rapidly. The phone rings again and Allen hangs up before the man answers.

Allen throws the phone back onto the chair and moves quietly down the narrow stairwell to the front entrance. He's about to radio Larry to ask if anyone is out there, but sees the dead bolt.

He stops. He stares in disbelief. It's an old keyed dead bolt that requires the key to open from the inside as well as the outside. Usually with this kind of lock people leave a key in, but Rick has not. Allen checks for alarms, then tries to open the door. Bolted. Incredible.

Larry radios, "Dude, got the tone. Now wrap it up."

"One sec," Allen replies. Rick probably leaves the key in when he's home, in order to bolt it, but then takes it out to lock the door from the outside. Although Allen has a pick gun, he isn't proficient enough to use it quickly, and he'll have to relock the dead bolt from the outside or Rick will definitely be suspicious. Allen looks quickly at the one window adjacent to this side entry. The window is new, with double latches and an inner sash bolt for extra security. Allen curses. If he goes out this way, Rick will notice all the latches open, and with the keyed dead bolt, he'll know someone couldn't get out. Everything will be blown.

Allen hurries back upstairs, moving toward the kitchen area. Larry says into his ear, "Yo, B. It's just a five-minute walk from the diner. Get your ass out of there."

"Copy that," Allen says, unlatching the window and opening it. He looks down and sees the thirty-foot drop, maybe closer to thirty-five feet. He peers up at the gutter about ten feet from the window. Impossible to jump up, and even if he could, the gutter wouldn't hold him. If the downstairs neighbors hadn't come out earlier, Allen would've had the rope and used an ascender and stirrup to climb back up. He shuts this window, latches it, and moves to the window in Rick's bedroom, which is close to the electrical pipe. But not close enough. He can probably leap over to it, but would almost definitely tear it off the wall.

"Subject in sight!" Larry whispers harshly into his ear. "Should I run interference?"

"Yes," Allen replies. "I need more time."

"Fuck, B. You're giving me a heart attack."

"Five minutes. Give me five minutes." Allen closes and latches the window and returns to the kitchen. He knows Serena is right, that this life is too dangerous.

Fourteen

The **Block is** in a storage closet underneath the stairs while Rick moves above him in the kitchen and bedroom, steps creaking. This closet shares a bathroom wall with the downstairs couple, and Allen can hear their toilet hissing, the water running in its tank. He tries not to panic. He will wait until Rick goes to sleep, then leave through the front door. Allen will have to risk the open dead bolt, and hopes Rick will just assume he had forgotten to lock it.

Allen couldn't have anticipated the dead bolt. The front face looks like any other keyed bolt, and it's unusual to take the interior key out, since it's a hassle to use a key whenever you need to unbolt the door from the inside. There's also the danger of losing the key while inside the house and finding yourself locked in. As he hears Rick move across the apartment, the low murmuring of the TV filling the silence, Allen clicks the TALK button on his wrist, and whispers, "Do you read me?"

Static. "You okay? Where the hell are you?"

"Stuck in a closet."

"Oh, shit. Inside? Shit."

"Downstairs. I can get out but I just have to wait."

"Jeez, B. You're killing me. What do you want me to do?"

"Sit a while. The FM is engaged. The Infinity isn't."

"I'll tune in."

"I left a tap in the trunk. See if you can hook it up to the telephone interface on the side of the house, use the VHF transmitter with it."

"Now?" Larry asked.

"Yes. Radio silence until later."

"Okay. Out."

Allen is getting warm in here, the bleach and insecticide odor stifling. He listens to the noises upstairs. When the TV sounds stop, he tenses. But he hears Rick moving from the living room to his bedroom. Allen knows he'll have to wait at least an hour or so until he's certain Rick has gone to sleep, and tries to get comfortable by sitting carefully on a tub of detergent. He calms himself by slowing his breathing and thinking of Kierkegaard.

When Allen read *Fear and Trembling* earlier this evening, occasionally looking over at Serena sleeping, he began connecting some of what he read to his relationship with her. The "movements of faith," Kierkegaard wrote, "must constantly be made by virtue of the absurd." He was referring to the story of Abraham, but Allen could see that all kinds of faith, even faith in a relationship, were premised on similar uncertainties, even absurdities.

This beautiful and loving woman was with him for some absurd reason. His job had caused Gracie's death, and yet she was trying hard not to blame him. He wasn't as outgoing or social as her friends—he was decidedly boring—but she still loved him. She was patient with him. Allen, moving next to Serena and holding her arm lightly, sought to comfort her in her dreams. He watched her sleep. Her face was relaxed, calm, and he brought the small lamp closer so he could read next to her.

Her eyelids fluttered at the sounds he made, and he stopped, resting his hand on her forehead; he whispered to her to go back to sleep.

He tried to return to his reading, but didn't want to remove his hand. He felt the warmth of her scalp passing into his palm.

Larry's voice breaks into his thoughts. "All hooked up. Over."

Allen checks his watch. Thirty minutes have passed, and he hasn't heard any more activity above. He stands up slowly, his knees cracking. He whispers into his radio, "No problems?"

"Needed to hook up a battery. No power source. So after a couple days we'll have to replace the nine-volt."

That won't be a problem, since the interface box is outside and easily accessible. He says, "What do you hear upstairs?"

"Nothing. I think he went to bed."

"I'll try to leave in about fifteen minutes. Keep me posted of sounds or if you see lights upstairs."

"Understood."

Allen inspects his gear and makes sure his pack and rope are secure. It's only ten feet to the front door, so all he has to do is walk quietly, open the dead bolt, and slip out. He considers trying to pick the dead bolt closed, since it would ensure Rick's not getting suspicious. Just in case, he has his pick gun ready. The pick gun is a triggered device that snaps a tiny wire inside a keyhole, forcing the pins up and acting as a temporary and aggressive key. It isn't the most nuanced way to open a lock, but Allen finds that with some patience he can open older, worn locks. Larry is much better at picking locks, and Allen decides at this moment that he has to learn more from him.

Allen plans his movement across the floor and to the door. The wooden floors creak, so he'll have to step near the walls, where the joints are firmer. The dead bolt will probably click once he turns the key. Wait. What if the key isn't in the lock? Allen opens the closet door slowly, peers out, and aims his flashlight at the dead bolt. Yes, Rick's entire key set is in the lock. That's why he doesn't have a key in there when he leaves the house.

He waits. It's 2:50 A.M. Allen and Serena had talked about running in the morning, because Allen's work at night has disrupted their usual schedule. And with her parents arriving, they didn't think they'd get many chances to run for the next two weeks. But he doesn't think he'll be up for a run in four hours. He'll have to cancel.

Allen radios Larry, "How does it look?"

"Quiet. Where'd you put the transmitter? I can't hear him."

"Hallway. Used an external power source."

"Looks okay from here. Be careful."

"Okay. Out." Allen opens the closet door, and listens. The toilet in the adjacent apartment continues to hiss, making it difficult to hear the sounds upstairs. He steps out slowly, testing the hardwood floor, hesitating with each step and easing his weight down. He moves at this excruciating pace to ensure silence. With the first creak he freezes. He holds his breath.

Allen waits for a few minutes, then takes another step. Needing ten minutes to travel ten feet, he reaches the door and touches the key ring with a half dozen keys attached. If he had a wax bed, he could make impressions for some of these keys and have a locksmith make duplicates. Something to remember for later. He turns the key slowly, his ear close to the dead bolt. He wants to hear the cylinder turning so he can anticipate the bolt clicking out of its strike plate. He feels the key engaging the cylinder and connecting with the bolt mechanism. He continues turning the key and hears the bolt about to slip over its threshold and fall into its open position. He stops. This could be loud.

Larry radios him, "Did you just make a noise?"

Allen can't respond, because if he lets go of the key, it might push the bolt all the way. He tries to listen for any noises, but he only hears the neighbor's toilet.

"Do you read me? There's something. If you can't respond, just hit the TALK button twice for yes. Do you hear me?"

Allen uses his chin to press the button twice on his left wrist. He keeps the key steady with his right hand.

"Okay. He might be up. Not sure. Are you making noise?"

Allen presses the button once. He doesn't want to stop moving the bolt, so he continues the slow, steady twisting and feels the bolt catching the key and flipping. He isn't able to stop the weight of the bolt clicking out of its strike plate and a loud, metallic *thunk* vibrates out of the door, the sound carrying up the stairwell. He winces. He unlocks the door handle and waits. Pulling out his pick gun from the side pocket of his backpack, he tests the trigger. The insertion point snaps quietly. The pick gun is shaped like a mini hand drill, the tip similar to a bobby pin, though the upper wire springs up at each pull of the trigger. Allen decides to relock the bolt from the outside. He opens the door slowly.

Larry whispers in his ear, "There it is again. Is that you?"

Allen doesn't think the bug upstairs can pick up the bolt click. He's about to answer when the light above him blinks on.

"What the fuck?" a voice from the top of the stairwell. Rick.

Allen yanks open the door, and hears a tumbling of steps heading for him. He jumps out of the doorway. Rick yells, "Busted, asshole!"

Allen gets three steps out when he feels his backpack yanked, the straps dragging him down, and then he's tackled onto the grass. He rolls, using his pack for cushion, and elbows Rick in the head, which makes him grunt. Rick's hand lashes out, and he tries to grab Allen's throat. Allen knees him in the chest and slams his fist into Rick's face. The grip on his shirt loosens, and Allen rolls away, leaps up, and sprints across the narrow lawn and around the side of the house. The coiled rope bounces against his leg. He presses the TALK button on his wrist, and says, "Chased. Get out. Meet me at Union and Van Ness. Out."

He hears Rick cursing and crashing through bushes after him. Allen easily hurdles over the side fence, and zigzags around patio furniture as he crosses another small yard and emerges onto Greenwich. He then runs east, toward Van Ness. He hears Rick falling behind. Allen's legs feel strong, energized, and he bursts forward. He glances back and sees Rick climbing over the fence, struggling. Allen has lost the pick gun, but that's it. Rick curses. Allen runs faster. When he looks back he sees Rick running with a limp, bent over, holding his gut and gasping for air. Allen turns a corner and runs lightly to the new meeting spot.

Larry and Allen circle the block, tuning in to both bugs: the one in Rick's hallway and the teletap with the VHF transmitter. The VHF range is limited, and the battery power supply weakens the signal, but as they drive closer, they pick up the phone conversation, static lacing the words.

Caught him coming in. Found the pick gun. Professional. That bitch probably hired the guy, Rick says.

To do what? Work you over? An older man's voice. Allen thinks it's the same voice of the redialed number.

Maybe. He had rope. Tie me up? Search the place? Not sure.

He only got into the door? He didn't get upstairs?

No. He didn't expect me to be awake.

That's fucked up. You think she hired someone to break you down?

She would. She'd do anything, man.

Did you ID the guy?

No. Too fast and too dark

Was it the PI?

Could've been.

Shit, you better check the phones. Get off the land line and call me back cell.

Allen hears the phone disconnect. Larry says, "He thinks you were trying to break in, not get out."

Allen asks, "You got the tape recording from before?"

"Yeah. I listened to it—a phone number?"

"It might be this guy he called. We'll need to find out who it is."

"No problem."

"What about intercepting the cell phone?"

"Tough, with the new digital encryption. I saw some new equipment online, but it's like fifty grand."

"Oh."

They hear through the FM receiver Rick walking across the apartment. Then he says, *It's me. I'll just be more careful. I'll search this place and maybe put someone watching the bitch.*

He's quiet, then says, *Yeah. I'll take care of it, Val. Don't worry about that. Frankie's safe.*

Allen sits up. He and Larry glance at each other.

Rick says, *Don't worry. I said I'll take care of this. They're just getting desperate. We knew they'd get dirty. We just get dirtier. I'll call Sid tomorrow. All right, I gotta get some fucking sleep.*

Allen says, "He knows where Frank is."

"Who's Rick talking to? Val? Who's Sid? There're others involved?" Larry scratches the stubble on his cheek. "The bug and tap are probably blown."

"But he knows. It's definite," Allen says.

Larry nods. "You better be careful. He's not just gonna let this go."

"I know." Allen leans back in the seat and sighs. He remembers the spiral notebook and pulls out the sheet of paper. "Here's something to check out."

Larry holds the note up to a slice of street lighting falling through the windshield. He says, "International number."

"Maybe a lead on Frank?"

"But if Frank's left the country . . ."

Allen says, "Yeah, we're screwed." He feels his body crashing. He says, "Is Linda waiting for us at your place?"

"I told her to go on home while you were in there."

He nods. "We'll sort through this tomorrow. I'm beat."

Larry starts his car. "Rick's got help; this is complicated."

"I know."

"There's definitely more going on here than a custody case."

Allen sighs. "I know."

Fifteen

The long-distance telephone number is for Nauru, a country Allen has never heard of, so before he tries to call the next morning, Allen does some quick research at the library. Nauru is an island that lies near the equator in the South Pacific, and is the smallest republic in the world. It's only eight square miles, with a population of ten thousand, and its natural resources have been decimated by phosphate mining, which has stripped 80 percent of its land. Nauru has four hundred banks and some of the most rigid banking secrecy laws in the world.

Allen stops reading. Four hundred banks in eight square miles? This is beginning to make sense. Frank needed to transfer and hide his assets, but why Nauru and why through Rick? Allen learns that Nauru is at the top of most international economic watchdog lists for money-laundering countries. The Russian central bank pointed to Nauru as one of the main destinations for an estimated $70 billion of funds leaving their country.

Taking notes and jotting down questions he has, Allen finishes his reading and drives to Rick's apartment. He parks around the block and turns on the FM and VHF receivers, but doesn't pick up the usual squelch of a quiet transmitter. He dials Rick's number on the cell phone, checking if the ring carries over, but it doesn't. Rick must have found both devices. Allen walks through two yards and checks the side of Rick's house. The telephone interface now has a small lock on its outer casing. Allen can probably pick the lock, but then remembers that he lost the pick gun. He returns to his car and heads to Larry's.

He's being outmaneuvered. Rick is slowly cutting the inquiry web, strand by strand. When Larry lets him in and asks him about the surveillance equipment, Allen shakes his head.

"Damn. Those were expensive," Larry says.

"It's coming out of the retainer, don't worry," Allen says. "I want to call this Nauru contact and check my e-mail."

"What about your computer?"

"They took it. Remember?"

"Shit, B. They're cleaning you out."

Allen nods. He takes out the slip of paper and sits down at Larry's desk. "Want to listen in?" he asks.

Larry picks up an extension. Allen calls the number, and gets a woman with a British accent: "World Nauru Bank. May I help you?"

"May I speak with Rafe Luong?" Allen asks, then hears his words echoing.

A pause, then the woman replies, "Please hold."

Then a man's voice comes on: "Rafael Luong. Can I help you?"

Allen says, "I'm working with Rick Staunton? I'm just following up the new contacts."

"One moment. Staunton. Staunton. You mean Frank Staunton?"

"Yes. Rick's his brother."

"May I ask who this is?"

Allen thinks quickly, and says, "My name is Mack Johnson. We're doing a little reorganizing and—"

"Can I have the account number, please?" Their words overlap in the odd long-distance echo.

"Oh, I don't want to access the account. I just want to verify—"

"I'm sorry, but for security reasons we can't proceed without the account number and verification code."

Allen waits until the echo stops, then says, "Can you at least verify Frank Staunton's address?"

A pause. Then Rafael says, "No. I'm afraid you'll have to call back with the proper account procedures. Thank you." He hangs up.

Allen stares at Larry, who puts down the extension, and says, "Well, at least you know where his money is now."

"You don't think he's there?"

Larry says, "No. You use those shell accounts to hide money while still living in the U.S. They're called 'pay-through' accounts."

"How do you know about that?"

Larry says, "What, you don't think I've thought about hiding money from the IRS? This Nauru bank opens a pay-through account with a U.S. bank, so you can write checks on the U.S. bank, but the money comes from Nauru. It's all legal."

"Doesn't the U.S. bank care?"

"Why should they? The Nauru bank could be a Nauru corporation or legit business. All the U.S. bank cares about is that the money is there to cover whatever checks or debits are recorded."

"It's that easy?"

Larry nods. "Something to think about if you ever get rich."

"And you can't trace it?"

"Because the Nauru bank doesn't have to give out any info."

Allen says, "Are we in the wrong business?"

"I'm thinking, yeah. At least as a chef I can have some fun and eat my work."

For the rest of the day Allen is at Larry's desk doing the kind of research work that he actually enjoys, and he focuses on deciphering the touch-tone phone number Larry recorded from Rick's cordless. After a few tone comparisons with the telephone, Allen figures out the number and begins a systematic reverse telephone number check.

There are different kinds of reverse directories online, beginning with the public cross-listings the phone company provides. It doesn't surprise Allen that this number is unlisted. Over 40 percent of telephone customers choose an unlisted number. However, Allen then contacts private locator databases that cull phone numbers from credit report header files and financial institutions. These companies then sell the data to people like Allen, who needs only to input the number, and the screen prompt lets him know that they have a listing. The name, current and previous addresses, and current and previous telephone numbers cost Allen $9.95, which he charges to B&C.

Val Pinetti's current address is in Potrero Hill, the next neighborhood over from Larry's, but Allen doesn't want to seek Val out until he does a deeper background check. He submits Val's name and address to B&C's usual information broker for a complete dossier, then logs off.

Larry walks in, still talking into his cell phone. He hangs up, and says to Allen, "Just got the briefing on Bascome from my New York PI. Want to hear?"

"Go ahead."

"Nothing really," Larry says, and tells Allen about the police reports, which his contact obtained. "It was open-and-shut. Bascome had old needle tracks, and they found next to him the syringe and paraphernalia. Toxicology reports showed the contents of the heroin mix to be 90 percent pure. He shot up near-pure heroin which, of course, would kill him."

"But someone could've given it to him, or even shot him up?"

"Sure, but the police had no motive. The guy quits his job, goes to New York, and falls into bad habits. Open-and-shut."

Allen nods.

"And I was just talking to our insurance guy," Larry says. "That bastard."

"Uh-oh."

"Not good, Block, not good. We might have to sue. They're dragging their feet."

Allen sighs. "Tell me about it later."

"I'll take care of it. Don't worry."

He wonders if it's always going to be like this—confusing, complicated, with a low hum of stress pulsing through his neck and back. Although he can't tell Linda and Julie exactly what he's been doing, especially since he's been breaking the law, he needs to convey the Nauru connection. That could help their lawyer Charlene with the legal front. But he also feels a small vindictive urge to withhold information as punishment. They lied to him.

Still, he can't forget about Nora. He leaves a message on Linda's voice mail, telling her he has an update. He then checks on Serena, who is at work, but will be leaving early to pick up her parents at the airport. When she asks how it went last night, since she hasn't had a chance to speak with him yet, he's intentionally vague, not wanting her to worry. He likes the sound of her voice, and tries to keep her on the line. "How are you?"

"All right. A little tired. You probably didn't sleep enough, as usual."

"By the way, I was reading last night. I'm understanding Kierkegaard more."

"Good. You can explain it to me."

He hears the clacking of a computer keyboard. He says, "It's all about the Abraham and Isaac Bible story. That's the key."

She says, "A Bible story?"

"It's the premise for his leap of faith, the movement into the religious sphere."

"Right," she says, her voice distracted. "Hold on a sec." Her muffled voice comes through as she speaks to someone, then she comes back on. "Allen, I've got to go. Dinner tonight, right? My parents?"

"Right. I'm looking forward to it."

"Liar," she says, and laughs softly, "but I appreciate that."

They hang up, her laughter still in his ears, and he's glad for the distraction of her parents. At dinner he'll suggest an out-of-town trip to the wine country. He'd just feel better with Serena away from all this for a few days, at least until he can get a stronger sense of Rick's offense.

Larry walks into the living room and tells him he's running some errands. "Lock up if you leave."

"How much should I worry about Rick?"

"Let's see. He hit your and Serena's apartments. He's dealing with money laundering and hiding assets, has too many contacts just to be hiding his brother, and can reach across the country to shoot up a washed-up PI. I think you best be careful."

"You think Bascome was killed?"

"Yup. Maybe not directly, but pushed along."

Allen rubs his forehead, thinking, What the hell am I doing?

Larry says, "If it wasn't for your connection to Linda, and if there wasn't a kid involved, I might even tell you to drop the case. It ain't worth it."

Allen looks up. "You? Drop a case? All that money?"

"I guess I'm reevaluating things, B. What's the point of money if you're dead?"

Smiling, Allen replies, "Since when did you become a philosopher?"

"Well, Block-o," Larry says, "I guess having a gun aimed at your pecker makes you think."

Allen nods. "I don't think Kierkegaard could've said that better."

Larry's intercom system chimes, jerking Allen awake. He looks down at Larry's book on money laundering, and a spot of drool has blotted a corner. He wipes it quickly, and jumps up. The buzzer goes off again.

He walks unsteadily to the front hallway and presses the TALK button, asking who it is.

"Linda. Larry said you'd be here."

He buzzes her in and leaves the front door open. His thoughts sluggish, his vision blurry, Allen tries to shake off the remnants of the nap and rereads the page on laundering money through high-volume cash businesses, like restaurants. Or a diner, Allen thinks. But this reading is so dry and technical that his eyes smart. He hears Linda approaching, and when she walks into the loft she says, "Are you still mad at me?"

She's dressed casually today—jeans, a leather jacket, and a red baseball cap. She gives him a tentative smile. Allen isn't sure if he's still mad. He says, "Annoyed, maybe."

"Larry told me things last night didn't go well."

"You don't want to know," he says. "But I have some updates."

"Are we okay?" She motions the air between them, something he's seen many times before. He's surprised by his recognition of her hand gestures, how the pattern of her movements hasn't changed, and how he knows them so well. He knows how she thinks.

"Allen?" she asks.

"We're okay," he says. "But no more lying."

"For what it's worth, Julie told me not to."

"Where is she?"

"Still trying to appeal to Diedre again, especially after what happened to your and Serena's apartments." Linda studies him. "You seem tired."

"I am."

She reaches into her pocketbook and pulls out a pink plastic bag. "I have something for you. A gift. A peace offering." She hands it to him.

Allen opens the bag and takes out a small box; he recognizes the smell. Sweet rice cakes. He smiles, and says, "You remembered."

"How could I not? You loved that stuff."

"You found an Asian grocery."

"Took a quick trip to Chinatown."

He leans against a table and quickly eats one of the sticky cakes, made of sweetened rice flour. They're cool and dissolve in his mouth. "Have one," he says.

"Nah. Never liked them like you."

He stops eating, struck sad by this gift, which reminds him of happier moments between them. One of the first times they had met he had been eating rice cakes, and since then she had often surprised him with a small box. He says, "Remember when I was guarding that software guy, and you gave me these?"

"At the hotel. I remember. You did push-ups to keep alert. Didn't that software guy offer you a job?"

Allen says, "Yeah. I never called him about that."

"I can't believe I was that green reporter back then."

"I was all gung ho about security. I took it a little too seriously."

"When did we get so . . ."

"Old?"

She laughs. "Jaded. We've been though a lot, Blocky."

He glances at her. She hasn't used any of his nicknames in years. He doesn't reply, but likes the sound of it.

"Will you tell me what's happening?" she asks.

Allen and she sit down on the sofa, and he begins to explain the link to Nauru when she pulls out her cell phone and dials. He asks what she's doing.

"Charlene needs to hear this." After a moment she says into the phone. "It's me. Allen's got something. Hold on." She hands Allen the phone.

Allen describes his conversation with the World Nauru Bank without explaining how he found the number and contact. Charlene makes a sharp sound, a breath of surprise, and he hears papers rustling. When he tells her the name and number, she asks him to slow down. Then she says, "This is perfect. We got him."

"Why?"

"Nauru doesn't comply with a new anti–money laundering act just passed. The Treasury Department can go after the correspondent bank and cut off the shell accounts. This is exactly what we need. You say this Luong person confirmed Frank Staunton's account?"

"Not quite. He knew the name, but when I didn't have the account number, he hung up."

"Doesn't matter. We didn't know which country to start with. I was tangling with Guatemala, but this is perfect. Put Linda on. Wait. Anything else?"

"No." He hands back the phone and watches Linda as she hears the good news, her eyes flashing with triumph. She says into the phone, "Damn, that's good. Julie will love this." She reaches over and squeezes Allen's arm, which makes him smile. When she hangs up, Linda moves away from the sofa and paces in front of him, pulling off her baseball cap, and shoving it into her back pocket. She says to him, "I hope he has all his money there. I hope we choke him." She makes a fist.

He hasn't seen her this excited in a long time, and tells her so. She turns to him, and replies, "I haven't had any good news in a while. Tell me what else you've got."

"I'm learning about Rick's friends, people who seem to be connected to all this. I'll know more by tomorrow."

"Tell me."

"There's this guy Val Pinetti who Rick talks to—"

"Wait a minute. Val Pinetti?"

"You've heard of him?"

"The name is familiar. Do you have Julie's notes here?"

"They were stolen, remember?"

She grimaces. "Was his name listed in there?"

"No. I would've remembered."

"Are you sure?"

He nods. "I think he's an older guy. Kind of raspy voice."

"San Rafael? He lives in Marin?"

"No. I think right here. Potrero."

"You know where he lives?"

"I think so. I'm still doing a background check."

"Let's go to his place. Maybe if I see him—"

"Whoa. No. I want to get background on him first, then do this alone."

"But I might know something. The name is familiar. Let me try Julie again." She opens her cell, and Allen walks to the desk to check his notes. He hears Linda leaving a voice message. He regrets mentioning this lead before he has checked it out himself. He's certain she will try to persuade him to act now; he's just not sure how she will do it.

She hangs up, and says, "It's not like her to turn off her cell."

"She's trying to talk to Diedre?"

"That's what she said."

Allen worries about this. "She's being careful, right? Rick is on to us, so she has to be careful."

"He's always been on to us. I don't know if Frank would let it get so far as to hurt Julie."

"Rick might."

Linda nods slowly.

"I mean we're turning it up on him. And now with this Nauru connection, it could get worse?"

"Worse?"

"If Frank gets squeezed financially, he and Rick could get desperate." Linda says, "Tell me where this guy Pinetti lives. I can do it myself."

"And tip him off? No."

"I can probably find the address myself."

He stares at her. "And I can drop this case."

"Allen," she says quietly, "don't punish Nora because of me."

There's the strategy, he thinks. Guilt. He says, "You'd be jeopardizing her by stumbling forward with this without preparation. You need to know who you're dealing with first."

"All I want is a look. Can't we just sit and watch? Maybe tail him? The name is familiar."

Allen wonders if casing the place first might be a good idea, but he glances at his watch. "I have to meet Serena's parents for dinner."

"Her parents? Really?"

"They're flying in."

"Hey, this is serious, then. You guys moving in and all. Now the parents?"

"How about this?" he says. "I have dinner with the parents. Later tonight you and I do a couple drive-bys. Just a sense of what kind of surveillance I'll want to do when I get the background info."

"Just a drive-by later tonight. Okay." She touches his arm again. "Thanks. I'm really glad for your help."

Sixteen

Allen hears on his answering machine at home that Serena is bringing her mother to her apartment around seven o'clock, and that they're planning on having Korean food for dinner. Allen showers quickly and drives across the Bay Bridge, feeling disconnected. Last night he was breaking into Rick's apartment, and tonight he is having dinner with his girlfriend's mother. He has trouble shifting his perspective. He keeps seeing Linda with her rice cakes.

Allen enters Serena's apartment and turns off the alarm. He notices how quiet it is, how acute Gracie's absence still feels. There's an awkwardly placed throw rug over the section of the floor where they scrubbed out bloodstains, stripping the wax. Allen walks around the throw rug, and even though everything else is back in its place, he still feels the hangover of intruders. The rooms have been tainted.

The lack of sleep and the long hours of research today have tired him, and he lowers himself onto the sofa with a groan. He turns on her stereo and listens to whatever she has in the CD player. Jazz. After a minute, he stands up restlessly, and paces. He searches through her bookshelf, amidst the computer-programming textbooks, the Jane Austen novels, and biographies, and finds one of the introductory philosophy books he left here. With this, he sits back on the sofa and reads. He skips to the section on Kierkegaard.

He skims the long biographical note about Kierkegaard, and is startled. Kierkegaard was engaged to be married to Regina Olson, a young woman he aggressively pursued. But for no apparent reason Kierkegaard broke the engagement and almost ruined Regina's life. The engagement had been published in the newspaper. Regina was deeply in love with him. She pleaded for him to return, and even had her father demean himself by begging Kierkegaard to reconsider. Instead, Kierkegaard fled the country. This was when he wrote *Fear and Trembling.*

Allen feels the gnawing sense of understanding, that these biographical details are important in understanding Kierkegaard's philosophy. When he reads on, he learns that Kierkegaard eventually changed his mind and returned to Denmark, only to find Regina engaged to another man. His journals were filled with jealous and mournful thoughts.

Allen stands up and begins to pace Serena's living room. This is the man who wrote about the wonderful benefits of marriage? A man who not only was never married, but screwed up the only relationship that meant something to him? And while he was in the throes of doubt and regret, he wrote one of his most important treatises on faith?

"This means something," Allen says aloud. He turns up the stereo, since the music seems to help him think, and he says to himself, "He was writing about religion, about getting to the third sphere, but he was thinking about Regina. This means something."

"Who's Regina?" a voice asks.

He turns around. He sees Serena and an older Korean woman standing there in the open doorway, watching him. The woman says, "And why does it mean something?"

Serena says, "Allen, this is my mom. Mom, this man talking to himself is Allen."

"Does he live here?" Mrs. Yew asks her daughter. "Are you two living together?"

Allen hurries to turn off the stereo.

Mrs. Yew is shorter than her daughter, but has a similar slim, energetic build, her movements quick and restless. She sheds her blue blazer and throws it over the love seat, and asks Serena for a glass of wine. The glare of the lights bounces off her silver wire-rimmed glasses, so Allen has trouble reading her eyes, and when she says, "That rug doesn't match," he's not sure if she's talking to him or her daughter. She says again, "That rug doesn't match, Allen."

"Oh, right," he says. "It doesn't. It's covering a spot on the floor. I have to find a stain and wax in the right color."

Serena has already told her mother that Allen doesn't live here, that he has his own place in the city, but he noticed how on her quick tour around the apartment, Mrs. Yew focused on the queen-sized bed. She didn't remark on it, however. Now, as Serena brings in three glasses of Chardonnay, Allen says, "Where's Mr. Yew?"

"At the hotel. Jet lag. My daughter told me not to speak Korean to you."

"Yes, well. I can't understand it."

"Hm," she says, looking around the apartment with a quick jerk of her head. To her daughter she says something in Korean.

Serena answers in English, "Do you know how expensive it is to buy a place in Berkeley?"

Mrs. Yew again speaks in Korean, and this time Serena answers back in Korean. Allen doesn't know what to do as they continue their conversation around him. He fiddles with his glass and gulps down half of the wine.

Mrs. Yew watches him and says something to her daughter in Korean.

"Mo-*om,*" Serena says. "Stop that."

Allen smiles. She suddenly sounds like an eight-year-old. Mrs. Yew notices Allen's expression and says, "*Aigoo,* you understand me?"

"No. I was smiling at Serena's tone. What did you say?"

"I said you seem nervous. Why are you nervous?"

Allen isn't sure how to respond to that, and glances at Serena for help. She says, "Mom, leave him alone. He's not nervous."

"He's very nervous. What did you tell him about me?" Mrs. Yew asks. "I'm not that bad."

"Mom." Serena sighs.

Mrs. Yew laughs; her eyes lock on to Allen. He doesn't know whether to laugh with her or pretend not to understand what's going on. Mrs. Yew suddenly stops, and says, "Where's that dog? Didn't you have that big dog?"

"Gracie wasn't that big," Serena says. "But she died recently."

"Oh," Mrs. Yew says. "I didn't know that."

"It's okay. It was fast. She was getting pretty old."

Allen waits for Serena to elaborate, but she doesn't, and he realizes that she's not going to tell her mother about the break-in. He wonders if it's because the break-in was his fault, connected through his work, and in some way Serena is protecting him. He turns to her gratefully. She meets his gaze and smiles.

Allen says to Mrs. Yew, "So are you looking forward to visiting the wine country?"

"Why is everyone trying to push us to the wine country?" She shakes her head, and says to her daughter, "I told you, I want to see the Bay Area, not the wine country."

"But the wine country is the Bay Area," Serena replies.

"You know what I mean," her mother says. "Is there something going on? Why don't you want me here?"

Serena answers quickly and smoothly, "Of course I want you here. I just thought it'd be nice up there."

"Is there a good Korean restaurant around here?" Mrs. Yew asks. She glances at Allen. "You do, at least, eat Korean food, don't you?"

"Mom," Serena says.

"I love Korean food."

"What's your favorite dish?" Mrs. Yew asks.

"Bibimbap," Allen says. "My father used to bring it home for me."

"Ah, a peasant dish. Did you know that?" Mrs. Yew smiles at them. "I had that all the time as a little girl as well. Did you know it originated from large-meal leftovers? After the rich people finished their meals, the servants would mix everything together and divide it up. That's why the dish now has all those different ingredients." She says to Serena, "Your father and I are peasants at heart."

"So is Allen, apparently," Serena answers. "There's a take-out place nearby. I'll call in the order."

As Serena calls the restaurant, Mrs. Yew asks Allen what his parents did before they passed away.

He tells her that his father drove a truck, and his mother died in childbirth and hadn't worked at the time. He then asks her what she and her husband used to do.

"My husband was with Chase Manhattan Bank, and I was in human resources for different companies."

"What's it like being retired?"

"It's driving us crazy," she says with a bluntness that makes Allen laugh. She turns to him, amused. "Yes," she says. "We don't know what to do with ourselves."

"What about traveling?"

"The first year that's all we did. But it's tiring, and after a while all the tourist attractions seem the same. Besides, I like staying at home."

Allen nods, and says, "I don't like traveling either."

"I know. You wouldn't visit us."

"Oh, I . . . uh, it's just that work . . ."

"It's fine, Allen. Serena explained how you are."

He says, "How I am?"

"Very shy. Quiet. You prefer not to be noticed."

Allen blinks. He wonders what else they talked about. He says, "I like my . . . routines."

"Your exercising? Serena is also like that. I exercise. Did she tell you? I go to aerobics three times a week."

He smiles, and says, "That's great. We all should go hiking in Marin."

"I'd love that. We might have to leave Serena's father behind, though. He'll just want to watch baseball."

This worries Allen, who knows nothing about organized sports. Mrs. Yew notices his expression and says, "Don't worry. You won't be expected to join him."

He says, "You seem to know my thoughts."

"I'm afraid I can't quite do that, though I spent almost thirty years in human resources. I interviewed applicants and dealt with people problems, so I've gotten good at reading people. It was probably similar to things you do. Did Serena ever tell you about the time I interviewed someone and I knew he was hiding something? It turned out he had murdered someone."

"No! You're kidding!"

Mrs. Yew begins telling him the story, and he finds himself relaxing. Perhaps it's the wine, but he recognizes this same trait in Serena, the ability to shift the focus onto herself and let him simply listen and witness. Mrs. Yew finishes her wine and pours herself another glass, still talking. She refills his glass almost to the rim, and tells him about finding the gaps in the interviewee's story, his work history, and connecting it to a prison term. With a few calls she found out who the applicant was. "He had spent fifteen years in prison for second-degree murder, and tried to hide this from me."

"I guess he didn't get the job," Allen says dryly.

Mrs. Yew leans her head back and laughs. "Oh, no, we hired murderers all the time. In fact, we recruited at the local prisons."

"You'd be a good investigator."

"That's nice of you to say. I've wondered about getting a part-time job because retirement just isn't very satisfying. Maybe you'll hire me."

He smiles. "The pay is lousy."

"Serena would love that, wouldn't she? Her mom working for her boyfriend." Mrs. Yew giggles, and Allen suddenly sees her as a young woman, as Serena is now. They have similar facial features—the dark eyebrows and sharp jaw—though Serena's nose and cheeks are harder, more angled. In a brief vision he sees himself with Serena thirty years from now, a retired couple, and he likes the image of them hiking—perhaps at a slower pace—in the Marin Headlands.

Serena then walks back in with the cordless phone. She glances at her mother and at Allen. Mrs. Yew says, "Allen was just about to hire me to work for him."

"She seems to have good people skills," he says. "She can spot murderers miles away." They laugh.

Serena says with a puzzled smile, "Okay. No more wine for you two. At least until I catch up."

Allen picks up their dinner from a restaurant in Albany and brings it back, finding the dining room table set and Serena and her mother laughing. As Allen and Serena lay out the heaps of barbecue beef and spicy pork, Mrs. Yew tells Allen what they were laughing about, that Serena at one point wanted to be a nun. Serena smiles and shakes her head. Mrs. Yew adds, "She also wanted to be a nurse."

"And a doctor," Serena says.

"And a doctor, then an actress."

"I was serious about the acting."

"I know," her mother says. "But I'm glad you left Hollywood." She turns to Allen. "Tomorrow you'll meet Serena's father. He's curious to see who is stealing his daughter."

"Stealing?" Allen asks.

"Keeping her out here on the West Coast. We always thought she'd come back to New York."

"Will he expect me to speak Korean?" Allen asks.

"No," Serena says quickly. "I told both of them."

"It's so strange that your parents didn't teach you," Mrs. Yew says.

"Mom," Serena says. "I explained that. His mother died when he was born, and his father worked all the time."

"It wasn't a priority," Allen says. "My aunt thought it important that my English be good for school."

"We did, too," Mrs. Yew says, "but we spoke both to Serena."

"And also made me study it in Saturday Korean school."

"That's true," Mrs. Yew says.

"And I went to Yonsei for two summers to study Korean language."

Allen says, "That's always impressed me."

"That's why I can speak it better than a mixed Korean-English hodgepodge."

"Where did you go to school?" Mrs. Yew asks.

Hesitating, and noticing Serena's uneasy expression, he replies, "SF State, but I never finished."

Mrs. Yew straightens up. "You never finished college?"

He smiles and shakes his head. There's an awkward silence. He knows what his aunt would say, so he anticipates Mrs. Yew's reaction, and adds, "It's not really needed in my profession. I mean, it's important, I know, but my field is kind of specialized knowledge, security and investigations."

"But a college degree . . ." Mrs. Yew turns to her daughter.

"He does a lot of reading on his own," Serena says.

Allen hears the defensiveness in her voice, and doesn't like it. He says, "A degree is a piece of paper. It's not a sign of anything except tuition paid and classes passed."

"But education is so important," Mrs. Yew says.

"Mom, he's fine."

"It's okay," Allen says to Serena. "I'd like to hear what she has to say."

"Allen, you can never get anywhere in America without education."

"I'm educating myself," he says, his cheeks growing warm. "And I'm doing okay."

Mrs. Yew studies him without expression, and Serena is about to say something when Allen's cell phone vibrates in his pocket. He excuses himself and answers the phone, trying not to get too annoyed at Mrs. Yew. He walks across the room, and says, "Larry?"

"No, it's me," Linda says.

"What's up?"

"You said we'd do a drive-by of Pinetti's."

Mrs. Yew and Serena are watching him closely. He grips the phone, and says "We will."

"When?"

He checks his watch. "A couple hours."

Serena stands up and folds her arms. Mrs. Yew's eyes flicker from Allen to Serena, back to Allen.

Linda says into his ear, "All right. Two hours. I'll be at my hotel."

They hang up, and he slowly turns to Serena, who is frowning at him.

Seventeen

The traffic into the city is snarled, and Allen coasts bumper to bumper along the Bay Bridge, but he likes the quiet inside his car. He listens to a classical station and feels as if this bridge is his buffer, a zone of peace that isolates him from Serena and her mother in Berkeley, and from the case waiting for him in the city. He's suspended over water, violin strings soothing him. He ignores the cramp in his left calf from using the clutch every few feet. An ache in the back of his head spreads slowly down to his neck. He still hears Serena's polite, cool response to his excuse for leaving her so late at night; she said, "You promised to be here tonight."

"For your mother," he said, lowering his voice. Mrs. Yew was in the bathroom, preparing to return to the hotel. "She's going."

"It's almost midnight."

"I know. I'm sorry. I'll be back in an hour or so."

"Why not do this tomorrow?"

"Linda's anxious to—"

"Well, then. If Linda beckons, then you must go. Isn't that how it works?" Her expression was cold. She shook her head, gave him a slight bow, and went to her mother.

Now, while going through a tunnel, Allen regrets giving in to Linda so readily. Client or not, ex-girlfriend or not, she shouldn't expect his entire life to revolve around her case. He is, however, glad not to be under Mrs. Yew's scrutiny any longer. She reminds him of his aunt, who also criticized his truncated education. He tries not to let this bother him. One of his biggest fights with his aunt was about quitting school, and she predicted he would never be successful if he dropped out of college. He replied as a teen would. "Successful like you? Like my father? Both of you finished college, and my father drove a truck, and you hate your job crunching numbers. How is that successful?"

His aunt flinched, then just said that he understood nothing.

She was right—he understood nothing back then. He sees now that it's never simple, that language problems contributed to their limitations, that his mother's sudden death forced his father to take jobs he hadn't wanted. And Allen learned almost twenty years after his father's death that his father hadn't forgotten about more education—he was studying medical textbooks on his own, hoping to attend medical school someday.

As Allen drives into the city he briefly considers going back to school for his degree. He should ask Serena about how night school works.

At Linda's hotel, he walks through the lobby without being stopped by the clerk, takes the elevator up, and finds her at her computer.

"You're late," she says, typing.

"Got a late start. Where's Julie?"

"Her cell phone battery died. She's on her way back. She talked to Diedre."

"And?"

"She'll fill us in later. But check this out. I found some clippings on Pinetti."

Allen moves next to her and peers at the screen. There's a list of articles in reverse chronological order, all from the *San Francisco Chronicle,* and Linda says, "Pinetti was charged with money laundering after some big heroin bust, but got off because the DA messed up the case." She clicks on the oldest article, and Allen reads the headline, "Heroin Ring Busted." The smugglers used shipping containers routed through San Francisco and Oakland ports, and it isn't until the end of the article that Allen sees Val Pinetti's name as one of the people charged.

"Rick's name isn't there."

"This is much bigger than Rick's crimes. Look, it says they made almost four million in three years."

"Rick did time for selling. Maybe he was just a street dealer."

"The later articles are about the prosecution, and Pinetti is mentioned there." She opens a new article and Allen learns that Pinetti was the only one who escaped jail time because the DA couldn't prove he was directly involved in any of the smuggling or selling. The IRS was brought in to trace the money and bring up more charges against Pinetti, who worked for Pacific Thrift, a small credit union that was unwittingly involved in the laundering. A jury found Pinetti not guilty, the only one of the ten arrests, with charges ranging from possession of heroin with the intent to sell, kidnapping, possession of firearms, racketeering, conspiracy, and money laundering.

Allen says, "So he gets off, the others don't, and Rick moves up?"

"And Rick maybe brings his brother in for help?"

"Right. That would explain Rick's deep interest in protecting his brother," Allen says.

"Did the background info on Pinetti come in?"

Allen checks his e-mail, but doesn't find the file yet. "It should be in soon, though."

"If Pinetti is higher up than Rick, then maybe Pinetti knows more about where Frank and Nora are."

Allen nods, seeing where this is going, that Linda wants to check out Pinetti's address. He says, "Just a survey. We don't do anything but look."

"To see if you can break in? Or some kind of surveillance?"

"Just a look."

He tells her to drive towards the 280 freeway, and near the Caltrain railroad tracks. The quiet between them feels awkward and strange. He's not sure why silence can take on different meanings—when they were dating the silences were comforting. It's the projection of themselves into the silences that must change it. He remembers those times at the beach when he and Linda would sit quietly, sunning themselves and watching the waves. He wants to ask her about the notions of silence, but can't.

She says, "So, how'd it go with Serena's parents?"

"I just met her mother tonight. It was okay."

"My mom really liked you. Remember? She thought you were my protector."

"I didn't do a very good job," he says, recalling how she had been injured with a serious concussion back when they were looking into her brother's case, and her family, especially Julie, blamed Allen's negligence.

Linda shrugs this off. After a moment she says, "Look, I want to apologize again about lying to you. Really, I am sorry."

Allen points ahead to a gray stucco building next to a small hamburger restaurant. Charlie's Burgers has iron bars over the windows, and a huge metal exhaust sits on the roof. Residual smells of frying meat leak into the car. He says, "Next to the burger place. I think that's his building."

"Do you know which apartment?"

He checks his slip of paper. "One-ten. First floor I guess. But drive around the block. I want to see the alleys." They pass the hamburger place, which is closed, but lit up inside. Allen says, "You know, the Bascome lie was dangerous. Bascome was most likely hit, and without my knowing anything, I could've been in jeopardy."

"You think he was murdered?"

"Most likely. The sequence of events is too strange. There might not be evidence, but I can see Rick bribing him, then having someone kill him in order not to pay. You put me in a really bad, blind situation."

Linda circles the block. Allen notices a large wooden fence separating the properties, the area filled with small apartment buildings. When they pass the building again, Linda pulls over to the curb. She turns to him, and says, "I'm sorry, Allen."

He shrugs it off.

She says, "This is no excuse, but I've been pretty unhappy."

In the darkened car, headlights from the approaching traffic drifting across their faces, Linda and Allen talk quietly. Linda tells him how after she stayed down in Marina Alta, she didn't feel like finding a new newspaper job and tried to write freelance articles, but had lost the ambition to write. She became depressed. She tried traveling. She spent more and more time with her sister, whose marriage was then becoming acrimonious. She flew back and forth from LA. She hung out with Nora. Deeply rooted within all of this, though, was a restlessness and dissatisfaction.

"Dissatisfaction with what?" Allen asks.

"With everything. My life, the people around me, the world," she says. She tells him that the money her late father had left her freed her from job worries, but this made her realize how little else she had. "I was all about work. Then it got worse. I went to my doctor for an unrelated thing, and she did some tests. It turns out I can't have kids."

Allen is jolted, and says, "What?"

"My fallopian tubes are screwed-up."

He says, "I thought you didn't want kids."

"I don't."

He puzzles over this. "But . . ."

"By choice. I chose not to have children, but this is different. It's no longer my choice."

"You considered changing your mind."

"I actually hadn't even thought about it until she told me that. Then I couldn't stop thinking about it."

"I'm sorry."

"And then spending all that time with Nora . . ."

"I'm really sorry."

"No need to be," she says. After a silence she turns to him. "I have no idea why I told you that."

He stares out onto the street, and says, "We used to tell each other everything."

"I remember."

He says, "Why did you lie to me?"

"I didn't want you to know I've been unhappy. That's why I made up a fiancé."

"But why? What do you care what I think?"

"Don't you know? Of course I care. I loved you. And I felt terrible about the ways things ended."

He freezes. She has never used the word "love" with him before, and it's unnerving that it would come up now. He tries to see her expression, but it's too dark. He doesn't understand what she wants from him. He says, "Don't worry about it. It was hard how it ended, but I'm fine now. And you should know that I just want you to be happy."

"Were you jealous when I told you I was engaged?"

Allen begins to feel uncomfortable, and says, "Surprised, maybe."

"Not jealous?"

He grapples with the truth and the fear of revealing the truth. Why does she want to know this? He has always tried to be honest with her, and despite her lies, he admits, "Maybe a little jealous."

"Did you like how I made him an investment banker?"

"A good touch, but I was disappointed that you went so conventional. Why not something more interesting?"

"Like what? A computer programmer?"

It takes him a moment to connect this to Serena. He turns to her. "Hey."

"Just kidding."

"It's a good job."

"I was kidding. Really."

Allen nods. "It would've been more interesting if he was an astro-physicist or some kind of scientist."

"Not believable," she says. "I had to come up with something you'd buy."

"An investment banker named Michael."

"Gabriel. You keep getting it wrong."

"Gabriel, Michael—it's fake anyway. What's the difference?"

"It's a matter of respect," she says.

"Respect?"

"Getting my fiancé's name wrong shows you don't think it's worth knowing—"

"But he's fake! He's made-up!"

"It doesn't matter. Before you knew that you kept calling him Michael—"

"Oh my God. I can't believe you're getting on my case for not remembering a *fake* name to a *fake* person!"

They stop, and after a pause they both begin laughing. Allen finds all this so absurd that he leans forward and rests his head on the dash-board, laughing so hard he can't breathe. It feels good, and the stress from the past few days quickly dissipates. He coughs and tries to inhale. When he sits up, Linda is smiling at him, the lights from a pair of head-lights glinting in her eyes. She says, "I forgot how much fun it is to argue with you."

"It wasn't always fun," he says.

"I know."

"So you haven't been dating?"

"Oh, I've tried. But you wouldn't believe how bad it is out there."

"I believe it."

"The stories I could tell you . . ."

"I've heard a lot of them. Serena's friends are all in that dating mode.

I've actually done background checks on some of their dates. One guy turned out to be married with three kids." He notices that mentioning Serena's name shifts her expression, but he continues, "I can't imagine myself going through all that."

They fall quiet, and although they have seen enough of the building, he wants to continue talking to her. He remembers his attempt to tell Serena's friends about Kierkegaard, and to fill the silence he tries it on Linda. He tells her what he's been reading lately, and says, "You want to hear about his spheres of existence?"

She shrugs. "Sure."

He tells her that Kierkegaard considered the spheres to be life stages, although someone could remain in one sphere his whole life. The first one, the aesthetic sphere, is the lowest arena—you're interested in pleasing yourself. The leap from this is to the ethical sphere, where you're trying to get more than selfish pleasure.

Linda says, "Like what?"

"Instead of thinking just about yourself, you choose to live by a moral code, any code. You move out of a neutral selfishness and think about others."

"Are you taking a class in this or something?"

"No. I'm just interested," he says.

"Just like the philosophy of removement."

"Oh. You remember."

She laughs. "I remember."

He smiles and shakes his head. This history they have together is nice. He says, "Do you remember when you did all that research for me when I was trying to get another executive protection job? You spent hours getting contact info and came home with an armload of printouts?"

She doesn't answer for a full minute, then says, "Of course."

"You were excited, and some of the papers were falling out of your arm."

"I was happy to be helping you. I found some really good leads."

Allen remembers her flushed face, her eyes excited. He says, "I never really thanked you. I was so surprised. That was one of the best things anyone ever did for me."

"You thanked me."

"Not really. I was so . . . touched. You must have spent hours."

"Almost that whole day, actually. I almost missed a deadline because I was so involved in getting you that data."

Allen says quietly, "Yeah, we had some fun."

Linda nods, but stares out the window. Allen thinks, I'm in the ethical stage. My moral code is not to hurt anyone. I worry about others. I love Serena.

Two darkened figures suddenly appear on both sides of the car, and Allen, not having seen anything in the mirrors, quickly locks his door and yells for Linda to do the same. But her door jerks open and a man points a .45 at her head, saying, "No. No. Don't do anything stupid. Both of you, hands on the dash."

Allen has his SIG in his belt holster, and his Raven against his ankle, but the man on his side of the window clicks the muzzle of a .38 on the glass and shakes his head. Allen can't see much of his features in the darkness, and the man on Linda's side says, "Eyes forward."

Allen has no alternative but to press a switch, and all the locks disengage. Allen's door flies open and the man shoves the gun into Allen's cheek and quickly frisks him, pulling out the SIG. He checks Allen's legs, but when a car turns a corner and approaches, the man misses the ankle holster as he looks back at the street. The car passes by. Both men then open the back doors and slip in quickly, their guns pressing into the backs of Linda's and Allen's heads. One of the men tells them to shut their doors and start the car.

"What do you want?" Allen asks.

The man behind him slams the gun into his head and Allen falls forward, his vision lighting up, and he swoons in pain. "Shit," he says.

The man behind him says. "Quiet."

The other man says to Linda, "Drive. Get onto Van Ness and head north. Do anything that attracts attention, and your friend gets a bullet in his head."

"Where are we going?" Linda asks.

The man behind Allen hits him again, and Linda yells, "Stop that!"

"No questions," the man behind Linda says. "Just follow my directions."

Allen keeps crouched over his knees, rubbing the back of his head. He knows he can reach his Raven and pull it out in two quick motions, but can't risk it yet. He doesn't understand how these guys sneaked up on him. Was it when they were laughing, his attention diverted? He's sweating from the pain and squeezes his eyes shut for a moment. He feels his shirt being pulled from behind, choking him, and he sits back up. The gun muzzle, cool against his sweaty skin, presses against his neck. "Easy there," the man behind him says.

They drive across the Golden Gate Bridge, and Allen catches a glimpse of the man behind Linda, his hand in black gloves. He has long, bushy sideburns, and a silver earring. Lights from oncoming headlights flash intermittently, making it difficult for Allen to focus. The man behind Allen presses his gun harder, and says, "Eyes front."

Linda says, "My sister's waiting for me back at the hotel. If I'm missing, she'll call the police."

"Shut up and drive."

Allen worries about the use of gloves—they're being careful about leaving prints. A simple warning, a scare, doesn't require this kind of preparation. He wonders if they were being watched before they even showed up at Pinetti's. But Allen had marked cars as they drove, looking for a tail. He had swept all the cars for bugs and tracking devices right after Gracie was killed.

"Now what?" Linda asks as they leave the bridge and head north on the 101 into Marin.

"Keep going."

The quiet unnerves Allen. It's more than the quiet—it's the professionalism of these two. Nothing revealed, nothing except directions. Allen also doesn't like leaving the city. The farther north they drive, the less populated it is. The only contact Rick has up here that Allen knows about is his sister, and Allen can't imagine why they'd be brought there. If they pass the San Rafael exits, moving into less populated areas, Allen will know this is a hit.

Linda glances at him, then faces the road. Her eyes are tense. She turns on the air conditioner, and says to Allen, "What are the other stages?"

"The what?"

"Quiet," the man behind her says.

"The spheres. Aesthetic, ethical, and what else?"

"I said shut the hell up!" the man barks.

They fall silent. After a few minutes Allen says, "Religious. The religious sphere is the final one." Allen leans forward, waiting for a blow, but none comes. He realizes that the two men are looking around, checking the sparse traffic. They pass Diedre's exit, and as they continue beyond the last San Rafael exits and head toward Novato, Allen tenses. They're looking for a quiet turnoff.

He tucks his left shoe behind his right leg, and tries to unclip the button on the holster through his pant leg. The darkness hides his actions, and he manages to open the button. He then slowly tugs at his pants, raising the cuff to make it easier to grab the Raven. Linda notices his hand motion, and she grips the steering wheel.

"Here looks okay," the man behind Allen says.

"All right. Pull over," the other man tells Linda.

They're along a quiet stretch of freeway on the edge of Novato, farmland to the right and dark hills to the left. A couple of cars speed by as Linda slows along the shoulder, rocks crackling and pinging beneath them. She stops the car. Allen's fingertips tingle. He knows the sequence of movements to pull out the Raven effortlessly, but needs the right moment. He turns to check the man behind Linda. Both are looking around.

The man behind Allen raises his gun, and says, "Open your door slowly."

"Here?"

"Do it."

Allen opens his door, which triggers the overhead light. The other man quickly turns it off. Allen tugs more on his pant leg, exposing part of the holster. He knows the man behind him will lose the line of sight in order for him to get out of the back, which will give Allen a second to pull out his gun. But he has to worry about the man covering Linda.

"Get out slowly, one foot at a time."

The other man says, "Do anything, and I put a bullet in her head."

Allen lowers his right leg out the door, pulling more on his pants. He waits. Then, lifting his left leg out, he struggles forward, leaning down, and he easily grabs the Raven from the holster in a fluid motion. Then he stands up slowly, palming the small pistol and hiding it against his leg.

The man quickly slips out of the back, aiming his gun at Allen, and says to the other man. "Okay. I've got him."

"Walk in about fifty feet and make sure you're clear."

"What?" Linda says. "What's going on? What are you going to do?"

"Shut up."

"Allen?" Linda says in a panicked voice. "What's happening?"

"You were warned," the man with Allen says quietly. "You were warned, and you didn't listen."

"Just go and do it," the man inside says. "Use his gun."

"Wait!" Linda yells. "Wait! I can pay! We'll pay you, then we'll back off! Just don't do anything!"

"You'll get your turn."

"Allen?" Linda says.

"Don't worry," he replies. "I'll be fine."

"Yeah, right," the man with Allen says. "Move. Slowly."

Allen keeps his gun in front of him, but it's too dark to see much anyway. He stumbles a few times, and the man says, "Slow down."

"You do this often? Execute people?"

"I said slow down, goddammit."

Allen hears him tripping over rocks and regaining his balance. Allen turns around and aims his gun. The man hesitates. Allen says, "Don't raise your gun. I have an automatic aimed at your chest. One move, and I shoot."

"What the fuck . . . ?"

"Drop the gun."

"How the—"

"I said drop it."

The man keeps still, then, in the blurry darkness, Allen sees him raise the gun. Allen shoots and feels the familiar kick of the Raven. The man staggers back, and Allen dives, just in case the man lets off a round, but the man trips and falls backwards. Allen runs toward him and yanks the .38 from the man's hand and finds the SIG in the waistband. The man is gasping, clutching at his chest. He starts to call out and Allen quickly covers the man's mouth and slams the butt of the gun into the man's forehead. He hears Linda calling his name. He hits the man again, and the man becomes still.

Allen pockets his SIG and Raven and runs to the car, hearing Linda cry, "You didn't have to do that! We just hired him—"

"Shut the fuck up."

Allen slows down, his steps crunching the gravel, and the man says to him, "All right? No problems?"

Allen opens the man's door and shoves the .38 into his cheek. He quickly grabs the .45 and pulls it away from Linda's head. "Let go of your gun, asshole."

"Allen? Allen?" Linda says, turning around. "You're okay?"

But the man is fast, and he twists away from Allen's gun, using his elbow to deflect the muzzle, and tries to pull his gun toward Allen, who holds tight and aims it up. The man grabs Allen's .38 and leaps farther into the car, pulling Allen with him, and they struggle on the seat, falling into the small foot area. Allen head-butts the man and pulls his gun free, and the man lets off two quick shots, jolting Allen's left hand, before Allen shoves his gun into the man's waist and shoots. The man yells and tries to jerk away, but Allen shoots again. The man's grip on his gun loosens, and Allen pulls it from him, and scrambles out of the car.

The man curses and breathes heavily.

Allen says to Linda, "You okay?"

She turns to him, her eyes puzzled. "I think he got me."

Allen stops, then rushes over to her, pulling open her door and reaching up to turn on the map light. She squints and looks at him. "You're not hurt."

"You're hit? Where are you hit?" He looks at her blouse and sees that it's wet. When he rips the buttons off, he feels the wetness, the blood. He looks at his palm smeared red. He says, "Shit. Come here. Let me lay you out here."

He helps her out of the car, and lays her on the ground, seeing in the dim light from the car the blood dribbling out of a wound in her stomach. He says, "I'm going to turn you over to check your back." He hugs her and rolls her on her side, pulling up her blouse, and feels more wetness. Then he feels the first bullet hole near her side—it went through and exited her stomach.

"Allen . . . I'm hit. I feel it."

His hands shake as he finds the second hole further up in her ribs, and he lays her back down. He raises her bra, looking for another exit, but there isn't one. "Shit," he says.

"I was so scared they killed you," she whispers, her voice thinning.

Allen can't find the exit wound, and the bullet went near her heart.

"Hey, man," she says. "Stop feeling me up."

"Oh shit, Linda. Just hang on. Where's your cell?" He stops when he sees her eyes dimming, losing focus.

"I'm really sorry about this," she whispers.

"Linda! You'll be okay! Look at me!"

She blinks and turns slightly toward him. She shakes her head. She tries to speak, but nothing comes out, and she grips his hand. Her lips move, then stop. She stares at him, blinks a few more times, her grip loosening, then remains still.

PART IV

THE KNIGHT OF INFINITE RESIGNATION

Eighteen

magine Allen as a teenager, stocky and muscular, shy, with a jagged, uneven haircut his aunt had given him because she didn't want to pay $12 to a barber. The sides were uneven—the left shorter than the right—but he didn't care. His hair was always uneven. His life was uneven. Although he was on the soccer team and seemed fairly normal, he never felt quite right. This was more than the usual teenage angst, more than the common ailment of pubescent alienation—Allen was different. He had no real friends, no real connections at his school, and he rarely saw anyone outside of the classroom or soccer field. He took exploratory trips by himself on BART. He began jogging miles through Oakland. He spent less and less time at home with his aunt, who seemed to be growing more strident with every one of his report cards.

He no longer made collect calls to strangers. He had grown tired of trying to convince callers to accept the charges.

His father, now dead for a handful of years, flitted along the fringes of his memory, and because of his aunt's efficiency, her ruthless cleaning of his father's apartment, there were no memorial artifacts. Everything, except for a few medical textbooks that Allen wouldn't find for another twenty years, was gone. He had to rely on his fading memory.

Allen preferred solitude, his penchant for moving quietly and unobserved through his life, where it seemed minor explosions and tornadoes and hurricanes erupted within his periphery. He has an image of himself crouched and poised, ready to run or dive for cover. Perhaps he always played defense on some level, and his entire adult career has been variations on this theme. Security, bodyguarding, private investigations. He is a fullback with an unstated goal to protect a vague net. He is the Block in all senses of that word.

As a teen he avoided his soccer teammates during lunch, since he had little else in common with them and was beginning to hate being in groups. Instead, he would leave the school grounds. He would also walk the three miles to and from school rather than take a bus. He would eventually quit soccer, angering his aunt even more because of his lack of extracurricular activities, something she believed colleges would frown upon. Instead, he'd want nothing to do with his classmates. They began taking on a strange, wavering glow. They seemed unreal to him, zombies shuffling from classroom to classroom, and when they spoke to him, he couldn't stand to listen. Their mouths moved, sounds came out, but everything seemed irrelevant.

During one of his trips into the city, he left the BART station and saw an elderly man walking with a briskness that evidenced purpose and direction. The man, white-haired and garbed in a worn gray suit, barely looked around him crossing the street. He was on the move. Allen followed him. There was no real reason why Allen did this, except he was curious and had nothing else to do. He kept far enough not to scare the man, who probably wouldn't have noticed Allen anyway, and ended up at the Civic Center, where the man met a young woman and hugged her. Allen moved closer and listened to their conversation. The man was her father, and they talked about where to get lunch. Allen watched the young woman hook her arm into her father's, and they walked slowly toward Van Ness. Allen continued following them. He had found a new hobby.

The contours of grief are textured and serrated, and if you run your fingers over them, Braille-like to read the trajectory of sadness, you find the ridges rising and falling with small snags and depressions. They are never smooth; they cut your fingertips. You will leave a thin trace of blood.

Allen is plagued by memories. They appear before him as a sporadic fever might during an illness, and exhaust him similarly. These aren't just memories of Linda, although those comprise the majority of the flashes, but of singular moments in his childhood that haven't surfaced in decades. He keeps thinking of his father.

The reality of Linda's death has grown with every passing day, so that now, almost two weeks later, Allen has trouble handling the quotidian details of his normal life. How could he worry about bills and refurnishing B&C's office when Linda's parents had to fly up here to take her body back to LA for a funeral—one to which Allen was not invited? Julie told Allen that Linda was buried next to her brother in a quiet, family-only service.

How could he have dinners with Serena's parents when the Marin County Sheriff's Department interviewed him five different times to go over the events, identify mug shots, then talk for four hours with local DEA and FBI agents?

How could he do anything but think of Linda?

Charlene also flew up from LA to help Julie deal with the aftermath, which included a press conference during which Charlene detailed the search for Nora. Julie and Linda had been careful in the past about going public for fear of driving Frank even farther underground, but now Julie doesn't care; she will try anything. She made her appeal to divorced mothers with custody problems. She kept B&C on retainer, and Larry took over the investigation. The police and Feds are now actively involved.

Allen went home and had trouble getting out of bed.

He had witnessed death before. He had killed before. But even his partner's death four years ago didn't come close to all this. The expectations of danger were omnipresent in his job, and Paul Baumgartner's death while he and Allen were working executive protection had shaken Allen, but it was something both of them had known might happen.

But this.

The Marin sheriff's deputy told Allen that the man he had killed on the side of the road was a convicted murderer, suspected of at least four other murders and linked with numerous marijuana and heroin dealers. The man Allen had shot in the car, the one who—after a brief stint in the hospital—was now in prison awaiting trial for the murder of Linda Maldonado, was a heroin dealer with two prior drug-related convictions, and this murder could lock him away for life. But the jail time doesn't seem punitive enough. Allen wants Rick dead. Simple as that.

There are All Points Bulletins for Rick Staunton and Val Pinetti, both of whom have disappeared, their apartments emptied of most personal and business files. The good news is that Charlene, working with the Treasury Department, has frozen the pay-through account Frank had established at Credit First, a middle-sized credit union, and she's currently searching for more accounts through the Nauru link.

But all this means little at the moment to Allen, who spends most days reading Kierkegaard and remembering small details about Linda. He doesn't sleep much.

In fact, right now, three in the morning on a weeknight, Allen is staring up at the darkened ceiling, listening to Serena breathe deeply beside him. The apartment is still. He's been staying at Serena's place at her request, because she's worried about his being alone in his tiny, depressing studio. Serena has been careful around him, not asking too many questions, watching and waiting. He can see her wanting to know more but holding back. He is grateful for this, though sometimes he just wants to hide away.

He climbs out of bed and drifts down the hallway, drawn to her bookshelves, where he has stashed his philosophy texts. He pulls out the latest and settles on the sofa, turning on the small lamp on the end table and aiming it at the pages. He's encircled in a cocoon of light, and feels a small twinge of relief to be back with Kierkegaard. The more he studies this, the more relevant it seems. He tries to understand Linda's death through Kierkegaard's analysis of Abraham and Isaac.

Describing Abraham's actions of almost sacrificing his son, Kierkegaard calls Abraham a "Knight of Infinite Resignation," renouncing everything before him—family, society, laws, love—to follow God's request. He gives it all up and is infinitely resigned to these losses. Allen suspects that Kierkegaard was thinking of Regina—his abandoned fiancée—as he wrote this, but this resignation is the first step of moving from the ethical sphere to the religious sphere. Give everything up to move forward.

This idea appeals to Allen. Free yourself of everything but the pure self. Free yourself of memories. Of guilt. He doesn't quite understand, however, how murdering Isaac could be a movement forward; he'll read more about it later.

Maybe Allen needs to be infinitely resigned to losses. He must renounce everything to move forward.

He closes his eyes and thinks about this, but the light seeps through his eyelids. He turns off the lamp. There's something about the Abraham and Isaac story that rings false to him, contrived. Death seems to come too easily, and the ramifications of loss are glossed over. He wonders about the veracity of the Abraham story, or at the very least he's curious about the elasticity of the events described, the authorial mutability of actions and motivations. Allen has doubts similar to Kierkegaard's, though he knows his conclusions will be ultimately different.

Allen suddenly sees Linda lying on the ground, trying to speak but unable to. He rubs his eyes, blinks out spots. The image fades.

Death is never so simple, never so easily accepted. Never. The way the story of Abraham is written, the way Kierkegaard glibly debates the ethics of this—did anyone really fathom the consequences of such a personal loss? Allen feels very alone right now.

Why hadn't he thought about the gun going off and passing through the front seat? Why hadn't he tried to pull the man out of the car before struggling with him? Why hadn't he at least aimed the man's gun up and away from Linda? He has a frightening thought: could he have unwittingly sacrificed Linda?

He says into the darkness, "Stop that."

"Allen?" Serena whispers from the far end of hallway.

He jumps. "Right here."

"What are you doing sitting in the dark?" she asks, approaching. The outline of her body shimmers, ghostly, and she stops in the middle of the floor, suspended. The air around her seems to crackle.

"I was reading, but got tired."

"Come back to bed." She holds out her hand.

He walks to her, and she leads him to the bedroom. He grips her hand, needing the physical contact. Electricity flows into him. They settle under the covers, Allen spooning her back, and Serena quickly falls back asleep. Allen strokes her arm, then rests his face against her neck. He tells himself that he can't renounce everything, certainly not Serena. He kisses her hair and listens to her inhale and exhale, deep, steady rhythms filling the room, and he synchronizes his own breathing to hers.

"I need you back on the case," Julie says to Allen as he tries to adjust to her presence. He buzzed her up, and she's standing in the doorway, having just woken him up from a midday nap. She glances at his rumpled sweat suit, and says with surprise, "Did I wake you?"

"I've been on a strange schedule." He notices that she looks even thinner than before, if that's possible. She has the hollowed-out face of an anorexic. Her wrists are those of a small child's, and he sees red pimples on her neck and upper chest.

"Larry is okay, but he's too busy with fixing up your office. I need someone more committed. I need you back."

"The police should be—"

"They're doing what they can, but Rick and Val have vanished, and the Feds are more interested in the smuggling connection than in finding Nora."

Allen waits for news about Linda. Julie hesitates, then says, "Rawlingson, the guy in jail . . ."

"The one who killed Linda."

"He's not dealing yet. He's not giving anyone up."

"He won't admit Rick hired him."

"No. He has a good lawyer, and they're trying to plead down to manslaughter."

"But that's still a third strike."

"I don't know. He's definitely going down for something, but he's just a hired guy."

Allen suddenly realizes what she's saying. "You mean Linda's real killers, Rick and Val and whoever, might not be found?"

Julie stares at him. "Nora is being lost in all this," she says, her voice weakening.

Allen asks, "How are you? Are you okay?"

She shakes her head. Allen invites her in.

They sit across from each other in Serena's living room, the windows bright and the sun beaming onto the floors. Julie pulls her hair back and knots it off, and Allen smells her faint body odor, surprising him. He tries not to stare at her spindly arms, her collarbone and shoulder jutting against her pale, freckled skin. He says, "You've lost more weight."

"I have trouble eating."

"I know. Me too."

"I'm sorry about the funeral. My mother wanted only family—"

"That's okay. I wouldn't have handled it well," he says, though he was hurt he hadn't been invited. He saw it as an indirect way of blaming him. He asks, "How's your mother?"

Julie lowers her head into her hands, and says through her fingers, "She's taking Valium. She's a walking basket case. Her last hope is that I find Nora and we move in with her."

"Larry told me about the bank stuff. So you cut off Frank's funds?"

"One source. He probably has more."

"What are you doing now?"

"Larry hasn't told you?"

"I've been a little out of touch."

She stares at him. "You don't look so good."

He jerks his head back. *She* is telling *him* that? He says, "I just can't believe she's . . ."

Julie's face tightens, and she says, "Don't."

"Don't what?"

"Don't do that."

Allen rubs his temples, avoiding her gaze.

Julie says, "Larry got more information on Val Pinetti, some of that background stuff you ordered but also the stuff the Marin sheriff shared. Pinetti has former associates in Seattle, but Larry's dragging his feet."

"Associates?"

"Business partners, corporate filings. And since both Frank and Rick grew up in Seattle, there has to be a connection."

"What are the police doing?"

"They're not interested in finding Nora. They have the murderer, and he's not talking. The DEA has been trying to stop smuggling through Oakland ports for a while now, so they're focusing on that. No one cares about finding Nora."

"I care," he says.

"I know. That's why I want you back."

He nods. "She and I were just talking about old times. She brought me rice cakes—"

"Please, Allen," Julie says, grimacing. "I can't do that. I have to focus."

"I can't mention her?"

"I need to concentrate on finding Nora."

He looks down. "It's just that I don't have anyone to talk to about this."

"What about your girlfriend . . . oh, well, I guess it might be awkward. Look, find Rick and Frank. Find Nora, and we'll get through this."

He raises his head, shamed by his self-indulgence. He tries to dislodge the heaviness in his chest by taking a deep breath. Julie just lost her sister, who was also her closest friend, and is now trying to find her daughter; here Allen is moping around. He shakes this off and stands up. "All right," he says. "I'm sorry. Let me shower and change. We'll drive over to B&C."

Nineteen

Allen grabs his seat belt as Julie swerves dangerously around cars on the Bay Bridge. She mutters a curse to a slow driver with his blinker who doesn't change lanes. She accelerates around him and glares past Allen to the elderly man. Allen slowly leans back in his seat and braces his feet squarely on the car floor. Linda was aggressive in a car, but never like this. He turns to Julie, not sure if he should say something, but then again, Linda always made fun of his slow, careful driving. She used to call him "Jeeves" whenever he drove.

He asks her for more updates about the case, and she tells him of the corporate information the police had found about Pinetti, that he's had a varied career with numerous banks, including Frank's credit card company. They found at least a dozen shell corporations, most of them now defunct, with Pinetti as an officer, and almost thirty credit cards with Pinetti connected to them in some way, either personally or through the shell companies. "Most of them were canceled, but it looks like it was a complicated money transfer and laundering scheme that used automatic payments of the cards from different foreign banks."

"Pay-through accounts. Like from Nauru."

"Yes. And the cards were a lot easier to use than checks or even cash. Some of the cards had no limits. They could buy a car if they wanted to."

"What are the police doing about it?"

"Nothing. The accounts are closed. They gave the info to the DEA, but in terms of Linda's murder, they have the killer. If he deals, they might get Rick, but it doesn't look good."

The mention of Linda jars Allen. He loses his train of questions and stares ahead at the line of cars leaving the bridge. He still hasn't had any sense of her being truly gone. Even on the side of the road when Allen performed CPR and called 9-1-1 on her cell, when the police cars and ambulance arrived, when he followed the ambulance in the San Rafael police car, and ended up at Marin General, and the doctors there declared her DOA, when Julie and Larry and Serena all arrived and took over while Allen sat on the hard plastic chair in the waiting room, trying to answer questions from the police and then the Marin County sheriff's deputies, when Julie sobbed and yelled at the deputies to do something, when Allen heard the police talk about an autopsy—despite the sequence of events that allowed no other conclusion about the cause of death, Allen still doesn't quite understand it all.

He had seen Linda in the hospital before. He had seen her hurt, even in a coma. She had always returned. In fact, when she was in that coma, with a bolt attached to her shaved head, she looked much worse than when she lay on the side of the road. There, she looked peaceful, tired. Allen just can't seem to accept that it could end so gratuitously. He wants to ask Julie about the funeral. He has no pictures in his head, no images of grief. He isn't even sure what kind of service it was.

There is a momentary lapse from the tangible realities around him. Julie is saying something, but he can't hear her. He closes his eyes and remembers his father's funeral, an occasion two decades old but suddenly embroidered with details he has never until now recalled. Some of the tactile memories like his fingering the Korean Bibles and the itchy wool suit are familiar to Allen, but now there are other details: his pants were too short, and he felt his shins exposed and cold; the stained-glass windows were deep red, images of angels and crucifixes brilliant in the setting sun, colors exploding in his memory. Reds and blues wash across his vision. The pastor's voice crackled through the small podium speakers. An electronic hum blanketed the silences. The mourners didn't cry, but sat rigidly, and Allen couldn't understand a word of anything being said.

Julie turns onto Ninth and heads to the office, the familiar liquor and deli storefronts yanking Allen back to the present. He suddenly feels the details of the case, of Linda, of all these things crowding him. He has trouble breathing, and opens his window. Cool air whips inside, mussing his hair. Although he recognizes the neighborhood, the narrow side streets and cars parked on the curbs, he hasn't been here in a week, and the buildings seem older, more run-down. Everything ages, especially during his absence. Everything decays.

"Allen?" Julie says. "Are you listening?"

He says into the wind, "I don't know if I can do this."

"What?" Julie asks.

He turns to her and repeats himself.

She doesn't reply for a minute. Then, as they pull up to B&C, she says, "You have to."

Larry stands up from his desk, startled by Allen's entrance. "B! You're back!"

Allen notices the new large metal desks with notebook computers centered on them, sleek oval telephones in the corners. New black leather chairs cushioned with high headrests glisten under the track lighting. Larry says, "I wanted to finish the place before you saw it."

"You've done a lot." Allen wonders how much all this costs.

Larry follows his gaze and says, "Don't worry. The insurance covered all this. As soon as I brought in a lawyer they began moving their asses."

The conference room in the corner, sectioned off by glass, has the entertainment system shelving Larry had mentioned before. Allen says, "No conference table?"

"Not yet. It's being made."

"Custom-made?"

"I got a good deal. It's iron and a special polymer plastic. It looks hot."

Allen smiles. "We're a fancy outfit now."

Julie says, "I wanted Allen back on the case."

Larry glances at her, then says to Allen, "You up for it?"

Allen shrugs.

"He's up for it," Julie says.

Larry nods, but tells Allen, "Not a whole lot since the police and Feds got into it. The guy I know at the Marin Sheriff's Department is going to call me as soon as they get more on Rick's whereabouts."

Allen says to Julie, "You mentioned Seattle."

"Yeah," Larry says. "It might be a long shot."

Julie shakes her head. "Two of the early corporations that Pinetti was connected to were based in Seattle. Frank and Rick grew up in Seattle."

"Maybe" Larry says. "But wouldn't they steer clear of their hometown?"

"Rick and Pinetti might, but not necessarily Frank." Julie turns to Allen. "I think we need to check out Frank's parents, maybe track down Pinetti's contacts up there."

Allen sees Larry shrugging his shoulders, and asks Julie, "Did anyone talk to Rick's sister in San Rafael?"

"I did, before . . . before everything happened. The police did afterwards," Julie says. "She and her husband are afraid of the connections, so they've told the police all they know, which isn't much. They spoke to Rick a few times before. Diedre heard from Frank only once, and that was months ago. Her brothers were trying to protect her."

Allen believes Linda's funeral must have been Catholic, since her parents attended Mass regularly. But was it held at a church or was it at a mortuary? Who gave the eulogy? Allen could've given a good one. He probably would've talked about the first time he and she met. He'd try to make it funny.

"B?" Larry says.

Allen turns to him. "Yes?"

"You okay?"

"What about farming this out to a Seattle PI?" Allen asks.

"No," Julie says. "I'm planning on going up there. I want you to come with me."

"Why? A local PI might get—"

"No. I need to be doing something more. Plus I hired you, not some unknown Seattle person."

Allen asks Larry, "Aren't vital records public in Washington?"

"Much more public than here."

"That could be helpful," Allen says to Julie.

Larry says, "I've got the latest status reports online. I'm moving us to filing everything on a remote server, just in case of fire."

Allen looks at Julie, and says, "Will you at least tell me if it was a nice service?"

"What service?"

"For Linda."

Julie and Larry share a look. Larry quickly says, "Dude, let me show you your new computer. You can watch freaking DVDs on it. It's very cool." Allen is still waiting for Julie's answer as Larry tugs on his arm.

Julie turns to him and nods. She says quietly, "It was very nice."

Abraham had renounced everything—even morality, since he was about to murder his innocent son—in order to do God's bidding. Kierkegaard called this the "teleological suspension of the ethical," putting morality on hold, something that Allen finds incongruous to Abraham's being the paragon of faith. Contradictions and paradoxes riddle this story.

Contradiction and paradoxes riddle Allen's existence.

He wonders if it's a paradox to worry about the lives of those around him when everything ends inevitably in death. The original impetus for this case, the search for Nora, seems so distant and futile right now that he has trouble focusing on the two updates Larry filed. Allen tries to read about the sheriff's investigation of Rick and Val Pinetti, especially the financial ties to Frank's company, but he isn't used to this new note-book computer and has trouble with the screen size. He looks up and watches Larry assemble a bookshelf. Julie is at the new receptionist's desk, on the phone, possibly arranging the flight up to Seattle. Allen has to ask Serena about this.

Guilt fills him as he realizes how difficult he has been, brooding and silent. Serena is too good for him. Her parents left without seeing Allen again, and he knows from a few hints Serena has dropped that they put her on the defensive, that they thought she shouldn't be in a relation-ship with someone in such a dangerous profession. Mr. Yew apparently had trouble understanding how Allen could make a living without a reg-ular paycheck, and definitely didn't understand why Allen chose to deal with criminals all the time. Allen still hasn't told Serena the full details of what happened in the car, of the confusing mix of guns and the two shots and the surprised way Linda had said, "I think he got me." And the way she seemed happy that he was okay, even as she was dying.

Allen lowers his head and takes a deep breath. He smells a hint of Linda's suntan lotion, the coconut oil she always used when they went nude sunbathing at Muir Beach.

He feels he's being watched. He looks up. Larry meets his eyes. "You okay?"

Allen nods, and tries to focus on the computer screen, and reads Larry's summary of his conversation with his Marin sheriff contact. A name toward the bottom of the dense paragraph in Larry's shorthand style stops Allen: "Sidney Olshan."

Allen goes back and reads the entire paragraph. Larry had talked to Lieutenant Kyle over the phone, taking notes while Kyle had read off the names of possible associates of Pinetti's.

Allen recognizes the name. He asks Larry, "Where have I heard this name, Sidney Olshan, before?"

Larry shakes his head.

"You don't know it?" Allen asks.

Larry says, "Don't think so."

"When we heard Rick talking on the phone. He called Val Pinetti, but didn't he mention a 'Sid'?"

Larry stands up slowly, his knees cracking. "He said something about calling someone else."

"A 'Sid.' I'm pretty sure of it."

"Yeah, that sounds right."

Julie turns to them, still on the phone.

Allen asks, "How do I log on from here? I want to do a background check on this guy."

"You're already online. That's how you're reading that. Just click the browser icon."

Allen begins searching for more header information on Sidney Olshan, and although he gets a few phone and address listings in California, none are local. Julie walks to his desk and scans the screen. She jots down the listings and says, "Check Seattle, too."

Allen types in a Washington search, and a few Seattle entries appear. He says, "Without more information on this guy, it'll be tough to pinpoint. He might not even be listed."

"You didn't hear Rick say anything else?"

Allen says no, but then asks, "Do we have a listing of all the corporate officers in those shell companies that Pinetti had?"

Julie snaps her fingers. "Cross referencing. Good idea. Larry has that info."

They turn to Larry, who says, "I just got the general stuff from Lieutenant Kyle, not the actual corporate listings. That might be tough, because he'd have to copy and fax them to me."

"Why's that tough?" Allen asks.

"He's not supposed to be sharing that with a PI. It's a police investigation."

"But we can get that information eventually, through the Secretary of State corporate records," Allen says.

"That's true. Let me give him a call."

Julie says, "I'm going to book us on a flight to Seattle for tomorrow."

"That soon?" Allen asks, alarmed.

"Yes."

"Shouldn't we do more prep?"

"I know where the parents live. And if Larry gets that corporate information, especially any Seattle contacts, we'll have more."

Allen says, "It would be helpful to talk to old friends or business contacts."

"I have some of those from Frank, but I can try to find more."

"Let me talk to my girlfriend before I commit to Seattle."

She hesitates. "Allen, I need your help."

"I'll call you tonight."

"When?"

"Tonight," he says. "Don't push too hard."

She's about to object, but then nods. "All right. Tonight."

I didn't like her at all when we first met, you know, Allen says in his imaginary eulogy. He smiles. She was an eager young reporter trying to pump Allen for more information, and he distrusted reporters. She had gone to his boss in order to get an interview with him, a tactic Allen found distasteful, and when they finally met he was as cold and professional as he could be, though in her enthusiasm for the story she barely noticed. She thought she saw something unusual in his partner's death, that it might have been more than a bodyguard taking a bullet for a client, and she was right. She was the one who prompted him to delve deeper, and he owed the subsequent revelations about his family to her persistence.

And it soon became more than a story to her. She had become invested in him.

Allen sits on the floor in Serena's living room, waiting for her to return. He tries to suppress the unsteadiness blossoming in his chest, a wavering of emotions, and he says, "Shit. Hold it together." He leaps up and punches the air. He does a few tae kwon do kicks.

Hurrying to the bookshelf, he pulls out not one of Kierkegaard's philosophy texts, but a translation of his journals, and searches for excerpts about his ex-fiancée Regina.

There. May, 1842: "And it was the delight on his eyes and his heart's desire. And he stretched forth his hand and took hold of it, but he could not retain it; it was offered to him, but he could not possess it . . ."

Odd that Kierkegaard referred to himself in the third person. Perhaps it was too painful for him?

Their situations are not analogous, Allen knows, but there's something about the sorrow in his writings and his subsequent ideas that appeals to Allen. He closes the book and sits back down on the floor, crossing his legs and closing his eyes. Right around now Gracie would usually walk over to him out of curiosity. Poor Gracie. Allen has brought such damage onto Serena. Did she suspect he'd be such bad luck?

Did Linda die because of him? He imagines different permutations of actions, and in all of them two stray bullets don't end up hitting her.

He jumps back up and does a few more kicks, cursing.

Serena enters the apartment, and Allen sits back down quickly, pushing Kierkegaard's journal aside. Serena calls his name, and he answers with a hello.

"God, what a day," she says, walking down the hall and stopping when she sees him cross-legged in the middle of the floor. "You okay?"

"Just thinking." He stands and kisses her. He slips his hand underneath her blazer and rubs her back.

"How are you?" she asks.

"Okay. I'm getting back to work."

She puts her bag down slowly, then says, "Already?"

"They need my help."

"If you think you're ready . . ." She gives him a half shrug, but her expression is tense, her eyes worried.

"You had a bad day?" he asks.

"No big deal." She studies him. "Tell me what's going on. You've got a look."

Allen says, "I do?"

"You do. I can also hear it in your voice. What's happening?" She takes off her blazer and lays it carefully over a chair.

He takes a deep breath. "Well, I might have to go up to Seattle with Julie to look into a few things."

"What?"

"It's not definite. I wanted to check with you first."

Serena has on a light blue blouse, which she pulls out of her slacks. She unbuttons the front slowly, her bra peeking through. Finally, she asks, "Will it be dangerous?"

He starts to lie, but stops himself. "Maybe."

"Maybe. Maybe. What the hell is that supposed to mean?"

He flinches. "It means I don't know."

She unbuttons her cuffs, then sits on the sofa, crossing her legs and watching him coolly. Her neck is long and slim, curved elegantly in the semidarkness. He's struck by how beautiful she is, and almost says this. He sits next to her. "I know you've had to put up with me and all this stuff recently," he says.

"You could've been killed. I just can't get over that. You could've been shot."

"I know."

"No, I don't think you do. Any sane person would realize that and stop. It's like being a cop—no, it's worse. At least they have some kind of support system. You've been depressed, and I don't know what to do."

"I know."

"Allen, I don't like this at all."

"I know," he says. "Let me finish this case. I'll go and help Julie. I owe it to . . ."

Serena shakes her head. After a long silence she says, "You owe it to Linda."

"Yes."

She lowers her face into her hands, and says in a muffled voice, "I can't compete with her."

"You're not."

"She's everywhere. She's in this apartment. You were obsessing about her when I came in."

Allen freezes. Shit. Then he raises his voice. "She just . . . it just happened for crying out loud. Can't I *recover*?"

"I'm sorry, but all I can think about is that it could've been you. I didn't really know her. I have no connection to her. But you—it could've been you, and I can't handle that."

He doesn't know how to reply, and after a long silence Serena asks, "How long would it be?"

"A few days."

"When would you go?"

"Tomorrow—"

"Tomorrow!" She whirls toward him. "Were you waiting until the last minute to tell me?" She stops herself, takes a deep breath, then, after a second, rubs her jaw with both hands. Her expression is tired, and she looks up at him. She says, "Have you had dinner yet?"

"No. I was waiting for you."

"Shall we order in some Chinese?"

Allen is unnerved by this change in tone, and asks, "Are we okay?"

She shakes her head, and says, "Of course not."

"I have to do this."

"Are you even thinking for a second what this means for me? How I feel?"

"I understand, but this . . . but . . . I need to finish this."

She says, "You're putting me in an unfair position. You want me to let you risk yourself. I can't just do that without reservation."

"But I have to do this."

"You've said that."

"You know I love you," he says. "You know that, right?"

"I know that. But you're not doing a good job of demonstrating it." She stands, gathers up her bag and blazer, and walks toward the bedroom.

He says, "What if you were me? Jesus, this is my fault. I've got to fix this. I've got to finish my job."

She stops in the hallway, and is about to turn around to say something else, but seems to reconsider, moves a few feet, then turns around again. She says, "If I were you, I would never have taken the case in the first place, because I know how hard it would be for my girlfriend." She continues into the room and closes the door behind her.

He thinks, I'm losing her.

Twenty

Allen became good at shadowing strangers, and throughout high school as he followed random BART passengers around the city, he developed an intuitive sense of how far back to lag, how long he could lose sight of the person before reestablishing the contact. He sensed unseen distances, the invisible tether connecting them being stretched around corners. He knew he was conspicuous—a bulky Asian teen lurking around BART stations—so he had to finesse a tail. He had to be ghostly.

He was never caught or even noticed, though a few times he had lost tails in waiting cars or cabs, and he deemed the shadowing successful if he found out something unusual. It was the sense of possibilities that intrigued him, the imagined lives and unknown destinations. He began reading people quickly, recognizing tourists or college students, bored retirees or harried office workers heading home. He tended to follow people who didn't fit into those categories.

He once followed a kid younger than him; the unusual sight of a school kid also cutting school piqued Allen's interest. The kid met his father for lunch, and Allen knew immediately that the kid's parents were divorced, from the tentative and almost embarrassed way the father patted the son's shoulder. The kid shrugged to most of his father's questions. The father's face had on a strained, uneasy expression as they walked to a restaurant. What surprised Allen, and what made this a successful tail was that after lunch the father bought the kid a sweater, which the kid accepted with another shrug; but once they separated, and the kid headed back to the BART station, he threw the sweater into the garbage.

Allen was shocked at this waste, but was also fascinated by the dynamics involved. The power that this kid had was obvious. Allen couldn't stop thinking about how the kid had looked at the sweater, looked at the garbage can, shook his head, and threw the sweater away. Allen considered retrieving the gift for himself, but didn't. It was cursed.

The Block has never been to Seattle, and the city will forever be suffused with the glaring hue of guilt and sorrow. He expects rain, he expects gloom, but not this: crisp blue skies, the streets glimmering in the sun. The air is cool and smells clean. He almost wants the clichéd images of Seattle before him, the darkened and wet pavements, the hunched-over and hurrying pedestrians avoiding another shower. Instead he sees happy couples and spandex-clad joggers. Everyone seems to be smiling. This reinforces his melancholy.

Allen and Julie walk along the "Ave," a strip of stores in the university district, searching for a private mailbox service where a few of the more recent corporations in Val Pinetti's and Rick's names are supposed to be located. It's the only common address listed in the corporate records, box 118, though the corporations were dissolved. They're also planning to visit Frank and Rick's parents on Mercer Island, and are waiting for Larry to call them with any updates on the search for Sidney Olshan. Larry had to special order more corporation information because the Marin sheriff's detectives didn't go back farther than three years.

"There," Julie says. "Mail and Copies." The narrow store with copper-colored cubby boxes in the front area is next to a drugstore and an African clothing shop. The front window has stenciled across the center "5¢ Copies" and "UPS + FedEx Here!" and there's a short line at the counter in back. Allen looks around, checking up and down the street. The Ave is scattered with teens, tattooed and pierced, some panhandling, some sitting on rolled-up sleeping bags and plastic milk crates. A few skateboarders practice along a curb. Large, extended buses roar through every few minutes, the storefronts busy with young pedestrians, possibly students. Allen knows the University of Washington is a few blocks away, but doesn't quite understand the geography yet; Julie has done all the driving in the rental they picked up at Sea-Tac Airport.

He scans the area now, tense in this unfamiliar city. He couldn't bring his guns on the plane, so he feels exposed. He says, "How do you want to do this?"

Julie leads him into the store, and answers, "Let's try the direct approach."

They join the line at the counter, and Allen checks box number 118, seeing a few letters through the tiny window. The clerk, a young woman with a nose ring and dreadlocks, rings up a customer buying packing supplies. Allen finds it strange to be working with Linda's sister. He finds it strange to be working at all.

As they wait he tells Julie about his hobby of following people when he was a teen. She says, "That's creepy, Allen."

He blinks. Linda would've understood. This realization darkens his mood, and he decides not to reveal anything else to Julie. They move forward in line, and when it's their turn, Julie glances at him, signaling him to begin.

Allen introduces himself and gives the young woman his card. He says, "We're trying to locate Ms. Staunton's daughter, who was abducted by her ex-husband. We believe he might have had a mailbox here through a corporation, number 118. Is it at all possible to find out who rents this box?"

The woman glances at Julie. "We're not allowed to give out that information."

"My daughter Nora is nine years old," Julie says. "She's been gone for almost two months. I really, really need your help."

The woman looks around, and says, "My manager is on a lunch break. . . ."

Allen asks, "To get a box, you fill out a form. Do you have to give an address?"

"Yes," she says. "In case we have to close the box."

"Is it on file?"

She looks behind her at a cabinet. "Yes. They're all on file."

Allen sees that they almost have her. He says, "Are you a student?"

"A senior at U.W."

"Let us help you buy some textbooks." He nods to Julie, who reaches into her pocketbook. He says to the woman, "You're probably working here to help with tuition."

"Yes," she says, eyeing Julie, who pulls out a hundred-dollar bill. She glances again around the store, which has emptied out. Julie places the bill on the counter. The woman takes it, and says, "I'm going into the back room for a minute. The files are listed by name, but see that clipboard?" She nods to the clipboard hanging on a string by the mailboxes.

Julie says, "Yes."

"That's a list of the box numbers and the owners." She walks through a narrow doorway.

Allen says to Julie, "Go behind the boxes and take the mail in 118. I'll get the file."

As Julie hurries behind the wall with the mailboxes, Allen checks the clipboard and sees a grid with the numbers in the left column. He flips the pages until he gets to 118, and finds the listing, "Denhold Corporation." He then hurries to the file cabinet, pulls out the "A-F" cabinet, and quickly fingers his way through the "D"s. He pulls out the Denhold sheet of paper, folds it, and shoves it into his pocket. Julie hurries out from behind the boxes, nodding to him. They leave.

Outside, as they move down the street, Allen skims the form while Julie rips open the mail. He's surprised to see "Sydney Olshan" spelled with a "y," and a second listing for an additional mailbox key is "Douglas Staunton."

Allen points to this. "Who's this again?"

Julie says, "Frank and Rick's father. What the hell is he doing on this thing?"

"There's an address here: Twenty-fourth Avenue. If this is legit, I can run his name and this address for a background report. Is this the parents' address?"

"No. They live on Mercer Island." She holds up the opened letters. "Junk mail, addressed to the occupant."

"Let me call Larry to have him run a check."

"I made reservations at a nearby motel. We should go and regroup."

Allen wonders if it's because she and Linda are sisters or if it's just his imagination, but her choice of words, the intonation, is exactly like Linda's.

They drive to the Portage Bay Inn, a small gray-shingled motel two blocks from the University Bridge, and Julie registers them into two separate but adjacent rooms. She tells him to come over in thirty minutes, giving her time to shower and change. He immediately calls Larry from his room with the new information, asking him to run a background check and a general name, telephone, and address verification on Sydney Olshan with a "y." He then walks to the window facing the marina, the crowded docks with small yachts and sailboats obscuring any kind of calming waterfront vista. Boat repair shops run adjacent to the motel, and Allen watches someone backing up a dinghy on a trailer, angling it into Complete Boat Repair's hangar.

He calls Serena and leaves a message, telling her he arrived safely and gives her the motel phone number. He waits, hoping she picks up, then says, "I miss you. I'm really sorry about . . . about all this." He hangs up and suppresses the fear that he's screwing up this relationship. He paces for a few minutes, splashes water on his face, then lies on the bed, glad to be working but still feeling the heavy pull of mourning.

He doesn't believe in an afterlife, so Linda is absolutely gone. He would like to believe in something more, but he can't. He's a pragmatist. He's a rationalist. His view of the world is that of a case file: he needs evidence, lists, summaries. He can't have unsupported conjectures and hopes and comforts. The narrative must move from fact to fact.

And the fact is that Linda is gone.

Larry calls back, and says, "Can you give me the address again? You said Twenty-fourth?"

Allen reads off the address, then asks, "Why?"

"Thought so. No such house number for that street. And the zip is wrong, according to the U.S. Postal site. I think Olshan just put down anything."

"All right. It sounded too easy. What about a general search?"

"Yeah. A couple hits in Seattle. Got a pen?" Larry says, then reads off two phone numbers and addresses for two Sydney Olshans. "But these are the listed ones, and unless we get more header info—"

"I know, unlisted will be impossible to get. Okay, thanks."

"You doing all right? That woman driving you nuts?"

"Julie? She's fine."

"What's next?"

Allen glances at his notes. "Check these two listings, also look up the parents."

"Be careful, B."

Allen says he will be, and hangs up. He calls the two phone numbers, asking for Sydney Olshan, and when Olshan comes on, Allen asks if this is the Mr. Olshan of the Denhold Corporation. Both callers have never heard of it, and Allen decides not to push this end of the inquiry just yet. He doubts the Olshan he's searching for would be listed anyway, especially if he was careful enough not to put a real contact address linked to the mailbox.

Julie knocks on his door, and he lets her in, telling her what just happened. She says, "Okay, so the parents, especially Doug, will be first. I just checked, and they seem to be home. I called and pretended to be a wrong number. You ready?"

"For them? Why?"

"They're not terribly pleasant."

Allen says, "No one in that family seems to be."

Mercer Island sits in Lake Washington, east of Seattle. As soon as they leave the narrow bridge from the city, the late-afternoon sun reflecting off the rippling water, and they wind into the upscale neighborhoods, he feels a strange familiarity with this area; it reminds him of parts of the South Bay, particularly the more expensive areas of Silicon Valley. Large two- and three-story sprawling houses with lush yards and gardens are spread along curvy blocks, shiny Mercedes and Lexus sedans glittering in the driveways. Oversized SUVs crowd the intersections. He notices bright white fences, seemingly freshly painted, encircling many of the homes. Allen struggles with the map, and Julie makes a few wrong turns based on his bad directions until she finally pulls over and looks at the map herself. She says, "We're heading down here," and points to the southern tip. "We'll take Mercer Way and then Seventy-second, then to their street. Okay?"

"Got it."

Julie says, "I didn't believe Linda when she told me you were totally clueless about directions."

"She said she wanted to buy me a GPS system for my car, my crappy Volvo." He smiles, but then they fall silent. He stops looking at street signs, no longer paying attention to the houses and small parks, and instead closes his eyes and remembers the way Linda used to laugh about not only his geographic confusion, but about his careful driving.

He opens his eyes and sees Julie watching him. She turns back to the road, and says, "Allen, maybe you should wait in the car."

"No. I'm fine."

"I know how you feel, but I can't stop thinking about Nora."

"I'm fine. Really."

"We're almost there. Look for 303."

Allen peers out at the houses, counting the numbers as they near the address, then he sees a white Colonial with dark brown shutters; a bright copper "303" sign hangs on a redwood gate. Julie notices it as well, and she parks in front. Julie climbs out of the car and flips open a spiral notepad, startling Allen—it's the same kind of pad Linda used. He stares. Julie follows his gaze, and says, "Oh. She bought a bunch and gave me some."

They enter the yard and ring the front doorbell. Allen thinks, Focus.

After a moment a woman's voice says, "Who is it?"

"It's me, Julie. Marilyn, I want to talk to you and Doug."

"Julie! What are you doing here?" Marilyn says, her voice tightening.

"Open the door, please."

A pause, then the sound of a security chain rattling, and Marilyn cracks open the door a few inches. "Julie," she says. "You shouldn't have come."

From this angle Allen only sees a sharp nose and freckled, aged skin. He steps back, and Marilyn turns sharply toward him, a head jerk reminding him of a startled bird. She opens the door farther, and asks, "Who are you?"

"I'm a friend of the family helping out," he answers, getting a better look: Marilyn is a tiny woman, no more than five feet tall, with thinning pale hair and nervous, frightened eyes. She blinks rapidly, continuously, and looks Allen up and down.

"A cop?" she says. "Oh, no, you two have to go before Doug comes back."

Julie leans into the door, keeping it open. "He's not here? He answered the phone earlier."

"He went to the store. He'll be back soon. Please go."

Julie pushes the door farther, forcing Marilyn back, and says, "It's no longer just about the divorce. Frank and Rick are involved in a murder now."

Marilyn's eyes widen. "Murder? I don't know what you're talking about."

"My sister Linda. They killed her."

As her face becomes even paler, she says, "I don't know what . . . I can't get involved. . . ."

"You have no choice," Julie says, stepping in. "Your sons are wanted by the police, but all I want is Nora."

"Please!" Marilyn's fluttering hands go to her throat. "Please, I can't get—"

Julie grabs her arm. "Have you seen Nora? Do you know where she is?"

Allen sees Marilyn shrinking, and she tries to pull away, but can't. She yells, "You're hurting me!" Allen touches Julie's shoulder, and she lets go of Marilyn. He remembers Linda's telling him that this woman had a nervous breakdown when Frank and Rick were young, and Allen can see why; she's like a hummingbird, easily crushed. Marilyn says, "I swear I don't know where Nora is."

He says, "Do you know Sydney Olshan?"

Marilyn turns to him, confused. "Who?"

"Sydney Olshan. He's linked to your husband."

Her eyes momentarily register the name, but then she shakes her head, backing away.

"She's lying," Julie says.

"I know," he says, still watching Marilyn. "Tell us, Mrs. Staunton, and we'll go."

"I don't understand. I haven't seen Syd in years."

"Who is he?" Julie asks. "A friend of Doug's?"

"Of Frank's. They grew up together, but I don't understand. . . ."

"Where is Frank?" Julie pleads. "You must know. He always told you everything. I have to see Nora."

Her eyes pained, Marilyn says, "He hasn't contacted us since he disappeared with Nora. He's trying to protect us."

A voice from the front doorway says, "What the hell is going on here?"

They all turn. Allen sees a huge balding man with gray stubble along his cheeks. His bearlike body fills the doorway, a bag of groceries in one arm, and he glares at Marilyn. "Who are these two?"

"Doug," Julie says. "It's me."

He turns toward her, then after a small jolt says, "You! Get the hell out of my house!"

"Wait, Doug, we need to talk—"

"You haven't said anything, have you?" he demands of his wife. "You better not have opened your mouth—"

"I didn't say anything!"

Doug lowers the bag of groceries to the floor, and lumbers his way in, moving toward Julie, saying, "Get the fuck out or I'm calling the goddamn police."

Allen steps in between them, holding his hands up. "Whoa. Hold on. There's no need for that."

"Go for it," Julie says to Doug. "I *dare* you to touch me."

Allen says calmly, "Yes, maybe you should call the police. They'll be interested to know you probably were in contact with two murder suspects."

"Murder?" Doug stops. "What the hell are you talking about? Frank just wants this nutcase out of his life."

Marilyn says, "They told me that Frank and Rickie killed her sister." She glances at Julie, then asks her husband, "That's not true, is it?"

"Of course not," Doug says. "They didn't kill anyone."

Allen isn't sure if Doug is lying. He says, "Ten days ago Linda, Julie's sister, was shot and killed by a man named Rawlingson, working under

Rick's orders. Rick and Frank's drug-smuggling and money-laundering scheme has fallen apart. The FBI and DEA are now dismantling the operation. It's only a matter of time before they find everyone who's involved." Allen sees something flicker across Doug's face, uncertainty perhaps, and he adds, "If you received any money in any way from them, you're certain to be implicated. If you don't believe me, just call the police. Rick is wanted."

Doug glances at Julie, then at Marilyn, who whispers to him, "This can't be true, can it?"

"They shouldn't have killed Linda," Allen says.

"You remember my sister," Julie says to Marilyn. "She was at Carla Feinstein's wedding. Rick had her killed."

Doug's cheeks are flushed, his breath labored as he considers this. He glances at his wife. Marilyn says, "Did you know this?"

"I don't believe it. They're trying to scare us."

Julie flips open her cell phone and presses two buttons. She holds up the screen to Doug and says, "That's the San Francisco FBI office number. Press SEND and ask for Agent Ed Washington, who's handling the case. He'll confirm everything."

Doug stares at the phone, but doesn't take it.

"Rick was here, wasn't he?" Allen says. "You know he's in trouble."

Doug turns to his wife. "What should we do?"

"Tell us how to find him," Allen says.

"Tell us how to find Nora," Julie says.

After a long pause, Doug says to Marilyn, "I don't know what to do."

Twenty-one

Everyone is quiet as they wait for Doug, who sits down on the sofa, the frame cracking, and lets out a long, slow breath. A car with a loud muffler drives by. Allen glances out the window, checking their car. Marilyn asks her husband what's going on, and Doug squeezes the bridge of his nose. His hands are blotchy. He says to his wife, "Rickie came by a couple of nights ago, but I didn't tell you."

"What? Why not?"

"He's in trouble, but I didn't know why." He turns to Julie. "He didn't say anything about your sister."

"Why would he?" Allen says. "Why would he admit to murder?"

Doug says, "I'm just telling you what happened."

"Where is he now?" Julie asks.

Doug slumps forward. "He said he was going into hiding. I didn't want to know where."

"What did he say? What did he want?"

"Just that he and Frank were going to hide out for a while, that we wouldn't hear from them."

"Why are you telling us this?" Julie asks.

Doug turns to his wife. "He said he would use Nora if he had to."

"What?" Marilyn says. "A child?"

"To stop them." Doug motions to Julie and Allen.

"Frank would never allow that," Julie says.

"It's not up to Frank. He's in too deep. Rickie is calling the shots."

Julie leans back against the wall, her body deflating. "You haven't heard from him?"

Doug says, "Not from Frank." He glances at his wife, who agrees with him with a nod.

"We don't like this any more than you," Doug says. "Kidnapping? Hiding from the law? Depriving our grandkid of a normal life?"

"It's your sons' doing," Julie says.

"You shouldn't have pressed the money issue," Doug says. "That scared them. That brought Rickie into all this."

Allen sees Julie's angry expression and cuts in, "Just tell us where to find them. What about this Syd Olshan? Why were you listed on his mailbox form?"

"I was?" Doug asks. "Oh, that was last year. Rickie asked me to check the mail once in a while."

"Where is Olshan now?"

"He lives in Wallingford."

Julie jumps up. "He's there now? He's still in Seattle?"

"Yes, but Rickie and Frank wouldn't be stupid enough to stay there."

"Do you have an address?" Allen asks.

"No, just in Wallingford. Rick mentioned it once."

"But where in that area?" Allen asks. "A street? A marker, anything?"

Doug says, "I don't know. I didn't want to know."

Marilyn says, "All we want is things back to normal."

"How are you involved?" Allen asks.

Doug sighs. "He bought us this house."

"Rick did?" Julie asks. "Rick bought you this?"

Doug and Marilyn nod.

"Didn't you find it suspicious that he could afford that?"

"We were living in a tiny apartment in Renton. How could we turn down this place?"

Allen asks, "Did you know about the drug smuggling, the money laundering?"

Doug shakes his head. "Not except the dealing he did a few years back, but Rickie was always headed for trouble. I'm surprised he hasn't been caught yet."

Marilyn says quietly, "Not Frank. Frank would never get involved in murder."

Julie snaps to attention at Frank's name. "You have no idea where Nora is?"

They shake their heads.

Doug says to Julie, "I've never liked you, but I don't want any harm coming to Nora. She's our only granddaughter."

"Tell that to your asshole sons," Julie snaps, and heads for the front door.

They return to their motel to regroup, but Julie seems sapped of energy. She turns on her laptop and checks her e-mail, then lowers her head into her arms, resting on the desk. Allen asks if she has eaten anything today, and she says, her voice muffled, "The airplane food."

"This morning? Jeez. I think I saw a minimart at a gas station a few blocks away. Let me buy us something."

She shrugs.

"Why don't you try some phone-listing searches for Olshan?" he says. "Use Wallingford as a reference, wherever that is."

"It's a neighborhood west of here."

"Can you do that? I'll be right back."

"All right," she says into her arms.

Allen checks the phone in his room but finds no messages. He leaves the motel and walks along Northlake Way, occasionally stopping at one of the marinas to stare at the sailboats and yachts bobbing up and down in rhythm. He has never been in a boat, not even a dinghy or canoe, and suddenly wants to go on some kind of ocean vacation, a cruise perhaps. He and Serena can escape all this by going to sea. This idea takes hold, and he imagines Serena and him lounging on a sunny deck.

He wanders a few more blocks, but can no longer find the gas station. He looks around. Which way is the motel? He backtracks, wondering why Serena hasn't called him back. Perhaps she didn't receive his message. He hopes she's not angry with him. He can never really tell with her. She has that enigmatic, cool expression that bewilders him. She's so unlike Linda, who was never reticent about her feelings.

Allen stops. He shakes off an image of Linda on the ground, trying to raise her head but unable to. He looks down at the dirty sidewalk, and for a moment can picture her lying there, her eyes confused. He quickly walks on, finding a small bench with a view of the water, and sits for a moment, collecting himself. He knows this is normal, but he doesn't want to keep thinking about her every time he's alone. He feels as if he can't ever quite get a deep enough breath.

How could she be dead?

He remembers a photo of her as an overweight teen, one he found by accident at her mother's condo. It was a family shot, with her brother Hector, Julie, and her parents, and Linda's first reaction when he told her about it was "Damn, I thought I burned all those."

He smiles now. She hated any evidence of what she called her "fat teen years."

Allen stands up, tries to inhale, and says aloud, "Goddamn all this."

And slowly, as he takes in more air, he feels a slow-burning anger filling him. This didn't have to happen. This was Rick's fault.

A car down the street honks. Allen turns. It's Julie, and she pulls up to the curb, opens her window, and says, "There you are. I've been driving around looking for you. The gas station and minimart are in the other direction, Allen."

"Oh. I thought so," he says.

"Get in. I found Syd's address."

Once, when he and Linda were in bed, long before their relationship had deteriorated, when they were still maybe a little giddy in love, they had discovered that Linda's family had visited San Jose around the time when Allen was living there with his father. They imagined what it would've been like had the two of them met as children. Would they have been friends? Would they have had anything in common?

Linda told him that she was just beginning to get overweight about that time, and because it was before her stepfather and Julie came to live with them, she and Hector were a little wild. "I would've picked on you," she said. "I would've probably been a bully."

"To me?"

"To you. You were a small kid, right?"

"Skinny. Not that small."

"Still, I would've pushed you around."

Allen didn't believe it, and still doesn't. He asks Julie now, while they drive into Wallingford, what she remembers about Linda when they first met.

Julie shakes her head. "I don't want to talk about it."

"I do."

"Well, too bad."

"Please, just tell me that, and I won't ask again."

Julie says, "Allen, why are you doing this? You're making it worse."

"By ignoring it? By pretending it didn't happen?"

She shakes head, but after a few minutes says quietly, "She was chubby, Hector was a little monster, and their mother looked like she was going to collapse from exhaustion. Linda was really wary, really careful, until she and I realized we were close in age and both suspicious of everyone. Her dad had abandoned them, my mom had left us."

"I didn't know that. Your mom left?"

"She was young, stupid, and both of them knew she couldn't take care of me."

"Is she still alive?"

"She's in Vegas. I haven't spoken to her in ten years. Marianne is my mother."

"So what was Linda like?"

She sighs. "Kind of tough, but you could see she was scared by all the changes, by us. She really tried to look out for her brother."

"How'd you know she was scared—"

"Can we not do this? Please? She told me you overanalyze everything, but give it a rest, okay?"

Allen, stung, says, "All right. Tell me how you found this address."

"Simple," she answers. "Telephone search online. Then I called the number and pretended to sell long-distance. He's home."

"Wait. This is a listed phone number?"

"Apparently."

"Larry gave us two numbers, both of Sydney Olshan—"

"Those weren't in Wallingford."

"Where were they?"

"West Seattle and Beacon Hill, south of Wallingford," she says. "Look, I know he's your friend, but he's a little lazy. I've seen it. He cuts corners."

"Maybe he checked an older edition. That happens."

"Maybe," she says dubiously.

"I'll talk to him."

She says, "I don't care. That's why I asked you along. I know you're thorough."

Missing a listed phone number can happen—there are usually different editions floating out there, with updates staggered depending on the vendor—and he knows Julie isn't being fair.

Allen turns his attention to the neighborhood. Wallingford doesn't look that much different from the U district except for wider streets, more upscale stores, and a Starbucks every few blocks. He notices young children with their mothers at the small complexes, a handful of clothing and gift shops crowded into small buildings. Julie drives aggressively around slower cars, and Allen asks how she knows where to go.

"I studied the maps, plus I know the area. I used to come up to Seattle on business before I was married." She turns off the main strip and begins heading up into a quiet residential neighborhood.

Allen says, "It's customary for visiting PIs to check in with the local police."

"You can do that later, can't you?"

"I'm supposed to before I do any work, like visit a potential suspect." Allen is supposed to register any weapons as well, but he's defenseless at the moment. He says, "We have to be careful. We don't know how much this guy's involved."

"We will," she says, making a few more turns. "Almost there."

He goes over what they know about Olshan, that Rick and Pinetti referred to him while talking on the phone, that his name appears on Pinetti's shell corporations, and that he's an old friend of Frank's. Not a whole lot to go on, Allen thinks.

When Julie pulls up in front of a two-story house, the front yard overgrown and covered with weeds and crabgrass, Allen feels unprepared. He's on unfamiliar ground, and wishes he had more background on this guy. Does he have a record? Could he be dangerous? He says, "At the first sign of trouble, we get the hell out of here."

"All right, but I'd like to get something, anything." She climbs out, and Allen follows her up the brick steps. The house is half-buried in a small hill, the garage and first floor shrouded behind overgrown hedges, the second-floor lights bright and uncurtained. He checks the street and driveway. There's a car in the garage, and a Honda parked by the curb. He doesn't see any neighbors around, and finds this odd. It's past five in the afternoon, and he expects people to be returning home from work around now.

Julie rings the doorbell, and Allen begins to tense up, the unkempt yard here an anomaly among the other houses, where the lawns are neatly cut, small vegetable and flower gardens lining the sides of most of the yards. Allen says, "Rick's father might have warned this guy."

Julie rings the bell again, and they hear footsteps inside. Through the closed door a man says, "Who is it?"

"Syd?" Allen asks. "Syd Olshan?"   .

"Who is it?"

"Can we talk? I'm Allen Choice, and I'm with Julie Staunton."

There's a pause. "Who?"

"Syd," Julie says. "It's about my daughter, Nora. Frank's daughter."

The door opens, and a thin man with scraggly chin hairs and oily skin looks out. "Who are you?"

Allen immediately sees that he's high on something, his eyes unfocused. "Syd, can we come in and talk?"

"About what?"

Allen says, "Thanks, we appreciate it." He pushes the door open, and Syd steps back, confused.

"Uh, wait," he says, as Julie follows.

Allen looks around quickly, prepared for an ambush, but there's no one else in the living room. The furniture is old and torn, the carpets stained. He sees syringes on the coffee table near the fireplace. An addict. He meets Julie's eyes, and she nods.

"You're Syd Olshan, right?" Allen asks.

He says, "Yeah."

"Friends with Rick and Frank Staunton?"

"Who are you again?"

"This is Frank's ex-wife. I'm a private investigator."

Syd's eyes slowly adjust on Allen, and he says, "Investigator?"

"We're trying to find Frank and his daughter Nora. Have you seen Frank or Rick recently?"

Syd shakes his head slowly, apparently thinking about this, then suddenly bolts. He leaps over a small chair and runs across the living room so fast that Allen is momentarily confused. Then he runs after him as Syd goes through the kitchen and out the back door. Allen yells to Julie, "Circle around outside!"

Allen flies out the back, jumping off a short wooden deck, and sees Syd flash around the house to the side. Allen curses because the man is fast, and Allen is wearing his dress shoes. He slips along the grass and hurries around the corner, tearing his shirt on thorny bushes. There's a loud yell and the sound of something breaking, and Allen appears in the front to the sight of Syd stumbling on the ground and holding his head. Julie has part of a flowerpot in her hands. She then kicks him in the ribs, and yells, "Where is she? Where is my daughter?"

Syd lurches toward the street, regaining his balance, and Allen tackles him to the sidewalk, Allen's cell phone flying out of his jacket and cracking on the street. He grabs Syd's thin arm and twists it back easily, making Syd cry out and stop struggling. Allen flips him onto his stomach and presses his arm farther up his back, feeling the joint strain. Syd yelps in pain, and says, "You guys are fucking dead!"

Allen pulls him up and drags him to the house. Julie retrieves Allen's phone, then opens the front door for them. Allen throws him onto the ground, and says, "When were they here?"

"Don't know nothing," Syd says, cradling his arm. He then touches his forehead and sees the blood. "Shit."

"You knew Frank and Rick as kids, right?"

He looks up, surprised.

Allen says, "Their parents told us."

"I don't know nothing," he says.

Julie asks, "Have you seen my daughter, Nora?"

He doesn't answer, rubbing his elbow.

She asks, "Do you know where Frank or Rick are?"

He says, "Go fuck yourself."

Julie turns to Allen, and says, "Do something!"

"I was going to give him another chance."

"Don't bother."

Allen walks over to Syd, who sits up, one arm hugging his body, the other hand splayed on the ground. With his shoe heel Allen stamps down on Syd's hand, directly on the knuckles, and feels them crush under his weight. Syd screams and rolls over. "Motherfucking chink! You fucking—"

Allen kicks him in the face, a low roundhouse that connects cleanly into his mouth and flips him back. He writhes on the floor, flopping in pain.

Julie yells, "Do it again!"

Allen stops, and says to her, "Go upstairs and see what you can find. Evidence. A trail. Anything."

Julie nods and hurries upstairs. Allen says to him, "A close friend was recently killed by people working for Rick. I could care less if you live or die."

"My fucking teeth," he whimpers, his mouth now bloody. "You knocked out one of my teeth."

Allen grabs his neck and forces his face into the carpet. "When did you last see Rick?"

"He'll kill me."

"He won't know you told me."

"I can't."

Allen remembers how Linda tried speaking, but was too weak. He remembers how she said she was really sorry about this, and he isn't sure if she meant for getting shot or for bringing him into the case. Allen pushes Syd's face harder into the carpet, then punches him in the kidney twice.

"Oh, fuck," Syd says, and begins crying. "Fucking stop, man."

"When was Rick here?"

"He wasn't here! I swear! I met him downtown."

"When?"

"Yesterday. Just for a minute! I don't know anything, man."

"Where?"

"Westlake Mall."

Julie runs back downstairs and says, "Found this stuff." She holds up a bag of powder and a handgun, a nine-millimeter. Allen takes the gun, a Smith & Wesson. He checks the magazine. Fully loaded. She says, "It's a pigsty up there, but I didn't see anything that could help us find them."

Allen raises the gun, and tells Syd, "Put your good hand out on the floor."

"I'm telling you! I saw him for like two minutes at the mall!" He wipes his face with his sleeve.

Julie says, "Frank?"

"Rick," Syd says.

"What did he want?" Allen asks.

"He needed some quick cash. Thirty grand. He told me he was hiding out."

"Where?" Allen asks.

"Didn't say. I swear."

"Where was Frank?" Julie asks. "Did Rick mention Nora?"

"No. I haven't seen Frank in a year. I always deal with Rick."

"Deal with him how?" Allen asks.

Syd pauses. Allen aims the automatic at him.

"I help him clean up money," Syd says.

"How?"

Syd looks away, and Allen backhands him with the gun, sending him sprawling on the floor and covering his face. Allen says, "How?"

He breathes into his hands, and says without looking up, "He buys shitty houses up here, and I pay contractors and builders to fix them up. Then he sells them and buys more."

Allen says, "And you pay the contractors in cash?"

He nods.

"He lets a junkie handle this?"

"I'm not a junkie."

Allen grabs his arm and exposes the needle tracks. He drops the arm in disgust. "How do you contact him?"

"I call him in San Francisco, but he's running now."

"What did he say when you met yesterday?"

"Nothing, man. He just called and said bring whatever cash I had, and when I met him he told me he was going to hide out."

Julie says, "How are you supposed to contact him?"

"I'm not."

Allen turns and kicks the coffee table, upending it and breaking one of the legs. "I can't believe this shit!" he says.

"What about Val Pinetti?" Julie asks. "Have you talked with him?"

Syd turns to her, hesitates, then says, "Yeah. He's the one who tells me how to handle the money."

Allen whirls toward him. "Where is he?"

"I don't know."

"When was the last time you talked to him?"

"Few days ago. He called and told me to stop using the credit cards."

"Why?"

"I don't know. Something about everything being too hot now."

"Where did he call from?"

Syd shakes his head. "I don't know."

"How do you contact him?"

He shrugs. Allen grabs the back of his neck and forces his head against the floor. He says, "How do you contact him?"

"Please . . . man . . . stop." He tries to turn his head, but Allen tightens his grip.

Allen asks slowly, "How do I find Val Pinetti?"

"I already told you too much, man."

Allen grabs Syd's bad hand and begins squeezing it. Syd screams.

Allen says, "My friend was killed by your boss. I'll ask you one more time: How do I find Val Pinetti?"

"He's in Bellevue," Syd says weakly. "He's at one of the houses we're fixing up, but just until tomorrow morning. Then they're all taking off."

"Rick is there?" Allen asks.

"No, but they're going to meet somewhere soon."

"Frank, too?" Julie asks.

"I don't know. I swear."

Allen glances at Julie. She says to him, "Tell us the address."

"He's going to fucking kill me."

Allen touches Syd's hand lightly, and says, "I'm not going to ask you again."

Twenty-two

They tie Syd up and lock him in a closet, since they are worried about his tipping off Pinetti, and they lie to him that they'll let him go after they find Rick. Allen intends to tell the police about Syd as soon as the address is confirmed. Syd moans into a gag. Allen looks down at him without remorse. He wants everyone connected to Linda's death to suffer. He finds himself numb to anything but revenge.

In the car he mentions the possibility of bringing in the police to handle Pinetti. "He's wanted in California, so the Seattle police will apprehend him."

"What if he can lead us to Nora? Can we trust the police for that?" she asks.

"I think so. They'll definitely want Frank and Rick—"

"No. Not until I see Nora, then we'll call the police. I don't want to jeopardize anything by bringing them in yet. You know what Doug said."

"That they'll use Nora?"

"Do you doubt it for a second?"

Allen says he doesn't. For a guilty moment he realizes he hasn't been thinking about Nora at all, but about Linda, about getting Rick. The priority should be finding Nora. He says, "What about the custody case?"

Julie laughs harshly. "Frank is going to jail. He's now linked to drug dealers and my sister's murder. There won't be any custody problems."

Allen's not sure if Pinetti will lead to anything, especially Nora, but he keeps quiet. He finds himself gratified that Syd is stuffed in a closet, in pain, that someone is suffering a little for Linda.

Julie drives over a long, floating bridge into Bellevue, and Allen asks if she needs for him to check the map again.

"No, I memorized the directions," she says. "He's right near the intersection of the 405 and 520."

"We just wait and watch."

"If Nora's not there, yes."

"Of course," he says. He remembers what Syd said about the money-laundering scheme, and asks, "If you sell a house, doesn't that get recorded by the IRS?"

"But it's legitimate. It's washed clean. The plan is perfect. You get a mortgage and put a down payment on a run-down house. You pay cash to contractors to renovate and rebuild—they even prefer cash because they can pocket it without taxes. Plus they can use nonunion illegals for the work. Then you sell the place, pay back the bank, pocket the difference, and the money is clean. You do it again, this time with a bigger house. Maybe you don't even need a mortgage. You pay for the house up front, and sell it for even more profit. If it's your residence, there's no capital gains tax. It's perfect."

"And you wire the money overseas, out of reach."

"On paper Pinetti just looks like a smart real estate investor, buying a house and selling it later for much more, but he launders hundreds of thousands of dollars. When Frank and I added a room to our Walnut Creek house, it cost us almost ninety grand. One room."

"Did he pay cash?"

She says, "Damn. I don't know. He took care of it himself."

"It's possible that a lot of your money might be—"

"I know, I know," she says. "But now it makes perfect sense why Frank panicked."

"You were getting lawyers to dig into his finances."

She sighs. "What a goddamn mess."

Allen sees how simple and straightforward his life with Serena is, and he misses her even more.

He checks the nine-millimeter and shoves it back into his waistband. His cell phone is completely broken; he throws it on the car floor. Memories of Linda crowd out his feelings for Serena. He feels desolate again and stares out the window. Allen thinks, It's so easy to kill someone. And it's so easy to die.

The ride into Bellevue takes longer than Julie thought, and they have trouble finding the house, the dark side streets off 116th Avenue difficult to navigate. Allen marks cars around him and makes sure they're not being followed. Julie says, "Help me read the house numbers. We're looking for 115."

Allen turns and peers along the street. "There's 103, and 105."

"Good." She speeds up.

"No, take it slow. You don't want to do anything out of the ordinary. Pass the house, then circle around. We should park at least three or four houses away, out of a line of sight."

She slows the car, nodding.

Allen notices her tense expression, her jawline rigid, but doesn't say anything. He sees the houses on this side street—narrow two-story clapboards and small ranch-styles—look well kept, though the proximity to the freeways might make the noise and traffic hard on residents. He wonders if Rick chooses certain kinds of houses for the money-laundering scheme.

Julie says, "We're passing it. It's this small one."

"The lights are on," he says, as they drive by the one-story ranch with a long, sloping roof. He sees a Jaguar in the driveway. "But only one car."

"How should we do this?"

"Circle and park. I'll go on foot and take a look. You'll watch everything outside."

"Jesus. What if Nora's there?"

"I'll disable their car, and we call the police."

"If she's not there?"

"We can wait, follow him to see where he goes."

"Oh my God. This might actually lead to her."

"Calm down. We have to be careful about this."

She nods quickly. She turns on a street angled diagonally from the one they're on, and makes a long loop back around. Allen glances back, looking around. Allen says to Julie, "Keep farther away. The street's too quiet."

Julie parks the car at the curb, about two hundred yards away from the target house. Except for the noise from the freeway above, there is nothing else stirring.

Allen says to Julie, "All right. You keep watch for any activity. I'll be out of sight and taking a look."

"What if someone comes?"

"I'll hear them. You just try to see who it is. Take down license plate numbers, including that Jag."

"Good point. If you see Nora, come back here right away. Okay?"

"Okay." He leaves the car and walks down the street, his heart thumping, his hands sweating. He thinks of Linda, and the anticipation of revenge energizes and frightens him. Some of Julie's hope infects his thoughts; he wonders if Nora is here, if everyone is here and all it takes is a call to the police. Then he can go home to Serena. Then he can rest.

Pinetti's windows are lit up, and Allen hurries quietly along the side of the house, trying to find an accessible window, but the thick and thorny shrubs block his way. He moves silently around to the back, which has been paved over with concrete and brick, and eases up the steps to the back door. There are sheer curtains covering the glass panes on the door, but Allen can still see inside into the darkened kitchen. The adjacent dining room is lit up, someone is moving back and forth across the entryway. Then a man comes into view, talking into a cell phone. Allen moves slowly away, and the kitchen light blinks on. This must be Pinetti, and Allen peers though the corner of a pane, frying to get a better look. Pinetti is pulling a beer out of the refrigerator. He's a tall, heavyset man in khaki pants and a red dress shirt that contrasts with his pale blond hair. As he opens the bottle, his head angled against his shoulder to free his hands, he says into the phone, "I hear you, but you're not getting it. We've got to suspend everything. We cut our losses and run. Rawlingson won't talk, won't deal. He knows he'll die in jail if he does."

Allen tenses. Pinetti's been in contact with Rawlingson?

Pinetti scratches his head, his hair cut close to the scalp. His flabby cheeks are shiny with perspiration. He says, "No. I'm packing, and we're taking off around midnight. We'll be at a friend's summer place. My cell might not work down there, so I'll e-mail you the phone number when I turn everything back on."

He nods, then says, "All right. Just lie low." He hangs up, finishes the beer, and returns to the dining room, where Allen sees him moving a small box into a hallway. Allen continues watching, hoping to see more people, but there isn't anyone else. He circles the house, and in the front corner finds an entry through the bushes. He climbs up to the window and peers in. Two suitcases, a duffel bag, and a few small boxes are lined up near the front door. There's no furniture except for an air mattress. The walls are bare.

Allen moves away from the window and hurries to the Jag. He uses the gun to press into the rear left taillight, cracking the red cover. Then he wedges a key into the crack, and pulls it farther apart, a small popping sound breaking into the night. He stops. He uses the key to burst the bulb inside, then walks down the street.

When he climbs back into the car with Julie she asks breathlessly, "Nora?"

"No. Just Pinetti. I heard him on the phone. He's leaving at midnight with someone else. They're going to a summer place to hide out."

She checks her watch. "A little over an hour. Should we wait?"

"I wish I had my tracking equipment. He might lead us to Nora. You sure you don't want to call the police yet?"

"Not yet. Could Nora be at the summer place?"

"He said he had to turn the phone on when he gets down there. It sounds like it's not being used yet."

"Who is he meeting here?"

Allen says he doesn't know. "And I'm not sure who he was talking to, but he mentioned Rawlingson not cutting a deal."

She says, "Damn."

Allen says, "We should follow him, but it could be a long drive. I broke his left taillight to make it easier at night to ID the car."

"What if it's across the country or something?"

"B&C has the perfect tracking system, but . . ." He pauses. "Maybe I can get Larry's Seattle PI contact up here to bring us one. We have time."

She hands him her cell phone. He calls Larry at home, waking him up, and explains the situation. Larry says, "Wait. You're sitting there right now?"

"Yeah. Can you get that PI to bring us a tracking system?"

"Shit. He's in the city. How much time?"

"An hour."

"Let me call him. I'll call you back."

"I'm on Julie's cell. Mine's busted."

They hang up. Julie says, "If they leave, we have to follow them."

"Wait until I hear from Larry. You might be able to meet with this PI to get the equipment. He's in the city. A tracking device would mean we wouldn't have to be anywhere nearby."

"What did you see inside?"

Allen describes the empty house and Pinetti's belongings. "He's probably hidden out here the past few days, maybe even with Rick."

"But no sign of Rick?"

"No," Allen says, "and no sign of Frank and Nora."

Larry calls back and warns Allen that this is going to be expensive for Julie, but he coordinates a rendezvous with Julie and the PI at her motel—a halfway point—within thirty minutes. Julie argues that she wants to stay, and Allen should go, but he says, "Can you disable the car if something comes up? Can you take Pinetti down if necessary? I stay. You go get the equipment. Leave me your phone, and I'll call the motel if there's any change. I'll call the cops at the first sign of Nora."

"I'll be fast. If the PI doesn't show up on time, I'm leaving. We can't lose them."

"If I have to, I'll disable the Jag."

She nods. Allen climbs out and moves across the street near a construction site with temporary fencing surrounding a deep long rut. Plastic pipes are stacked besides the rut, and Allen, shrouded in the darkness, crouches by a SIDEWALK CLOSED sign. He has a good view of Pinetti's house and car, but is far enough not to be seen himself.

Julie drives away. Allen sits on the ground. He rubs his arms, the air chilly. He obsessively checks his watch. The best thing to do now is unfocus and wait for any changes. He stares at the house, then prepares himself by running contingencies. If it looks like Pinetti will leave early, he'll call the motel, then kill the car. Pinetti has too many belongings to load the car in one trip, so Allen will have time to slip underneath the Jag, reach up, and pull a fuel line. If Rick arrives early, Allen might have to disable both cars. If Rick arrives at all, Allen will have to try very hard not to go in and take him. Rick is Linda's murderer, even more so than Rawlingson.

He remembers meeting Rick at the diner, and Allen wonders if the place was another method of laundering money, though the police haven't found anything yet. He needs to get Larry to find out exactly where the police are in their investigation at this point. It seems like everything has halted with Rawlingson in jail, awaiting the preliminary hearing.

Allen sees movement in the window, then one of the lights in the living room goes off. He checks his watch. Plenty of time. Pinetti is probably resting up.

He wonders if everyone blames him for Linda's death. Julie was being very careful about that, but he knew their mother Marianne, a direct woman, wouldn't be so considerate.

But it doesn't matter. He *is* to blame.

Allen wonders, When can I rest? When can I stop thinking about this?

Exhaustion fills him. He has no answers to that. He wishes he'd brought his Kierkegaard with him.

Allen hears about death all the time on the news, in his PI and security newsletters and magazines. He killed the man who was going to kill him. Life seems to have little worth, yet he can't grasp the finality of death. The absoluteness of the end. He feels Linda is just on the fringes of his vision, about to round that corner. Even though he had performed CPR and tried to stop the bleeding of her bullet wounds, even though he had seen her dying and couldn't hear her breath or feel her pulse, he had known her to survive so many close calls that something as random and sudden as this—as meaningless—just *couldn't* end her life.

Their last conversation was about how she had helped him find contacts for his job, jeopardizing her own deadlines. He felt a familiar attraction to her, but then guiltily repressed it. He wonders if on some level he had gotten careless because of this. He was still attracted to her, and he punished himself for it by missing the two men approaching, by foolishly fighting for a gun.

No. He had done what he could. He was almost certain of that.

More movement in Pinetti's house. Another light goes off, and the dining room lights suddenly fill the windows. Allen sits up. He sees Pinetti closing the blinds, the slats of lights abruptly winking off.

He misses Serena. She's the only constant in all this, and he wishes he could've spent more time with her parents; Allen never even met her father. The Yews left a few days after Linda was killed, their visit cut short at Serena's request. She still hasn't revealed to Allen the extent of their disapproval. This adds to his depression. He's infinitely resigned to all kinds of losses.

It makes sense, though, to give in to losses. It frees you for the next step.

The movement into this next step, the religious sphere, begins with a Knight of Infinite Resignation, but it's more complicated than Allen first thought. During one of his long sleepless evenings, he read that Kierkegaard separated the religious sphere into two phases. First was the infinite resignation, but then the next step involved a paradox. He used Abraham as the example; not only was Abraham filled with infinite resignation, but he was simultaneously filled with faith, believing that God would make everything all right, that he *wouldn't* have to give up his son. Abraham believed that Isaac would die, but that he wouldn't really die, and to believe in both of these at the same time made Abraham, in Kierkegaard's eyes, crazy. The final movement into the religious sphere was then this paradox of loss yet believing that the loss would be prevented, and this is why it's a leap of faith—it's beyond logic and rationality. With this leap, a Knight of Infinite Resignation becomes a Knight of Faith.

But Allen isn't convinced. He cannot embrace that deep a paradox, and madness, even "divine madness," doesn't seem like a good foundation for a belief system. He feels some glimmer of understanding, however, something embedded within these concepts that's applicable to him. He just can't finger it quite yet. He will mull it over. He will pick it apart. He's resolved to learn this, since it's the last thing he talked to Linda about.

A car pulls up to the house, and Allen freezes. It's a quarter after eleven, and Julie is probably still on her way to the U district. He can't see who's driving, but after a moment the passenger door opens, and Allen realizes with a jolt that it's Nora. She's thinner than he remembers, but he's certain it's her.

He pulls out the cell phone and calls the motel, dialing in Julie's room number at the automatic prompt. After five rings a computerized voice tells Allen to leave a message, and he says, "Julie. A car pulled up. It's Nora. I'm going to disable the cars once they go inside and call the cops. I'm positive it's Nora."

He hangs up and checks the nine-millimeter. The driver's side door opens, and he thinks he recognizes Frank, who has slimmed down since Allen had last seen him. Frank used to be apple-shaped with an oversized gut, and moved slowly, almost painfully, but now he jumps quickly out of the car, slamming the door, and hitches up his loose pants. His oversized shirt flaps around him. He's wearing a baseball cap and carries a large backpack on his shoulder. Nora waits at the side of the car, and Frank points to front door of the house. She skips up the steps and rings the doorbell. She has grown a few inches, and has that preteen willowy look, her hair in a pixie cut.

Allen almost can't believe that they are right there, fifty yards away. He dials 9-1-1 on the cell phone and tells the operator who he is, where he is, and that there's a kidnapper with his abducted victim here. "Please send the police immediately. I can't talk anymore." He hangs up and watches Pinetti open the door and shake Frank's hand. Pinetti then pats Nora on the shoulder and guides her in. Frank and Pinetti talk for a few moments, then enter the house, closing the door behind them. Allen waits a moment and hurries across the street.

Twenty-three

Although the Block is not a car buff, and changes his own oil only because he's too cheap to spend the thirty dollars for a professional job, he has learned enough about engines to diagnose quick problems. Part of the defensive driving courses he has taken in the past for his executive protection jobs included basic car maintenance and repair, necessary if his vehicle breaks down or is tampered with. So he understands cars better than the average layman, but his expertise is limited to on-the-fly assessments and repairs. And to disable a car, it's simply the reverse process of repairing one.

His choices for disabling the Jaguar and the Ford Taurus are essentially electrical or fuel-related. Fuel-related problems are fairly easy to diagnose, since it's usually a matter of following the fuel from the tank, fuel line, pump, filters, and fuel injectors or carburetors. A breakdown along these lines would take a few minutes to check and repair. However, electrical problems are more difficult to pinpoint, since there are many possible causes, and electricity can be impeded in numerous ways.

Without an ohmmeter or voltmeter, most people won't know where the problem is.

He slides underneath the Jag and feels for the engine block. He doesn't have a flashlight, so has to go by the texture of the wires and the approximate location. He's not sure, but he thinks he locates the general area of the battery housing, and strains his arm to find wires leading to the ignition coil. He's worried about electrical shock, so he pulls out his belt and threads it over a series of unknown wires, then, hoping that the Jag isn't alarmed for engine tampering, yanks the belt down and tears the wires from their terminals. Because he's not sure if he actually disconnected the ignition coil, he searches for the distributor, but can't find it. So he crawls deeper in, his chest squeezed by the chassis, and yanks out a fuel line. Gas dribbles onto the pavement.

He scuttles out before getting splashed and considers letting the air out of the tires, but decides to work on the Taurus first. As he circles the sedan, the ground clearance uneven because Frank has parked on a sloping section of the driveway, he hears the front door of the house opening, and voices floating out. Allen runs to the side, diving into the bushes, the thorns cutting his arms and back. He keeps still.

Frank is saying, "It depends on what Rick decides, but we don't have much time." Both Frank and Pinetti carry boxes, and Frank opens the trunk of the Taurus. They load it and keep the lid open. Pinetti says, "They may have gotten Nauru, but Manila is safe. And this time no fuckhead clerk will give out goddamn leads."

"I don't like how close everyone is," Frank says.

"Shit. You think I do? We lost 750 grand in Nauru."

They walk back into the house, leaving the door wide open. The front foyer light shines brightly onto the steps. If they're loading up the car, Allen doesn't have much time. He climbs out of the bushes, about to get to the Taurus, but Frank reappears. Allen steps back into the shadows. Frank carries a duffel bag, and says, "Nora, just use the bathroom now. You'll regret it later if you don't."

"But I just went," Nora's high-pitched voice cuts into the yard.

"We're not stopping for a long time. I'm telling you now," Frank says, and throws the duffel bag into the trunk.

Allen is poised, but Pinetti comes out as Frank walks back into the house. Shit. Allen isn't sure what to do. He considers grabbing Nora at some point, but worries about scaring her. She probably doesn't remember him, and she seems fine with her father. No, the best course of action is to kill the Taurus and wait for the police to arrive.

Pinetti presses a remote control device on his key chain, aiming it at the Jag, then says, "Stupid thing." He shakes it and presses it again. He sniffs the air, looking around.

Frank comes out with another box. Pinetti says, "Locks aren't working. Is that gas I smell?" He uses his key to open the driver's side door, then pops open the trunk. Allen sees that they are both going to enter the house at the same time, giving him at least a few moments to go underneath the Taurus and pull the fuel line. He crouches low and waits.

But Pinetti stops and returns to the Jag, opening the back door and taking out a jacket.

Allen's pocket rings.

He freezes, realizing it's Julie's cell phone.

Allen fumbles with it, feeling the blood rush into his head. His own cell is always set to vibrate, and he had forgotten this was Julie's.

At the second ring, Pinetti drops the jacket and yells toward the house, "Someone's out here!" A gun appears in Pinetti's hand as Allen turns off the cell. Allen pulls out the nine-millimeter, and hears Frank yelling at Nora to get away from the door. Pinetti peers into the bushes, and yells to Frank, "Turn on the security lights!"

Allen jumps away from the bushes and runs around toward the back. Pinetti curses and chases him. The lights all around the house blaze on, temporarily blinding Allen as he stumbles into a fence and scrambles around it. The back door bursts open, and Frank has a shotgun in his hands, looking wildly around.

Allen can't take this on by himself, and he turns away from the house, heading for the back fence. He hears Pinetti yell to Frank to finish loading the cars. Allen scales the fence quickly, knowing that Pinetti probably won't be able to clear it without trouble. Allen stops after a few yards, turns, and lowers himself on one knee; he aims the automatic at the fence with two hands. He slows his breath and keeps his gun steady.

But Pinetti doesn't appear. Allen hears movement from the house, and when he approaches the fence and peers over it, the back door is closed. They're leaving. Allen climbs into their yard and runs around the other side, hearing a car starting. The engine roars. He hears more voices and car doors slamming. Allen then sees the Taurus back out of the driveway so fast that the front end bounces and crunches against the concrete. Pinetti bolts out of his Jag, kicking the door, and waves down the Taurus. Frank stops. Pinetti dives into the backseat. Allen runs toward the Taurus, getting a better look at the license plate, and memorizes the Washington number. He aims his gun at the rear tire, but the car races away. He takes one low shot, and misses. The car turns the corner. He hears sirens in the distance.

Allen quickly searches for Julie's cell phone in the bushes. He calls the motel, and Julie picks up immediately. "What's happening? What's going on?"

"Why the hell did you call me? Your cell phone rang and almost got me killed!"

"Did you get Nora? Is Nora okay?"

"They got away!" he yells. "I was going to disable the car, but the phone rang, and they pulled their guns! They got away!"

"I just wanted to check—wait, they got away? Nora's not there?"

"They ran. They're in a blue Ford Taurus. I got a license—"

"You let her get away? You saw her and you let her get away?"

"I was trying not to get shot—"

"I can't fucking believe this! They were right there! How could you—"

"You don't understand—"

"Allen, you had them and let them go! What's there to understand? How hard is it to . . . You and Larry are so . . . I can't believe this."

"Calm down. We got this far—"

"No. You and Larry have done shit. Both of you keep fucking up. I can't take it anymore."

He sees the Bellevue police cars arriving, lights flashing. He says, "The police are here."

"I'll be right over, but you and Larry are through with this. I'll find someone else."

"What?"

"You're fired. You two can't do this."

She hangs up.

He drops the phone and the gun. He pulls out his wallet with his PI license, hooks it onto his waistband, and raises his hands. He kneels to the ground, still holding up his hands, and the police jump out of their cars, guns drawn, yelling at him not to move. Piercing spotlights from the cars blind him, and the world is suddenly white and chilly, his body damp with sweat. He closes his eyes and waits to be taken down and handcuffed.

PART V

THE KNIGHT OF FAITH

Twenty-four

The Block can't rest. No longer working for Julie and busy with the transition to being the new president of B&C Investigations, Allen still follows the Rawlingson case closely. Rawlingson has pleaded first-degree felony murder to avoid a trial, but the DA reduced the sentence when he implicated a few middlemen in the drug-smuggling organization. It never reached Rick and Pinetti, though, and this rankles Allen. It gnaws at his heart. Almost two weeks have gone by, and there has been no progress in finding them. The license plate for the Taurus had been stolen off a truck in Seattle. Larry has learned from his contacts at the Marin Sheriff's Department that the case has been relinquished to the DEA and FBI, and the lead investigator at the FBI has admitted that unless there's a break, they're focusing on the Oakland shipping connection with the US Customs Service.

After being fired, B&C deducted its expenses, then returned what was left of Julie's retainer, though everything was handled through Charlene. Allen hasn't spoken to Julie since that night. Frank and Nora are still missing, the case is still open. Charlene worries that they might have fled the country. Allen wants *Rick* in jail. Allen wants revenge.

He has nightmares about Linda. Serena often finds him sweating and breathing unevenly while he sleeps, and when she wakes him up, he retains vivid images of Linda with bugs crawling out of her eyes and mouth, and she screams for him to help her. He doesn't tell Serena this, however. He just says he dreams of drowning.

The Block runs late at night, often without Serena, and tries to exhaust himself. Years from now, when he will remember this time as pivotal in his life, he will picture these late-night runs since he is usually the only person on the street. Except for the blinking red stop lights, which in Serena's neighborhood seem to go on automatically after midnight, Allen finds himself disrupting the stillness of Solano Avenue at two in the morning. Twice the Berkeley police have driven by slowly, checking him out. He waved, and said, "Insomnia." The officer nodded and continued on.

He runs from Berkeley through Albany, up into El Cerrito, around Kensington, and back down into Berkeley again. Bright storefront signs and streetlights blur across his field of vision. The moon lays pale light along his path. He's up to eight miles a night. By the time he returns to Serena's apartment, showers, and slips into bed next to her, his thighs are trembling. His ears pound to his slowing heart rate. This helps him sleep a dreamless sleep.

Tonight, when there is a glistening sheen on the streets from a light drizzle, and the air is cool and calm, he pushes himself even farther. He splashes through shallow puddles, reminding him of the times he used to play in the rain. He rarely dwells on the past, though, when he runs. His mind immediately falls into a rhythmic stasis, a blanking of everything except keeping his pace even. He sings marching songs in his head. He counts nursery rhymes: one-two buckle my shoe, three-four knock at the door.

When he returns to Serena's, he walks quietly down the hall and strips off his shorts and T-shirt. He seems to have moved into her place with most of his belongings here, not that he has much to begin with. Books, clothes, toiletries, work-related files . . . that's about it.

He showers, brushes his teeth, then stretches out on the living room floor, thinking about what he has to do tomorrow. He's interviewing candidates for a part-time receptionist, meeting with the bookkeeper to learn the way B&C handles and records its cash flow, and he'll be discussing with Larry two new prospective clients. Allen's first mandate as incoming president: no more dangerous cases. Both prospectives are insurance-related investigations.

Something else that Allen is doing on his own, without telling anyone, is a systematic search through all the corporate filings Val Pinetti and Rick Staunton were associated with. He remembers Pinetti talking on the phone about a "friend's summer place." Allen told the police about this, but it seems to have yielded nothing.

Allen isn't giving up this lead, however. He has a Statement of Officers record for every corporation the Marin sheriff discovered, plus the search Allen conducted on his own, cross-referencing Pinetti's and Rick's names with the Secretary of State corporate certification unit. The records, for a walk-in request in Sacramento, cost him almost two hundred dollars, but he's not charging B&C. He doesn't want Larry to know; he doesn't want anyone to know.

With each corporate officer listed, Allen is doing an address and background search, hoping to find some connection to a vacation home. He guesses that if a friend of Pinetti's is allowing him access to the home, harboring a fugitive, then this friend might be linked in some way to the shell corporations and listed as an officer. The problem is that each of the twenty corporations has three to twelve officers, and the background searches take time and money. And the vacation home could be anywhere. Frank and Pinetti were going to drive there, but that didn't narrow the area down much.

Still, it's a start, and Allen plugs away. While he was being handcuffed and interrogated by the Bellevue Police that night, he had promised himself that with or without Julie's help, he was going to find Rick.

Allen finishes stretching out and walks quietly into the bedroom, slipping under the covers and feeling Serena's warm leg sprawled on his side. He rests his palm on her thigh. Her warmth spreads through him. He is thankful for her presence. She stirs. She asks in a sleepy voice how his run went.

"Fine," he whispers. "Sorry to wake you."

"I'd join you if it wasn't the middle of the night."

"I know. I'll go back on a regular schedule soon."

"I hope so." She leans over and kisses him, then rolls over and falls back asleep.

Allen lies there, tiny muscle spasms in his calves, his heart quieting, and feels the faint prodding of guilt that he hasn't told her he's still working on Linda's case. She believes he's finished with it, and she has admitted to him she's glad. "Let's get our lives back to normal," she said.

Normal, he thinks now. He closes his eyes, hoping for no nightmares.

The renovation of the B&C office is almost complete, with only the final touches of the kitchenette and the conference room remaining. Larry is pressing Allen for a TV in the conference room, since they could give computer presentations on that screen, but Allen is resisting this. A whiteboard is all they need. The kitchenette was Allen's idea, though, since he's trying to entice Larry to stay with B&C as long as possible. They already had a ministove and refrigerator, so expanding the counter space and adding a larger sink was easy.

Allen goes to the office early to check his e-mail, knowing that more background and credit reports on the corporate officers are waiting in his mailbox. He has been the first to arrive here these past two weeks, liking the early-morning stillness of the office and neighborhood. For an hour Allen feels as if he's the only one alive. The first disruptions are the motorcycle engines sputtering and roaring as the shop down the street prepares to open, the clerks warming up display bikes and moving them to the front sidewalk. Then the traffic on Sixth picks up, and the offices and studios around B&C begin opening.

As he sorts through his e-mail, half the messages are the background and credit reports, which he prints out and files for later review, the folder now over an inch thick, and the other half are forwarded business items Larry wants him to take care of, such as signing up for a new long-distance service and sending a "past due" notice to a client who hasn't paid for the final expenses of a closed case.

Allen takes care of these things for the next hour, and when Larry arrives, he says, "Hard at work, boss?"

"All this busywork—what a pain," Allen says.

"Hey, last night I talked to T. J. at Sunset PI. Looks like Julie hired them."

Allen stops typing. "Same job? Find Nora?"

"Same job. T. J. wants to know how far we got. You okay about giving him the file summary?"

"Sure. Tell him we're interested in his progress if he has any."

"Will do. I don't think he'll get anywhere. Them dudes are air."

"Maybe," Allen says.

Larry points to the Linda file, and says, "What's that?"

"Personal stuff I'm working on."

"A personal case?"

Allen debates whether or not to tell him, then says, "Something like that."

Larry nods and walks toward his desk, then stops and turns around. "Wait. That isn't what I think it is, is it?"

"What do you think it is?"

"Something with Linda?"

Allen says, "Sort of."

Larry raises an eyebrow. "Sort of?"

"Just some odds and ends I'm looking into."

"But Julie fired us."

"It's not for her."

"What kind of odds and ends?" Larry asks. "They got the shooter in jail."

"They don't have Rick."

Larry sighs. "Block-o, you know I'm really sorry about Linda—"

"I don't need a lecture. I'm doing this on my own time, my own expense."

Larry thinks about this, then says, "All right. I understand. If you need any help, just let me know."

"Thanks."

Smiling, Larry says, "And I thought you were coming into work early and leaving late for the company. I was like, 'B.'s going to be a good president.'"

"I am doing B&C work. This other research I do at night."

"And Serena's okay with that?"

"She doesn't know."

Larry raises an eyebrow but doesn't reply.

He has never told anyone how important Linda was to him during the time when he was investigating his father's twenty-year-old-death. Everything he had known about his family was incomplete or simply wrong, and as he learned more, he felt the ground shifting beneath him—his base of knowledge was cracking. But Linda kept him centered; she listened, she analyzed, she pushed and prodded. When he had trouble with the police, Linda helped him, jeopardizing her job, even her life. In the aftermath and recovery, Linda was his lover. Yes, she dumped him; yes, they lost touch for a while; but she had her own problems at the time, and he couldn't blame her.

Did anyone really think he'd just let this go? How could the two people closest to him right now—his partner and his girlfriend—believe that having Rawlingson in jail would satisfy Allen? Didn't anyone know him?

Strange. The only person who would really know this is dead.

Linda loved to kid around, he would say in his eulogy. She loved to tease everyone. She would tease Allen for his driving, for his nickname, for his routines. She would poke his ribs and ask if Blocky was feeling blockable tonight. She would puff up her chest, grunt, and make fun of his bodyguard and PI colleagues, calling them "He-men." "Ugh," she'd say, "I am He-man PI. Look at my guns."

Allen laughs at this now, glancing up at Larry, who is on the phone, his feet kicked up on the desk. Allen knows he's forgetting the difficult fights he and Linda had, the brooding tension, the long silences. He doesn't care. He wants to remember the happier moments.

He meets Serena for dinner in the city at a tiny Vietnamese restaurant off Market, a busy, noisy kitchen counter with a picture of Julia Child on the worn and stained menu. The entrees are cheap and huge, and Serena likes their vegetarian dishes. They sit at a narrow table a few feet from the counter, the stove just two feet beyond that, and their conversation is periodically interrupted by the sizzling of fried vegetables and the eruption of a flaming pan. The smell of fried rice makes Allen's mouth water, and he immediately orders that, while Serena asks for a tofu curry noodle dish. Allen asks why she wanted to meet out here.

"Craving for this place," she says. "The last time we were here was over six months ago."

"You didn't come from work," he says, nodding to her clothes. She's wearing jeans and a sweatshirt.

"I left early and changed. I also wanted to talk to you."

Allen keeps still, worried by her tone. He hears two men at the counter speaking rapid Vietnamese. He says, "About what?"

"Larry e-mailed me."

Allen needs only a second to realize she's referring to the case file Larry has seen. He's not sure how to explain this and stalls. "What did he e-mail you about?"

"Is it true that you're still working on Linda and Julie's case?" She holds her red plastic chopsticks in one hand and taps them against the edge of her plate. "You were fired, weren't you?"

"Yes. I'm just following up a lead."

"But why?"

"Because it might yield something."

Creases between her eyebrows deepen as she stares down at her plate. A young couple two tables down breaks out into laughter, and the old cook at the stove glances over to them and smiles broadly, revealing a silver tooth. The silence from Serena takes too long, and Allen says, "It's just one lead. I'll hand it over to the new PI if I find something."

"Why not just give the PI this now? Let them handle it."

Allen thinks, Because it's too labor-intensive, because T. J. and Sunset PI might not consider it worthwhile, because it's a long shot. He says, "It's just one last thing I want to do."

"You've done your best."

"And Linda got killed."

Serena starts to reply, but stops. She says, "When will this end?"

"When Nora is found. When Rick is in jail."

"I was glad you were fired, but now I see it's made it worse. You're not yourself."

He almost says, "What is my self?" but doesn't want to sound combative. He asks, "Can't you see that I need to do this?"

"I can see it."

"Can't you see that it was my fault?"

"I can see that you *think* that. I don't agree."

"But if I believe this will help, shouldn't I do something?"

She nods. "But how far do you go?"

"Just this research. It's all I can do anyway."

"But I just don't understand—" She stops herself, and shakes her head. She says, "There's another reason I wanted to talk."

"What?" He tenses, preparing for anything. He rushes through a list of disasters—death, sickness, breaking up with him? He looks up at her, waiting.

"My father's coming back into town for a stopover. He's flying to Seoul but will be here for two days."

"What's in Seoul?"

"A sick friend, someone he grew up with. But he wants to meet you this time."

"Your mom?"

"Not coming. She's tired of traveling."

"I'll be there. Dinner?"

"Tomorrow night."

"Already?"

"He just heard from his friend, who doesn't have much time. But he's going to be a little difficult."

"Difficult how?"

"He's a little concerned about us."

"About you."

"About me," she says.

"He's going to give me a hard time?" Allen asks.

"Yes."

Allen rolls up his sleeves, and says, "I'll handle it."

Allen runs nine miles that evening, and as he stretches out on the living room floor, his knees aching from the hills, he grapples with a growing sense of panic about his life. Everything is too murky, too undefined. His job is in flux, his relationships tenuous, and he can't seem to get a good night's rest. Someone important to him is gone. He can't stop thinking about loss.

Now that Serena knows about his extra research, he can work on it at home, so he studies some of the files before he goes to sleep. He spreads out the reports on the floor, and draws diagrams on scrap paper, linking common names to different corporations, roughly five or six names reappearing on the more recent filings. Val Pinetti and Richard Staunton are on almost all the records, whereas Frank only appears on three. Sydney Olshan appears on one. Although Allen and Julie told the Seattle police about Syd in his Wallingford house, Syd had freed himself and fled. The police notified the local hospitals, warning them about a man with a hand injury, but no one of Syd's description has appeared yet. Allen sprawls out on the floor and reads the credit reports of the various names.

The reports reveal the addresses of the past five years, and Allen slowly compiles a long list, since most of the names have multiple addresses. He flags the addresses that might be a summer vacation home, though he isn't sure where some of the locations are. This will require more research, and after an hour of lists, Allen pushes this aside and stands up painfully. His back cracks.

He limps to the bookshelf and pulls out his notebook next to the philosophy texts. He has been jotting down notes from his readings, trying to grasp Kierkegaard's concepts of the Knight of Faith. Being a Knight of Faith in the religious sphere is a pretty desolate state. You are divinely mad, embracing the paradox of giving up everything, yet believing God will provide. And this kind of faith is unintelligible to anyone but God, so everyone else thinks you're crazy. It's completely isolating and utterly unappealing to Allen.

He resists the presupposition that this final sphere is the highest and most desirable one. There's something hypocritical about these writings, since Kierkegaard penned this under the pseudonym Johannes de Silentio, who claims not to be a believer. This is the man who gave up his fiancée and regretted it for the rest of his life. He did not seem infinitely resigned to that loss.

Then Allen has a thought: why must faith be faith in God? Weren't there other abstractions that were fulfilling and meaningful? Allen wonders, Was religion a substitute for the loss of Regina?

He writes this down and closes his notebook. Now both his mind and body are exhausted, and he limps off to bed.

Twenty-five

Thirty minutes before he's supposed to meet Serena and her father for dinner, Allen receives a credit report on one of the corporate officers with an address in Tahoe. Allen has been working in reverse chronological order, checking the officers of the more recent corporations, so this new report is for a corporation that went inactive four years ago and had only three officers, Rick and two unfamiliar names. One of these unfamiliar names, Baxter Pons, had four different addresses within the past five years, and one of the recent addresses is in Olympic Valley, which Allen knows is a vacation area. Serena went skiing up there last winter with her friends. Of the two dozen names he's looked up, this is the first address that could possibly be a vacation home. All the others are post office and private mailboxes in the city and local Bay Area addresses, with a few exceptions in Los Angeles and Seattle.

Tahoe is far enough from Seattle to require a long car drive, but not so far as to need an airplane. Allen checks the clock. Mr. Yew is staying

at a hotel near the Embarcadero Center, so Allen can drive over there in
ten minutes. Serena had already spent the afternoon with her father, no
doubt trying to soften him for the impending dinner. Allen studies
Pons's credit report more carefully, seeing that the most recent address
is in Orinda, with a telephone number. Allen dials the number, and a
woman's voice comes on.

"May I speak to Baxter Pons, please?" Allen asks.

"Oh. Uh, may I ask who's calling?" the woman says.

"My name is Mack Johnson."

A pause. "Were you a friend of my father's?"

Allen thinks, Were? He says, "I'm calling about the Olympic Valley
place."

"The . . . Oh, my father sold that house years ago. My father passed
away about eight months ago."

"I didn't know that. I'm sorry." Allen then wonders how old Pons
was, and checks the birth date on the credit report. He realizes with a
start that Pons was almost eighty years old. He says, "Was it natural
causes? I remember his getting on in years."

"I'm afraid so. His heart had been giving him trouble for a while.
Maybe I can help you. He hasn't lived in Tahoe for a while."

Allen thinks quickly, and says, "Actually I'm looking for a mutual
friend, Val Pinetti?"

"I remember Val. He and my father invested in real estate together."

Allen grips the phone. "Right. Val mentioned a vacation home, and I
thought he might be in Tahoe."

"My father bought and sold dozens of houses in the Tahoe area. Val
might be there, but I have no idea."

"Dozens?"

"Sure. That's how he made his living, buying and selling houses in
vacations spots."

"Where else did he have houses?"

"All over that area, mostly skiing places."

"You wouldn't happen to have a list or anything like that?"

"Sorry."

"How would you contact him, then, if he kept moving around?"

"He had a base office in Sacramento. He didn't necessarily live in all the places."

Allen sighs. "Well, can you give me an idea of what other towns?"

"Wherever there was skiing: Tahoe, Kirkwood, Bear Valley, Mammoth, Truckee. That whole area."

Allen says, "Can I call you back if I need to ask more questions?"

"Sure. I didn't know much about his business, though."

Allen thanks her, and hangs up. It's a start, and it makes sense that Val used someone else to help funnel the money out to Seattle and Tahoe, areas that he might already have been familiar with. And there must be records of Pons's purchases and sales, especially county property tax records. The Recorder of Deeds office will list the owners of property. Allen will need to find the quickest way to get this kind of data, but he'll have to do this tomorrow. Serena and her father are waiting.

Mr. Yew is a barrel-chested man in a tailored blue suit and rimless eyeglasses that seem to float in front of his face. Allen immediately notices how well-groomed Mr. Yew is, freshly shaved and barely a hair out of place. His skin is smooth and tan, and his clothes—from his sparkling black shoes to his Windsor-knotted tie—are immaculate. Allen tries not to look down at his own rumpled khakis and button-down shirt, and greets Serena's father as warmly as possible.

Mr. Yew gives him a brief smile and tells them he has made reservations at a restaurant at one of the Embarcadero buildings. His eyeglasses glint under the hotel lobby lights as he motions down the street and leads them away. Serena takes his arm. Allen follows a few paces behind them.

"How are you?" Mr. Yew says to him, glancing back.

"Fine, sir."

"I understand you had some trouble recently."

Allen hesitates. "Yes, sir. A case became complicated."

"You were in danger?"

"A little," he says, then adds, "sir."

"Seems like a risky way to make a living."

"Dad," Serena says.

"It can be," Allen says, "but I'm taking over the firm and will be moving us in a more conservative direction."

"Taking over?"

"I'm the new president of B&C."

Both Serena and her father turn to him. Serena says, "Already? I thought it was going to take a while."

"Larry kept pushing the paperwork through. It's going faster than we both thought."

"Conservative how?" Mr. Yew asks.

"Working more with law firms and insurance companies for worker's comp cases and fraud investigations."

"That could be lucrative."

Allen says, "Sometimes it is."

"I still have ties to JP Morgan Chase. Maybe I can check with the local offices here and see if they can use your company."

"That would be good," Allen says. "We've done some work for Sutro in a corporate espionage case."

"Really? I know people who used to work there before the buyout."

Serena meets Allen's eyes and gives him a puzzled but pleased grin. This annoys Allen, though, since it makes him feel as if he's being graded. He says, "But I don't think we'll ever stop doing missing persons or small cases. It's one of the reasons I like the job—helping people."

"But I imagine it's hard to make a living from small cases," Mr. Yew says.

"Depends on what kind of living." Allen has never been good with tests.

Serena interrupts them with a question about the restaurant, and Allen wonders if this preoccupation with money and careers is something all parents have for their children, since he remembers his Aunt Insook similarly concerned. But Linda's parents weren't like that; they just seemed grateful that Linda was seeing anyone.

Why does he keep bringing Linda into his thoughts? Allen turns his attention back to Mr. Yew, who is directing them to the elevators and telling Serena about an old friend whose son lives in the city.

"He's a pediatric surgeon in private practice now," Mr. Yew says. "In fact I was going to see if he would join us, but he's in South America for Doctors Without Borders."

Serena glances at Allen. He says, "What's that?"

"They volunteer to teach doctors down there about various procedures," Serena says.

Mr. Yew says, "Yes, John makes something over a million a year but he still volunteers to operate on kids."

"Wait a minute," Serena says. "This is John Kim?"

"You remember."

Serena rolls her eyes. "Not him again."

"What?" Allen asks.

"My parents and John's parents have been trying to fix us up for years."

Allen feels a jolt of jealousy, and turns to Mr. Yew, who is pressing the elevator buttons. Serena says, "What the parents don't know is that Dr. John Kim, M.D., only goes for tall leggy blonde models."

"His father tells me he's beginning to settle down," Mr. Yew says.

Serena laughs. "John is more interested in his Porsche collection than women."

Allen sees Mr. Yew's mouth tighten, but Serena doesn't seem to care. Then Allen registers what Serena has just said, and he wonders, Does everyone have money except me?

The filet mignon special costs seventy dollars. Allen stares at the menu, then glances up at Serena and her father, wondering if these prices amaze them as well. Apparently not. Although Serena mentioned that her parents live well, he never thought *this* well. Serena closes the menu and asks her father to order a nice Cab. Allen's not sure whether to order something expensive or to show thrift. Wait a minute. Is *he* supposed to offer to pay for this? Jesus. Is there room left on his credit card? He can't remember the balance. Do they even take his credit card here? He has only one card, Discover, and a lot of places still don't accept it. He suddenly feels his palms sweating, imagining the embarrassing scene.

The waiter breezes to their table, and asks if they'd like a drink. Mr. Yew says, "Your wine list doesn't have that really nice Cabernet my friend recommended. What was it, Diamond something?"

The waiter smiles. "Diamond Creek. We still have a bottle or two."

"The Cab?"

"Yes, 1981, Three Vineyard Blend. Very nice."

"We'll have a bottle."

Allen asks Mr. Yew, "Your friend?"

"John's father," he says, nodding to Serena. "He told me about this restaurant."

"The wine must be great. It's probably expensive," Allen says, trying to sound casual.

Mr. Yew replies, "Certainly. You have to pay for quality. The last Cab I had that was really good was, I think, more than two hundred a bottle."

Allen smiles. "Interesting."

Serena watches him, glances down at the menu, then says, "Dad, I want to thank you again for treating Allen and me to this nice dinner. We usually don't eat out at such fancy places."

"No problem. My pleasure."

Allen turns to Serena, who gives him a warm smile. Allen thinks, My God I love this woman.

———

Mr. Yew orders the filet mignon special, Serena the grilled salmon, and Allen chooses a chicken dish he can't pronounce so simply points to it on his menu for the waiter. Now that he knows he doesn't have to pay he relaxes and looks around at the darkened restaurant, etched glass partitions separating the window booths and low sparkling lights shadowing the face of the diners. He realizes he can't hear any ambient noise—no music, no chatter, no clinking utensils. The glass partitions are acting as sound barriers, and he notices that they reach up to the ceiling. Yet he still has clear views across the room to the other windows, the Bay Bridge lit up nearby.

Mr. Yew asks Allen, "So, is it true you can't speak any Korean?"

"Dad." Serena sighs.

"It's true," Allen says. "Never learned it as a kid."

"You were orphaned, correct?"

"Correct. Raised by my aunt from age ten."

"But your aunt was Korean."

"Yes, and I even went to a Korean church for a short time, but everyone always spoke English to me."

"I imagine if you learned Korean, you'd have a whole new client base for your firm."

Allen hasn't thought about that, and nods. "Maybe."

"The fact is that Koreans, especially immigrants, wouldn't trust non-Koreans with private matters to be investigated."

Allen isn't sure what he's getting at, and says, "Makes sense."

"And speaking Korean would certainly help that trust."

"Certainly."

"So why don't you learn Korean?"

Allen, startled, says, "It seems like it's too late."

"Too late? Is it too late to go back to school for a degree?"

"I guess not," he says. Mrs. Yew must have reported Allen's stats back to her husband. "Korean seems pretty complicated, though."

"Serena could help you," he says. He turns to his daughter and speaks in Korean.

Serena answers back, then says, "Can we drop this? Can we not hound Allen tonight?"

"Your mother wants to know if Allen is going back to get his degree."

Allen sighs.

Serena says, "Does it really matter? Bill Gates never got his degree."

Mr. Yew smiles. "Bill Gates was running a company out of his freshman dorm at Harvard. By the time Bill Gates was thirty he was a multi-millionaire. How old are you, Allen?"

Serena says in a low voice, "That's enough, Dad."

"No, I want to know. How old is Allen?"

"I'm thirty-three, and will be thirty-four in a few months." Allen stares at Mr. Yew and adds, "Sir."

"What about your kids?" Mr. Yew asks. "Will they learn Korean or will they get even further away from their heritage?"

"Dad!" Serena yelps. "What are you doing?"

Mr. Yew turns to her, and says, "I just don't want all that history lost."

Allen feels his stomach tightening. He says, "I understand, Mr. Yew. I understand what you're saying."

Mr. Yew answers, "I'm not sure you do."

A spasm of pain travels down his abdomen, and he flinches. Serena asks if he's all right.

He says, "Actually, I'm not feeling very well."

Mr. Yew turns to him.

"I haven't been sleeping well, and my stomach has been hurting. Maybe I should get going."

"No, wait. Allen . . ." Serena begins, but she sees his face, and says, "You actually look a little pale."

"I think I've been running too much."

"I apologize," Mr. Yew says. "I hope I—"

"No. I really don't feel so well." Allen stands. They begin to rise as well, but he says, "No. You two have a nice dinner. I'm sorry. I think I should go back home and rest."

"Should I come with you?" Serena asks. "I should come with you."

"No, really. I'll just take BART. I'll meet you back at the apartment."
He holds out his hand to Mr. Yew, who stands up and shakes it. "Nice
meeting you. Sorry."

"Just promise me this," Mr. Yew says.

Allen waits.

"Promise me that if you marry my daughter, you'll have a traditional
Korean wedding."

"Dad! Jeez!"

Allen says, "I promise." Serena turns to him, surprised.

The rumbling in his stomach doesn't subside, and while on BART to the
Berkeley station he feels stabbing pains traveling deep into his bowels.
He cradles his stomach and closes his eyes. Yes, he definitely needs a
vacation. Maybe after he finds Rick, and the transition at B&C is finished.

What happened to those days as a teen when he would ride BART
and follow strangers? He didn't seem to have many worries back then,
except for his aunt. Allen opens his eyes and checks out the other passengers, almost tempted to try following one of them. He remembers on
a few occasions seeing familiar riders, BART regulars, and trying to
learn their routines. He had to be careful not to be noticed by the passengers, since they'd recognize him, but he was pleased to find the same
person to follow. They'd be like old friends.

Allen thinks now, What a weird kid I was.

At the Berkeley station, Allen trudges up the steps and begins the
walk back to Serena's apartment. Shattuck Avenue is crowded with Cal
students, backpacks slung over their shoulders, young couples holding
hands. A few homeless men curl up in sleeping bags in doorways. Allen
worries about John Kim, MD, obviously Mr. Yew's preference, and considers running a quick background check on him at work. Know your
adversary.

He cuts over to Martin Luther King on University, and picks up his pace, jogging in his work shoes. Maybe he *should* learn Korean. He could probably take a class at Cal, or even find some local Korean church and hire a tutor. It actually might be useful for B&C.

The thought of work reminds him of all he has to do tomorrow, including beginning a preliminary review of the case he and Larry decided to take—an insurance company suspecting worker's comp fraud.

He finally arrives at Serena's place, sweating, tired, but at least his stomach doesn't hurt anymore. After a quick shower, he goes over the notes for Linda's case, wondering what else he can do about Baxter Pons. Tomorrow he'll check one of the online sources, the TRW REDI Property Database, which lists almost every property owner in most states, and he'll also call the Recorder of Deeds Office to check if they have any information of property bought or sold by Pons. What else? Probate records, possibly. He could ask Pons's daughter about that.

His thoughts race, and when he feels a sourness returning to his stomach, he puts away the file and stretches out on the floor. He rereads his notes on Kierkegaard while lying on his back, wondering if being a Knight of Faith also applies to relationships. When you are in love there is a teleological suspension of the ethical. Allen couldn't care less about moral or social norms when it comes to Serena; he would break laws and hurt others to make sure Serena was all right. When you are in love there is also the paradox of being selfish and selfless at the same time. Allen likes how Serena makes him feel, yet he also wants to make her happy, even at the expense of his own happiness.

Just as he is thinking this, Serena walks into the apartment with a paper bag, and says, "I brought you your chicken capillotade. It's delicious. Are you feeling okay? I'm sorry about my dad."

He looks up. "You're wonderful."

She stops, then smiles. "You're delirious."

Twenty-six

The Block's personal case begins to unfold after repeated calls and e-mails to the Property Data Research Center, where Allen signs B&C up to be a subscriber to the database. With step-by-step technical support on the phone, he configures his computer to access title searches, condo and co-op sales, and county property tax records. Allen realizes that some of B&C's regular information brokers use this service, and that by going directly to this database, he'll be bypassing the middlemen. A quick title check of Baxter Pons yields a condo in Sacramento and an apartment complex in Lafayette. Since neither of these is a vacation area, he calls tech support again and asks how to do a history search. The rep talks him through it, and after a few tries and callbacks, Allen finds that he has to do the searches by county, and then go year by year.

He starts in the Tahoe area, and immediately gets hits with Placer and Eldorado Counties. Allen will have to search these addresses for current residents, then compare that with the corporate officer lists, hoping to find a match. The more counties he searches in, the more hits he gets. Pons has owned houses in Alpine, Mono, and Nevada Counties. The list of properties going back a decade reaches fourteen, and Allen decides to begin with these. But B&C work intrudes, and he puts it aside to accompany Larry to the insurance company client meeting.

Allen lets Larry handle the Q&A, since he has done this kind of work dozens of times, and Allen itches to return to his own research. It's a tenuous connection—an alleged vacation home that might be connected among old associates—but the relationships could feasibly involve Rick. It seems prudent to hide out in someone else's home in a remote location, leaving no paper trails.

Last night he admitted to Serena the details of his investigation while eating his chicken leftovers, and she sat cross-legged in her chair, shaking her head slowly. She leaned on her elbows and didn't say anything for a while. Finally she said, "My father was sorry he goaded you."

Allen needed a moment to adjust to the subject change. He said, "It's okay."

"He thinks you're under a lot of stress."

He nodded.

"Do you really think this investigation is worthwhile?" She pointed to the files on the floor.

"Yes."

"You promised to stop after this." She held her finger up, a warning.

He nodded and took her hand. "Yes, I promised."

But now, as he listens to Larry give the standard B&C speech about the retainer agreement, he wonders if this is true. He meant it at the time, but now doesn't really believe he can stop until Nora is found, and Rick pays for what he has done.

He works late, turning off all the lights in the office except for his desk lamp, saving electricity. For the first time, Allen sees the overhead costs of an office, and the bills are shockingly high. The PG&E electric bill alone for this office averages over a thousand dollars a month. The phones, Internet service, security system, various equipment leases, insurance, and, of course, the rent make Allen wonder how they've stayed in business for this long.

Spread out on Allen's new desk are index cards representing houses or condos that Pons once owned, the addresses listed and the dates during which Pons was the title holder. For each card Allen has to do another title search to find the previous and current owners, and he jots these down on the card, comparing these names with the corporate officer lists he has relating to Rick and Pinetti. Because it takes time to get a title record, and depending on the house location Allen might order a background and credit report on the current owner, he spends hours filling in the cards.

Then, while moving onto Mono County and searching the past titles for the two condos that Pons had once owned, Allen finds a match. He squints at the name, his scalp tingling. The name on the current title of a condo in Mammoth Lakes matches the name on the statement of officers for a defunct corporation, Garrison Inc. The name, Sebastian King, an officer with Garrison Inc., stares back at Allen. There it is. King was part of this corporation before it was assigned forfeiture status in 1997. And King currently is the deed and title holder of a condo in Mammoth Lakes. King is the link between the corporation with Rick and the condo with Pons. Allen traces the connection: Baxter Pons bought and renovated this condo, then sold it to a friend, King. King now lends it to Rick.

Allen pulls out a northern California map and locates the town, about eighty miles south of Lake Tahoe. This is still no guarantee that this is a current link to Rick, and definitely no evidence that Rick will be there, but it would make sense.

The question is, Now what?

———

"**You have *got*** to be kidding me," Serena says, sitting up in the bed. Allen is standing in the center of the bedroom in the dark, unwilling to turn on the light. He sees multicolored spots floating in the darkness, his vision adjusting. The fluorescent digital clock reads 2:45 A.M.

"Once I get there, I can see for myself," he says. "Then I can call the police, Charlene and Julie, everyone."

"After all that has happened? What if he *is* there? Then you'd be putting yourself in more danger."

"I won't do anything. The thing is, it's not like I can call and ask if he's there, and I don't know anyone in the area to check for me."

Her face is shadowed, the dim night-light from the hallway barely reaching her, but Allen can see her inhale and exhale slowly. She says, "You promised. You promised that it'd end after the research."

"The research is still going on."

"You were fired, Allen."

"I may have been fired, but I can't close this case until Rick is in jail."

"All you have to do is call the police now. Or Julie. They will take care of it."

Allen has prepared for this on the drive over. He says, "First, I don't know if he's there. I don't want to look stupid and tell them about this if I'm wrong. Plus I'll have to tell Julie that I'm working on this even though she fired me. Second, if I'm right, and I tell them, I don't want anyone to mess this up. Rick could have a friend in the police department to tip him off. I mean, he always seem to be a step ahead of everyone. Or he could have someone tapping Julie's lines. I will call everyone once I mark him, and make sure I can follow him if he runs. I had Frank and Nora twenty feet in front of me before, and, because I wasn't prepared, I lost them."

"Why not just tell the police that it's a possible lead? You can even give an anonymous tip." She reaches over to the night table and turns on the light. Both of them wince at the sudden brightness, and Allen has trouble focusing on her.

"Too many variables," he says, squinting. "I need to get it as tied up as I can before calling them."

"But it could be dangerous," she says.

Allen says, "I just need to see for myself. Then I'll call the whole world."

Serena is quiet. Then, after what seems like a full three minutes, she says, "This isn't going to end."

"It will."

"You loved her," she says.

Allen pauses. They've never really talked about this. "She was important to me. She helped me when no one else would."

"I would've, if I'd known you."

"I know."

"Allen, I can't take this anymore."

"What?" he says, dread filling him.

"I can't do this."

"Do this?"

She says, "Come here."

He walks to her bedside, and she pulls him to her. She holds his cheeks with her warm palms and stares at him. He tries to lean forward to kiss her, but she holds him firmly. He asks her what she's doing.

"We should spend some time apart until you've worked this out."

"Why?"

"Because it's too hard for me."

"What about helping me? What about supporting me?"

She lets him go, and says, "Jesus, I've tried. You don't want to talk about it. You research it in secret. You go for runs in the middle of the night. Do you expect me to sit here and watch you obsess about her and eventually get killed?"

Startled, he says, "What do you mean?"

"You keep putting yourself in danger, and nothing I say or do changes your mind. I just can't . . . I can't watch this anymore."

"I'm telling you that as soon as I—"

She holds her finger to her lips, silencing him. She pulls him forward and kisses him on his cheek. "I can't live like this," she whispers in his ear. "Figure out what you want, then let me know."

Allen, angry at Serena for doing this to him now, drives to his apartment to pack a change of clothes, pick up his SIG and Raven, and a replacement cell phone. He drops by B&C and opens the new fireproof storage container that holds some of their surveillance equipment. The first thing he takes is the Doppler 890 vehicle-tracking system, with a tracking transmitter that has one week's worth of battery life, and the direction receiver he can use from his car. There are four magnet Doppler antennas that he'll have to position precisely on the roof of his car, so he grabs a precision tape ruler. He takes a parabolic long-distance microphone, a miniature night-vision pocketscope, an FM transmitter, and a Walkman as an FM receiver. He also grabs the mini digital video camera on his way out.

He knows Serena is right, but what choice does he have? He *has* to finish this.

He gasses up his car, pulls out his maps, and heads east. The advantage of driving at three o'clock at night is the lack of traffic. He'll cross the Bay Bridge and get onto 580 within thirty minutes. He's never driven to the Tahoe area, but he estimates a four-hour trip, and settles in for the ride.

Yes, he did love Linda. In a strange way she was the closest thing he had to family, and when he visited her parents in Marina Alta he felt they were welcoming him in. It wasn't until Linda was injured that he was edged out, but there was a moment when he was sitting with Linda's stepfather in the living room, listening to the news from the TV mingling with the chatter of Linda and her mother in the kitchen, that he felt a hint of family life, and he liked it. He had never had anything close to it.

That seems to Allen to be the highest sphere of living—communion, family, connections. The religious sphere is alien to him, unfathomable and inaccessible. Religion was a Kierkegaardian premise that seemed to go unchallenged by the nonbelieving alter ego author, Johannes de Silentio. Maybe instead of a religious sphere there's a communal sphere, one which isn't intertwined with moral implications, but familial and personal development. Allen recalls in *Either/Or* the leap into the ethical sphere is one that involves commitment to self-perfection and to others, a ridding of hedonism. But the need for a moral system, a demand for a choice between the selfish aesthete and the ethical, seems less an end in itself than a means toward the religious sphere. The entire enterprise seems geared toward highlighting religion. The bias is clear.

Allen has trouble figuring out how he feels about this. Maybe Kierkegaard did this because after he dumped Regina he turned to religion. Maybe the reason he was so fascinated by the Abraham and Isaac story was that he felt as if he had sacrificed her for religion. Allen could never do to Serena what Kierkegaard did to Regina. In fact, he fears losing her. He knows he wants that sense of family with her. He tells himself that everything will be all right, that Serena was just annoyed with him. When he gets back, they'll work this out.

A Knight of Faith, Allen concludes, is one who has faith in the contradictions and paradoxes of love, faith in others, in families and partners, but not necessarily in God.

He becomes sleepy as he leaves the Bay Area and drives through the long stretches of farmland and grasslands through Tracy and Manteca. Miles and miles of what seem to be peach, nectarine, and almond farms line the 120 freeway through Oakdale. He drives in complete blackness through the Stanislaus National Forest, his Volvo becoming sluggish as he heads up steep mountainous highways. He drives toward Yosemite National Park. At times, even with his bright headlights shooting far ahead of his car, he feels as if he's moving underwater, only the road signs glowing in the distance and the lane markings keeping him from veering off the highway. The radio stations fade in and out. He begins talking to himself to keep awake.

Maybe it's time to find Aunt Insook, he thinks. If she's the only living blood relative he has, then he can't lose touch with her completely. Her involvement with his father's death is something he is beginning to understand. Nothing is clear-cut. The assignment of blame is murky. Yes, she can be petty and small-minded, and she only helped him when she felt she had no choice, but she did raise him. She didn't dump him in a foster home. She fed and housed him. She even would've paid for college if he'd stayed.

His last image of her is her sitting at her kitchen table, head bowed. Four years ago. She had then fled to Korea, and Allen somehow knows she's still alive. She's a fighter, a survivor, and he imagines her thriving. She would've been happy that he's with Serena, a Korean American.

He enters Yosemite National Park at dawn, and is surprised by the twenty-dollar entrance fee. His car shudders as he climbs the long winding uphill Tioga Pass. The landscape has become dense and mountainous, thick with sequoias and majestic granite rock faces. Allen knows these are some of the best sights the country has to offer, and yet he's strangely unaffected. He has a job to do. He looks out at the dawn sun illuminating the sheer white mountains, and has the odd sensation of driving through a postcard. He's so tired that when he looks at his gas gauge, he's surprised that the tank is full. Then he remembers refueling an hour ago at a roadside Shell. Everything seems dreamlike, and to prevent an accident he pulls over at the Tioga exit and naps in the small parking lot.

He wakes up with a jolt thirty minutes later. His first thought is of Serena and how he knows what he's been doing to her. He would feel the same way if the situation were reversed. He starts his car, and speeds down 395, then heads toward Mammoth Lakes. But he has to do this.

He owes it to Linda. He arrives at the edge of town as the midmorning sun blankets the wide, newly paved streets, construction cones lining the side. He suddenly knows that he's right about this lead. Somehow he knows Rick is hiding out here.

Twenty-seven

The first thing he notices when he stops in front of the Visitor Center and Ranger Station at the Mammoth Lakes entrance is the cool, sharp air. It cuts into his lungs and energizes him. A few RVs and a dozen cars are parked in the large lot, families and retirees streaming toward the entrance. Allen realizes that he has arrived a few minutes after the eight o'clock opening. A line forms at the door. A family with three young girls sits on the picnic tables in front, the mother snapping at the eldest daughter, telling her to stop complaining. Allen checks a map displayed on a bulletin board, positioned above rows of brochures for hotels, condos, and local businesses. He searches for Sebastian King's street, but can't find it. He inhales deeply, feeling the city smog wash away. The map reveals that the town is only a few square miles, with Mammoth Mountain to the west. He waits on line and shuffles into the small office and gift shop.

When it's his turn at the counter, he approaches a smiling, gray-haired woman with a flower print blouse. He asks for a street map, which puzzles her. "Don't you want a day hike map of the trails?"

He shows her his slip of paper with Sebastian King's address. "I'm looking for this place."

"That's in Old Mammoth," she says, tearing off a map from a large pad on the desk. She points to a neighborhood south of the town. "It's off Tamarack Street. Down here." She then points to where they are right now and traces a route with a yellow highlighter. "Just take Old Mammoth Road all the way down."

Allen thanks her and returns to his car. He drives along a commercial strip with restaurants and mini malls. There seem to be gas stations on every corner. He checks his cell phone, charging in the car lighter. The reception is weak but manageable. He has everyone on speed dial memory. The ring is set to vibrate.

As the sun rises higher in the sky, he sees the mountains in the distance lit up with morning light, then passes a golf course with bright manicured green lawns, a driving range, and golf carts parked in neat rows. The juxtaposition of colors—glaring green against a background of muted gray-and-olive-colored mountains—jars him. Construction sites appear every few hundred yards. As the road narrows, the condos and commercial buildings thin out, and houses ranging from log cabins to sleek modern homes with high windows sit surrounded by tall pine trees.

Allen turns onto Tamarack, then finds Sebastian King's cul-de-sac with two newer houses and a converted trailer. Allen, in his Volvo, feels conspicuous in the quiet, sleepy neighborhood. Instead of pulling into the cul-de-sac, he turns around and parks on a dirt shoulder at the first turnoff. He grabs his cell phone and walks through the woods, heading for the back of the houses that fill the cul-de-sac. Leaves and dead pine needles crunch under his shoes, the strong smell of pine sap and smoke around him. King's address is 204, so Allen walks to the house closest to him, and checks the number on the mailbox—202. He walks to the converted trailer on the left—200. He then retreats back into the woods and focuses on the gray-shingled two-story house to his right. He checks his watch. Eight-thirty.

He moves farther back into the woods, finds a tree to rest against, and settles in. He could find out the phone number and call the place to see who answers, but he doesn't want to make anyone suspicious. A hang-up, a wrong number, even a telemarketer could set off warnings. No, Allen is just going to sit and wait and observe.

He shivers, but can feel the sun already warming the air. He checks his phone reception and calls Serena, and her machine picks up. He says quietly, "Just wanted to let you know I'm here and I'm fine. I won't be answering my phone, but I'll call again later, maybe tonight." He hesitates, then adds, "I love you. I know you're right, and I'm sorry. I have to do this." He hangs up. The battery is fully charged.

He remembers promising her father that he and Serena would have a Korean wedding, but he doesn't even know what that means. Is that a wedding in Korea or a wedding with Korean customs? Has Serena hinted to her father that she and Allen might get married? Allen is curiously pleased, and hopes she still feels that way when he returns. To be a family with Serena is something he has considered on an abstract level, but the reality of it doesn't scare him as he thought it might. Whatever doubts he might have had a few weeks ago seem to have dissipated. He realizes that his seeing Linda again and dealing with her loss have strengthened his attachment to Serena. He loves her, and he knows he's got to fix all this.

Is it that simple? He has no models of marriage, of relationships. He has no instruction manuals. All he has is a bastardized version of Kierkegaard, suited to his own needs.

It pains him to think of the times Linda was unhappy, which, toward the end of their relationship, was frequently. She always seemed to be searching for something to ease her restlessness, a feeling that things weren't right. Whether it was her job, her apartment, her relationship, her family—any of these aspects of her life at any given moment offered only barbs that pricked her skin, irritations that grew the more she dwelled on them, and Allen could do nothing to help her. Sometimes *he* was the barb that needed yanking.

So when she told him about how unhappy she had been the past two years, he wasn't surprised. He knew that she probably wouldn't have kids because she always liked to be free. Then again, she seemed to have been changing.

Her death was senseless, like his parents'. The difference was that he didn't witness theirs. In fact, despite his father's funeral, which the ten-year-old Allen never quite saw as an acknowledgment of death but rather a strange Korean gathering, Allen sometimes felt as if his father were on a long trucking haul. For many, many months, Allen could catch himself wondering when his father would be returning home.

Allen sits up when he notices more activity in the cul-de-sac. A neighbor throws out trash, and another neighbor drives off in a Jeep. King's place is still quiet. The garage doors don't have windows, so Allen can't tell if there's a car inside. If there's no movement in an hour or so, he might go in for a closer look.

But after thirty minutes Allen hears the automatic garage door whirring, and a green Subaru SUV pulls out into the street, then stops. The garage door closes. Allen notices the new car dealer plates. Pinetti's Jag was impounded, so he'd have had to replace it.

Allen waits until the SUV drives away, then he moves closer to the back of the house. There's a small patio area and a second-floor balcony. If he wants to break in, it'll be easy for him to climb to the second floor and jimmy open the sliding glass doors. Those are never more than a simple latch. He'll have to check for alarms.

Then, the curtain in an adjacent window rustles, then pulls open. Allen keeps still. The face in the window looks up at the sky, and Allen recognizes him: Rick. He has shaved his goatee and mustache, but it's definitely him. Allen holds his breath. Rick leaves the window and after a moment the curtains in the first-floor patio windows slide open. It's the kitchen, and Allen watches as Rick makes himself coffee and turns on a small television. Allen has to fight the impulse to run in there with his gun, while Rick is obviously off guard. Where are Frank and Nora? If that was Pinetti in the SUV, then where is Sebastian King?

He says to himself, Calm down. You need more information. He doesn't want to call the police until he knows exactly where Nora is.

He returns to his car, arms himself with his SIG and Raven, and loads a small backpack with the tracking transmitter, the bug and Walkman, the mike, and the video camera. Until he knows where Frank and Nora are, he doesn't want to do anything. He needs to have Nora pinpointed, to have Frank and Rick bull's-eyed. Then he'll be able to present the whole package to the police and to Julie. He must redeem himself. He must do this for Linda. He imagines Julie apologizing to him, grateful for his help, and her parents thanking him, asking his forgiveness for excluding him from Linda's funeral. He imagines Larry slapping him on the back, congratulating him for keeping with the case. And he imagines Serena telling him that he was right to push forward on this.

Allen finds a better vantage point in the woods, moving farther back but angled to see the entire driveway. He nestles in, making sure no one on the second floor can see him from a window, and the neighbors' windows aren't in any direct line of sight. He turns on the video camera and zooms in on the second-floor window, hoping for a better view of Rick.

The SUV returns, this time backing up and parking in the driveway. The rear hatch pops open. Allen records Pinetti climbing out of the driver's side and checking the grocery bags in the back. He pulls one out, leaving the hatch open, and walks to the front of the house.

This time Allen isn't going to make the mistake of losing them by hesitating. He turns on the tracking transmitter, a small black box the size of a paperback book with a flexible antenna and magnetic fasteners, and moves quickly to the side of the house. He hears voices coming through a screen window on the second floor. He runs to the SUV and attaches the transmitter to the chassis underneath the rear bumper. He then hurries back into the woods, keeping the trees in between him and the second-floor windows. When he returns to his spot, he turns on the parabolic mike, adjusting the gain on the amplifier and slipping on the mini headphones.

Parabolics aren't perfect, but help cut out ambient noise, and the dish in conjunction with the amplifier can pick up distinctive sounds, like quiet voices in the woods. Allen aims the dish at the second-floor window and turns up the amplifier. He immediately recognizes Rick's raspy laugh as it fades, the same laugh he had used when telling Allen about Bascome, the New York PI that Linda and Julie had hired first. Allen's throat tightens. He has to remind himself that he needs Frank and Nora's location before doing anything.

The voices grow louder for an instant, and Allen hears Pinetti say, ". . . drop off the groceries and split up the cash . . ."

Rick replies, but Allen can't make it out.

Pinetti says, ". . . weekend, when there're more tourists."

"I'll . . . to the kid," Rick answers, his voice moving in and out of range.

The voices die out, and after a few minutes Pinetti returns to the SUV with a suitcase and slides it into the back. He shuts and locks the hatch.

Drop off the groceries? Something about Nora? Allen quickly packs the gadgets and returns to his car. He pulls out the directional receiver, plugs it into the car lighter, and threads the antenna wire out to the roof. There are four whip antennas with magnetic bases, and he needs to position them precisely with the connecting cables taut, and check the base labeling. He measures the distance of the diagonals, making small adjustments. He then connects the wires to the receiver and turns it on. The LED display lights up. There's a motion detector on the transmitter, and Allen sees the SUV is still parked. He starts his car and drives farther away from the cul-de-sac.

The antenna uses a Doppler system of triangulating the signal, so

Allen sees on the display an arrow pointing on a 360-degree grid, with the signal strength on a one-to-ten scale, and a blinking picture of the "target car" positioned in relation to the tracking car, his Volvo. He turns on the Vari-tone option, which rises in pitch the closer he gets to the target.

He parks, finding a dirt shoulder away from any condos and houses, and leaves his engine running. The transmitter is still in "slow mode," which means the SUV is stationary, and the transmitter is conserving its battery.

The beep is low and steady. He waits.

As soon as the beeps change tone, and the transmitter goes into "fast mode," Allen turns the ignition key, not realizing he has left the engine running, and jolts the transmission, the loud grating sound making him wince. He checks the directional grid and sees the SUV heading away from him, the arrow pointing left. Allen turns the car around and drives in that direction, the beeps steady at first, then slowly rising in pitch.

Without a partner to monitor the directional grid, Allen has to rely on the pitch and an occasional glance at the arrows. Since there aren't many complicated streets here, he's not worried about dead ends or losing the general direction. Allen remains on Old Mammoth Road, and slows his car when he thinks he sees the SUV in the distance. No need to be so close.

The arrow changes direction and the pitch rises for a moment—a turnoff. Allen slows and waits until the pitch lowers, then continues. He checks the arrow, which is now pointing almost behind him, then sees the dirt path leaving the main road. There are no signs, which makes him uneasy, but he turns off the road. The pitch increases.

Branches and bushes scrape the side of the car, and Allen slows. The path is too narrow for him to turn around, and he doesn't like driving blindly on an unmarked road. He listens to the pitch falling, but then it remains steady, and the "slow mode" switches on. The SUV has stopped.

Allen begins backing out. He estimates the SUV went about a quarter of a mile in, possibly less. The bottom of his Volvo grinds against rocks. He slows, trying to maneuver around the ruts in the road. Once he reaches the main road, he drives around a bend and parks on the shoulder. He grabs his backpack, checks his guns, and walks toward the turnoff.

Worried that the SUV might be coming out this way at any moment, he prepares to run into the brush at the first sound of a car. He checks his cell phone, and the reception is uneven. But all he has to do is confirm the location of Frank and Nora, and he can leave here and make the call.

The dirt road widens. Allen smells wood burning. Then, after a hundred feet, he sees the edges of a small log cabin coming into view. He moves off the road and into the bushes, finding narrow paths leading around the cabin. The chimney lets off a thin, lazy stream of smoke.

The SUV is parked in front, and an old Ford pickup truck in back is partially covered with a tarp. The cabin's roof is sagging, and the windows seem warped, gaps along the edges stuffed with putty. Allen checks the perimeter for alarms or dogs and sees nothing. In fact, he wonders if there's any electricity in the cabin, since he can't locate any wiring. There's a small shed adjacent to the cabin, and he moves toward it, checking inside. A generator. But no phone lines.

Voices murmur through the walls. Allen crouches and moves quietly along the side of the cabin, stopping beneath a window. There are gaps in the molding, and Allen hears Pinetti talking to someone about splitting up. Allen pulls out his FM transmitter from his backpack, connects the nine-volt battery and turns it on. He wedges the bug into the small crevice under the window, then retreats back into the woods. He circles to a view of a window on the other side of the cabin and pulls out the parabolic mike. He turns on his Walkman and tunes it into the high-end frequency. He and Larry set the FM bugs to transmit in the 108-megahertz range, since most people don't have their stereos set to stations up there. He has only one set of headphones, so listens in on the bug for a minute, then turns on the parabolic and plugs his headphones into the amplifier and listens. Slightly better. Pinetti is closer to this window, and Allen hears him talking about driving cross-country to Florida.

"No, I should stay for a while," a new voice says, and Allen thinks it's Frank, but isn't sure.

"You trust that old woman with the kid?" Rick asks.

"Yeah. She'll be quiet."

"Tell her good-bye for me," Rick says.

"I'll be bringing her back tonight."

Pinetti says, "Can we split the cash now? I'd like to get the fuck out of here."

Rick laughs. "Val wants to be an old geezer in Miami."

"How much is this?" Frank asks.

"This is about five hundred grand," Rick says.

"What about the money in Manila?" Frank asks.

"I'll wire that to your new accounts once everything cools off."

"That fucking Nauru money," Frank says. "I can't believe it."

"That bitch wife of yours—"

"Ex-wife, goddammit"

Someone sighs.

A cell phone rings. Rick answers it with, "Yeah?"

After a moment, Rick says, "Wait, you're cutting out. Let me go outside." Rick appears at the front door, and Allen aims the parabolic at him. Rick says, "What? You got to be fucking kidding me. Here? Oh, fuck me. How did he . . . ?" Rick lets off a string of curses then says, "All right. You earned it. Keep me posted."

Rick hurries back into the cabin. He says, "That fucking PI is on his way."

"What? Here?"

"Which PI?"

"The chink one. He left last night."

"How the fuck did he find us?"

"No idea—"

"Last night?" Frank asked. "He could be here now? Were you fuck-ing followed?"

"No. Absolutely not," Rick says. "We're being really careful. Val, you didn't leave a trail, did you?"

"No way."

"Shit," Frank says. "That means I've got to run again. Split the cash now."

"Wait until tonight," Rick says.

"What if he goes to the fucking police!" Frank yells. "Who the fuck *is* this asshole anyway?"

"Linda's ex," Rick says.

After a brief silence, Frank says, "Split the cash now. We can't waste any more time."

Allen flips open his cell phone and calls the police. He tells the dis-patcher that he's a private investigator and that there are three men wanted for murder in a cabin off Old Mammoth Road, about two hun-dred yards in the woods. He ticks off their names, so the police can ID them, and gives Sebastian King's condo address as another hideout. He says, "Please call Special Agent Edward Washington of the San Fran-cisco satellite office of the FBI for confirmation. I can't talk anymore." He hangs up.

He's not going to screw this up this time. If they split up now, he'll certainly lose two of them. They might sweep the SUV for the transmit-ter; they might jump to different cars and disappear. He tries to decide what to do, when he hears Frank say, "I'll leave it to you guys to set aside my share. I want to get my daughter."

"Wait up," Rick says. "This will only take a minute. I don't want you getting on my case about shorting you."

"We should hurry."

Allen pulls out his SIG and hurries to the front of the cabin. He needs to keep them here until the police arrive.

Twenty-eight

The Block hears the three of them talking inside, but they don't seem ready to leave yet. He has no idea who could've called Rick's cell and tipped them off. No one knew he would be here except Serena, but even she didn't know exactly where he was heading. He had only mentioned Tahoe in general, but then again that would be all Rick needed to know.

No, the connection to Serena is ridiculous, and it's more likely that Rick has someone keeping tabs on Allen, possibly eavesdropping or tracking him. He hasn't swept his car in a while; he hasn't checked Serena's phone lines since Gracie was killed. A tap? Possibly. He didn't name the location in his last call, but it would be easy to link it with any previous surveillance. And the fact that he was heading to Tahoe would be enough to alarm Rick. Allen feels a momentary tug of exhaustion; it's impossible to keep up with these men.

Movement inside. He hears Pinetti say, "You want the groceries?"

Frank answers, "Can you load them into my truck?"

Footsteps approach the door. Allen moves to the side and waits.

The door opens, and Pinetti says, "Not your damn delivery boy, Frank."

Pinetti steps out, and Allen shoves the gun into his neck, and whispers, "Quiet now. Don't say a word."

Pinetti freezes. Allen pulls him away from the door and guides him away from the front windows, pushing him to the side of the cabin. He whirls Pinetti around, forces his face into the logs, and says quietly, "Where is Nora?"

Pinetti hesitates, then shrugs his shoulders. Allen gives him a rabbit punch to the kidneys, which forces Pinetti down onto his knees, coughing. Allen hits the back of his head with the gun, and says, "Don't fuck with me. Where is she?"

He shakes his head. "I don't know. A babysitter. Someone Frank hired to watch her."

"Where?"

"I don't know. I don't care."

Allen stops. He notices that the cabin is quiet. Then he hears the floorboard creaking inside near one of the windows. Allen slams the gun into Pinetti's head, knocking him to the ground, and the front door bursts open, Rick running out and seeing Allen at the side. Rick raises a pistol and shoots, splintering the wood near Allen. Allen dives and rolls. He hears another gunshot and there's the shatter of glass. Allen shoots, and sends Rick back inside. Rick yells, "Go! Get the fuck out of here! I'll take him!"

Allen runs into the woods, circling the cabin, and sees Frank coming out a back door. Allen shoots out the front tire of the pickup. He aims and shoots out the rear tire, and the truck begins sagging to its side. Frank jumps back in and slams the door. He hears Rick yelling, "Split up! He's alone! Take my car and get the fuck out of here!"

Allen rushes behind the truck and toward the rear door of the cabin.

He pulls it open, hearing the SUV in front starting. He looks in, but Rick yells something and shoots at him. Allen pulls away. He runs along the side of the cabin, and when he reaches the front he sees the SUV lurching down the narrow path. He's about to aim at a tire, but he hears Rick running out the back, following Allen's route. Allen races into the woods, taking cover, and Rick fires two more shots at him.

"The police are coming!" Allen yells. "I called them five minutes ago!"

"Then they're going to find you dead," Rick says. He calls out, "Val! Come on! We can take this asshole!"

Allen listens. He's certain he didn't knock Pinetti unconscious. Where is he? Then he realizes that Pinetti probably ran. Allen laughs. "He took off! You're stuck here with the police on the way!"

Allen sees a blur as Rick runs from the cabin into the woods. Allen, startled, chases him. Rick turns and takes a quick shot, forcing Allen to stay farther back. He hears Rick cursing and crashing through bushes. Allen, remembering the time he got himself lost in the Santa Monica Mountains, wants to stop Rick from going too far in. He veers to Rick's right, moving quickly around trees and up a rocky slope, listening to Rick's movements. Allen leaps over a fallen tree trunk and dashes closer toward Rick, hoping to cut him off. He then sees through the brush Rick's blue jacket, and Allen aims his SIG low and fires.

"Fuck!" Rick yells, and falls. Three shots quickly follow, aimed at Allen, who dives to the ground and crawls behind a tree. Rick curses again, and tries to get up, but falls.

"Drop your gun," Allen yells.

"Come and get it."

Allen says, "The police are coming. You're screwed."

Rick fires another two rounds at him as an answer. Allen stays hidden. He says, "All I have to do is keep you covered until they show up."

"Son of a bitch." Rick fires another shot, and gets up. He limps a few yards. Allen aims at his other leg and fires. Rick collapses with a yell.

"It's over," Allen says. "You're not going anywhere."

Rick breathes heavily, and yells, "I'm going to kill every fucking member of your family before I get to you!"

Allen says quietly, "I have no family."

"Goddamn this!" Rick fires one more shot, then collapses with a shout. He struggles up onto his arms and checks his leg, cursing.

Allen stares at him through the shrubs. After a moment he says, "Why did you kill Linda? Didn't you know killing her would push everyone harder to get you?"

"Stupid fuck. You're such a stupid fuck."

"You're the one who brought all this down on you."

"It was that bitch Julie, goddammit."

"You shouldn't have killed Linda," Allen says.

"She wasn't *supposed* to die, asshole!" he yells. "*You* were supposed to die!"

"What?"

"Go to hell."

"What are you talking about?"

"Fuck you."

"Linda was going to be executed," Allen says.

"I'm glad she's dead, that bitch."

Allen feels a coldness seeping into his hands and arms. He thinks, Suspend the ethical.

Rick says, "Rawlingson told me that you cried over her. He said you were giving her mouth-to-mouth and crying." He laughs. "I hope she died in pain."

Allen steps out from behind the tree and aims his SIG. "What do you mean she wasn't supposed to die?"

"You think I'm fucking crazy? You're just some shit PI, but I wasn't going to kill that bitch. Hell, if I was going to kill anyone, it would have been Julie, who started all this shit."

"What are you talking about?"

Rick quickly raises his gun, but Allen fires his SIG and hits Rick in the chest. Rick shoots a round, misses wildly, and falls back. Allen approaches slowly, still aiming, not sure how many rounds are left in his magazine but he doesn't care. He says, "Those two men were going to kill us one by one."

Rick breathes heavily, struggling to raise his gun, but can't. He can barely turn his head. He coughs blood, then says, "Hope she died screaming. . . ."

Allen walks closer to him, saying, "What do you mean she wasn't supposed to die?" Rick suddenly manages to lift his gun, and Allen shoots him once more in the center of his chest. Rick jerks back, dropping his gun, then sinks to the ground. His face twitches with fear. Allen stares at Rick as he stops breathing. Allen feels absolutely nothing.

The Mono County sheriff picks up Val Pinetti at a rental car company on Meridian Boulevard, trying to pay cash for a rental. Allen shows the sheriff his car-tracking system, and leads the sheriff and four deputies to a condo on Lakeview Boulevard, where the SUV is parked. Within fifteen minutes the sheriff and the deputies locate the condo where Mrs. Henrietta O'Brien, a seventy-year-old retiree, lives. Neighbors say she occasionally babysits their children. Frank gives himself up quietly while Social Services explains to a confused Nora what's happening.

But what Allen will always remember is not the calm and civilized way the sheriff arrests Frank and brings Nora to the police station while they sort everything out. Years from now he will barely remember the Social Services woman trying to play cards with Nora while Julie flies into Mammoth Lakes airport on a chartered private plane. He will soon forget the details of the interview and debriefing with both the sheriff and the FBI agent who arrives within two hours. He's in a fog of aftermath.

No, what Allen will always remember is when Julie comes to the police station. It's early evening. Frank is in a holding cell. Val Pinetti is being questioned by the FBI agent. Both Pinetti and Frank want their lawyers, and will be taken to San Francisco in the morning. Allen has told the Mammoth Lakes police sergeant everything he knows. The Mono County coroner and crime scene unit are going over the cabin, confirming Allen's sequence of events. He told them Rick would not surrender his gun, even after being shot, and Allen had no choice but to defend himself.

Julie bursts into the police station, calling for Nora. The sergeant jumps up and stops her, telling her that she has to wait for the Social Service liaison to question her, and that the custodial procedures must be followed precisely to prevent legal problems in the future. Julie yells for her daughter, a vein in her neck bulging. Charlene appears behind her, surprising Allen, who didn't realize she was up from Los Angeles. Charlene tugs at Julie's arm, telling her to calm down. Julie yanks her arm from Charlene and again calls out Nora's name.

Nora comes out of a side room with a young woman, the Social Services liaison, and Allen sits up. He expects a loving reunion; he anticipates watching them run into each other's arms. But the moment Nora recognizes her mother and Julie straightens up, inhaling quickly and saying, "Honey?" Allen sees Nora's face tightening, closing up. She backs away. Julie says again, "Honey?" Nora then screams, "Get away from us! This is all your fault! Why can't you leave us alone!"

Julie almost falls back. Her arms curl up against her chest.

The Social Services woman tells Nora to be nice.

"Where's my father?" Nora yells. "She ruined everything!"

Julie rushes to Nora, saying, "Please, honey! I love you! I've been trying so hard to find you—"

Nora shrieks and tries to hit her with her fist, but the Social Services woman grabs Nora's wrists. Nora goes wild, her head lashing back and forth, arms struggling, feet kicking, fingers clawing, and a deputy runs over to help restrain her. Charlene grabs Julie's shoulder.

The Social Services woman says, "We should do this tomorrow. Let her rest. It's a shock. She's confused."

Julie sinks to her knees, watching her daughter being carried screaming into another room. Julie covers her face and cries. Charlene rests her hand on Julie's head. "We expected this," she says quietly to Julie. "We knew this might happen."

Julie shakes her head, speaking into her hands. "No. I didn't think *this* would happen."

Nora continues shrieking down the hall, "Where's my father! I want to be with my father!"

Twenty-nine

The image of Julie kneeling on the floor, her face in her hands, haunts Allen as he drives back to the Bay Area that evening. He tries not to think about Julie's dulled expression when she turned to him, the way her face seemed devoid of hope. How did the family degenerate into that? Frank poisoned his daughter against her mother, but to that extent?

Allen heads home, but calls Serena on the cell. Her answering machine keeps picking up. He tries again, and says, "I want to talk to you. Please."

Finally, after the sixth or seventh message, she stops the machine, and says, "I'm here."

He says, "Why didn't you answer the phone?"

"I don't know."

"Are you mad?"

"No. I don't know. A little. You said you're all right."

"I'm all right." He tells her briefly what happened, leaving out the exchange of gunfire with Rick.

She listens quietly. When he finishes, she says, "You did it. You found her."

He answers, "I did, but no one's happy."

"And you're done?"

"Yes. I'm the main witness in the case, though. I'll be testifying before the grand jury, then helping the US Attorney's Office in the case against Pinetti."

"What about Frank?"

"He's pleading some of the charges. Rick was obviously the head guy. But I'm done with that family. I'm done."

"I was worried," she says.

"I know."

"I tried to be supportive, but I just couldn't see you get hurt. . . ."

"I know. It won't happen again. I'm done with dangerous cases. I promise."

"I just kept getting angrier that you were doing this to yourself and weren't thinking of me. . . ."

He says, "I know. I completely understand."

"I'm glad you're okay."

"I love you," he says.

"I love you, too, Allen."

"Listen," he says. "I've got to ask you something."

Serena waits. Allen hasn't had a chance to sweep his car and the apartments for bugs, but he realized on the drive back here that if he were being monitored, Rick would've known immediately that Allen was tracking them down. Rick would've known before Allen even arrived in town. He can't figure out who called Rick, but it had to be a leak. He says to her, "It's about how Rick knew I was in Mammoth."

Serena says, "Yes?"

"Someone called him and tipped him off that I was heading over there. I don't know how he knew."

A wave of static passes between them, then fades.

He says, "The thing is, I was wondering if you mentioned the fact that I was heading there to anyone, even casually."

"Wait. You think I tipped someone off?"

"Accidentally. I didn't tell anyone except you, so I just can't figure it out."

"You don't think I had anything to do with them—"

"No, of course not. But who did you tell?"

"No one," she says, then stops. "Wait. You didn't show up for work in the morning, so Larry called here."

Allen stiffens. "Larry called and asked where I was?"

"He said you usually come in early, but you weren't there in the morning."

Allen asks quietly, "What did you tell him?" Sadness trickles into his chest, the answer obvious.

"That you left in the night for Tahoe."

He grimaces. "And you didn't tell anyone else?"

"No."

"Are you sure?"

"Yes."

"Positive?"

"Positive."

Allen feels the weight of this, then tells her that he has to talk to Larry.

"Why?" she asks.

"He's mixed up in this. He almost got me killed." Allen realizes with a start that Larry could've been involved in Linda's death. He says, "I think he could've been bribed by Rick."

"Did you think I had something to do with this?" she asks quietly.

"Never. Not for a second," Allen says.

"All right," she says. "I miss you."

"I miss you, too. I'll see you tomorrow? We can talk more?"

"Okay."

On his way to Larry's loft, Allen pieces it together. Who suggested quitting the case early on? Who missed the obvious address search of Sydney Olshan? Larry had given Allen two Olshans, but not the correct one, which Julie found online on her first try. Julie called him sloppy and lazy, which is why she wanted Allen back on the case. He remembers Rick's MO, trying to pay Allen off first. Rick in fact got the previous PI to back off, then killed him. Rick probably went to Larry after it became clear Allen wouldn't be stopped.

Allen thinks, There might be another explanation.

It seems that B&C has had a lot of money recently from the insurance settlement. But then again, Allen has never seen the actual check from the insurance company. He has seen the deposit in the bookkeeping program, but that can be easily fudged.

"No way," he says, but he keeps remembering small things, like Larry's uneasiness with Allen's research despite being fired off the case. Larry told Serena about this research. Did he think Serena would stop him?

Fighting Bay Bridge traffic into the city, Allen realizes how simple Larry's involvement would be. Larry wants out of the business. Rick had already tried paying off Allen, but it hadn't worked. How much would it take for Larry to sell his partner out?

Whoever broke into his and Serena's apartments knew exactly what to take—the case file and the computers.

Then it hits him: how did those two men know where he and Linda would be, casing Pinetti's apartment? Allen had dug up Pinetti's address while at Larry's place. He had used Larry's computer. Jesus. He might even have left the printout on Larry's desk.

Could Larry have been responsible for Linda's death?

It's not anger he feels when he arrives at Larry's building and rings the buzzer. It's not rage or bitterness. He feels sorrow. Larry comes onto the intercom and asks sleepily who it is.

"Me. I'm back."

Larry says, "Block-o! Congrats! Julie's lawyer filled me in earlier."

"Let me in," Allen says, which Larry does.

Allen goes through the gate, and Larry meets him outside his front hallway. He's wearing a sweat suit and baseball cap, his hair in a long ponytail. He says to Allen, "You okay? What's the problem?"

Allen thinks about the expensive furniture and office equipment in the office. Would an insurance company cover all that? He says, "How much did the insurance company pay us again?"

Larry makes a face. "What?"

Allen repeats the question.

Larry answers, "In the twenty grand neighborhood. This can't wait until the morning?"

"I never saw the check. You think it's all right if I call them later and ask to send confirmation of the payment?"

"Why? We got the money."

"For the sake of neatness. Won't we have to have evidence of payment for the IRS?"

"Don't worry about that, man. The bookkeeper will take care of it. What's this about?"

"Let me call the insurance company. Just to check things out."

Larry says, "What's going, on, dude? You okay?"

"Did we really get the money from insurance?"

Larry answers, "Of course. I can get the confirmation if you want." He motions back to his apartment. "I can call first thing. It might take a while, because you know those assholes were dragging their feet—"

"Larry, look at me."

Larry turns to him.

Allen knows that he's lying, feels it. Allen sighs. He says, "Why?"

"What? What are you talking about?"

"You sold me out."

"What the hell are you—"

"Do you really want me to go through it one by one? Do you want me to call the insurance company myself and prove that you're lying?"

Larry hesitates.

Allen says, "They knew I was in Mammoth. The only people who knew were Serena, then you."

Larry says, "Serena could've—"

"Don't. For chrissake. I thought we were . . . How could you sell me out?"

He looks down. "I don't know what you're talking about, man."

"Linda? Linda was killed. Were you involved in that?"

Larry sighs heavily. "You're not making sense," he says.

Allen says softly, "Please tell me you weren't involved in that. Please."

Larry keeps still for a moment, then shakes his head. "No. I swear I wasn't."

"But you knew we were going to look into Pinetti? I left the records on your computer."

Larry nods.

"What happened? How did Rick get to you?"

"Fuck, B." He takes off his cap and rubs his forehead.

"Tell me," Allen whispers. "Tell me why you did this."

Larry squints. "You got to believe that I had nothing to do with Linda. I swear to God. All I was supposed to do was slow things down and let them know what was happening. That's all."

"How much?"

Larry hesitates. "Almost fifty grand."

"The insurance?"

"None. The fire was suspicious enough to delay payment until an arson investigation was done."

"Did you set the fire?"

"Hell, no! I'm positive the Jamaican guy did it. In fact he's still out there, which don't make me feel too good."

"Why did you . . . ?" Allen turns away, too many questions in his head. He doesn't know where to begin.

Larry says, "B., this is a shifty business. You see that, right? We deal with fucking scumbags all the time or cheating insurance companies trying to scam the small guy. We deal in the gutter, and I'm sick to fucking death of it."

"What about Julie and her daughter?"

"That chick is a nightmare. *I* would've snatched the kid and run if I was married to her."

"But Linda . . . She was my friend."

Larry shakes his head quickly. "Look, I swear I had nothing to do with that. I didn't know anything about it. I'm so fucking sorry about that."

"Rick mentioned something about not intending to kill her. That I was supposed to die, not her. What did he mean?"

Larry says, "It's over, man. Forget it."

Allen grabs his arms and shakes him. "You tell me, you son of a bitch. You know we're finished. B&C is over, right? You know that? I'm trying to decide whether to turn you in. Now, tell me, asshole."

Larry pulls away and holds up his hands. "All right. I found out later that the two men were supposed to shoot you and scare Linda into backing off. She wasn't the target. You were. I swear I didn't know that they were planning it. I thought they were just going to warn you."

"But they were going to execute us, one at a time."

Larry looks down at his hands. "No, man. Rick didn't want to touch Linda because he knew Julie would never stop. But he knew Linda could cool things off if she got scared enough."

Allen realizes what he's saying, that if Allen hadn't fought, he would've been dead, but Linda would be alive. He says, "You're lying."

Larry doesn't move. "I'm really sorry."

"So, I killed her?" Allen says.

"No way. Rick killed her. You did what you had to."

Allen is tired. He hasn't slept in forty-eight hours. He turns toward the gate, and Larry says, "What are you going to do? Are you turning me in?"

"I don't know," he says. "But you want out of the business? You're out."

"I just wanted a little extra money, Allen. That's all."

"I hope it was worth it," he says, and leaves.

Allen returns to his bare, quiet apartment off Clement and tries to stop the buzzing in his head, the chain of thoughts leaping from Linda to Serena to Julie to Larry dizzying him. He showers for a long time, letting the hot water scald his back, then climbs onto his futon, exhausted but unable to sleep.

There was no way he could've known that Linda wasn't a target, that only he was supposed to be killed. Everything that the two men had done pointed to an execution. And even if he had known, he would still have fought with the gunmen, still tried to take both of them down. Otherwise, he'd be dead. But maybe there was something he could've done differently. Maybe he could've pulled Rawlingson away from Linda.

Stop. He stares up at the ceiling. Stop thinking about this.

He searches for something to read and picks up the journals of Kierkegaard that he left by his bed a while ago. He flips through the various entries, focusing on the dates when Kierkegaard was approximately the age Allen is now. Early thirties. Kierkegaard lived only until he was forty-two.

Around this time in Kierkegaard's life he had finished some of his most famous books, including *Fear and Trembling*. He was working on the religious sphere. He was becoming a Knight of Faith.

While skimming the entries, Allen reads something that stops him cold:

May 17, 1843: "Had I had faith I should have remained with Regina."

Allen stares at this, then says, "No way." He rereads the line a dozen times. What happened to the infinite resignation? What about accepting those losses? What happened to being a Knight of Faith in God and giving everything else up?

Had I had faith I should have remained with Regina.

Privately, in his journals, Kierkegaard had acknowledged what seemed self-evident to Allen all throughout *Fear and Trembling,* that there is no faith greater than that of love and communion, that the connections between family, between friends, and between lovers supersede all the abstractions of the unknowns, and no matter how sophisticated the latticework of argumentation is for lofty ideas, it always comes down to one thing—the connection with others.

Kierkegaard couldn't resign himself to the loss of Regina. He couldn't console himself with an irrational belief similar to Abraham's, that Regina, like Isaac, must be sacrificed, that true faith would somehow reconcile everything. No, Kierkegaard knew he had screwed up.

This is the communal sphere that Allen strives for, and in this groggy, traumatic moment, when the events of the past few weeks—no, the past few years—have sent his life spinning from one mess to another, in this moment when he simultaneously grieves for Linda and in a small way for Larry, when he thinks about what keeps him steady and sane and blockable in the tumult of his life, he knows with certainty that it's Serena.

The only thing he wants right now is to be with her.

He climbs out of bed and dresses quickly. He rushes to his car and speeds back to the East Bay.

Perhaps it's the lack of sleep. Perhaps it's the fact that he just misses Serena so much. But he knows now exactly what he needs to do. He will not screw up like Kierkegaard had. He will never renounce what is so obviously good for him, and never, like Kierkegaard, fear the unknown. That's what it comes down to. Kierkegaard got scared. Then he tried to rationalize his actions, only to admit privately he had made a terrible mistake.

In his own way Allen has been adopting similar strategies, formulating his philosophy of removement, abandoning it, then searching for something else to replace it. He dove into Kierkegaard, he buried himself in books. He tried to structure his life and thoughts and relationships around abstractions. But the solution isn't an abstraction.

There is only one answer.

He drives into Berkeley and parks illegally on Martin Luther King. He runs up to Serena's apartment. He lets himself in with his key, and walks to her bedroom, calling her name. She sits up, reaches for the light, but stops. "Allen?" she says, her silhouette poised toward him. "What's wrong? Are you okay? I thought you were coming over tomorrow."

He kneels by her side and takes her hand. The pale glow of the moon falls softly onto her arms. She's luminous. He says, "I had to see you."

"Is everything okay? What's the matter?"

He kisses her hand. "I want you to know something."

She's quiet. She sits up and touches his shoulder. He remains kneeling and presses her palm against his cheek.

He doesn't know where to begin. He says, "I know now that *you* are my family."

"Okay," she says, curiously.

"I want to be with you."

She doesn't answer right away. "Yes," she says. "I want to be with you, too. I just don't know to deal with—"

"No, listen. I wasn't thinking about you. You were totally right. I was so wrapped up in all this . . ." He stops. "I'm so sorry."

"It's okay," she says softly. "I understand."

He pauses, takes a deep breath, and says, "Let's move in together. I mean it, and it's not a reaction. I want to have a great life with you. I want to be with you forever. I love you."

And in the moonlit darkness she nods, whispers, "I love you, too," and leans over and kisses him.

Epilogue

Allen is walking around Lake Merritt, something he hasn't done since he was a teen. It smells much worse than he remembers, the foul stench of geese droppings and rotting algae blowing up around him. He remembers everything being cleaner—the water, the pavement, the playgrounds. The feeding pen is busy with kids throwing bread crumbs to the geese, and the smell is even worse here; he hurries past it, disappointed that reality so abruptly contrasts his reminiscence.

He's taking the day off. For the past two weeks Allen has been converting B&C Investigations to Choice Investigations, dismantling the limited partnership agreement with Larry and incorporating the new business. Allen hasn't spoken to Larry since the split, but through their mutual lawyer Allen learned that Larry is letting everything go, including the remaining cash in the B&C bank account, of which he has a right to half. Allen considers it guilt money, but will use it to cover the overhead while he pays for the changes and figures out what to do with his new business. Although he still has one client—the insurance company worker's comp investigation—he's being careful about taking on new work right now. He's fielding a handful of inquiries from parents with abducted children, referrals from Charlene, who also listed Allen in one of the national child abductee organizations. He's not sure if he wants to take on more of this kind of work right now, since he's still a little shell-shocked from Nora and Julie's reunion.

Charlene has told Allen that Julie and her daughter are in intense family counseling, but the damage is substantial. Julie and Nora had had problems in the past, and Frank exploited this, telling Nora that her mother was trying to destroy both of them, using the police to get his money and break them up. Nora is having nightmares about her father in jail. Frank is still working on a plea agreement, but is looking at an extended prison term. Pinetti's case is heading for trial, and the US Attorney's Office has told the press that they have an extremely strong case, possibly even stronger if Frank's plea agreement works out.

Rawlingson, no longer worried about retribution from Rick, is now telling the DA even more information, pointing to Rick as the ringleader.

Allen considers specializing in this kind of investigation, family skip tracing. He can see himself trying to bring families back together. But it's fraught with the venomous feelings that members of families often have for one another. The look of terror on Julie's face as her daughter screamed, "I hate you," is something Allen doesn't want to witness again.

He reminds himself that he doesn't want to think about work today. He has been at the office almost twelve hours a day for the past two weeks, and Serena ordered him to take a day off, to which he agreed when he found himself winded after walking up the steps at a BART station. He hasn't been running and lifting with Serena lately, but tonight he's supposed to go for a short run with her.

They're searching right now for a larger place together, maybe even a small cottage, and Allen likes the idea of this, a home for both of them, sharing dinner every night, going to bed together.

Had I had faith, I would've remained with Regina. Kierkegaard broke his engagement with Regina, then regretted it for the rest of his life. In some ways Allen sees Kierkegaard's philosophy as compensation, justification, even punishment for his actions that would reverberate through everything he wrote. And even though Allen feels a little nervous about the changes coming, even scared at the thought of having to deal with Mr. and Mrs. Yew more often, he knows he won't make the same mistake as Kierkegaard. It's a cold, desolate world, and Allen won't be moving through it alone.

Allen walks toward a sandy playground and sees among the small crowd of kids and parents a father and son throwing a Frisbee. The father is trying to teach his son how to keep the Frisbee level. The son, about seven or eight, sticks his tongue out in concentration as he curls his arm and flings the Frisbee smoothly to his father, who praises him.

Allen watches them for a while, wondering how Kierkegaard's philosophy would've changed had he married Regina. Would his notion of infinite resignation to losses be tempered by what he would've gained? Allen thinks so.

Allen once saw the bonds of family as tenuous and even irrational. He thought the very idea of random circumstances of birth determining lifelong connections ridiculous. But he sees now that his perspective was that of a bewildered orphan trying to find his bearings, his coordinates in the world. He sees now that the beginnings of those lifelong bonds are not random at all, but chosen, as he and Serena have chosen each another. The family, from his perspective, begins now. The bonds are very rational.

Allen walks by a pay phone splattered with bird droppings. He pauses and circles back, picking up the receiver. He had left his cell phone at the office, trying not to be tempted to check his voice mail, but he wants to talk to Serena. He doesn't have enough change, but knows another way to contact her. He dials "0" and tells the operator he'd like to make a collect call, giving Serena's direct line at work.

The operator connects him to an automated system, which asks him for his name. He says, "The Block," and waits. He watches the kid catch the Frisbee with one hand, look down startled at this trick, then dance up and down, pumping his arm into the air. The father claps. Allen hears Serena voice float into the phone, laughing, "Honey? Why are you calling me collect?" Rather than answering her right away, he savors her laugh and closes his eyes, feeling the warm sun beaming on his face.

Acknowledgments

Thanks to my agents, Nat Sobel and Judith Weber; to my editor, Sally Kim, and Associate Publisher John Cunningham; to my early readers, Frances Sackett and Jen Temple; to the Unis family for the use of their Mammoth Lakes condo; and a special thanks to the many booksellers, like J. B. Dickey, Ed Kaufman, Barbara Peters, and Elaine Petrocelli, for their early and vocal support of Allen Choice.

About the Author

Leonard Chang was born in New York City and studied philosophy at Dartmouth College and Harvard University. He received his MFA from the University of California at Irvine, and is the author of two previous Allen Choice novels, *Over the Shoulder* and *Underkill*. His short stories have been published in literary journals such as *Prairie Schooner* and *Confluence*. He lives in the San Francisco Bay Area, and is working on a new Allen Choice novel. For more information, visit his Web site at www.LeonardChang.com.